P9-DEQ-585

Cat in a Sapphire Slipper

A MIDNIGHT LOUIE MYSTERY

Carole Nelson Douglas

A Tom Doherty Associates Book
New York

NOTE: If you purchased this book without a cover, you should be aware that this book is stolen property. It was reported as "unsold and destroyed" to the publisher, and neither the author nor the publisher has received any payment for this "stripped book."

This is a work of fiction. All of the characters, organizations, and events portrayed in this novel are either products of the author's imagination or are used fictitiously.

CAT IN A SAPPHIRE SLIPPER: A MIDNIGHT LOUIE MYSTERY

Copyright © 2008 by Carole Nelson Douglas

All rights reserved.

A Forge Book
Published by Tom Doherty Associates, LLC
175 Fifth Avenue
New York, NY 10010

www.tor-forge.com

Forge® is a registered trademark of Tom Doherty Associates, LLC.

ISBN 978-0-7653-5829-5

First Edition: September 2008
First Mass Market Edition: July 2009

Printed in the United States of America

0 9 8 7 6 5 4 3 2 1

*For all the dedicated animal lovers who help feral cats lead better lives
through Trap, Neuter, and Release programs across the country,
and particularly for Alley Cat Allies and Feral Friends,
which helped advise me on our first feral rescue.*

Contents

8 · CONTENTS

Cat in a
Sapphire Slipper

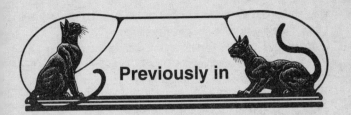

Previously in

Midnight Louie's
Lives and Times . . .

There are lots of fat cats in Las Vegas.

These glitzy media-blitzed streets host almost forty million tourists each year and a ton of camera crews. If lights, action, and camera are not recording background shots for *CSI: Crime Scene Investigation,* they are taping any of thousands of personal videos. People think they know this town—from film if not firsthand experience—know it from the flashy hotels to the seamy side of the Strip.

And a good number of them know one particular Las Vegas institution.

That would be me.

Every last neon bulb and grain of sand in Greater Las Vegas is my personal territory. Oh, I keep a low profile. You do not hear about me on the nightly news. That is the way I like it. That is the way any primo PI would like it. The name is Louie, Midnight Louie. I like my nightlife shaken, not stirred.

Nowadays, though, I am in an unprecedented position. I am torn between two assignments. Usually I am torn between two Persian showgirls, so this is a new predicament for me.

On the one mitt, I am worried about the once-significant other of my roommate, Miss Temple Barr. Mr. Max Kinsella was last seen performing incognito as a masked magician and hitting the Neon Nightmare nightclub wall at fifty miles an hour on a bungee cord. Not even an ace illusionist could survive an impact like that. He has not been seen since and is presumed dead by all and sundry who might know about his masquerade as the Phantom Mage. That includes only me and my business partner-cum-purported daughter, Miss Midnight Louise.

That this tragedy coincides with my ever-lovin' roommate going over to the Light Side (our handsome blond neighbor and former priest, Mr. Matt Devine) in her romantic life only adds to the confusion. I believe there is a film of recent vintage called *Two Funerals and a Wedding*. In my estimation, the current situation is *One Funeral and Two Weddings*.

Because here I am, Vegas's most macho gumpad (and, boy, do I step in a lot of that stuff) and I am overhearing talk about nothing but upcoming nuptials.

Well, you will soon have to suffer from all that drippy sentimental stuff yourself. I will console myself by summing up the much more dudely and dastardly events that have happened to me and mine previously.

I am a noir kind of guy, inside and out, the town's top feline PI.

I am not your usual gumshoe, in that my feet do not wear shoes of any stripe, but shivs. Being short, dark, and handsome . . . really short . . . gets me overlooked and underestimated, which is what the savvy operative wants anyway. I am your perfect undercover guy. I also like to hunker down under the covers with my little doll. My adventures would fill a book, and in fact I have several out. My life is one ongoing TV series in which I as hero extract my hapless human friends from fixes of their own making and literally nail crooks.

That is why my Miss Temple and I are perfect roomies. She tolerates my wandering ways. I make myself useful looking after her without letting her know about it. Call me Muscle in Midnight Black. In our time we have cracked a few cases too tough for the local fuzz of the human persuasion, law enforcement division.

So when I hear that any major new attraction is coming to Las Vegas, I figure that one way or another my lively roommate, the petite and toothsome, will be spike heel–high in the planning and execution. She is, after all, a freelance public relations specialist, and Las Vegas is full of public relations of all stripes and legalities. In this case, though, I did not figure just how personally she would be involved in a bizarre murder far from the madding Strip.

After the recent dramatic turn of events, most of my human associates are pretty shell-shocked. Not even an ace feline PI may be able to solve their various predicaments in the areas of crime and punishment . . . and PR, as in Personal Relationships.

As a serial killer finder in a multivolume mystery series (not to mention an ace mouthpiece), it behooves me to update my readers old and new on past crimes and present tensions.

None can deny that the Las Vegas crime scene is a pretty busy place, and I have been treading these mean neon streets for twenty books now. When I call myself an "alphacat," some think I am merely asserting my natural male and feline dominance, but no. I merely reference the fact that since I debuted in *Catnap* and *Pussyfoot,* I then commenced to a title sequence that is as sweet and simple as B to Z.

That is where I began my alphabet, with the B in *Cat on a*

Blue Monday. From then on, the color word in the title is in alphabetical order up to the current volume, *Cat in a Sapphire Slipper.*

Since I associate with a multifarious and nefarious crew of human beings, and since Las Vegas is littered with guidebooks as well as bodies, I wish to provide a rundown of the local landmarks on my particular map of the world. A cast of characters, so to speak:

To wit, my lovely roommate and high-heel devotee, Miss Nancy Drew on killer spikes, freelance PR ace MISS TEMPLE BARR, who had reunited with her elusive love . . .

. . . the once missing-in-action magician MR. MAX KINSELLA, who has good reason for invisibility. After his cousin Sean died in a bomb attack during a post–high school jaunt to Ireland, he went into undercover counterterrorism work with his mentor, GANDOLPH THE GREAT, whose unsolved murder while unmasking phony psychics at a Halloween séance is still on the books. . . .

Meanwhile, Mr. Max is sought by another dame, Las Vegas homicide detective LIEUTENANT C. R. MOLINA, mother of teenage Mariah . . .

. . . and the good friend of Miss Temple's recent good friend, MR. MATT DEVINE, a radio talk-show shrink and former Roman Catholic priest who came to Las Vegas to track down his abusive stepfather, now dead and buried. By whose hand no one is quite sure.

Speaking of unhappy pasts, MISS LIEUTENANT CARMEN REGINA Molina is not thrilled that her former flame, MR. RAFI NADIR, the unsuspecting father of Mariah, is in Las Vegas taking on shady muscle jobs after blowing his career at the LAPD. . . .

In the meantime, Mr. Matt drew a stalker, the local lass that young Max and his cousin Sean boyishly competed for in that long-ago Ireland . . .

. . . one MISS KATHLEEN O'CONNOR, deservedly christened Kitty the Cutter by Miss Temple. Finding Mr. Max impossible to trace,

Kitty the C settled for harassing with tooth and claw the nearest innocent bystander, Mr. Matt Devine . . .

. . . who tried to recover from the crush he developed on Miss Temple, his neighbor at the Circle Ritz condominiums, while Mr. Max was missing in action. He did that by not very boldly seeking new women, all of whom were in danger from said Kitty the Cutter.

Now that Miss Kathleen O'Connor has self-destructed and is dead and buried, things are shaking up at the Circle Ritz. Mr. Max Kinsella is again apparently lost in action. Mr. Matt Devine had nosed him out on the run for the roses, anyway, the prize being the heart and hand of my lovely roommate, Miss Temple Barr.

Her maternal aunt, MISS KIT CARLSON, ex-actress and current romance novelist, came to visit and stayed to hook up with ALDO, the oldest of the fabulous Fontana brothers, hitherto all bachelors save for the youngest, NICKY, who runs the Crystal Phoenix Hotel and Casino with his lovely wife, MISS VAN VON RHINE.

You would think everything is lovely in Las Vegas from my last paragraphs.

But there are almost forty million potential victims in this old town, if you include the constant come and go of tourists, and everything is always up for grabs in Las Vegas 24/7: guilt, innocence, money, power, love, loss, death, and significant others.

All this human sex and violence makes me glad that I have a simpler social life, such as just trying to get along with my unacknowledged daughter . . .

. . . MISS MIDNIGHT LOUISE, who insinuated herself into my cases until I was forced to set up shop with her as Midnight Inc. Investigations, and who has also nosed herself into my long-running duel with . . .

. . . THE SYNTH, an ancient cabal of magicians that may deserve contemporary credit for the ambiguous death of Mr. Max's mentor in magic, Gandolph the Great, not to mention Gandolph's former onstage assistant as well as a professor of magic at the University of Nevada at Las Vegas.

Well, there you have it, the usual human stew, all mixed up and at odds with one another and within themselves. Obviously, it is up to me to solve all their mysteries and nail a few crooks along the way. Like Las Vegas, the City That Never Sleeps, Midnight Louie, private eye, also has a sobriquet: the Kitty That Never Sleeps.

With this crew, who could?

Chapter 1

A Surprising Scenario

The after-dinner crowd was exiting the Crystal Phoenix Hotel and Casino's revolving rooftop restaurant, the Crystal Carousel.

Temple and Matt still stood at the head table, watching the last stragglers file up to Temple's aunt Kit and Aldo Fontana farther down the table, congratulating them on their surprise engagement announcement. The nine bachelor Fontana brothers had been a Vegas institution until Temple's novelist aunt from Manhattan, sixty and scintillating and devotedly single all her life, had hit town and hit the eldest Fontana brother, Aldo, "in the eye like a big pizza pie," as the old song went. That's *amore*.

The dinner had celebrated Temple's public relations triumph for her employers at the Phoenix: solving the murders at the Red Hat Sisterhood convention and saving the hotel from Bad Press Hell.

"We still could have said something about us," Matt whispered to her.

That "something" would have been the surprise announcement that Miss Temple Barr, Vegas's premier freelance PR woman and occasional crime-solver, was engaged to be married to Mr. Matt Devine, more widely known as "Mr. Midnight" on a syndicated late-night radio counseling show.

This engagement had been more than a year in coming, since Matt, an ex-priest, had first come to Vegas searching for an abusive stepfather. He had subleased a condo in the same building Temple had lived in with her significant other, the missing magician, Max Kinsella, aka the Mystifying Max.

A lot had happened in a year. Max had returned after almost a year away, but Temple had already sympathized with the handsome ex-priest trying to settle old family matters and exchange his longtime celibacy for an enduring new love.

It had looked like Temple might be the one until Max—Temple's earlier, tempestuous love—had turned up again. But Max was a man with a secret mission. A counterterrorism operative since his teens, a man with a price on his head was in no position to maintain a serious relationship, even with Temple trying her best to warm the embers of her old love.

Now, Max was mysteriously missing. Again. Now, Matt and Temple had committed the sin of full emotional and physical commitment. She had the engagement ring. All that was left was to arrange the church ceremony, blessing and legalizing their love.

Temple the woman could live with that. She would always love Max and wish him well, but a girl had to move on. Matt was a dream of a man, not only attractive, but decent and caring in the extreme. And she'd secretly wanted him, bad, for a long time. Ever since Max, for good secret agent reasons, had abandoned her so long for her own safety.

Temple the crime-solver chafed at the idea that Max could vanish for good and all this time, and she'd never know why. Or where. Or whether he was alive or dead.

Matt squeezed her hand. "A Sacajawea dollar for your thoughts." He knew where her feminist sentiments lay. But he didn't need to know her still-raw regrets about Max.

She needed to tell Max her decision herself. She needed to say good-bye.

"Hey." A couple was coming up to address her and Matt, not the official lovebirds.

Some couple. It was Lieutenant C. R. Molina's two top homicide detectives, the seasoned Morrie Alch and the petite but persistent Merry Su.

Su sparkled in her black sequin-trimmed riding jacket and thigh-high-slit slim black skirt. She looked like the Dragon Lady and had been acting that way toward Temple since Molina had asked the PR woman, and not Su, to go undercover as a teenager at a reality TV show shot in Las Vegas, on which Molina's teen daughter was a contestant.

Alch, always the diplomat, drew Matt into conversation and edged away as if glad to escape his partner's company for a bit. Su was a tenacious detective, but she could be abrasive. Temple understood that. Short, petite women like her and Su had to compensate somehow. Temple did it with an extensive high-heel collection. Su did it with nerve.

"I suppose," Su said, "you miss your pal Lieutenant Molina being here."

"Hardly my pal," Temple said. She and the tall, no-nonsense lieutenant had wrangled over Max and why he went missing and whether he'd committed an unsolved murder on the way out of town for more than a year.

Still. She would have loved Molina being in the audience when her engagement to Matt was announced. The half-Latina detective might have harbored a hankering for the dishy

Polish-American ex-priest. They were the same religion, after all, and Molina had never married and must be pushing forty. Temple was on the cusp of thirty-one, and Matt was thirty-four.

Su smiled, always a bad sign. "The lieutenant hasn't been in to work the last couple of days."

"Really," Temple said, unwilling to admit she was interested.

"The flu, they say."

Temple frowned.

"The Iron Maiden of the LVMPD never is out sick," Su continued.

Temple wasn't surprised. Molina had never let up in her vendetta against Max. They'd even duked it out mano-a-mana (if there was such a thing) in a Strip club parking lot. Molina had finally caught Max and he needed to get away fast because he knew Temple was in danger of becoming the next Stripper Killer victim.

Su's piquant face had a sly, triumphant look.

Payback time for Temple, a rank amateur, copping a prime undercover assignment she had wanted. It didn't matter that it had frosted Molina's tortillas to ask such a favor of an antagonist. Temple had gotten the job, not Su, who was as capable of looking sixteen as Temple was, if that was an advantage when one was almost thirty-one and aching to be taken seriously in life and love.

Su leaned close to whisper, at just the right level of Temple's left ear.

"The rumor is that the lady lieutenant flipped and eloped with that hunky magician you used to call yours. *That's* why Max Kinsella is missing. She is too! They're off together on a quickie marriage license and making whoopee in some cheap motel."

NO!

Temple fought to look unruffled. *No. Max would never— Molina would never—*but look at Shakespeare's *The Taming of* *the Shrew.* Men like a challenge, and nobody liked a challenge more than Max. Strong women like stronger men. And Molina was a strong woman.

It made a kind of crazy sense.

Temple's pulse was pounding in her . . . temples. She moved away from Su, who slunk into the waning crowd like a snake relieved of its poison. Temple was aghast. Disbelieving. Stunned. Betrayed. Jealous.

She looked for Matt, for a glimpse that would restore stability, remind her how much she loved and desired him.

He wasn't there. Nobody still lingered at the head table. Everybody had drifted away without her noticing.

It wasn't just Max anymore. It was everybody.

She gazed around.

The entire room was empty.

She was alone at the banquet table with its abandoned dessert plates and crumpled peach linen napkins.

This was a nightmare!

She needed somebody to tell her so, and nobody was there for her.

Not even the malicious Su anymore.

Max and Molina. Max and Carmen.

No!

Temple swallowed. She wanted to shout the word, but she couldn't.

She couldn't move. Couldn't speak, shout.

No.

This *was* a nightmare.

Her nightmare.

She blinked her eyes open in the dark.

A warm hand was on her arm.

"Are you all right?" Matt's voice came from the dark. "You were making almost strangling noises. Temple?"

Was she all right?

Obviously not, if she was still dreaming about Max.

Maybe this dream was the real good-bye. Her unconscious had paired Max with her worst enemy, the woman of her nightmares, and bid him adieu. Said good riddance to them both.

That was it. The dream was a sign any feelings for him were over. All gone. Gone with the Molina.

So revolting! *Ugh.*

She shuddered.

"You're cold," Matt said, tightening his grasp. "Let me warm you up."

Chapter 2

Shallow Wound, Deep End

Morning, after another long, fitful night.

Carmen Molina could hear her daughter and Morrie Alch talking in the other room, through a fog, darkly.

Mariah's light, girlish voice made a pleasant counterpoint to Morrie's low, street-cop growl. Carmen smiled. Making detective had never softened that rumble-busting vocal grumble. Then she took her own inventory.

She wasn't used to being helpless. Ever. Yet she'd lain here for three days on antibiotics and Vicodin, like some zonked-out druggie. Matt Devine hadn't swooned into bed like a Southern belle when *he*'d been stabbed.

But his had only been a short superficial slice. Hers was superficial too, but long. Sitting up, even breathing and talking and eating, were darn unpleasant.

A homicide lieutenant ought to be up for a stronger adjective than "darn," but she habitually watched her language around Mariah. Besides, it unnerved the unit that she'd always been so eternally in control. A lot of females in male-dominated jobs tried to relax their male subordinates by matching them curse for curse, shout for shout. A couple of football coaches, notably Super Bowl winner, Tony Dungy, went the opposite route. That's why they called her the Iron Maiden. Quiet but unflappable, invincible. Silent as cold steel.

Not very iron lately.

The voices were coming closer. Mariah bearing her morning slop: canned soup! But Morrie had done it: whipped her hormonal, edgy, unreliable teen daughter into a meek little nurse.

Molina pushed herself up against the piled bed pillows, trying not to grimace as the eighty-six stitches in her stomach and side screamed bloody murder at the motion.

A deep wound knocks you out. A shallow one tortures you to death.

Morrie turned on her bedside table light, leaving the shutters closed. He didn't want Mariah seeing or guessing any more than she should.

"Something new from your friendly neighborhood grocery shelf," he said. "Mac and cheese."

"Great." She meant it. The thin soups were getting old. "Thanks, honey, but you better get to school."

"You guys just want to talk about something I'm not supposed to hear." Mariah ruffled her blond-highlighted hair into a suitably unkempt appearance for Our Lady of Guadalupe Catholic school. Her uniform jumper was a rigid navy-and-green plaid over a crisp white blouse, but her hair was now as punk as the school rules would allow.

She still looked like a pretty decent kid.

"Thirteen," Morrie commented after Mariah had eased out

of the sickroom, then slam-banged through the house and out. "Around seventeen you can expect some relief."

"I can't believe she's buying the Asian flu excuse."

"She's probably relieved to see you helpless for a while. Not going to question her luck."

"Or yours?" The first spoonful was so hot she had to dump it back into the bowl.

He chuckled. "Even Superwoman has to run into a little kryptonite now and then. It was too bad you had to miss the Crystal Carousel shindig, it was quite a party."

"I didn't plan on getting knifed."

"While breaking and entering Max Kinsella's empty house."

"What a wasted effort," she said. "The bastard was gone and now I have to figure out who hated him enough to trash his house and clothing, even with him not in it."

"Besides you."

"I don't hate him, Morrie. I despise his lawless, laughing attitude. But it's moot. This time I believe he's really gone. For good. End of story. I can't get him on the old Goliath Hotel murder, but he doesn't get to slink around Vegas in secret screwing his girlfriend and laughing at law enforcement."

"No screwing anymore. Except the law. Temple Barr is pretty cozied up with Matt Devine now. I would have expected their engagement to be announced before one for her visiting aunt, Kit Carlson, and Aldo Fontana."

Molina frowned. "I'm not sure that's the best combo around."

"Carlson and Fontana?"

"Well, any one of the playboy Fontanas, but I meant Temple and Matt. He doesn't seem her type. Too nice."

Morrie shrugged. Molina's judgment on the Circle Ritz residents had always been skewed. "So. You think you can come back to work Monday?"

"I do," she said. "You ever been cut?"

He shook his shaggy Scottish terrier head, gray at the ears.

"It's quite a trip, Morrie. Every move you make tears everything. I'm seeing the doctor again Thursday."

"Good thing she knows your job title. Civilians always expect us cops to engage in regular fracases. From the TV shows."

"This is pretty obviously a knife slash. And I am pretty obviously *not* in a domestic violence situation. But I still had to get the damn third degree about it."

Morrie pulled the dining-room chair doing bedroom duty by the window closer to the bed. "Better eat your noodles while they're still hot."

"Yes, Nurse Alch."

"Speaking of domestic violence, just what is between this Rafi Nadir guy and you?"

She nodded toward the empty main rooms. "Only Mariah. And that wasn't by my choice."

"Regrets?"

"Lots. But not Mariah."

"The guy raped you?"

"God, no! I was a street cop then. They sicced me on all the black brothers in Watts. Women got the shit details; we were supposed to fail. Rafi and I . . . we lived together. Don't look so shocked. I was a half-Hispanic woman; he was an Arab-American man. We were both predestined to flunk Street 101."

"So Mariah—?"

"Not a planned pregnancy. I found a pinprick in my diaphragm. Not my doing. Yeah, laugh. I was more Catholic then. Couldn't quite go against the Pope and use the pill."

"So why'd Nadir want you pregnant?"

"I was moving up faster than he was. He's Christian, but from a culture that ranks women with pack donkeys and pariah dogs. I assumed it was a ploy to build his ego two ways. He probably thought it would make me quit the force."

"You mean you *assumed* he thought that."

"You are a wicked interrogator, Alch. Act so easy, but go right for any narrow window of opportunity. You're right. Motivation rests on assumptions, but they need to be proven. Yes, I'm no longer so sure that he sabotaged my birth control. It's just that I was so careful about using it."

"Could have been a manufacturing flaw, or some drugstore smart-ass product-tampering."

"I've been considering that. Thinking about the infamous 'lot of things.'"

"Thinking is always good."

She gobbled the rest of the cheesy noodles—an apt description two ways—set the bowl and tray aside, then pushed herself higher against the pillows.

There were two things wrong with that. It made her grimace with pain, and she was wearing a long T-shirt with no bra. She had not been seen by a man with no bra in a long time, except when she was performing occasional gigs as Carmen, the torch singer at a local club. She wore vintage thirties and forties evening gowns for that and they didn't allow for much underwear.

Still, she could talk better from a sitting position and she had to start rebuilding her stomach muscles for Monday morning.

"Morrie, I owe you for helping me out with this. With the captain, the doctor, and Mariah. I also owe you some explanations."

"No, you don't. But I *am* curious enough to take them."

"One, Rafi Nadir. When I realized I was pregnant, I was cooked. My career was shot. I was too Catholic to get an abortion, but a patrol officer is at too much personal risk and I wasn't going to subject a child to a dead mama. I was damned if I'd let a man put me in a corner like that. I secretly resigned the LAPD, grabbed what I could, and ran. I had a good record despite my brutal 'initiation.' I used my mother's maiden name, got a patrol job in Bakersfield, and eventually worked my way to Las Vegas."

"And Nadir?"

"He didn't take to being low minority on the totem pole. I had ways of checking. He really blew it after I left, and got kicked off the force."

"It takes a lot to get kicked off the LAPD."

"Tell me about it. Along with New Orleans, Chicago, and Minneapolis, L.A. is considered one of the most minority-unfriendly forces in the country. Maybe it's changed by now. I did make lieutenant in Vegas."

"This Nadir guy turning up here must be a nightmare."

"Worse. I'd never dreamed of such a thing. Now he's found me, and therefore, Mariah. He's not stupid. He knows he's her father. He wants her to know it."

"I see your problem."

"That's not the only one. I may have been wrong about Rafi. I may also have been wrong about your pal Temple Barr's long-time sweetie, the Mystifying Max Kinsella."

"You did have a hard-on to nail him for that old Goliath murder."

"That's how you saw it? *I* was too convinced he had done the murder? Look. He had just finished his magician act contract at the Goliath Hotel that very night. Then this dead man dropped from the ceiling above the gaming tables, where only a cousin of a garter snake could go. To top it off, Kinsella was not to be found or heard of after that for more than a year. Any judge would have issued a warrant on probable cause, but he skipped town right after that murder, which is obviously still unsolved."

"Obviously, he came back to haunt you. As did Nadir. Why?"

"My rotten luck?"

"You don't believe in luck, Carmen. You believe in hard work."

She patted her stomach gingerly. "Whoever did this was running amok in the Mystifying Max's well-concealed house. I finally traced Temple Barr to the place and went in on my own to check it out. I interrupted, or just preceded another Max Kinsella fan as disenchanted as I was. Maybe more. Someone was going through the rooms, slicing his clothes into shreds in the closets. And I thought *I* despised the guy."

"Maybe it was that big alley cat of Miss Barr's, Midnight Louie, miffed at the man for vanishing on her again."

"Nice try. A knife did the slashing, a big butcher knife from the block in the kitchen. That's what grazed me. It probably had a ten-inch blade."

"Four inches can kill you." Alch picked up the empty food bowl, then donned his purse-lipped thinking hard expression. "Seems to me your biggest problem is keeping your B and E secret. That could kill your career. You could go the lawyer route with Nadir, hold him at bay for a while."

She thought too. "Maybe I should do something even more draining about him."

"What's that?"

Molina picked at a loose thread on the bargain percale sheet hem. "Maybe I should talk to him first." She sighed, and it hurt. What didn't these days? "When I can stomach it."

A Deeper Shade
of Black

Black. Black.

Everything was black.

He was in a tomb. Or a tunnel.

Did he see a flicker of light? No.

Did he feel anything?

Only the slightest twinge of consciousness after long uncon-
sciousness.

Or could he be sure of that?

He was either blind, or his mind was a blank, like a blackboard with no writing on it.

Wait. Blackboard. That was a concept. He had a mental picture of it, framed in wood.

His mind was not black. Only his senses were.

No feeling, no sight, no hearing, no smell.

But taste. A bad, dry taste in his mouth, like he'd tried to swallow a toad.

Toad. Another concept. Another mental picture.

Something or someone was keeping him prisoner like this. Sense deprivation.

An abstract concept. Not a thing, like a blackboard or a toad.

He could think in concrete terms, in concepts and analogies.

He just couldn't see, hear, taste, smell.

But he could think. That was a hopeful sign. A spring, a feather, a dove . . .

Ideas were spinning in the blackness of his blackboard mind, but he felt even that feeble grasp on beingness fade to a deeper shade of black.

There was no where, no what, no when.

No who.

No one else.

Nothing.

Chapter 4

A Winning Pair
of Diamonds

"Oh! I almost squashed Midnight Louie again." Kit jumped up again before sitting on Temple's living-room sofa.

"He's hard to squash." Temple watched the big black cat stretch luxuriously, claiming even more territory with his long muscular body and extended legs and tail. "He's reclaiming the sofa because you used it for a bed before Aldo exported you to whatever hidden love nest you've been calling home lately."

Kit sat where Louie wasn't. As petite as Temple, she could fit in the small space the resident alley cat wasn't hogging at the moment. Temple perched on the sofa arm.

Their elfin figures and pose made them look like mother and daughter, and they sounded like it, with their matching slightly raspy voices. But they were aunt and niece, roughly thirty years apart. Temple was thirty about to turn thirty-one, and Kit was roughly sixty and planned to stay that way for a good long time.

Right now they were both going on eighteen.

"I never saw yours up close at the Crystal Phoenix party," Temple said, peering hard at Kit's left hand.

"I never saw yours at all that night."

Midnight Louie suddenly stood, arched his back like a Halloween cat, and thumped his twenty pounds down to the parquet floor.

"Guess he doesn't like girl talk," Kit said.

They watched him stalk into the adjoining office with its tiny adjacent bathroom and the open window he used as an informal doggie door. Temple had long since given up treating Louie like a cat. He was more like a resident furry godfather, the Mafia kind. She sometimes wasn't sure who was letting who live with whom. The only certainty was that Louie knew his way around Las Vegas inside and out, turning up as regularly as CSI personnel at crime scenes.

Letting him roam was less like letting a house cat loose in Sin City than exposing the town to feline muscle of the first water.

Speaking of the first water, which was a term for diamonds of the greatest purity and perfection, Temple slid into the spot Louie had vacated—*hmm*, warm—and fanned her left hand alongside her aunt's. They both sighed.

"Yours is fabulous," they said in concert, then laughed.

"Does 'yours' refer to the ring, or the donor?" Kit asked.

"Both, of course!"

"Temple, why didn't you say something the night of the party celebrating the successful close of the Red Hat–Pink Hat case! You didn't even wear your engagement ring."

Temple sobered. "I had mixed feelings. What with Max so recently . . . missing."

"Gosh, what has it been now?"

"Almost six weeks."

"Six weeks, really? Aldo and I have lost track of time flying between my condo in Manhattan and looking for new digs here. And still no word?"

"Kit, a guy who sells his house and leaves town without mentioning it to his girlfriend is not likely to send homesick text messages."

"It's a mystery. You'll solve it."

"I will. Someday. But, meanwhile, we have to get you married to the eldest Fontana brother. All Vegas will be agog at this foreign New York City woman who skimmed the cream of the town's deeply committed bachelors into her web of bewitchment in a few days flat."

Kit, an ex-actress who could look as demure as Miss Muffet when called for, eyed the glittering square diamond solitaire on her petite knuckle. "He did go all out when he finally went over to the wedlock side."

"The stone is huge!"

Kit batted her eyelashes. "I've never bought the idea that small women should wear small hats and jewelry, have you?"

"Absolutely not."

"Besides"—Kit leaned in to examine the intricate ruby and diamond ring on Temple's left hand—"who'd a thunk an ex-priest would come up with a vintage ring ripe for appearing in the original cast of *Broadway Babies of 1935*. That's a work of Art Deco."

"He got it at a little shop around the corner of the Strip. Fred Leighton. The wedding ring itself is a pair of ruby circle guards."

"I'll be right there, ogling it at the ceremony."

"My matron of honor."

Kit teared up. She'd been a big-city career woman since college, and single. Who'd a thunk a Vegas hunk years her junior (who was counting exactly?) would be Mr. Right?

"Why can't *you* be *my* matron of honor?" Kit said. "That would be so deliciously unexpected. Aren't you and Matt getting a civil wedding here before going formal and letting your mom and dad back in Minnesota know?"

Temple sighed. "Maybe. Whatever we do, I don't want to rush it."

"Probably wise," Kit said, "given the large dangling loose end." She saw Temple's expression wilt. "Oh, sorry! Slap me so I bite my tongue! I didn't remember that Max's old magic act used suspended animation and bungee acrobatics."

Temple nodded, not able to speak for a moment, secretly afraid that Max wasn't just missing, but dead.

"Listen, kitten. Just think how flabbergasted Karen will be when she comes for the wedding and gets a load of Aldo. Her old maid sister marrying a devastatingly eligible Fontana brother."

"*Mom's* coming?"

"Sure. I mean, she *is* essential family. Isn't she? Look, I know you've been kinda distant, and I don't know why, except the same thing happened to me thirty-five years ago when I left Minneapolis for a bigger, more exciting city."

Temple had her hands to her face, which made the ring's dazzle explode in the daylight from the room's row of French doors. "Mom's coming! Oh, my God. I hadn't dreamed of that. I thought Matt and I would fly up to see her and Dad and everyone in Minnesota . . . later."

"I doubt your brothers will come. Weddings are too girly. Bad enough they had to be at their own."

Temple laughed shakily. "Oh, God, yes. Men in flannel shirts, wearing Frye boots."

"Why did you leave Minneapolis for Vegas a couple years ago?"

"Yeah, but I did, love. I was doing PR for the Guthrie repertory company when he came through with his magic show."

"He must have been some barnstormer to shake you loose of your Midwestern roots."

Temple smiled nostalgically. "And . . . it was pretty overprotective up north. When my four older brothers stopped dodging me as a hopeless tagalong, no one would let me go anywhere on my own. Max was the Big Bad Wolf who stole Little Red Riding Hood."

Kit reached out to stroke Temple's shoulder-length hair. "Semi-red now. I love that strawberry color you put in over the blond dye job. How many PR women in this town go undercover for homicide lieutenants, I wonder?"

"You think the hair came out okay?"

"Great!"

"Why not? It's our color, our Pink Lady color." Temple was referring to her and Kit's masquerade as Pink Hatters at the recent, and deadly, Red Hat Sisterhood convention at the Crystal Phoenix Hotel and Casino.

"My blushes, Watson." Kit put her hands to *her* cheeks this time. "As an actress I just can't bear to advertise my age to one and all."

"Wearing a red hat does announce one is over fifty these days. Besides, red is not really your color."

"Damn right. Unless I've put a foot in my mouth again and am emulating a beet. So you do like lilac. We'll have to hit the high-end shops. No bridal shop regalia at my wedding. Something different."

"Maybe vintage?"

"Maybe. Maybe Italian designer. Aldo is springing for my duds and price is no object."

"Ivory leather? I saw a fabulous suit at Caesar's Apian Way shops."

"A leather wedding suit? Love it! You are radical."

"It's a pearlized ivory leather, with the jacket's puffed

sleeves and bodice leather done in cut-lace detail. It has a short skirt with a detachable bustle train that ends in just trailing lace. That would be too long on you, but all the more bridal."

"Wonderful! Let's go get it. We'll find something for you along the way. I can't believe I got talked into a formal wedding within six weeks of the engagement."

"No problem, Kit. Van von Rhine could mount a British royal coronation in five days flat. All you have to worry about is showing up dressed."

"Well, if I wanted to make trouble for myself, I could worry about the bachelor party the other nine Fontana boys are throwing for their eldest brother."

"When is it?"

"Tomorrow night. It's a Monday, Matt's night off at the radio station, so he can attend."

"Where is it?"

"That's the problem. It's a secret. I know boys will be boys, but these 'boys' have been men on the town for a long time. I expect it will be bawdy, involve cigars, and strippers jumping out of things a lot more interesting than giant cakes."

"Hey, Kit. Aldo's not going to blow his first attempt at matrimony."

"It's not Aldo I'm worried about. It's those fun-loving, hunky brothers of his." Kit looked closely at Temple. "You're frowning. You're worried about the bachelor party too?"

"Well, Matt will be there, and that's not exactly his scene. But, no, my mind was moss-gathering."

"You're too young for 'moss-gathering.'"

"Issue-gathering, then. I just can't believe Mom is coming to a place like Las Vegas on such short notice."

"Kid, with us, the notice is always 'short.'" Kit mugged the line, with an elbow to Temple's ribs and a wink. Both were five feet flat, which is why they wore high heels. "Your landlady runs a wedding chapel, for heaven's sake. She'll help. The ceremony's going to be held at your main hotel account, the Crystal Phoenix. Everything's in place."

"Except . . . except I wasn't anticipating introducing Matt to my family so soon."

"Why the hell not? He's as presentable as Prince Charming. An ex-priest, for God's sake. Any overprotective family has gotta love that. I mean, as Universal Unitarians, they're very ecumenical, and he comes shrink-wrapped. What's safer than that?"

Temple was blushing again. "Don't remind me. They'll worry about that. Ask embarrassing questions about his sex life. Matt isn't used to family interrogations."

"Un-huh. He handles anonymous callers with every kind of hang-up imaginable at the radio shrink line six nights a week. What makes you think he can't handle your mother?"

"Because I can't?"

"Gracious, girl. You're all grown-up now. You're a maid of honor for a mature bride. An engaged woman. You have been the paramour of a world-class magician and have an ex-priest lover. You have unmasked murderers."

"Kit! You're plotting a romance novel, not reality."

"However you put it, I'd say maybe you're grown-up enough to face down my sister, Karen. Who can be a teensy bit conservative."

"You skipped town to get away from family pressure too."

"True. Look, I'll back you up. She will hit the roof over any off-white, high-end, train-trailing bridal gear of mine. I won't tell her it was your idea. That ought to take the heat off. And we'll get you something Miss Muffety in voile and satin with a Victorian high-collar neckline and a bow on the butt."

Temple dissolved in laughter. "Kit, why am I having worse bridal nerves than you over this?"

"Because you're next?" Kit cackled. "And I do expect to be matron of honor. I can wear the suit without the train, because of course you'll be in pure, pristine white."

"You're sure?"

"Your mother, and Matt, wouldn't have it any other way."

Chapter 5

Cleanup Detail

Carmen didn't tell Morrie what she'd finally decided to do.

Father figures were great in theory, but her fathers had been confusing.

The Anglo mystery man who'd sired her had been driven out of the Hispanic family circle before she was born, her mother caving to ethnic, church, and family pressures. He was a literal ghost: pale, Nordic, blue-eyed. He lived on only in Carmen's eye color, which had singled her out in every barrio and church and school photo of her early life. She would have hated him just for that if she'd had a chance to know him.

Her mother had married after her "mistake," Carmen Regina, girl-child out of wedlock. Carmen had never bonded with her stepfather. As the eldest, she'd been half a mother to the many children they'd conceived in unfettered Catholic Hispanic certainty.

Every darling toddler seemed a rebuke. She'd loved them, and they her, but it was a sad charade of the half-life she lived. Carmen the half-breed.

She'd discovered some soul mates, old ladies she'd crossed paths with. They were the eldest children of men killed in World War II. Only children, only survivors. Their young, widowed mothers had remarried and started large fifties families. The lone older daughter who didn't remember a father became the stepchildren's quasi-mother from a very early age.

It didn't make her crazy to go out and multiply on her own, whatever the church decreed.

Her liaison with Rafi Nadir was born of mutual alienation.

And then she'd ended up the mother of an only child in her turn.

Except she didn't see hooking up again in her case, having more children.

Just this one. This precious one.

So her own only daughter was also a half-breed. Half Hispanic-Anglo, half Arab-American. Really, a quarter-breed.

People were supposed to say it didn't matter. Ethnic origin. Skin shade. Eye color.

It did.

The knife wound had cut a swatch across Carmen's olive skin.

Hatred was equal opportunity.

She felt the severing in her soul.

She'd been angry, anxious, insecure. Had let it pile up into a mountain of mistakes.

Why had Max Kinsella become such an obsession?

He'd gotten away without a scratch. Gotten away in a smart, slick, easy, painless way.

He hadn't gotten stuck, as she had. He'd eeled out of a murder rap and even a miffed girlfriend he'd bailed out on for a year. Any other mortal would have paid, and paid big for being at the scene of the crime, skipping town, and coming back an uncatchable shadow. Not Max Kinsella. She hated people who got away with behaving badly. That had been her whole law enforcement life.

Maybe because she'd never dared to behave badly herself.

Until now. Breaking and entering. Arranging clandestine surveillance with an undercover cop who might be okay, might be rogue. Getting knifed, goddamn it, off the clock.

Now that her wound had forced her to lie still and think, alone at home, hurting physically, she realized that she'd made as many unwarranted assumptions as Max Kinsella ever had.

And she had been wrong! Kinsella was a target, as Matt and even Temple Barr had hinted. Not a perpetrator. He was an undercover operative? Kinsella! Holy Mother of All Things Annoying! She'd been chasing a shadow of herself.

Her attacker had knifed her while shredding Max Kinsella's Las Vegas life to bits.

She'd thought *she* despised the man. She was a piker. Someone seriously whacked was out there.

Was Temple Barr safe? She had to think about that. Matt? Or . . . worse. Her attacker didn't know who she was, just someone there. What if she'd been followed home? What if Mariah was now a target? She, Carmen, and her one-woman pursuit mission, had exposed her daughter to terrible danger perhaps.

Sitting up in bed made her belly burn as if she was in childbirth again.

Thank God for Morrie. He'd left her some ground to stand on: her job. She had to start using that better.

Number one: neutralize Rafi Nadir. He wasn't going to go away, and if he really hadn't tampered with her birth control device, why should he? Number two: distance herself from Dirty Larry. He'd come in handy for her, but you had to ask why. She didn't need an ambiguous boyfriend. She needed . . . Morrie Alch. He was shrewd, loyal, and more than she deserved. Daddy dearest. She swallowed hard. Yes. She needed someone to look out for her. Yes, she still needed someone. Someone to watch over me.

The lyric and music played in her head. So what if she was a little feverish, a little Vicodined out.

She had a lot of catching up to do when she felt up to it in a few weeks.

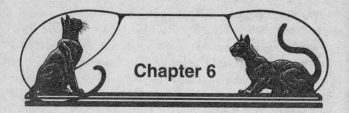

Chapter 6

Here Comes the Ride

Naturally, I have not been invited to the Fontana Family bachelor party for Aldo.

Naturally, that does not make a bit of difference to my intentions and actions.

I intend to be in on the action, however juvenile and rowdy.

It is not often that one gets to see a Fontana brother tie the marital knot in this town. I was there when the youngest brother, Nicky, got hitched, and I will be there when the eldest falls to the blow of domestic bliss.

It is a snap for Midnight Louie to crash a party of this nature.

Obviously, ten brothers, their notorious uncle, Macho Mario Fontana, and Mr. Matt will be transported in one of Gangsters' famous theme limos. The boys own that company, and only their vehicles are long and large enough to transport so many in such luxury.

The key is to anticipate which model will have the honor to-night.

I stroll among the cast of custom vehicles in the Gangsters' lot.

First, I had to customize two overzealous guard dogs. I had nailed their noses with a one-two to each long German shepherd snout. They were whimpering when the human guard called them off.

"Bruno! Horst! That is only a stray cat. What is the matter with you two tonight?"

I can answer that better than they can: quarter-inch-deep tracks on their hypersensitive German schnozzles. If they were weiner dogs you could call them "Weiner schnitzel" after I got through with them.

So now I am car shopping, sniffing tires for hints of where these glamorous vehicles have been. *Umm.* The scent of French bread. Must have been at the Paris last. A dude can travel the world just from sniffing the Gangsters' tires.

Since the Fontanas favor pale summer suits of Italian design, I am torn as to whether the stretch Lamborghini or the stretch Maserati will be the lucky ride tonight.

Then I hear the scrape of many feet on asphalt.

Rats! (Not the cause of the skittering sounds, but merely an expletive dear to my kind.) My keen ears pick up the sound of custom-leather loafers surrounding a vehicle the whole damn lot away.

I skitter myself over there just in time to shadow the last pair of black Bruno Maglis into the last closing door on a stretch vintage Rolls-Royce Silver Cloud. Was I wrong about the ride!

Luckily, the open interior is carpeted in black-like-me. Also, everybody is joshing Aldo and doing that kind of human arm slapping and feet milling that is very hazardous to my health.

I dodge size eleven shoes to hunker down by Mr. Matt's more

sedate size tens. A family of all brothers can be a high-spirited bunch. It occurs to me that Mr. Matt, until not long ago a man of chaste and churchly ways, could use a bit of backup among this mob. Oops! I did not mean that last word personally. Macho Mario Fontana is the last of the red-hot capos in this town, but no one likes to comment on that.

I dig in my four-on-the-floor as the huge Rolls lurches into gear and motion. The interior is one big conversation pit studded with built-in bars. Corks are popping like firecrackers and Cristal is foaming over a dozen champagne glass rims.

Nobody offers me even a sip.

However, a lot of it oozes floorward, and I polish a few shoe tips unseen. *Hmm.* Excellent vintage. Airy and impertinent, like me, with a smoky hint of Italian leather.

I return to hide behind Mr. Matt's less expensive and also less damp shoes.

Macho Mario Fontana leans forward to address us. Or only Mr. Matt. Little does he notice it is now an "us."

"So, *compadre.* This is your first time at an Italian bachelor party. I understand you will be the guest of honor at another one soon."

"Yes, um, Sir."

Mr. Matt is clearly befuddled by Macho Mario's girth under the silk-screened vest that depicts in fine art detail naked ladies on red velvet swings. He is also no doubt taken literally aback by the pungent cigar smoke and the fiery tip that gestures at Mr. Matt's chest on every other word.

"Call me Uncle," Macho Mario insists, clapping Mr. Matt on the shoulder so hard he inhales a lungful of blue smoke and starts coughing. Even I am coughing and I am on the floor where the smoke is last to go.

"Are all the people at the party relatives?" Mr. Matt asks.

"People? Hell, have you never been to a bachelor party? It will be just us guys, and a naked girlie or two we smuggle in as a surprise for the poor dear Intended."

Mr. Matt looks a little sick, whether from the cigar smoke or the promise of undressed entertainment I cannot say.

"Aw, that is right, son." Another clap to the shoulder and a hearty, "Hi-ho, Silver." "You are kinda new to this guy stuff. You were a man of the cloth. Dontcha worry about that. My nephews will get you togged out right for your own, er, festivities."

"I do not know that many people in town, working nights at the radio station, as I do," Mr. Matt says with relief, "I will not need a bachelor party."

"Well, you are going to get one. Worry not. Macho Mario Fontana knows enough good wiseguys to fill a football stadium. Man, I cannot believe that Aldo fell for that little New York gal enough to marry her. I thought Nicky was going to be the only married Fontana of his generation. I tell you, Mike—"

"Matt."

"Matt. Better name. You cannot trust micks named Mike. I tell you, Mack, marriage looks a lot better on paper than in practice. But since you too are among the poor dear Intendeds, I can advise you to drink up and enjoy the parties, because the forty years afterward is not so much fun."

Macho Mario quaffs his champagne and leans back to eavesdrop on his favorite nephews, who are razzing Aldo something fierce.

Mr. Matt is murmuring something under his breath. It sounds like "Holy Mary, mother of God. No one in seminary mentioned a mobile mob riot."

I am tempted to provide a consoling shin rub. I agree that civility is sadly lacking among the rowdy bunch already . . . and they are not even tipsy yet.

I figure we are heading to a racy striptease club. However, I confess that I am looking forward to the forthcoming scantily clad ladies. (They are never really naked, but clothed in bits and pieces, and those bits and pieces are often sparkly and feathered. Right up my alley cat!)

I do like to see how the other half lives, even if it is rude, loud, and rather tacky. That is the heart of rock 'n' roll and also Las Vegas. And sometimes, me.

Chapter 7

Girls' Night In

Van von Rhine's glass desktop in her Crystal Phoenix office was no longer bare and sleek.

It was littered with fat photograph albums displaying everything from the chosen floral arrangements to napkin designs.

Two huge boxes spilling gouts of gilt tissue were open on the navy Milan leather sofa.

Van, Temple, and Kit gathered reverentially around them.

"Kit, that ivory leather wedding suit of yours is gorgeous. Aldo will flip. I'm thinking bronze and the palest mauve orchids for the bridal bouquet. Simple, exotic, and expensive. What will you do for shoes?"

"I was thinking some sexy ankle boots. Bronze, you think?"

"Perfect. You need a firm foundation for the leather suit." Van turned to Temple. "And you! Those shades of lilac and mauve are stunning."

"I love purple shades," Temple said, stroking the filmy gown. "And Matt seems to agree with me." The dress was simple. It had spaghetti straps, so appropriate to an Italian wedding, an Empire waistline, and a flowing skirt that was short in front and longer in the back, all the better to showcase her Midnight Louie Austrian crystal shoes. This would be a White Carpet occasion.

Van actually produced a sentimental smile. "It'll be perfect with your softer strawberry hair color, Temple. You'll look adorable. Anyway, Kit, now that I've seen the gowns you two have chosen, and the bridesmaids' rainbow of pale metallic colors, it'll make the chapel and reception color themes a snap. We have everything on hand. I must say that outfitting eight bridesmaids for eight groomsmen has been a . . . diplomatic feat."

"It seemed easiest," Temple said, "to let the brothers invite their girlfriends."

"I obviously don't have any girlfriends in town," Kit noted.

"So," Temple said, "we have instant *Eight Bridesmaids for Eight Brothers*. What could be handier?"

"Is that a reference I should know?" Van asked.

Temple exchanged a knowing glance with her aunt. "Kit knows. It's a famous fifties movie musical, based on a Stephen Vincent Benét story."

When Van continued to look puzzled, Kit explained. "Benét was a poet. He updated the legend of Rome's founders raiding the neighboring Sabine tribe for brides on whom to found their dynasty."

"A musical based on mass rape?" Van said, shocked.

"Not really," Temple said. "Benét transferred the plot to the America frontier, where women were rare. The seven brides are kidnapped, true, but to be wooed, not raped."

"Some of the best musical choreography of the twentieth

century is in that chestnut," Kit added. "The late Michael Kidd. Great fun."

Van raised her pale eyebrows, unconvinced. "Whatever their numbers, and in whatever age or locale, bridesmaids always have issues. That's why I planned a pastel metallic rainbow of colors for them; every girl should find some shade she likes. The wedding is less than a week away. We need to fit them all in the next couple of days. I've been leaving voice mail messages all over town for them." Van frowned. "I'm not getting calls back yet."

While Temple and Kit reboxed their outfits, Van checked her watch. "The 'boys' should be arriving at the secret location of their bachelor party about now."

"I hope," Temple said, "Matt isn't overwhelmed by all that big Italian family energy. He's an only child from the conservative Midwest."

"Aldo won't let him get overwhelmed," Kit said with a hug. "He takes his responsibility as the eldest seriously."

"When's your bachelorette party?" Van asked her.

"I don't know a soul in town besides Temple and you and Electra. No party."

"Nonsense," Van said. "Call Electra over," she told Temple. "We're going up to the owner's suite to drink ourselves silly on Cristal champagne. The boys didn't get all the bottles into the Gangsters' stretch limo without me copping a couple."

Van stroked her smooth French twist and then winked. "We're going to have a girls' night in while they're having a boys' night out."

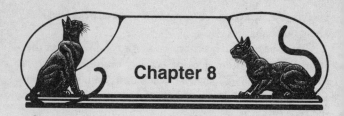

Chapter 8

High Anxiety

The view out the spotless window glass was spectacular.

He leaned closer to see more of the snow-topped mountain peaks. They ringed a valley that plunged into the lush green slopes of early spring, wildflowers scattered everywhere like confetti. It was almost like looking out on a painting. Unreal.

He leaned even closer to the glass, as close as the wheelchair would permit. His head twisted left, then right, then up. Ah, huge eaves above. To take the snow in the winter. The building must be set into a hillside. The outside wall of his room was almost all glass. Supernaturally clean glass. That took money, that took pride, that took a certain fussy perfectionism that he understood, that pleased him.

The door to his room *whooshed* open. All the doors here were on air hinges so they wouldn't shatter anyone's nerves with an ill-timed bang. Or so they wouldn't alert those inside who was coming and going.

A lot of people had been coming and going in his room, but he knew he'd been drugged and out of it probably for days or weeks, he could hardly remember any of it. Still, he was conscious now and was a quick study. Pain was throbbing in his legs and head, but no pain medication was fogging his brain. He'd palmed the pills once he'd become conscious for longer periods. He could let them think he was woozy, and he was, for purely natural reasons. He preferred pain to ignorance any day.

He turned the chair wheels toward the latest person who had *whooshed* into his territory. They never knocked around here. Medical personnel were like that.

He cocked his head at the visitor. Someone new. Someone not all in white scrubs. (He thought hospital personnel wore figured scrubs now, whimsically colorful, to put patients at ease, but in this place both doctors and nurses wore wedding-gown white.)

Having the light from the huge window at his back was an advantage. He could assess his latest visitor.

Tallish. Female. Wearing a pale green silk runway suit worth a couple thousand with a Hermès scarf as carelessly arranged as her tawny blond hair. A professional, surely. But what kind? Chorus girl legs and knows it. Skirt hem just at the knee. Clipboard? Short, polished nails. Not a nurse, for sure. Doctor? Too upscale. Too silent. No "Good morning, how are you today?"

He could play that game. He observed her taking him in. He had no idea what he looked like. Felt like hell, but he wasn't going to cop to a weakness.

"May I sit?" she asked.

He nodded. *What the hell—?* The accent was slight, but European. He'd overheard a babel of languages since he'd been brought here, barely conscious. English. French. German. Some others. . . .

"My name is Schneider," she said, leaning forward to reveal a tantalizing glimpse of cleavage where the suit lapels met, holding out one hand.

Nobody medical shook hands in a hospital. Her hand was warm where his was cold, and her grip was solid. He returned it, even though that sent a spasm down his shoulder to his spine to his damned useless legs.

"Doctor?" he asked.

"In a sense." Like a doctor, she studied his chart on the clipboard, putting him in uneasy suspension. "Your case is most interesting."

"Tell me about it. Nobody's thought to mention how interesting I was to me."

She chuckled. "Americans. So direct."

"Since I'm direct you might as well tell me who and what you are and what right you have to read up on my blood pressure and bowel movements."

"*Challenging*, not direct," she corrected herself. "All right, Mr. Randolph, I'll tell you what you ask and then you can answer some questions for me."

Randolph. That *wasn't* his name. He knew *that*. When you're at a disadvantage and don't know what's going on, act as if you do. Let *them* tell *you*, when they think all along that *they're* conducting an interrogation.

"No one quite knows what happened to you, Mr. Randolph. Do you?"

He shrugged. *Ouch.* Apparently he couldn't move much of anything.

"Obviously," she went on, "a climbing accident, but what kind? Were you alone on the mountain? Was it equipment failure? An avalanche? Carelessness?"

He felt the wince cross his features before he could stop it.

She caught it and threw it back at him. "You resent the implication that you could have been careless. You're not the sort of man to make mistakes."

"And you know this how?"

"It's my job to know what you think."

It's my job to keep you from knowing that, he thought. *I'd do it better if I weren't in so much pain. As you well know, you leggy blond bully.*

"My name is Schneider," she repeated. "Revienne Schneider. I'm here to find out about your accident. Temporary memory loss about the details is to be expected."

Her voice was soft, yet rich. He'd heard women announcers on German radio who purred over the airwaves that way, amazingly seductive for a language that seemed harsh. Yet she dressed like a Frenchwoman. And her first name stemmed from the French verb for "returning, haunting." Odd name. Odd that he should remember such oddments of French.

"You don't speak much, but you think a lot," she said.

"A man with temporary memory loss wouldn't have much to say."

"*Hmm.*" She licked her lips judiciously as she studied the unseen chart again. "It's quite remarkable that you survived a fall of so far. The surgeons said the violence of the impact was severe."

Surgeons. How many? For what? What was wrong with him, other than temporary memory loss and the fact that his legs were in heavy incapacitating casts? And the pain all over, of course. No one had told him anything. He wasn't sure how long he'd been unconscious, or conscious. Shards of motion, conversation swirled around his brain, yet his first clear memory had been of looking out the window. Just now.

"I fell here?"

"In the Alps? No. You were flown in."

"From—"

"Nepal."

"I am quite the climber, aren't I?"

Nepal! That didn't sound right. Falling, yes. Something in his gut twisted and fell again. Falling.

She smiled so slightly he might have been imagining it. "Climbers are a breed apart. I can't say I understand the sport myself. The ego must be as high as the mountain to be conquered."

He said nothing. She was both criticizing and admiring him, appealing to his ego, appealing to his . . . libido, whatever he had left of it after the fall and the pain and the medication.

"You're a . . . psychiatrist," he said. "You think you can manipulate my memory of the fall to come back."

Her slight shrug didn't pain her shoulders, but it did wonders for her bodice. He *did* have some libido left, after all. Since he was forgoing the pain pills, he might as well sample some alternative medication. . . .

"You're a man used to being in control, Mr. Randolph. If you weren't wealthy, you wouldn't be at this sanitarium. If you weren't willing to risk, you wouldn't be in a wheelchair." She leaned closer again, flashed her subtle cleavage, hardly worth it. "Were you drunk?"

"No!" The response was instant, emphatic. He surprised himself.

"As I say. You are a man using to being in control. Or believing that he is. Or it could be denial. Do you know?"

He was silent, thinking. So much was foggy, even without drugs. Drunk. The accusation repelled him. Why was this his strongest reaction yet? Why was he so sure?

"If you have to ask, *you* don't know," he said.

Chagrin flickered over her annoyingly serene features.

"They'd have taken blood tests right after the accident, yes?" he asked.

She nodded. "No alcohol or recreational drugs in your

system. At that point. But you were flown in from another continent."

He nodded, in turn, to the window and the panorama of what he now knew were the Alps. But which Alps? French, Italian, Swiss? The Alps snaked across Europe like the rim of a massive crater.

He said, "Any climber, especially a control freak, would be crazy to drink anything but water up there."

"'Control freak.' I do love American expressions. They always cut to the . . . pursuit."

"Chase. Cut to the chase. The expression is based on early filmmaking. Directors of cheap thriller movies would skip the exposition, the dialogue, and cut to the action scene: bad guys chasing good guys."

"And which guy are you?"

He smiled at how formal the word *guy* sounded in her overprecise English. "We don't know yet, do we? So why'd you ask if I was drunk, when you knew the tests proved me sober?"

"I wanted your spontaneous answer."

"Just to be mean? Taunt the invalid?" He almost added, "Get a rise out of him?" but decided that was too close to reality.

Actually, he was enjoying this in more ways than one. He'd heard only solicitous murmurs in the far back of his mind for a long time, maybe even weeks. It was good to exercise his brain on something, someone not treating him like a helpless child.

She pursed her lips while examining the chart he suspected was a meaningless prop for her inquisition. Psychiatrists always thought they could outthink their patients, and she was exactly what he'd suspected she was. But what kind of psychiatrist?

"Actually, Mr. Randolph," she said at last, "being drunk is the only rational explanation for why you weren't more seriously injured. The surgeons said your fall had the impact of a car crash at sixty miles an hour. You should be dead, or in a cast up to your cerebellum. Instead, you have a couple of broken legs. Not fun, but not as lethal as it should be."

"You'd prefer me dead?"

"Of course not. But the surgeons said that the only way you could have come off so lightly, the only way anyone did from an impact like that, was as a drunk driver. The kind that walks away from a crash that kills his victims because he was so inebriated his body was utterly limp during the crash. Senselessness saves the sinner."

He didn't like hearing how bad it could have been. Or being compared to a drunk driver. He knew he hadn't brought this on himself. Why was she trying to make him feel guilty? Some shrink! She was doing everything she could to rile him. Weren't there laws against this kind of patient abuse?

He gazed out the window. From this distance the majestic peaks seemed only postcard pretty, not lethal. And he couldn't picture himself attacking those sharp icy teeth with pitons and a pickax. Not his thing. But it must be.

He glanced back. Her eyes had never left his face.

"Maybe," he said, "I'm just a relaxed kind of guy."

"That doesn't go with the control freak."

"Maybe I'm more complex than you think."

"Oh, I think you're very complex, Mr. Randolph. Too much so. I don't want to keep you. À bientôt."

Until later.

He watched her leave, relishing a future tête-à-tête. His legs were broken, maybe not badly, thank God, but she was right about his need for control. He hated this wheelchair.

He propelled it into the adjoining bathroom, through a bland blond door wide enough to accommodate it. Brushed steel assistance bars were everywhere, but he was interested in the shower rod above the—nice, if his casts were off!—Jacuzzi bathtub.

Pushing himself upright against the white-tiled wall, he

studied the rod and its attachments to the tile. Solid. Everything here was for security and safety. German-built. Like Revienne Schneider.

He grasped the pole underhanded and then hauled up against his imprisoned legs. If he was such a gung ho mountain climber, he didn't want to lose any upper body strength. He guessed he'd been doing this during every conscious, unchaperoned moment. The first pull-up was still agony. The second worse. He did ten. Twelve, twenty, then stopped and lowered himself on trembling arms into the wheelchair.

He'd forgotten to check himself out in the mirror over the sink while he'd been upright, but it was probably just as well. He had a feeling he wouldn't recognize his face. He knew "things," could think, but he didn't know a damn thing about himself or how he'd got here. What really bothered him was the name "Randolph." It had a vague familiarity, but it wasn't his. It didn't feel like his name.

Nothing did. Surnames tumbled through his brain— O'Donnell . . . Kinkaid . . . Bar . . . Bartle. Moline. But that was a town in Illinois. His brain had salvaged lots of general information, but no specifics. No faces and places. He'd have to analyze himself before that tight-lipped shrink pried out more than he wanted her to.

He knew a lot about mountains and foreign languages and attractive interrogators, but he didn't know a damn thing about himself except what he could weasel out of his shrink.

Nothing.

Not even his name.

Matt, maybe. The name just came to him! Matt?

Matt Randolph. Didn't feel right.

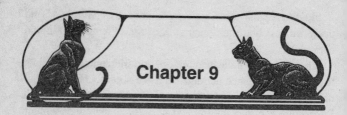

Chapter 9

From Here
to Urbanity

Even long, lean Fontana brothers, Las Vegas's own Magnificent Ten, have to disembark from the Rolls onto the desert sand when we arrive at the party destination in the dark of evening.

Wait a minute. *Desert sand?*

I am not the only one befuddled, although I am the only one who is licking sand grains from between my unshod toes.

"Hey," says one plaintive voice. "This isn't the strip club, is it?"

By now three rounds of champagne have sloshed in the gathered glasses, except for Mr. Matt's and mine.

That extra-dark tint on the Rolls's windows may have been disorienting.

"Naw, that must be the place," Emilio announces, gesturing with his still-full champagne glass.

Indeed, amidst the Stygian darkness that surrounds the party we can see the illuminated glitter of a large entrance canopy.

(This Stygian darkness is like super-dark shades and refers to some ancient place underground, like a cave. Or a wine cellar. Or a tomb. Even now I do not quite grasp our situation. And I am the only one in the party fit to grasp anything, except for Mr. Matt, who is starting to frown just before the Rolls headlights go out and we are all truly in the dark.)

The sound of leather soles grinding on sand guides me forward. Mr. Matt and I have been abandoned to trek along behind the brothers ten and Uncle Mario.

By now I have been noticed, and, in fact, had about six toasts made to my unexpected presence en route to the bachelor party. That is why I and Mr. Matt are sober and surefooted, and all the Fontanas are lurching along like hail-fellows-well-met.

I am starting to feel the hairs on my spine stiffening and standing upright.

It could be the cooler night air.

It could be the off-key chorus of "O Sole Mio," that is drifting back on the desert air.

It could be the fact that the convivial singing comes to a sudden halt on the warm, lamp-lit threshold before us all.

I, of course, was born to see in the dark, so I swagger into the lead. That is not hard to do. The brothers Fontana are already swaying instead of swaggering. I have never known them to be the tipsy sort, but this is a landmark occasion.

I gaze into the light, my pupils slitting to laser-sharp focus long before the humans in the party can stop blinking blindly.

And a little cat shall lead them. . . .

I march into the glare, having spotted all the hallmarks of bachelor bliss awaiting our party: several human little dolls of the leggy sort, attired in skimpy wisps of sheer fabrics decorated with sequins and rhinestones and (my favorite) mounds of marabou feathers.

Let the games begin!

Chapter 10

Perennial Partner

Matt was trying to be a good go-along guy.

Mob scenes, figurative or literal, weren't his thing.

Stag entertainment wasn't on his horizon or in his history.

An ex-priest had a hard time regarding women as sex objects.

Large amounts of bare female skin still made him uneasy.

Intimately, it was a turn-on. Publicly, it was . . . gross, crude, blatant. Exploitive of both gawker and gawkee.

And, of course, all en route to this bachelor blowout, he wondered, not what Jesus would do—He'd probably be okay with it; witness the woman at the well and the wedding at Cana; Jesus had been the Prince of Peace and the Soul of Mercy and Tolerance—but what Temple would think.

Of him.

This did not promise to be an easygoing evening.

So when he saw the peep show backlit at the entrance to wherever they had been driven, he thought, *Holy mackerel!*

Butch Cassidy and the Sundance Kid could not have been greeted by a perkier array of corseted, feather boa–strewn, high heel–booted saloon girls in their heyday.

He'd expected to suffer through this supposed festivity. He hadn't expected to be as badly ribbed as the guest of honor, bridegroom-to-be Aldo Fontana.

"Pretty good goods," a Fontana brother commented, jabbing his ribs.

"You get what you pay for," Matt answered, meaning every shade of the words.

They bounced off Fontana brother bonhomie.

"Right. This is way spicier than I expected, now that Aldo is giving up his wild, womanizing ways. We're gonna actually have fun. I can tell. Let the par*tee* begin!"

Matt and, of all not-people, Midnight Louie were the last to move into the dazzling light. The cat had been first, but now hesitated on the threshold.

Temple's black cat, a last-minute hitchhiker, finally trod in delicately, forefoot by forefoot. Matt could have sworn the cat was as much taken aback by this Wild West saloon scenario as he was.

"We'll both have to keep a sober eye on the proceedings," Matt told Louie under his breath.

It disturbed him immensely that the big black cat winked at him.

Okay. One eye closed momentarily. Maybe he had a hair caught in it.

Twelve men and cat had entered a *Wild Wild West* fantasy of a Victorian brothel. The flocked floral wallpaper wasn't scarlet woman crimson-colored, but it was velvet-flocked: deep blue against a silver foil background.

The carpeting was a field of Victorian, full-blown roses (so appropriate to the feminine residents). The shades were blue and green with touches of gold.

Beyond the foyer in the parlor, on various blue velvet love seats and settees in the Victorian style, lounged, lay, and reclined about a dozen women attired in bits and pieces of corsets and lingerie, all in shades of blue.

If there were eight groomsmen in the party, there was a shade of blue for each one: baby blue, aqua, sky blue, periwinkle . . . lavender-blue, Dilly, Dilly . . . teal, ice blue, royal blue, sapphire blue, and even navy blue, in the form of a sailor suit with a bikini bottom and a skimpy sea-shrunken top.

While the groomsmen leapt to the task of inspection, Matt was interested to see that Aldo and Nicky were loitering in the foyer with frowns on their faces.

One was almost wed, one married, so Matt approved of them showing at least some discretion. Uncle Macho Mario Fontana was accepting a cigar the size of a submarine sandwich from the madam of the place, the only woman fully clothed. She wore some Mae West blue-sequined gown rimmed in pale blue feathers at the shoulders.

Matt edged over to the frowners because they most closely reflected his own confusion.

"We were supposed to go to the G-String Club on the Strip," Nicky was saying under his breath, "with the nude harpists. I mean, fun's fun, but this place is obviously—" He shut up as he noticed Matt approaching.

Aldo's back was to Matt and he kept talking. "Kit will have my nose hairs in a vise and our Miss Temple will have all our heads on pikes outside the Crystal Phoenix if she finds out about this. The guys said they'd arranged a first-class venue with one discreet, cake-popper-out-of stripper. The usual harmless prank."

"This," Matt said, "doesn't look 'usual' to me, and I've never been to one of these before."

Nicky's upper lip was actually dewed with tiny dots of sweat. He had his cell phone to his ear.

"Sorry, Father," he murmured absently. "Damn!" he spat at Aldo. "I'm not getting a signal. We are screwed. What's going on here? That drive was way too long."

Aldo was chewing his lower lip. "I thought we were deliberately being driven around town so we'd have time to do our duty by the champagne."

The eldest and youngest Fontana brothers were clearly dealing with an unexpected situation.

"Why don't we ask the driver?" Matt suggested.

Nicky and Aldo exchanged a long stare.

"Good idea!" Aldo strode toward the door, Nicky and Matt behind him.

Aldo opened it on someone on the other side. Someone in a nifty black chauffeur's cap and jacket, and nothing else but fishnet stockings, four-inch black heels, and an Uzi cradled in her uniformed elbow.

"*Holy shi—shazam!*" Nicky breathed, glancing at Matt midway through his expletive.

"No need to get huffed," the caramel-skinned chauffeurette said, caressing the Uzi's trigger with her forefinger. Her nails were long and lacquered crimson. "You all look so cute standing out here with your mouths hanging open, but you'd better get back inside before this big mean gun gets too heavy for little me to hold and I grab onto the wrong part."

Nicky and Aldo backed up quickly. Maybe it was her remark about the wrong part. Matt stayed put.

"You drove us out here?" he asked. "Why?"

She looked him over, mostly his face and blond hair. "You may be an innocent bystander, mister, but an Uzi isn't very discriminating."

"Jesus!" Aldo breathed behind him. "I for one don't underestimate the 'weaker' sex. This is as serious as that chest-stapler she's holding. What the hell—?"

"Get back inside," Nicky ordered. When Matt didn't move, he shouted at the girl, "You'd off a priest?"

"Ex," Matt tossed over his shoulder without taking his eyes from the woman. He was used to talking to suicidal and sometimes homicidal people on his call-in radio advice show. This girl didn't strike him as either.

But her next words and tone changed his mind. "A priest," she purred. "Now isn't that interesting. Maybe we can use you for some ceremonial necessities later."

"They don't do extreme unction anymore," Aldo said, jerking Matt back inside the foyer by the jacket sleeve. "Hold your trigger finger, lady. We're all inside."

Matt shook himself loose as soon as the door slammed shut. "She's not for real."

"That Uzi sure is," Nicky said. "Never argue with a fully automatic gun that can kill your whole damn family in one strafe." He redialed his cell phone. "Nothing. You take this," he said to Matt, slipping it into his jacket pocket. "It's an auto-dial to Van. I have a feeling this is a Fontana affair." His face and voice were grim.

"Some gangsta hoods have heisted us," Aldo said. "Don't let the James Bond girl in fishnet hose fool you, padre. This is a sharp operation. They've got Fontana Inc. in the palms of their machine pistols. The whole enchilada. *Shit!*"

"Yup. The whole Mama Fontana pasta factory." Nicky turned to Matt. "Play along. Don't make any fuss. We're the target, obviously. They may overlook you."

"They?"

But the two brothers were separating at the double doors to the parlor, drawing Berettas and waiting like cops about to storm a crime in progress.

"Mr. Fontana and . . . Mr. Fontana?" came the madam's once-booming voice, sounding quivery. "Please come in."

"And drop your weapons before you do," a second voice commanded.

Consulting each other with a glance, Nicky and Aldo lowered their guns to the floor and kicked them inside onto the field of blue flowers that carpeted the place.

Matt stood, shocked, in the foyer as the two men vanished into the Victorian sitting room at some unseen gunpoint.

This must be act one in a Vegas mob war.

From Temple's talk of the Fontana brothers, he'd considered them hunky comic relief on the Las Vegas scene. Apparently it was a lot more serious than that. Thank God Temple was safe at home at the Circle Ritz. *Sweet Jesus. Louie!* Her precious alley cat was here, in danger of getting caught in the crossfire. Anything happened to him, it'd be worse than the current anxiety she was feeling about Max. She tried to downplay it, but he knew.

Nicky was right. Nobody had mentioned him. He glanced to his left and the floral-carpeted staircase leading into shadows above. Thank God! Midnight Louie stood five steps up, waiting for him. Looking like the cat was concerned about *him*, rather than vice versa. That was a cat for you.

But Louie was right. Matt got it. In this crowd of large, dark-haired men barging into that crowded and armed and dangerous brothel sitting room, an effacing blond guy might get lost. He had been. Along with an alley cat. The driver-gangster girl wouldn't forget him, but she was pulling guard duty outside, perhaps for the duration.

He moved swiftly to the stairs and cautiously up the treads. The place may have looked like it dated from the last days of the frontier, but the steps were solid and creakless. All the better for serial hanky-panky in the night. Not that sex was on anybody's mind anymore. Just its perennial partner. Death.

Only when he reached the dark at the top of the stairs did Matt notice that Midnight Louie was no longer anywhere to be seen.

Chapter 11

Déjà Vu

I am relieved that Mr. Matt Devine takes my hint and pulls an instant Mystifying Max–like vanishing act. Time to hang loose and regroup. What we have here is a cast of dozens with no guide as to who's who and what's what.

What I do not like is seeing such heavy artillery in little dolls' hands. Some may call me sexist, but some may also call me "Kitty," so I do not apologize for anything. Clearly, the Aldo Fontana bachelor party has been driven to, and walked into, a serious kettle of sharks.

First, I do my duty by my Miss Temple and stash her amour, Mr. Matt Devine, safely out of sight. That is not hard. He is taking the situation very seriously, and follows me like a lamb. He has never been one to underestimate a cat, especially *moi,* just like the F Boys do not underestimate the Female of the Species. Felines and females. Together we can tame Homo sapiens.

Next, I ankle back down into the teeth of the "situation."

Like Nicky and Aldo Fontana and Mr. Matt, I find my way blocked at the bottom of the stairs by a dame.

She is even dressed in a cute little outfit that shows off her gams and high-heeled little claws and her perky little face and figure. She has long black hair, green-gold eyes, and one white vibrissae in a field of black. (Vibrissae is the scientific name for the airy front feelers that allow a fellow or a gal of my persuasion to know where we are going, even in the dark. The human word "whiskers" is too rough-and-ready a name for such a subtle and sensitive attribute of my kind.)

We joust vibrissae for a moment or two, getting to know each other.

"Where are you going?" she demands.

"I take it from your tone that this is your territory. Are you also in the employ of the armed forces occupying the place?"

"Never," she hisses. "But you are an invader too."

I eye my soon-to-be conquest. She is wearing a turquoise cape rimmed in matching marabou feathers. This is an irresistible lure for one of my sensitive yet macho nature. I have heard of these show cats in their Elizabethan collars and enhancing capes, but have never encountered one in the fur and flesh so closely. Usually they are caged to protect them from overmuch mauling. If this were a bachelor party for felines, she would be the icing on the fishcake. *Merrrow!*

Still, something criminal is going down here, and it involves my friends, or friends of my friends, and I must stick to duty.

"Stand aside, my dear lady. I am almost the only one of my party who is still free and free-ranging. I must protect my humans."

"And I mine!" she spits back. "Until I know you are to be trusted I am not turning even one more Las Vegas scoundrel loose in this place."

"Ah. Before I ask what you mean by 'Las Vegas scoundrel,'

which strikes me as a case of blatant geography-ism, I must know what 'this place' is."

"Fair enough, Furface. This is the Sapphire Slipper, the finest and classiest little licensed brothel in Nye County."

I inhale deeply. A mistake. This kit is drenched in nip and Chanel No. 5. *Umm.* From what I can tell, she is fully pheromoned and furious, a bad combination.

"And you are the cathouse—?"

"Cat," she snarls, as if daring me to make something of it.

I take another deep breath, maybe just to inhale that hypnotic and potent blend of feline catnip breath and human high-dollar perfume. I scent something else as well. A scintilla of memory. I have met this lady before, in her younger days, on the Strip.

For a moment I cannot speak, smell, or think. *Can it be?*

"What do they call you here?" I ask, braced for a shock.

She sighs. "What else? The clichéd cathouse cat."

"I mean, by name?"

"Here? Baby Blue."

Baby Blue. It is not a bad name. But not the right one.

"So, before you were a Satin," I hazard.

Her eyes grow round and amazed. Then she really looks me over.

There is a long silence while our vibrissae tremor.

"Louie?" she says at last.

"The very one."

"But, but . . . they said you had been run down by a Brinks truck."

"Almost. It was a close shave and a haircut. I was hitching a ride downtown when I was discovered. The guard managed to sock me in the gut with a bag of nickels from the slots. I hit the pavement at twenty-five miles an hour. Between one thing and another, I was off the streets for a few weeks before I finally recovered."

"No wonder I could not find you. I had to go to a shelter to have my litter."

"You were with kit?" I feel as if my gut has taken another shot of nickels. What I most fear may be what I have to face as the truth. "What happened to them?"

Satin shakes her head. "They took them all away, but nobody adopted me. My coat was thin and dry from caring for five kits. I was doomed to a quick exit via the needle until the Sapphire Slipper head lady came in . . . and now they are all in danger—"

"*Shh*," I hiss gently. "If these Sapphire Slipper ladies saved your life, I will save theirs."

"How can you? Outsiders with firearms and issues of their own are all over the place. They invaded and took over our premises before your bachelor bridal party arrived."

I cringe a bit to hear my associates, the formerly fearsome Fontana brothers, described as my "bachelor bridal party."

Satin continues her under-the-breath report. "I managed to slip away unnoticed, but all my Sapphire Slipper ladies have been under guard since two hours before your limousine of humans arrived. That is a most impressive vehicle. You must have become a major entertainment figure to travel in such style. I have seen some fancy rigs pull up to the Sapphire Slipper, but never a stretch Rolls-Royce."

"Stretch Rolls-Royce Silver Cloud," I correct gently. "Yes, I have been in the personal appearance game . . . New York . . . television."

I do not mention that my moments of fame were shilling for a cat food brand I would not touch with an infected toenail. "But now I am back home and working freelance. This is your lucky day. I am a professional. I am founder and CEO of Midnight Inc. Investigations."

"You are a private dick?"

"So they tell me. You can see that I am not exactly at a loss here. Yes, you are right about the Limey limo, ducks. My Las Vegas posse travels only first class, and that is how I will bust us all out of this trap."

"Your posse is large and many, but now they are disarmed and helpless."

"Not usually. But *we* are armed and dangerous, are we not? You still have your shivs, right? These ladies of the night were not so foolish as to disarm you?"

She flashes them with a sudden spurt of street spirit. That is my black Satin! After my recovery from the Brinks job, I found no word of her on the Strip, although I hunted for months. A classy lady like Satin does not disappear unless she is kidnapped for domestic servitude, or worse, dead.

I take a deep breath, like Mr. Matt in a crisis. I do not doubt that Satin lost all her offspring to adoption, but some placements may not have, er, taken. I have a horrible feeling that I know one of her lost litter. There is a chilling likeness about the nose.

Miss Midnight Louise would not be able to keep her claws out of my hide if she knew her assumption of my paternity was right, and that her mother survived to become the house cat at a hooker emporium.

I shudder, which Miss Satin mistakes for regret, rather than fear, thank Bast!

"It is all right, Louie. I do not blame you for my condition and fate. We knew so little about safeguards in those days."

"Right," I say.

I do not know much about them these days either, except that I am surgically sterilized so I can play without paying. "Let us pad into the parlor and see who has the guts and smarts to take down the whole Fontana family at once."

Chapter 12

Cell in Solitary

Matt listened hard in the dark at the top of the stairs. The silence downstairs was reassuring, for the moment. No gunshots and crashing bodies or furniture.

He slipped out of his loafers, stuffed them in his side jacket pockets as best he could, and moved slowly down a long, low-lit hall like a hotel's.

Actually, the layout of this place should come pretty close to a hotel.

The first room—a bedroom—he ventured into was a fussy Victorian affair: high four-poster brass bed with a lot of knobs and curlicues, dressing table, upholstered ottomans, fringe, and feathery dried floral arrangements.

He spotted an oil lamp on the dresser and found a box of long farmers' matches beside it. The oil broadcast a heavy floral scent once the flame was going. Matt stifled a sneeze and went back into the hall, using the flickering light to search for a rear exit. There had to be one, thanks to fire safety standards.

He surveyed each room he passed, making sure they were vacant.

It was like opening the doors onto a series of stage sets. The entrances were set back in niches. Every room had its theme, although shades of blue decorated each one. The colors reminded Matt of the Virgin Mary, hardly the idea here. After three "visitations," he realized that a blue glass Cinderella slipper was a feature in every vignette.

Some rooms teemed with vintage froufrou from the Gay Nineties to the 1940s. After that, nostalgia faded and the décor was showy modern, furnished with sleek mirrors and stainless steel and suede. Every room was pristinely neat, lavish and gaudy in whatever its style, and empty.

How unnerving to think that each room had hosted a paid-for thousand-and-one one-night stands . . . several times over if the bordello was a few decades old.

Some rooms had Jacuzzis and brittle little fountains everywhere. Some rooms, both Victorian and modern, housed strange devices of leather and metal that looked as if they'd been imported from Inquisition Warehouse.

Matt was glad his knowledge of the darker shores of sex for sale was pretty limited.

As he suspected, the hall ended in a back service stairway. He eased the heavy metal fire door open and padded down a few steps. Muffled voices!

He crept down a few more risers.

Several voices. The captives wouldn't be jawing away like this. The gang must have taken over the back rooms as their headquarters while the Fontana party and the residents were held hostage in the front parlor and the adjoining barroom he'd glimpsed through the double interior doors before he'd ducked out.

Not good. He leaned against the wall, holding up the oil lamp and hitting redial on Nicky's cell phone. No bar graph showed up, nothing but a message that the phone was "searching for a signal," and then nothing.

Matt was searching for a signal too.

Call it a sign.

Chapter 13

Courtesans on Parade

Of course, nobody notices a couple of cats roaming the premises.

Some of my breed might be a bit miffed that humankind is so ready to overlook the species the ancient Egyptians worshipped. Unfortunately, any remaining Egyptians have lost the faith. Besides, being overlooked has always been my ace in the hole. Especially if you are black and low-profile. Now we are two.

So Satin and I ankle into the main parlor. I must say I shudder at what I see.

One by one, the Fontana boys have been gestured at major gunpoint into this room. All I see of the gangsters are black boots, leggings, turtleneck-sweater sleeves, and leather gloves. And black 9mm guns to match. I must admit I admire the unknown perps' color choice, although it has long been the uniform of cat burglars, including myself.

Satin and I follow the latest Fontana brother to suffer this in-dignity, unnoticed.

One of them, maybe Ernesto, is being patted down, front and back—intimately—by agile gloved hands, and relieved of his sig-nature Beretta.

I shiver as I observe this. This is not something a guy ought to undergo in front of witnesses, particularly several older brothers.

I growl my protest to Satin.

"Yes, Louie," she comforts me. "It is most ignominious. My ladies here exist to coddle the male ego. They devote their lives to it. Such violation is . . . unthinkable. Males egos are such del-icate flowers."

"Uh. I am a catclaw cactus kinda guy myself. Violate me and I dig deep. These guys are merely playing along for the moment until they figure out the who and why of this high-handed, high-artillery assault. The Fontana family goes back to the days of Thompson submachine guns. True, these bozos got the drop on them, but that will not be all she wrote. Trust me. This is not over."

"So who are the gangsters who hold your male *compadres* captive?"

A good question.

Inside the room, I see the perps are wearing spandex masks that would make them as unrecognizable as Spider-Man's evil twin. However, they have accessorized even that full coverage with large sixties-style black sunglasses, which gives them a creepy bug-eyed look.

Additionally, they range from tallish to six-foot size and say not a word, letting the long lean metal barrels of their guns do the gesturing for them.

All in all, this is a very disturbing and sinister mime act.

Beyond the fussy parlor, I glimpse an empty bar area with the usual clubby look, carpet and leather chairs, mirror and bottle glass. I suggest we remain in this "debriefing" room in our guise of helpless domestic pets.

My description is not half wrong. The masked thugs stripping the Fontana brothers of their weapons are also making unwarranted searches of their underwear.

"Oof!" Emilio objects, avoiding an illegal forward pass with a swiveling hip movement that would do any running back proud. "There is nothing resembling lead there."

I bite my tongue. The nature of this disarming is suddenly all too evident to my super feline senses. The "gangsters" are all of the female persuasion.

I spot the long nailed hands under the leather gloves and watch them add another Beretta to the impressive pile, and shudder. Wait until the boys discover they have been disarmed by women. That is not a macho position to be in.

"The gangsters have very agile and clever claws," Miss Satin allows.

That is the thing. This gang of masked women have high-end manicures and their claws are all utterly false, the glue-on kind adapted in envy of my kind.

Why do these dames need these guys disarmed and dangerous?

I am detecting a certain barely veiled lust.

I must admit that I am used to that reaction among the female faction, as are the Fontana boys. It is just that we are not used to being disabled because of it. I do not know how to convey these ugly realities to poor little Satin.

While I dither, so uncharacteristically, she is coming to her own conclusions from her years in the brothel.

"These women do not want hostages," she merows in my ear. "They want mates."

This wafts a vibrissa too close to our own once-upon-a-time relationship.

I huff up my collar into an impressive ruff and growl.

No one notices.

"All right," one of the masked and clawed dames (you would

think she was the homicidal Hyacinth, a Siamese of my acquaintance) snarls. Yes, she snarled, just as you and I would, if we were both feline.

"You boys can settle down here now that your claws are clipped. Sit down. Look and do not touch. Say nothing. We will let you know what comes next."

Puzzled and disarmed, the Fontana boys sit gingerly on the froufrou pieces of furniture. I understand their conflict. A macho guy doesn't do blue satin, but neither does a gentleman poleax a lady, not even an armed and dangerous gang of them.

"Now see here," Macho Mario says, not moving a muscle. "You do not know who you are tangling with."

"It is you who are ignorant of the fury of your opponents," one dame says in a credible baritone growl.

"Sit. Don't move. We have business elsewhere in the establishment, but are leaving guards at each archway."

A gentleman does not poleax a lady, but Macho Mario's expression as he drops his weight into a pale blue velvet upholstered Victorian chair indicates he may now be willing to make an exception.

After the gang presence withdraws, I notice that Mr. Nicky Fontana, the youngest and only married brother, and the only CEO among them, is missing.

So I inform Miss Satin, sotto voce. (This is an operatic term meaning under my tuna breath.)

After she reels away, she comes up with a rejoinder. "Why would they single out your Mr. Nicky?"

"I do not think they did. They are interested in the *bachelor* party. He is not a bachelor and thus escaped their notice, like my Mr. Matt."

"Tell me again about 'your Mr. Matt.'"

"He is the only cream in the all-black flock, also not a Fontana. He was just along for the ride."

"So were you," she points out.

"So, they got a couple of ringers in the bunch. Let us remain in the parlor and see what the Fontana boys and the ladies of the house have to say to one another."

While we creep farther into this Suite in Blue, we see the house ladies sitting up straighter than the Teetotaler Ladies Tea Society on one side and the Fontana boys staring at their polished shoe tips and their buffed nails on the other, with a couple of the black-clad posse in between.

Aldo is checking the ticking old-fashioned mantel clock every thirty seconds. He is calculating that this was supposed to be a boys' night out, an all-nighter. No one will miss them until at least one P.M. tomorrow, Tuesday, give or take a hangover or twelve.

I see that the gang has removed all of their Rolexes as well as the Italian hardware. So is profit the motive, or something more personal?

"You know who these women are?" Aldo asks the madam.

"We do not usually entertain women."

"You recognize any of them?"

There is a rustle of taffeta and tulle. My nails itch for a good rip, but I hold back.

A girl done up like the Blue Angel speaks hesitantly. "I recognized one voice."

"Yes?" the madam encourages the damsel in question.

"I think she called a couple days ago, inquiring about our . . . hours."

The madam barks out a laugh. "Pretty much twenty-four seven, like the rest of Las Vegas. What did she think?"

"She asked if we . . . handled . . . groups."

"And—?" The madam was frowning now.

"I said we can do groups up to twenty, and she booked us for tonight for a twenty-four-hour exclusive."

"*Shii . . . take* mushrooms," Aldo explodes, suddenly mindful of the female company. A Fontana boy is always the soul of courtesy. "That means no one else is going to show up here until tomorrow night. Why'd the gang need that much time?"

"Scary," Emilio says mournfully. "I do not even slot in my best girlfriend for a full twenty-four exclusive."

"Have you had such a booking before?" Rico asks the madam.

She shakes her lavender-blue tinted head.

"I thought it was a corporate inquiry," the angel-baby in blue woman says in defense. "The woman who called sounded like an executive assistant. I thought it was one of the big hotels going all out for a celebrity high roller and his posse."

"She was an executive thief," Emilio grumbles. "They have got a hundred thou in our Rolexes alone. Rolexi?"

"You never were any good in Latin class in high school," Rico says.

"Who needs more Latin than '*veni, vidi, vici*'?"

The madam, who must have had high school Latin too and learned Caesar's boast: "I came, I saw, I conquered," laughs again.

"Not tonight, boys. Besides, surely the Fontana brothers can disarm an army of men in tights."

That is just it. The madam has not had a close look at our captors. These are not men in tights, but girls in guns, an even uglier thought. Those delicate ladyfingers are not used to packing trigger-sensitive iron. They could break a nail and spray the room with bullets without even meaning to.

"It sounds," says the madam, "like we all will be here for a while. We should introduce ourselves. I am Miss Kitty."

Satin and I exchange a glance. It is sad how often our kind's various nicknames are borrowed for ladies of the night and shady activities. The ancient Egyptians stuck to a simple "Meow" when naming us.

The ladies give their first names in turn. There is an Angela, Babette, Crystal, Deedee, Fifi, Gigi, Heather, Inez, Jazz, Kiki, Lili, Niki, and Zazu.

Satin hisses into my ear. "Only thirteen are working tonight, a bad sign. The reservation was for that number."

Meanwhile, I am doing some math of my own. There are the ten Fontana brothers, Mr. Matt, and Uncle Mario, the big kahuna, who has been detained, bound, in the archway to the barroom. That is twelve. "Who is the thirteenth of these ladies for?" I wonder.

"The limo driver," Satin hisses back.

But the limo driver was replaced, so why order the full house? And where is the limo driver, anyway? Obviously, someone else took over for him and drove the whole crew here to this unexpected destination.

Was he bribed, led astray, or waylaid? I can only hope they knocked him out back at Gangsters' and he is now raising the alarm in Vegas.

Except who is he going to call when the whole clan Fontana is under lock and key and gun sites here at the Sapphire Slipper? And he would not know where to send anyone, anyway.

Who you gonna call? Crimebusters!

I turn to Satin. "I am going to, uh, deputize you for the duration. Midnight Inc. Investigations needs a little beefing up at the moment." I notice the airy vibrissae over her eyes waft. "Nothing personal. Just an expression we use in the private cop trade."

"I will be your undercovers partner, Louie," she says, rubbing the side seams on my slinky black satin coat the right way.

I swallow. "*Undercover* partner, Satin. That is the expression we use in the private cop trade."

I must admit, though, that the atmosphere here puts a wild hair up my nose. And it is black satin.

Chapter 14

Name Day

"Mike, my lad!" The greeting boomed from the doorway with theatrical gusto.

There'd been no name on the chart dangling from the foot of his bed. He'd checked after the psychiatrist had left. There had been no chart left. Strange.

The late-middle-aged man beaming at him from the doorway looked nice enough. A civilian in rumpled suit and tie; good quality but rode hard and put up wet, like a saddle horse. A little overstuffed he was, but with a sharp, shrewd nose and chin. He was clean-shaven, but the graying hair was longish in back. Sharp hazel eyes were packed in weary pouches. Looked a little like a brilliant conductor focused on so much the rest of us—we the audience—didn't see, that he appeared a bit scattered.

"Glad to see you sitting up." The fellow bustled over to sit on the bed's foot and dig in the net grocery bag he carried. "Chocolate, some English-language newspapers."

He studied the chocolate wrappers handed to him. "Swiss. I thought so."

"Of course, my bright boy. Only the best for your recuperation."

"And just how am I 'your boy'?"

The man froze, then leaned in to whisper, so he was forced to wheel closer to hear.

"I know we need to be discreet," the man said, "but I doubt this room is bugged."

"I don't." Suddenly his feeling of unease made sense.

"Ma . . . Mike?" The furrowed brow was a washboard of worry lines now, the man's eyes darting around the room. "When I last saw you, you were out cold, but—"

"When did you last see me? After I fell off a mountain?"

"No. Here. After you were flown in."

"From Nepal."

The man ducked his head in vague agreement. "Mike, don't you remember the accident?"

"No. I don't remember Mike either. Or you."

"I'm Garry Randolph."

"A relation, then?"

"More of choice than of blood."

"Then why the bloody hell did you give me your surname when you checked me in? Don't I have any relatives, family?"

"You've been estranged from them for almost two decades."

"Why? What did I do to estrange my entire family?"

"It was more something that was done to you."

"You're talking in riddles," he said sharply. "What would lose a man his whole family?"

"A boy. You were just seventeen then. I've been your family ever since. It was . . . your choice. The situation was dreadful, but you chose another path than falling back into the old life and trying to forget."

"What path did I choose?"

"Justice."

The word made him draw back. It was a weighty responsibility he wasn't quite ready for. "And justice involved my climbing mountains?"

"You really don't remember . . . anything?"

"Oh, I know where Switzerland is, and that it's famous for chocolate." He tossed the thick bar onto the thin white bed-spread, even though it looked good to his medication-dry mouth. "I know what mountains are, and pain. I know I need to be care-ful. But with who, old man? And why?"

"Not with me. Trust me on that. I've been your friend for a long time."

"Not 'Michael' Randolph's friend?"

"No. You're right. That's my last name. You've been almost a son to me, this old bachelor."

He saw the man's eyes fighting moisture at not being recog-nized. At having to state their relationship, give it a context. This man wasn't a psychiatrist. He wasn't wearing an expensive French suit.

He, "Mad Mike," may not know who he was, but he recog-nized genuine emotion.

He clasped the man's hand, hard. "I'm better than they think," he whispered. "Physically, if not mentally. We've gotten out of tight corners before?"

Garry Randolph nodded, once.

"We'll do it again."

The old man embraced him. Whispered something for his ears only.

"We will, Max. But you didn't hear that name from me."

Max.

It was strong, that name. Short for what? Maximilian? Germanic. Teutonic. A European name. Not quite . . . right. But he had a name and this man knew it. This man trusted him with it.

No one else could know this. Tight corners. But a real name was something he'd needed to know. It felt right. Max. He was Max. In time, he would remember all that Max had been. And known. Including what kind of justice he had fallen off a mountain hunting.

Chapter 15

Bridesmaids Revisited

By now the parlor scene has settled down.

The Fontana brothers and Uncle Mario have been stripped of all the heavy metal on their persons, which I see includes a few switchblades. These weapons and primo examples of the watchmaker's art are piled on the big round table with a fringed cloth. They are guarded by a single sylph in black spandex bearing a single Uzi.

A whole lot of tall, rangy Fontana brothers are hunched un-happily on the various blue velvet Victorian settees intended to be draped by skimpily-clad ladies of the night. And day, here in Las Vegas.

Macho Mario Fontana is established in a low-slung Victorian chair, attended by the madam herself.

The resident "girls" are arrayed along the walls, eyeing the Uzis at the archways to the bar and the foyer with edgy respect.

Only us felines are cool. Like the kidnappers. Wait! How can you "kidnap" a roster of fully adult brothers? An interesting question.

I send Satin to the kitchen to eavesdrop on the other distaff kidnappers and remain to see how the men of the party are reacting.

"This is ridiculous," Macho Mario blusters. "We have a lot of outside firepower to call on."

"If you could call," a guard in masked spandex purrs, pointing to the pile of RAZR cell phones on the table. "Take a gun, a watch, and a cell phone from a tough Las Vegas wiseguy, and he is limp linguini."

Yup. This dame purrs. Like the lead femme fatale on a soap opera.

A lot of Fontana fingers twitch at that taunt. They not only are *not* trigger fingers, or itchy cell phone fingers, but well-buffed champagne bottle fingers. I must admit it makes the hair on my hackles rise to see so many dudes cowed by a bunch of distaff desperados. *Desperadas.*

Then out from the kitchens via the empty barroom strides the full posse again: I count seven altogether. They are all either anorexic muscle boys, or women.

I notice the Fontanas notice the same thing, and breathe out mutual sighs of relief.

Premature.

"We can cuff you if you need it," a woman's voice says. "There are plenty of cuffs around here."

"Even gentle baby blue–dyed, rabbit fur–lined cuffs," another lady desperado lisps, flaunting a few pair. "We like *live* rabbits."

A few Uzis focus rather unnervingly on both the Fontana boys and the brothel girls.

"Faux fur!" the madam shouts, like a team coach crying "Foul." "No rabbits were injured in constructing our erotic handcuffs! I have a paper that guarantees that."

"What about the *girls* in those handcuffs?" one black-clad figure asks, twirling the silly artifact in question.

I will never understand the human notion of naughtiness. If they had ever had to wear a collar for real, or get their ears clipped or rear branded for identification purposes, they would see that S&M is really just Sad and Mean. But maybe these toys are for B&D. My canine cousins know about Bondage and Discipline all too well. Luckily, we felines are usually the S part of S&M.

However, the whip hand, so to speak, is held by the little ladies with the captured Berettas and switchblades and even metal nail files, oh my.

Well, Satin is hissing along with the commando girls now, and we dudes—the Fontanas and myself—are seriously outnumbered.

Aldo takes the lead and answers. "We were bound for a harmless little bachelor party at a harmless little bar. Not here. Not for a brothel, however well staffed and really well decorated and, er, manned by such lovely ladies. If you want to condemn anybody, condemn yourselves. You picked this place."

There is a long sentence.

Then one clear soprano answers, "But you *didn't* pick us!"

The nasty black spandex masks peel off.

I gaze upon beauty bare, an octet of lovely ladies in the prime of their twenties and thirties. Their expressions are intense.

"Why are we always the bridesmaids and never the brides?" another demands.

"Aldo may be tying the knot—the only real man among you!—but you younger brothers are still playing the field. And we, the field, don't like it," says another.

Silence prevails.

The Fontana brothers eye the women they chose to play bridesmaids to their groomsmen in the imminent wedding.

"Hey!" shouts Macho Mario. "I'm not even *in* the wedding party.

I am an innocent victim. Take my nephews. They are philandering dogs! But I am innocent. I should be sprung."

"He is 'sprung' all right," one woman says, sashaying over to cluck Macho Mario under the chin with the business end of a confiscated Beretta.

While he sputters his indignation, she eyes the ladies of the house arrayed along the walls.

"Okay. Here's the deal. This is between us and these handsome but sadly maritally backward guys. We can confine you in the house B&D room, or you can put these sweet baby blue and pink faux rabbit–fur cuffs on our hairy-wristed guests. It is up to you, ladies. Nine ought to do it, if we include Mr. Macho shaking on the lounge chair over there."

Fontana brothers pale in unison as the blue and pink fuzzy handcuffs are flourished.

I sympathize, observing with a low growl to Satin, "These rogue bridesmaids are mean. Real guys do not wear pink. Especially in fetish wear!"

"Really? I think the baby blue at least goes rather well with black hair." She bats her eyelashes at me.

Yes, we felines do have eyelashes outside of cartoon representations of our kind. Take a close look at yours sometime, if you can do so without a faceful of shivs.

Me? Bound in baby blue? Pretty in pink? I do not think so!

One thing I find consoling: Mr. Nicky Fontana is also missing. In a blitz of brothers I can understand how the berserk bridesmaids overlooked a married one they seldom saw. Those full-coverage masks and bug-eyed sunglasses do not permit much peripheral vision. And these little dolls are totally focused on the objects of their frustrated affections, not any spare and ineligible dude.

"This is just a girls' idea of a bachelor party they can control," Miss Satin sniffs. "They have no criminal intent and are paying for the staff's time."

"Fur-covered or not, those handcuffs are effective," I say. "I do not like to see dudes of my gender, if not my species, lose their dignity, not to mention their hardware. What do these dames hope to gain by this?"

"Have a little fun at the guys' expense and remind them that the girls have been taken for granted. That is why many of our gentleman callers visit the Sapphire Slipper. They feel taken for granted."

Satin slips me another long-lashed look. I have a sick feeling that she is also referring to my amorous attentions back in the day when we were an item on and off the Strip.

It is likely true that no real mayhem is intended here, except that Mrs. Nicky Fontana will be anxious if her wandering spouse is not home by the wee hours of the morning, and it sounds like this captivity is shaping up to be a twenty-four-hour deal.

I would not want to be hanging around the penthouse suite at the Crystal Phoenix when Miss Van von Rhine discovers that Mr. Nicky is not only *not* coming home tonight, but the Gangsters' limo is lost in space.

Chapter 16

Champagne Suite

"What do you think the rascals are up to tonight?" Van von Rhine asked as she refilled her three guests' champagne glasses. Electra had come when called, leaving the Circle Ritz on the Hesketh Vampire motorcycle. Her helmet sat at her feet, the words SPEED QUEEN printed on the front.

Next to it sat the Crystal Phoenix's house cat, a gold-eyed black stray named after Temple's cat, Midnight Louie. Midnight Louise was smaller, had longer hair, and didn't share Louie's eye color, but she was as prone to push through open doors into other people's parties as her namesake.

She also had that same odd air about her of appearing to understand what people said. Or, at least, she listened intently, as if there was something to learn. This was odd, because Temple would swear that cats never condescended to learn anything from human beings.

She bent down to pat Midnight Louise's attentive black head. She wished Louie himself were here. She always felt more at ease in his formidable presence, and on more than one occasion he had attacked a human on her behalf. Hard.

Of course, she wasn't the one in peril tonight.

Temple didn't want to admit it aloud, but she was worried about Matt. He was venturing far from ex-priest territory tonight. She assumed a Fontana brothers bachelor party could be pretty wild, in a harmless sense. Surely, Aldo would look out for Matt. After all, they were soon to be pseudo brothers-in-law. Surely.

Omigod! Would she have to call him *Uncle* Aldo?

"I don't have to guess," Electra said smugly. "I know."

"Know what?" Temple had forgotten what the conversation was about.

"Where the rascals are going for Aldo's bachelor party."

"You do!" they all shouted at once.

Every woman here had someone near and dear off in the desert night partying hearty, except Electra.

Electra pleated the full floral folds of her muumuu.

Seeing her whizzing by on a sleek vintage motorcycle, engine screaming like a banshee to live up to the model's name, would be pretty scary, Temple thought.

"What are twelve *men* going to come up with in terms of party arrangements on such short notice?" Electra glanced at Kit. "Although I do understand why you don't want to delay your nuptials to the adoring Aldo for one more day than necessary."

"What did you come up with, Electra?" Van asked. "A private performance of Cirque de Sole Mio?" The disciplined pale blond hair in Van's French twist was separating into loose tendrils. The champagne hadn't dented her dignity, but had added a certain flair.

"The Shemale Review at the Goliath," Kit suggested with an arpeggio of airy laughter.

"A private wake at the city morgue," Temple put in.

"Please." Electra fluffed her helmet-flattened white curls. "Give me credit at least for being appropriate. No, it's a private party at the G-Strip Club. A program of Elvis impersonators performing, with a wedding dress–garbed Priscilla popping out of the traditional cake. Elvis and Priscilla were married here in Vegas, after all."

"A bride stripper?" Kit asked, incredulous.

"She's only a slight flaunter, not a stripper." Electra glanced at Temple. "Nothing an ex-priest couldn't see on television."

"Have you *seen* television lately?" Temple asked. "That blond fifties cabinet model in your penthouse doesn't look fully functional. Network is getting as racy as cable. I will admit, though, that since the brothers helped me out as Elvis impersonators a while back, that is an appropriate form of entertainment for Aldo's bachelor party."

Electra waved a plump hand. "Would I let you ladies suffer a moment of insecurity? Even the Priscilla is a wholesome little wisp of a thing."

Temple narrowed her eyes while sipping her third glass of champagne. They could all crash in Van and Nicky's place tonight. When he finally stumbled into their pajama party, he could sleep in the bathtub. Or so Van had stated.

Of course it was a roomy two-person, jetted tub.

"'Wholesome little thing.'" Something had penetrated Temple's bubble-lulled brain. "Electra, you didn't! You didn't hire that poor, pathetic juvenile delinquent stepdaughter of miserable Crawford Buchanan's? Quincey?"

"I did. She's still pursuing a performing career, and it's running away from her faster than she can cat-walk. You know our guys will be perfect gentlemen all."

"Well, mostly," Van conceded with a ladylike hiccup. "Nicky promised to be home by one A.M. and to bring Matt with him. To drop Matt off at the Circle Ritz, rather."

They all glanced at the tall crystal plinth of an ultramodern grandfather clock against one wall of the huge living room. Past midnight.

"Boys will be boys," Kit remarked apropos of nothing. "I can't believe I'm finally getting married."

"Let's see," Van remarked, speaking slowly as one mainlining unaccustomed champagne should. "I've been married once. You and Temple have never been married but are hurtling toward the altar, or the justice of the peace, and Electra has been married—"

"Five times." She shrugged her floral-swathed shoulders. "It took practice in the old days. Here." She raised her glass. Van filled it. "A toast to our blushing brides."

"Do you blush?" Kit asked Temple.

"Unfortunately, yes."

"*Ooh!* I can't wait to take pictures at your wedding. You and Matt will make the most swooningly precious couple."

"Aunt. You're sloshed. Please do not apply the word *precious* to me and mine."

"Not even to that old softie, Midnight Louie?"

"Especially not to Midnight Louie!"

"Where do you suppose he is tonight?" Kit's gaze grew sentimental. "Out on the town himself, courting some feline fatale."

"Gag," Temple said. "I sincerely hope this champagne makes us forget everything we said tonight. A bachelor party may be a little gross, but a bachelorette party is Soupy Central. Why do I sense the guys are having a lot more fun than we are?"

Van topped off her glass, which had somehow gone dry.

"They'll have hangovers to enter *The Guinness Book of World Records*, but they'll feel pleased with themselves and their one-night rebellion. Men!"

"Men!" Kit echoed, lifting her glass. "You can't live with them, and you can't live without them."

"Men," Temple said. And smiled.

"Men." Electra frowned. "I wish you girls better luck with 'em than I've had."

"It's kinda nice," Van said, sliding down onto her usually steel spine as she cosseted her champagne glass, "to know they're having a last bit of brotherly, boyish fun tonight. Nicky could use a break from the executive suite. And Aldo . . . Kit, he is a Prince Charming. They are all."

"To all Prince Charmings," Temple said, lifting her glass. "Wherever they are!"

She thought immediately, with an unwanted, slightly tipsy pang, of Max.

Then she chugalugged the champagne. There was nowhere she had to be tonight. Nothing she had to do.

Nothing but relax and enjoy.

So why was she worried?

Chapter 17

Garden of Lies
and Spies

The air outside his window was crisp, fragrant. Wonderful.

He inhaled deeply as Garry Randolph wheeled him around the terraced gardens in the clear mountain sunlight.

The man wasn't a matinee idol, but he had a silver tongue. He'd convinced the dubious nurse that the patient could use some fresh air.

No one else wandered these high mountain meadow paths. The views at great heights above and depths below were breathtaking. He knew this must be alien terrain for him because it enchanted him so much. But Randolph would have told him the hills were alive with the sound of listening devices.

Once they were behind a sheltering stand of pines, Randolph quickly knelt and examined the wheelchair to the rims. Then he'd pantomimed a request for "Mike" to pat himself down, though the loose hospital gown didn't allow for concealment.

Then Randolph had inspected his casts, thoroughly enough to cause pain, and felt the gown tie-strings.

"Why would my room and I be bugged?" he asked when Randolph nodded the okay for speaking.

"You're here because someone tried to kill you."

"Not on a mountain."

"God, no. You'd never waste your time risking your neck just for the heck of it."

"But I *have* risked my life."

Randolph nodded. "You've always worked without a net, but never without an escape plan. Listen, until you're able to get around on your own, I don't want you knowing too much about yourself. If someone should get ahold of you and start asking questions, I want you to retain a certain amount of honest ignorance. That can't be faked. Not even by you."

"What am I? Who?"

Randolph shook his head. "Can't say yet. I can say someone meant to kill you, and you survived. As soon as you can walk, we're out of here."

"For where?"

Randolph lowered his voice. "I've got some very interesting leads in Ireland."

"That where I live?"

The man shook his head. "I've been your handler for seventeen years. Trust me. I know best."

" 'Handler.' I'm some kind of . . . pet? A spy?"

Randolph chuckled and patted his shoulder. "Much more interesting than that, dear boy. No, your job here is to get better and hold the foxes at bay. The longer you appear to be the victim of total amnesia, the safer you'll be."

"I *am* the victim of total amnesia!" In frustration, he launched the wheelchair forward when his legs wouldn't do the job. The mechanism was slick. The chair shot toward the walkway's edge.

Randolph followed and stopped it with a speed and agility that surprised him, even as his stomach twisted to feel the chair teetering on the edge of a sharp fall into the deep green valley below.

"Don't be impetuous," Randolph said. "You never were. I understand your frustration, but you can't afford theatrics here. Slow and steady win the race. The longer you can play the medical staff along, the better off we'll both be. I can get you out of here PDQ, if I have to."

"Can the staff be trusted?"

"No. Anyone can infiltrate any medical facility, and has."

He frowned. Maybe he wasn't a mountain climber, but he must have taken some heavy risks to be this valuable—or dangerous—to someone.

"What do you remember?" the man asked.

"About me, my life, my friends, my family, where I lived, went to school? Nothing."

Randolph's expressive face puckered with distress. Personal distress.

He felt obliged to console the old fellow.

"I do know a lot of things about the larger world. I guessed where I was. I seem to be . . . highly observant. I don't like to be helpless. I don't trust. I've been building my upper body strength to compensate for the casts on my legs. I've started moving them from the hip, though it hurts like hell. I'm not taking my knockout meds like a good little boy."

Randolph was nodding sagely. "Your instincts are inbred. That's what saved you in the . . . accident."

"How?"

"You saw the brutal impact coming. You did what few people can manage in a crisis. You let your body go limp so it didn't fight the blow. You also bowed your head into your arms, avoiding brain injury."

"I seem to have scraped my pellucid skin pretty damn hard."

"And your vocabulary doesn't seem to have suffered."

Old man Randolph grinned. He felt his scabbed cheek stretching painfully to grin back. Still, it felt good.

"So I knew what I was doing. I wasn't an incompetent ass."

"Never."

"What *was* I doing? Where did I fall?"

"I don't want to give you specifics, although you've trained to resist truth serums. You intended to 'drop out' from your current life, your current role, because some very nasty people were after you. You arranged your own accidental exit. Then someone else lent you an unsuspected helping hand. Only your lightning reflexes, superb physical condition, and raw nerve saved you from instant annihilation."

"Lightning reflexes and raw nerve. You think I still have them? The superb physical condition is shot."

"Indubitably. Trust your survival instincts. You'll recover the rest with time. But trust no one, except me. I've brought you a world away from the scene of the attempted murder, but we're dealing with an international . . . force here. I want you out of here as soon as you can limp away. Meanwhile, play the slowly recuperating invalid. Especially in the area of your memory. The more you remember, the more you endanger yourself."

He nodded. The advice was useful . . . if he was really James Bond. See. He remembered all the petty, pop culture stuff, the learned-in-school stuff, just nothing about himself.

He considered further, then nodded. "They've sicced a psychiatrist on me to work on my memory."

Randolph sighed. "The formidably brilliant and attractive Doctor Schneider."

"You think she's an enemy?"

"She is if she teases your personal memory back too soon. Do you think you can keep her dangling without learning anything?"

He thought. "A challenge. She's very good at what she does.

I'm not quite sure what exactly that is yet. I'll enjoy finding out." He glanced at the older man. "Apparently I'm heterosexual?"

The hazel eyes twinkled. "Seriously."

He smiled. Max whoever-the-hell-he-was smiled. Even though it hurt.

"Let the games begin."

Chapter 18

Boys Just Want to Have Fun

Once the Fontana brothers and Uncle Mario are bound (but not gagged), their captors pause to shake out shiny heads of variously colored hair like show cats flaunting themselves before a captive audience.

And the Fontana brothers start spitting out a series of feminine first names. Obviously, this is not stranger-on-stranger crime.

And, just as obviously, the boys are not one bit amused by the revelation.

"What kind of cockamamie deal is this?" Uncle Mario demands of the women and his nephews. "I do not care who knows who, nobody disarms the Fontanas. If you know these dizzy dames, boys, you better get some bridles on them before they ride you all to the branding station."

While the women boo and hiss Uncle Mario, the guys fight their bonds, no longer respectful of the firearms and furious at being corralled by their own girls.

"We used to know them," Ernesto says coldly. "Before we found out what crazies they were. I am not kidding. Let us loose, or you will be sorry."

"We are sorry already," one woman says. "You are all ready to mount up and celebrate Aldo's getting married, but you would not consider any of us for the altar to save your lives."

"Maybe to save our lives," Aldo puts in. He gives his brothers and uncle a cautioning glance. "We know who still holds the fire-power, and the keys to our handcuffs, and maybe our hearts."

One of the women dangles a set of keys small enough for a jewelry box.

The brothers boo her.

"Now, guys," Aldo says. "I can see why they are so steamed. I am getting married, but we all went off to party without them, and I have not exactly seen you buying any engagement rings and doing likewise."

"That is no reason to take us prisoner," Julio grumbles.

"Prisoners of love," one girl coos.

I feel a hairball coming on.

But Aldo leaps on opportunity. "See, guys! The girls just want to prove to you that they can give you a better time than any bachelor party paid escort. It is a matter of hurt pride."

"You think?" Ralph asks.

"They are sure not doing this because they want me or Uncle Mario in their manicured clutches, right, girls?"

Uncle Mario curses under his breath, but the girls' cries and whispers overwhelm him.

"Girls just want to have fun," a breathy blonde promises, step-ping nearer the bound brothers.

Cocking their dark heads en masse, the Fontana brothers

begin to see the light. They produce a chorus of persuasive pleas to release them so they can start having some of that "fun" the girls crave.

The women respond by sitting en masse on their laps.

I turn my head away. This scene is getting way too kinky for a street dude.

"It is just the prelude to a friendly lap-dance," Satin tells me. "I would think that you would be relieved that your friends have been hijacked for hanky-panky rather than murder and mayhem."

"Please, Satin! You do not mean to say you are familiar with such inappropriate intimacies?"

"I am a mother of five, however long removed from the domestic scene. This is nothing, Louie. My many mistresses do this several times a day."

"I am busting you out of this sordid environment as soon as I free the Fontanas! You are riding in a stretch limo with me, back to the Circle Ritz."

"Circle Ritz? Is that a rival brothel?"

"It is not! It is a quaint, classy residence off the Strip. My human roommate, the clever and tenacious Miss Temple Barr, and I share quarters there. Purely platonic, of course. She sometimes helps me with my cases. A human ally can come in handy for the foot and phone work."

"There is a lot of foot and phone work at the Sapphire Slipper too."

I watch in horror as the captors push their tootsies out of their black cowboy boot–style mules to rub their naked feet up the ankles of the helpless Fontana boys.

"Louie! They are merely teasing."

In fact, the Fontanas are watching the revealed faces of their tormentors with sudden interest and smiles.

"What is going on, girls?" Aldo asks. He is the only brother not occupied by, and with, a latter-day Charlie's Angel hussy.

"This was supposed to be a stag party, and it certainly was not supposed to be held at a men's entertainment emporium."

"Like you mind," one girl jeers, twining her fingertips in Ernesto's . . . or Emilio's or . . . who-knows-who's shiny black hair. (I have to admit dudes like me are pretty irresistible to the feminine contingent.)

"I mind," Aldo says simply. "I am the bridegroom-in-waiting. My bride would not appreciate this ambiance. She would kick major butt over it. Yours. Not mine."

"He is just lonesome," pouts another girl, running her forefinger down Rico's or Eduardo's or Ralph's chest, no doubt in search of the thick black well-groomed chest hair the Fontana brothers and I share. Females of any species cannot resist that.

"I am *not*," Aldo spits out. "This is supposed to be my party. You and my cappuccino-foam-headed brothers owe me an explanation for ruining it."

"That is telling them, Aldo," Macho Mario spits out even louder.

He also is unharassed, but, unlike Aldo, is looking none too happy about it.

Meanwhile, the ladies of the establishment pout along the walls in an unhappy clot, watching outsiders usurp their usual role.

Manx! Two whole sets of rival women for one large litter of dudes. For all the protestations of innocence, this could get ugly! And the Fontana boys are the territory that will be fought over.

Hey. I kind of like the role reversal. I usually have to fight all comers for the feline fatale of my choice. Might be nice to have the ladies tussle over me for a change. . . .

"Forget it, Louie," Satin says softly, sounding way too much like Midnight Louise. "This is a very odd situation. Nothing good can come of it."

"You are serious?"

"I have changed my mind. I want the Sapphire Slipper back to the sleazy, raucous, venal, boozy place I know and love. This sexy stuff here is not the paid-for kind. It is really dangerous."

What can I say? I am speechless, like the Fontana brothers. Of course even I know that the safe, state-regulated brothels are not a substitute for love and marriage. What can Satin be talking about? She has been corrupted by the sex trade. Imagine, finding her after all this time? A fallen feline!

"So," Eduardo says slowly to his personal lap attachment. "What is the point? You wanted us off all to yourselves?"

"Right," she says back. "In front of an altar like your gutsy older brother here."

"Exactly," another one tells her hog-tied man. "We are tired of always being bridesmaids and never brides."

"Hey," says Rico or maybe Ernesto. "We asked you to the wedding."

He gets a (luckily) playful slap on the jaw.

"Yeah, you get to wear these color-coordinated fancy gauzy dresses. You girls like that," Ralph says.

"We would like gauzy white dresses even better."

"It is not like you, um, qualify."

Another slap.

"You guys do not qualify for wearing tails like an English butler, either, but you will do so for Aldo's wedding. Why not for your own?"

"Aldo is older. He . . . flipped over some visiting foreign female."

"We know all about it. She is a mature woman. This Kit Carlson has *never* been married. We do not want to live to be old enough to be our own mothers and say we have never been married. If Aldo can do it, so can his younger, dumber brothers."

Brother! This is a fine kettle of koi! My sleek Italian posse is being hustled into servitude most unfeline. It is okay if Aldo wishes to give up his life as a street dude. He is about to get gray around the whiskers anyway. But the whole litter should not be forced into domesticity.

I stare hard at Macho Mario Fontana, who has been as macho on this scene tonight as a limp eel. He is the paterfamilias. Time to dredge up some pater and slap these slaphappy, up-start girls down the way they have been disciplining his nephews.

This whole scene is on the edge of turning from a prank into something prosecutable.

Satin rubs against me. "We have got to do something, Louie. Those bridesmaids are getting bitter. At least they are not in jeopardy of being left with a litter to support."

I cringe a bit at the reminder. You can never tell when a dame is rubbing it in or really on the warpath. I sympathize with the Fontana boys.

Miss Kitty, the madam, chooses that moment to appear from the kitchens behind the bar with the biggest bottle of cham-pagne I have ever seen.

Behind her comes a blue lady bearing a silver tray with a gadzillion champagne glasses. It all looks very festive, even, er, bridal.

Satin chirps with satisfaction beside me. "Our housemother al-ways knows when to calm a crowd. Usually it is the men she has to sedate, but in this case the women are getting a bit rowdy."

"I hate to tell you, but I have seen a lot in Vegas, and women in general are as capable of getting as rowdy as anyone, prop-erly motivated by spite, jealousy, and hurt feelings."

"They are silly! It is as clear as the fangs in your face that your compadres are enjoying the idea of a night in a bordello with their girlfriends. Except for Mr. Macho and the one called Aldo who is spoken for."

Before I can correct her several erroneous assumptions, Miss Kitty steps up to the girls in black. "I need a pair of male hands free to liberate our champagne. And you might tell me your names while we are at it. I won't remember them all, but it will be a bit more civil for drinking partners."

"Champagne! All right!" says a redhead who's about a foot taller than my Miss Temple.

The women's variously colored heads confer. In a clot they much resemble a litter of calicos. Almost all are showgirl tall, I notice. No wonder the Fontana brothers treat my Miss Temple like a litter of adolescent Dobermans escorting a Yorkshire terrier.

The women quit buzzing and straighten up. "Aldo. He is the man among you. He is getting married."

Aldo offers his wrists to be freed from the gaudy bracelets with an air of relief.

As he rises to address the champagne bottle the way a golf pro would contemplate the lie of a ball, I notice he skims a look at the parlor table bearing all the Fontanas' looted hardware.

I can see what he is thinking. Shake the bottle a little while working on uncorking it, then spray the female felons in charge and reclaim the upper hand, bearing a Beretta.

"Come on, girls." Miss Kitty gestures to her crew in blue. "We will all relax with a glass of champagne, and then we can take the ladies upstairs to select the room of their choice for their later entertainment. After all, they paid for it."

"When do *we* get a glass of champagne?" Ernesto asks.

The invaders like the madam's idea. Several grin. "If you are good, you will get yours upstairs. After we pick out just the right . . . setup for you."

That sounds like a threat and a promise. The Fontanas are still hot to play along, as this is definitely an amorous dude's bonus.

Aldo has concluded the same thing, because he uncorks the bottle with the signature pop known the world over. Only a tiny bit foams over the bottle lip. I am thinking Aldo wants Charlie's Angels and their sisters-under-the-silicone tipsy and off guard.

And from the way his eyes flit around the parlor and adjoining bar, he has not forgotten for a minute that his youngest brother, Nicky, and Mr. Matt Devine are not present, cuffed, or anticipating horizontal romps.

"I am sorry," says the pouting brunette bearing the turquoise fur handcuffs. "You did a great job with the champagne cork, but we really cannot leave you alone down here unsecured."

Aldo sighs, extends his arms, and shoots his impeccable suit coat sleeves and shirt cuffs. And then he is. Cuffed. Again. Sure does ruin the line of his tailoring, especially across the shoulders.

Meanwhile, seven gals in concealing black and thirteen in revealing blue trip up the stairs, the same stairs I herded Mr. Matt up an hour ago.

Their combined boot heels and stiletto heels sound like a herd of rhinos on the rampage as they clatter up. I know Mr. Nicky must be a past master at hiding out, but what about Mr. Matt? He is such a direct and honest sort. Surely even an ex-priest will figure out some surefire place to hide from invading hordes of women being girly.

"This is outrageous," Macho Mario complains to the madam, who has remained behind. "We would be the laughingstock of Vegas if this got out. A bunch of chorus girls tying up Fontana Inc. Boys, I am putting this on your heads. If you could control your women we wouldn't be here."

"Yeah," Ralph says with a goofy grin.

Upstairs, a lot of stomping and giggling commences.

"It sounds like a sorority house up there," Aldo grumbles.

Miss Kitty smiles. "Just girls having fun, playing dress up. My staff usually doesn't get to cut loose on a work night." She eyes her parlor full of handsome but reluctant clients. "I should not wonder if my team would join in on the room parties. There are plenty to go around."

A serious silence ensues. Fontana eyes consult Fontana eyes.

These dudes have never needed to hire female company, that is for sure. The idea of their girlfriends being coached, even abetted, by pros is both . . . insulting . . . and inciting.

"Males!" Miss Satin hisses beside me.

"What can it hurt?" Emilio asks. "They are not serious kidnappers. It will all be over by this time tomorrow night. Aldo's virtue is safe, and his chick is bunking at Miss Temple's place. It should make for some very mellow bridesmaids in the wedding party. Girls just want to have fun."

"Idiot!" Satin spits beside me. "They are dead serious. They want their own ownership rings."

"Uh, that is wedlock rings. I mean, wedding."

"Our kind does not go in for ceremony, other than the usual mating dance, and we have no choice whatever about that. 'Wedlock' is right. Human females never joke about craving marital yokes."

Satin is right. Humans have to tie everything up with red tape and paperwork. No wonder the Fontana boys are enjoying relinquishing the reins to their girlfriends for a boys' night out.

Myself, I never give the female of the species, any species, an inch.

They have too many good reasons to take revenge on the male.

I listen to the latest stutter of high heels above, and shrieks of laughter.

I think of Mr. Matt, hidden and penned like a hunted tiger, in that room-to-room rampage for just the right lustful setting.

And shudder.

Chapter 19

Peep Show at the Chicken Ranch

Matt had heard the women toasting with champagne and planning to invade the upstairs. He'd figured out from the loud phrases that had drifted up the staircase that they must be intimate enemies, if not rival mobsters. That didn't mean they weren't formidable.

Problem was, they sounded ready to raid every bedroom.

Problem was, he needed to find a hiding place for a good half hour, at least. And then they'd be coming up again, with their captives.

Matt could get stuck in some closet, party to who-knows-what intimate fun and games all night long.

He knew he didn't like bachelor parties, without ever attending one, and now he *really* didn't like them.

He started cruising the bedrooms, trying to remember one that had offered a likely place of concealment. One where he was effectively blind and deaf too. Someplace as dark as an old-fashioned confessional.

He had to find one *now*! Before he was found out and subjected to who-knows-what hanky-panky. He shut the door quietly, when he ached to slam it, on a Victorian boudoir with only a stand-alone wardrobe for a closet. Even if he was willing to hunch for hours in a crouching position, the wardrobe was crowded with lacy, feathered apparel doused in cloying scents. He was sure to sneeze, like a cuckolded husband in a French farce.

Under the bed? Embarrassing, but at least he'd be able to stretch out.

But searching under the brass four-poster in the next room, he fished out such intriguing treasure as peacock feathers, a small riding crop, something long and rubbery that plugged in . . . no, under the bed was no sanctuary.

Another room had a rococo, painted standing screen. Diving behind there, he found pegs with numerous changes of lingerie. Not here.

By now the women's giggling sounded like the baying of bloodhounds.

Matt opened the door on another room. This had to be it. He had to go to ground.

It was one of those sterile modernistic rooms full of metal and leather and odd accoutrements. The laughter came closer.

But, wait! That far mirrored wall didn't match up panels evenly.

He rushed toward his own foggy reflection like a man in a nightmare, fingered the beveled seams. One gave way to his desperation. He was in a small black-painted room. With a chair. He could sit all night if he had to.

The mirrored wall clicked shut on him.

He'd been wishing for a small, dark, old-fashioned confessional.

Oh.

On this side, the mirror was a window. This room was a peephole for the perverted. It could see the entire outer room as through amber glass.

A woman with a champagne glass was pausing in the doorway.

"Oh, this looks kinky," she said. "This'll really give my guy the creeps, and a huge thrill, I bet. This one!"

"Too austere," another girl said. "The next room has a Jacuzzi."

Matt brushed his hand over the walls, looking for a latch that would release the door. His palm found a plastic rocker panel, like for a light. Light he didn't need. It would expose his hiding place.

He pressed it anyway.

The mirror went black.

He was in absolute isolation in the dark.

He couldn't see a thing.

Thank God.

He sat down in the chair, feeling like he'd taken a seat in an X-rated theater, with a certain "ick" factor, and went into meditation mode.

Temple would never believe what this outing had turned into, and he'd never tell her what he did the night of Aldo's bachelor party. So help him God. Amen.

Chapter 20

Dirty Laundry

Lieutenant C. R. Molina was not used to huddling in her dark-
ened bedroom nursing a knife wound under the guise of it really
being a rugged case of flu.

A really rugged case of flu had never gotten her down and
kept her from work before.

She had holed up in her bedroom to hide the discomfort a
long slash across her abdomen caused with every move she made.
At thirteen, Mariah was more than old enough to be suspicious
of unusual behavior in a parent.

Damn that sneaking, anonymous mortal enemy of Max Kinsella who'd dared to break into his house the same night she
had taken the law into her own hands and done likewise!

Now, she was no wiser to what had happened to Max Kinsella
than she was to who hated him enough to slash his wardrobe
into pieces in his absence. Absence, in his case, did not make

the heart grow fonder. Even Temple Barr had finally given up on the man and made Matt Devine the happiest man in the world.

Carmen tried to cushion her shoulder on the piled bed pillows. A rip of fire along the eighty-some stitches in her side erupted like Vesuvius. She yelled.

She could because she was home alone. Mariah was in school and Mama Molina was watching the inane fare that passed for daytime television programming. Right now she was tuned to a rerun of one of the half hour Hollywood gossip shows that usually sullied the pre-evening news slot.

Excess Hollywood or something, it was called.

The helmet-haired hostess actually breathed a word that caught a cop's interest.

"Former Hollywood madam Heidi Fleiss has opened a Laundromat in Pahrump, Nevada," the woman announced as if hailing the Second Coming. "It's called Dirty Laundry and is a prelude to her breaking ground for the first chicken ranch for women, also in Pahrump."

"Just what I need!" Carmen moaned. Would women really run with the wolves and flock to a joint with men for sale? Not in her jurisdiction anyway, but this was yet another sad sign of the coming Apocalypse in Vegas and environs.

On the breathless news went: "This gender-breaking establishment was originally titled the Rooster Ranch, but will now be called the Stud Farm."

Carmen patted the rumpled covers, desperately seeking the remote control. If she never heard about another Nevada chicken ranch it would be far too soon.

Once the TV was off, she could hear her distant doorbell ring. Great. She had no hope of getting there before the ringer had left, and risked irritating her stitches into a fevered snit.

She lay back, huffing with effort more than sighing. Sighing hurt. No way could she pretend to normal movement at work for a few more days. Luckily, Morrie Alch was so straight-arrow that the brass would believe him if he swore the Pope was Mormon. If he said she had the flu bad, it stuck.

The doorbell was silent now. Who had to bother hapless housewives at midday anyway?

She was trying to shift to a more comfortable position when her bedroom door opened. Someone was in the house! Someone unauthorized. The front door had been locked.

She patted the covers for her ankle piece, the small Colt semiautomatic. A cop on her back who's been attacked by an unknown person does not tumble into a sickbed with just a TV remote.

Her heart was beating hard enough to tear out her stitches as she aimed at the tall shadow against the hall light. "Morrie?" she said hopefully.

"I figured he was in on it," the shadow answered.

"Larry?" She wasn't exactly relieved.

"Yeah."

"Who said you could break and enter at my place?"

"No breaking. I have a key, remember?"

She didn't, but she couldn't remember a lot on Vicodin. Her mind tended to wander. One minute she's hearing about Dirty Laundry, and then Dirty Larry shows up at her door. That was the undercover cop's nickname. He'd bullied his way into the edges of her professional and private life in the past few weeks, but now that he knew she'd mangled the law, she found him less amusing and more alarming.

His turning up at Kinsella's house just after she'd been knifed by an intruder in the dark had turned on her suspicions. The intruder could be anyone, including Dirty Larry. Why? She had no idea, but she was finding it harder to believe that he'd pursued her lately just because she was so darn cute.

"You're not telling anyone about this." Her words were an order.

"Of course not, but I wanted to make sure you were okay."

"I hurt like hell, I'm on enough painkillers to get busted if I didn't have a doctor's prescription, and I don't feel like talking."

"Whoa! Got it. Didn't mean to scare you." His shrewd eyes glanced at the Colt, still in her hand.

"I wasn't scared," she said. "Just cautious. And you know better than to walk in on a cornered cop."

"Right. Now you know what it feels like to have something to hide, just like an undercover operative. Can't ever tell anyone the truth. Can't ever stop watching your back. Can't ever trust anyone."

"Larry—" His litany of undercover problems had sounded more like a subtle threat than an expression of sympathy. But she could very well be paranoid about everyone now.

"I'll lock the door on the way out," he promised, "so your kid won't even know I was here."

The bedroom door shut. Carmen risked a small sigh that ended with a hiss of pain.

Larry had a hard-bitten manner; that's why the bad guys so readily took him for one of them. Now she had to wonder if he *was* one of them and if he'd tried to sucker her, maybe even stabbed her, in the dark. If he was more stalker than suitor.

One thing was certain: she was still in the dark.

Chapter 21

Hen Party

So there I am in the hall, trying to avoid the stomp of boots and high heels from twenty champagne-sipping human females milling around.

Do they glance down at the carpet to see if there is any stray resident around? No. Speaking of stray residents, I have seen no trace of Mr. Matt, which is a big relief. Nor do I see Mr. Nicky Fontana lounging about either. Although I think Mr. Nicky would be better at hiding out in a bordello than Mr. Matt.

Miss Temple will have *my* hide if her fiancé is found in a compromising position in this house of the rising libido.

Meanwhile, it is all one big chicken ranch party up here. The Fontana bridesmaids are *oohing* and *aahing* at the settings and accoutrements of the cathouse trade.

I finally am spotted, of course, but they are all so wrapped up in French ticklers and the like than I am taken for the house cat,

Satin. People are just not very observant when it comes to presumed domestic slaves like us. This blind spot is very useful to the
undercover investigator.

I am just glad Miss Midnight Louise is not in on this gig. I know
she would take the strongest exception to the harmless fun the
girls are having as two very different worlds of feminine wiles
cross trails momentarily.

"No offense, ladies," says one girlfriend. "The boys were not
supposed to come here. They were going to be driven to an Elvis
impersonation, with a teenage-bride Priscilla popping out of a
cake. Lots of rock 'n' roll music and that one tame peekaboo bit."

The residents hoot it up. "Really? You are kidding! Well, we
will take the night off, since you have paid for it, and you have
the run of our facilities," says Gigi. (I have a photographic sniffer
and can match each hooker with her perfume from the roll call
in the parlor.)

Another now tipsy bridesmaid confides to a girl in blue, "I know
the bride-to-be did not want her fiancé kicking up his heels or
anything else interesting tonight, but the groomsmen are fair
game."

"Pretty game, I think," Angela says, "from their expressions
and certain other signs."

"They are all single!" a bridesmaid says, pouting. "Why
should they not have fun at a bachelor party? As long as it is
with us, their loyal girlfriends."

"You really hope to get them to commit after tonight?"

"Who thought Aldo would ever get married? Now he is all
grins and domesticity. If one can fall, so can the others."

Not this "other."

Midnight Louie does not get 'napped, trapped, and whapped
with a wedding ring. Never. No way. If the formerly freedom-loving
Fontanas want to be sucker-bait, fine. It is nice to see Satin again,
and know she is off the streets and safe, but I am not throwing my
ruff in the ring for her paw in perpetuity.

The plan for the evening seems pretty clear at this point. The bound-but-not-gagged—and certainly at this point not terribly resisting—Fontana boys are going to have a prenuptial honeymoon in whatever setting their particular girlfriend chooses.

Macho Mario is going to be kept prisoner in the parlor, surrounded by a bevy of beauties who have no interest in catering to his needs or druthers, along with the madam, with whom he seems to have a nodding, but not intimate acquaintance.

Satin and I will have lots of time to catch up on old times.

And Mr. Nicky and Mr. Matt will continue to hide out, as emerging now would be rather embarrassing.

One good thing: given the amount of champagne being consumed by the bridesmaids, I am guessing that the festivities will end in a snoozer long before daylight blinks its eyes open over the desert and shows us all where the heck we are.

I follow the giggling bridesmaids down the stairs for another round of boyfriend teasing before they herd them upstairs for more serious business.

Humans! Cannot live with them, cannot live without them.

Unfortunately.

Chapter 22

Dead Spot

Matt heard the commotion in the hall and had hardly dared breathe since, despite being in the place's best-kept secret room.

The unmistakable sounds of girly celebration were confusing. Apparently the . . . er, pros workforce wasn't at all threatened by the amateur takeover. Maybe they were all in on it.

His immediate problem was worse than whatever fix the Fontana brothers were in downstairs. God! To be caught lurking in a peephole in a brothel like a perv or a juvenile delinquent.

It was beyond contemplating. He'd have to risk being spotted to find a literal closet to hide out in until he figured out what was going on. He set the spy window to see-through mode. The room looked unoccupied and the last high heels were clattering down the staircase.

It was now or never.

Matt edged through the concealed door, remembering to shut it quietly.

There must be a regular closet somewhere in this place. Certainly a linen closet, he thought with a wince. That would be the safest place until he figured out what was happening.

He moved as stealthily as possible over the bedroom floor, glancing back at the door to make sure no traces of his stay remained.

Then he forgot everything. Safety. Secrecy.

A woman lay on the bed that had been vacant. A half-clothed young, beautiful woman.

He couldn't think. Maybe she was . . . only a prop. One of those blow-up dolls he'd first learned about only a month ago. This place was a fantasyland of forbidden sex.

He couldn't just leave her without making sure.

Retracing his steps, he saw with every one that she was real; a young, beautiful, dead woman. She wore a corset missing the cups for her breasts and a garter belt with the silver garters loose and glittering. She was naked enough that he'd hesitate to approach her, but the black stocking wrapped tight around her neck assured the dead part. Or near dead.

There was spittle on those ripe red lips, and her staring eyes were bloodshot.

He put his fingertips to her neck, searching for any spasm in her carotid artery.

Her skin was soft and . . . warm. Like living flesh.

CPR was worth a try. He depressed her breastbone in rhythm until the bed bounded obscenely under her. Then he pinched her nostrils shut and blew into those parted lips, hard. Again and again. The Kiss of Life was not gentle.

"Jesus Christ, Matt! What are you doing with that woman?"

He turned to find Nicky Fontana in the doorway. "You got free? Help me! She's still warm. She could be revived."

"Yeah. But—" Nicky came over, swift but quiet, taking in the scene. "Good God, what happened here?"

He pressed the side of her neck, frowning.

Matt took another breather. "I don't know."

"Give it up. No pulse. You don't know?"

Matt was breathless, and now Nicky's diagnosis had taken his breath away again. It took a few moments for him to straighten up, to look dispassionately down on her as unrevivable, to give up the ghost.

He finally said, "There's a secret room behind the mirrored wall. A peephole room. I ducked in there to hide, and when the hubbub outside died down, thought I needed a better hiding place. I only saw her when I turned to give the room a once-over before I left."

Nicky glanced at the mirrored wall, then nodded. "You were in there, and saw nothing?"

"There's a switch that closes the view window, like some kind of internal blind. I shut it. I didn't know if anyone could see me with the window operational."

"Probably not. The whole kick is not being seen."

"It seemed like the perfect hiding place."

"It was. Someone felt free to commit murder, never suspecting there was a witness."

"A possible witness. I was totally in the dark. What are we going to do?"

Nicky washed his face with his dry hands, thinking. "You figure out what's going on here?"

"The abduction, the laughing women, this? No."

"I was in the linen closet, under a hell of a lot of scented sheets. I was also a lot closer to the hallway action. I'm getting that this whole thing is a prank. My brothers' girlfriends decided to crash the bachelor party and railroad them here for some semi-serious ribbing about them not following Aldo into the bonds of holy matrimony. Instead we get unholy murder.

Damn! It's a bitch that you didn't have some normal curiosity or self-preservation and keep the viewing window open."

"I don't know how these things work. I figure if I can see, someone can see me. Maybe it's magical thinking, but I'm not used to places like this and figure the less I know about them, the better."

"Not in this case."

"If the kidnappers are only a bunch of annoyed girlfriends, we just have to tell them what happened and that the lark is off and we need to call the police."

Nicky was pacing now, not caring if anyone downstairs heard him.

"Not exactly, pal. What police? Where are we? Who has jurisdiction? And you've just found a dead woman in a bordello. She's been killed in a way that screams 'sex crime.' You are a semi-celebrity in this town, a radio personality. An ex-priest. Someone might hear the whole scenario and think that you flipped out and went psycho-religious at being exposed to the sleazy side of Vegas."

"That's ridiculous."

"Not. Plus, we have Uncle Macho Mario bound downstairs. He was a major mob figure in his salad days. Sure, he's only minced parsley today, but some cops, and some robbers, would really like to see him brought down.

"And then there's me."

"You? You have nothing to do with it."

"I, like you, got away from the girl kidnapping ring. I hid out up here. Alone. Like you. I have a good rep as a businessman in this community, but my name is Fontana. The police always like to hassle a Fontana. We have no alibis, Matt. We call the police, the least we get is humiliation and suspicion and rotten publicity. The worst we get is a murder rap."

Matt got it. The whole picture. Not blacked out at all.

"Molina—"

"Yeah, she'd probably give us the benefit of the doubt, but the weirdness of us all being here, and now, this murder . . . front page, instant online podcast, paparazzi up the wazoo, no wedding, no reputations, no way out."

Matt felt his head spinning and it was champagne-free. "What'll we do?"

"You have my cell phone."

"I've tried using it. We're out of range."

"It can be rough out in the desert where these chicken ranches operate."

"Chicken ranches?"

"An old term. Legal Nevada brothels are way more sophisticated now. Have Web pages. Sell certified once-worn thong panties. Give me my cell phone. We need to ditch the murder scene. I'll see if I can find a spot where the signal will work."

Matt did as Nicky said, following him into the empty hall. The other man had his cell phone on and was watching the small screen as they walked.

"This area is a dead spot. If we can find an outside wall—"

Nicky led Matt to a closed door that opened into shelves heaped with pillows and bed linens and lots of strange toiletry items. He ducked inside, up against the back wall, and hit the cell phone buttons again.

"Got a signal. One bar. Here goes nothing." Nicky squeezed himself against the wall, and then walked his back down it, watching the cell phone screen all the time.

He listened intently. "Van? Van, baby? Can you hear me?" He pushed down until he was sitting on the floor. "Can you hear me now? Great. I've barely got a signal. Now listen hard and fast. It's a matter of life and death and it's all up to you now."

Chapter 23

Rescue Party

"It's Nicky," Van said, giggling. "I guess he just can't stand being away from me for even one night."

Temple smiled indulgently.

They were all smiling indulgently. They were all rosy-nosey high. Tipsy. Happy. Girly.

Kit took advantage of the interruption to rise and refill all their champagne glasses. As her left hand hesitated over the Lalique crystal flutes her ring sparkled like the light blazing out from the top of the Luxor pyramid, a light that could be seen in outer space.

"I bet those Fontana boys are getting rowdy," Electra said. "That many brothers have got to be a handful."

"I have four older brothers, and they are," Temple said. "Total teases. It's nice to be on my own here and not be overprotected and underrespected."

"The Fontana boys are all darling with you," Kit said. "Like the world's sexiest big brothers."

"I would never," Temple said with the kind of slow solemnity several ounces of champagne produces, "flirt with a Fontana brother. We have a special relationship. They respect me, and I respect them. You will be marrying into all those brothers, Kit."

"I can use some brothers-in-law, especially if they treat me the way they do you."

"They're pretty . . . nice," Temple said. "I don't know why some lucky girls never got their claws into them . . . I mean, converted them to matrimony."

"Overrated," said Electra, the much-married, and divorced, woman. She was frowning at Van. "That girl is getting sober. Fast."

"Van's always so dignified," Temple said. "It's nice to see her loosen up."

"Van's never as white as a Halloween sheet," Electra said, her fingers patting the air to quiet Temple and Kit. "Something's going on."

Van was making writing motions with her right hand and looking way not tipsy. Or happy.

"The Sapphire Slipper. I've heard of it, but—"

Kit ravaged a distant desk for pen and paper. Temple pulled a two-inch-thick *Vanity Fair* magazine off the coffee table to offer it as a writing surface. In a few seconds, Van was jotting down frantic phrases.

They were all listening hard now, memorizing the words Van repeated as she made huge, sloppy, slanting notes.

"Isolated. Iffy cell phone. Temple. Take the . . . Rover. Kidnapped! By whom? Murder?"

While Temple and Kit stared at each other in utter shock, Electra disappeared.

"Nicky," Van was shouting. "I'm losing you! The connection. *Nicky!!!*"

Cool, cool Van von Rhine was shaking when she reluctantly snapped the cell phone shut. Her hands were smoothing her mussed French twist.

"Nicky swears it will soon all be under control," she said, "but he says we have to get out there ASAP."

"We?" Temple asked. "Not the police?"

"He says the bachelor party—him, Aldo, their brothers, Uncle Mario, and Matt—" Van glanced sympathetically at Temple. "They've all been kidnapped. Even Midnight Louie is there!"

"My cat? Who'd kidnap a cat?"

"He must have been along for the ride. They were hijacked to a different location than the expected bachelor party in town. This . . . notorious brothel in the desert. Somebody look up the address—"

Electra bustled in. "I've got the coffee on and found the telephone book. Just give me a minute. Van, you need to get online and get a map to this Sapphire Slipper place. They're sure to have a Web site."

"Of course. Online." She stood up. "Nicky said—"

"What did he say?" Temple demanded, jumping up.

"He said they need you out there to solve a murder. They need a cool head and an outside eye. He said that Matt discovered the body, and Nicky discovered Matt with the body, and they're the most likely suspects. We get a jump on the police, or they . . . jump on them. It was a prank. Just a prank. The bridesmaids went berserk. It was supposed to have been funny. Now maybe one of them is dead. Murdered."

"Who can drive?" Kit asked.

"Me," said Electra. "I was planning on 'cycling home, so went light on the champagne. Plus, I've got the extra poundage to metabolize it. Sometimes fat girls *do* have less fun. Van, you get the map and order the Rover from the valet captain. If cell phones don't work out there—"

"There's a satellite phone in the Rover," Van said, racing for her home office and the computer.

Temple sat down. Everybody seemed to have it together.

All anyone needed from her was on-scene detective work.

All?

Matt? A suspect. Matt at the Sapphire Slipper brothel? Oh, my. Oh, Matt.

She was starting to shake like Van had at first. Nicky vulnerable, too.

Something soft intruded on her crazed, anxious mental soliloquy.

Midnight Louise was rubbing against her calf, looking up through serious, round, gold eyes.

And Midnight Louie out there too!

Midnight Louise spoke. One meow. Loud and strong.

"We'll get them all out of it in the twitch of a cat's whisker," Temple said, stroking the little cat.

She didn't believe one word of what she said.

Chapter 24

Hitchhikers

Sorry, Miss Temple, I do not need a pat on the head, I need
wheels and some armed and dangerous backup.

The women are still a bit shocked and shaky despite their brave
talk, but it is no surprise at all to me that a midnight phone call re-
veals that the old man is ruff deep in a hotbed of shady women,
dangerous men, and murder most sleazy.

I am surprised, though, that Mr. Matt Devine, who provided
my first temporary shelter after I showed up as a stray at the
Crystal Phoenix, would be in any danger of a murder rap.

No way, Bombay! That is not going to happen with Midnight
Louise around.

I let the women-behind-the-men on the hot seat out in the
desert run around and mount what passes for a rescue party.

I take careful note of their urgent shouts and consultations.

My sharp ears (both in their external appearance and aural effectiveness) twitch this way and that to take it all in. This Sapphire Slipper is tucked away on the backside of any reasonable distance, but where there is a will, there is a way.

"Won't we need, uh, weapons?" Miss Kit Carlson asks, sounding as fierce as her frontier gunslinger namesake.

"No. Nicky said not." Miss Van von Rhine is her sharp, efficient self again, her hair slicked down and smoothed for a rumble. "The brothers were traveling fully loaded, and the mock-kidnapping has turned into a hysterical hen party, he says. The boys will soon be in charge again."

"When were they ever not?" Miss Temple Barr asks.

Miss Van von Rhine lifts an almost-invisible eyebrow. These pale human show cats have barely any vibrissae over their eyes, unlike my lush black spidery lashes.

"Apparently for a few hours tonight they have been disarmed, bound, and held utterly helpless."

Miss Temple gives a disbelieving cry.

I agree. No wonder murder was afoot if the Fontana brothers were tied hand and foot. Who would be so stupid as to take the only decent muscle in Las Vegas out of action?

"I do not care what you say," Miss Electra says. "We can stop at the Circle Ritz on the way for a couple useful switchblades I got from my motorcycle club guys. Forearmed is forewarned."

Now we are rockin'! My switchblades are built-in, and I do not go anywhere without them. They are my American Excess card.

I follow the rescue party down in the elevator and into the blare and glare of the hotel's busy gaming and public spaces . . . unnoticed.

Naturally no one would think to take me along, but I cannot allow the senior partner of Midnight Inc. Investigations to stew in his own aging juices. Besides, I can hardly wait to see the old buzzard held captive in a brothel. He will never live that down. Not while I am around.

I must admit that Miss Electra is a pistol at the wheel. She wrangles that well-mannered Brit Rover through the Vegas traffic like a broncobuster. We run over a few curbs and dust a few fenders, but what the hell. We move too fast to hear the curses in our wake.

While the big vehicle purrs on idle in the Circle Ritz parking lot and the ladies race inside to round up items suitable for an impromptu kidnapping-murder party, I hop out of the door behind Miss Kit Carlson and dive into the attractive shrubbery. The oleander bushes, though poisonous to us, make great cover for our kind.

"Paging Ma Barker," I yowl.

She is in my face faster than a fistful of switchblades. Which she happens to be carrying.

"Who goes there?"

"Your putative granddaughter."

The word *putative* stops her colder than *granddaughter*. I pick this vocabulary up from lawyers around the Crystal Phoenix.

"You are who?"

"We have met. Midnight Louise. Full partner in Midnight Inc. Investigations. I need backup on a freshly cold case with a hot corpse in the desert. It might involve making a certain Midnight Louie look like a pretty lame duck."

"This would also involve—?"

"A wild ride in yonder Britmobile, maybe some discreet claw work, crime-solving, and saving Mr. Midnight Louie's assets."

Ma Barker snorts. "And he has any?"

"A few."

"Yeah. I have a certain lingering maternal memory of the little imp before he was a big wheel around town. I am game. Let us hop to it. Oh. This Britmobile is a far bound upward for an old dame."

"Hey! The Brits are *ruled* by an old dame. Come on, old girl, up and at 'em."

I give her a friendly spur-prick on the hindquarters and we clear the running board together and hunker down on the dark carpet of the third row of seats.

"Where are we headed?" she inquires while laving her stinging pads.

"The Sapphire Slipper. The finest little whorehouse in the state of Nevada, which supports quite a few."

"Sapphire Slipper? Shoes," Ma Barker sniffs between paw licks, "are highly overrated."

Once we are under way, I loft up onto a third-row seat back. Miss Van von Rhine is now at the wheel, Miss Temple Barr is in the front passenger seat, cursing and trying to operate the built-in map screen, Miss Kit Carlson is leaning over the front passenger seat, backseat driving, and Miss Electra Lark is loading lead into a nasty big black revolver behind the driver's seat.

"So we are going out to this remote murder scene to do what?" Miss Electra asks.

I admire a dame who can mix bullets and leading questions.

Miss Van von Rhine heaves a sigh large enough for a sumo wrestler.

"Nicky said the kidnapping situation was under control, but that they needed Temple there to solve a murder."

"Whose murder?"

"One of the 'girls.' The connection was riddled with static. I do not know whether he meant one of the girls who work at the chicken ranch, or one of the girls who kidnapped the bachelor party."

"Chicken?" Ma Barker hisses from behind and down. "I could use a little snack."

Now I sigh, but a lot quieter than Miss Van von Rhine. Ma Barker may be a tough old bird, full of street smarts, but she has no Strip sophistication. Hang out at a high-end Vegas hotel and casino for a few nights, and you know that sex in all flavors is for sale all over town, and you hear about the legal brothels called "chicken ranches" that dot the outskirts.

"These chicks are not edible," I hiss back, "unless you like lime-flavored leg-shaving cream and nail enamel with a dash of glitter."

"That is a funny way to dress a chicken."

"These are the human variety. Chicks. Pretty women. Ladies of the night."

"Oh."

Ma Barker hunkers back down to lick her own toenails. I have been a street cat. There is not much time to master the finer points of human misbehavior when one is scrambling for a mote of food and a drop of water or avoiding imminent death under radial tires.

Meanwhile, in the front seat a debate has erupted over our direction and speed. Of course it is as black as the old man's nose hairs out here off the main freeways. I risk lifting up to brace my front mitts on the roll of, yum, black leather upholstery under a side window. Full leather interior. My, my.

The night is as dark as always, with those pinpricks of light humans delight in. Starlight is good for nothing. At least the moon can illuminate an outside faucet dripping a little water on the grass. Finding water in a desert city is no picnic for the homeless of any species.

I have never been so far out into the empty desert. It is scary to look back and see Las Vegas as a star-small twinkling oasis in our wake. I am not frightened of much, but immensity. How will we find one small chicken ranch in this Big Uneasy Empty?

Taking Back
the Night

"We two guys may know what's going on around here," Nicky said in the hall, where he and Matt stood breathing deeply. "But that is still a hostage situation downstairs. My brothers and Uncle Mario are not going to like being taken for a ride by nobody. And when they find out that someone was killed while they were hog-tied, they'll be seeing blood-red. We gotta change it before reinforcements arrive."

"That why you told your wife things here were under control? They aren't."

"They will be by the time she gets here."

"And I doubt Temple can solve a murder among strangers in a few hours."

"At least she, and we, can sort out the suspects. It'd be good to have someone else to point a finger at. I'd have to testify that I found you in a very compromising position with the dead woman. It's your hide that's in real jeopardy. I know that Temple would drive to Mars and back to make sure no damaging whispers get out about your involvement in this. You're the perfect fall guy. You were truly 'just along for the ride.'"

Matt took another deep breath, and nodded.

Nick went on. "Those daffy bridesmaids are not going to give up on their empowering little kidnap scheme unless we make them. The only bloody 'murder' they wanted to hear about tonight was my brothers crying for mercy and marriage."

"How are two guys who don't want to hurt anybody going to stop this crew of up-in-arms women?" Matt asked.

"Excellent point. We have to take out the ringleaders."

"How? Punch them? They didn't teach that in seminary."

Nicky winced. "At least I got through to Van. She's bringing Kit and Temple and Electra. That ought to diffuse the situation."

"Kit too? Here as well as Temple? Are you crazy? They are these women's worst enemies, engaged women."

"True, but Van's coming. She's no one to fool with. Well, yes, she is, in my case, but sheer executive steel outside the family circle. We've got to get control of the weapons, period. These women think they're kidding, but they don't know how dangerous that firepower is, or that someone has used their prank as a shield to commit murder. Can you imagine how wrong the police could go with a mob scene like this? And having it in for my family? We don't want a SWAT team outside."

"Agreed." Matt felt that certainty deep in his soul. Besides the terrible danger of a misunderstanding escalating a wacky prank into a deadly standoff with the law, even an orderly intervention would be a disaster for Temple's aunt Kit. And Temple.

So he talked himself into this gun-grabbing scheme of Nicky's. The Fontana brothers' arms were usually show-and-tell. Mostly. He hoped. But they were surely loaded and needed to be somewhere safer than piled on a Victorian table.

He still pictured the pale, dead body of the woman upstairs. She looked so unhappily like any woman in any brothel, anonymous, half-dressed, laid out. . . . He couldn't think more about it, he got too angry.

"So," Nicky said. "I stroll into the parlor, upsetting the game. The missing Fontana brother who nobody noticed."

"Sounds like a diversion. And I—?"

"You slip in near the table, commandeer the weapons, and hold everybody hostage until I can uncuff my brothers and we take our own back."

"Uh, this scheme relies on me totally turning the tables in about two seconds flat."

Nicky pounded him on the shoulder. "You got it. All eyes will be on me, and you get all the glory."

That's when Matt realized that "all the glory" was a relative term.

He wasn't going to scoop up eight or nine Berettas in one armful.

"Your gun is in the pile too?"

"I don't carry," Nicky said.

Matt resisted commenting. Apparently, there were Fontana brothers, and then there were Fontana brothers.

"Fine," Matt said. "Everybody's overlooked us because you're married and I'm as-good-as, besides not fitting the family profile. You appear in the archway between the bar and the parlor. I'll sneak in through the entry hall and take control of the weapons table . . . if you trust a midnight angst disc jockey with all that firepower."

"Absolutely." Nicky punched Matt on the shoulder to show

his confidence. "Just don't freeze. Grab the nearest gun and look like you mean business and aim."

"At whom?"

Nicky shrugged. "Try me. I'll be the center of attention."

Chapter 26

Eight Berettas
for Eight Brothers

Of course they have not figured me into their plans.

I am the lowly foot soldier.

The guy at one-foot height. Literally. And literally.

I have been all over this crime scene like a cheap suit. I have been downstairs, upstairs, and in my ladies' chambers. I have scoped out the place from parlor to *pissoir*. (That is a fancy French term for what you can figure out all by yourself.)

I have sniffed the trails of several interesting parties from kitchen to boudoir to powder room to weapons dump. I have seen the swains of my two headwomen—Miss Van von Rhine of the Crystal Phoenix, where I used to be house detective, and Miss Temple Barr of the Circle Ritz, where I am chief security officer—play hide-and-seek amid a harem of bedrooms and come up the sole possessors of a dead body.

Where to deploy my awesome abilities where most needed? *Hmm.*

Obviously, Mr. Matt Devine needs a sidekick.

Mr. Nicky Fontana's plan is okay for the first two seconds of shock, but that is a lot of hardware on the Victorian table and Mr. Matt is a smart guy, but not your average gun dealer.

I figure if twenty pounds of snarling alley fighter jumps to the tabletop at the right psychological moment, threatening to snag the hose and snarl the hairdo of any rogue bridesmaid thinking about reclaiming a firearm, that will take the plan from lame to game . . . set . . . match. Checkmate. Although the mating game is what has got all us guys into this murderous mess.

I tail Mr. Matt down the creaking stairs.

Luckily, there is a lot of palaver going in the parlor. No one knows, of course, that a woman lies dead upstairs. No one but the murderer, that is. I will watch the assembled company closely for someone whose surprise seems manufactured.

But first I have to shadow Mr. Matt down the stairs in the dark.

He is so concentrated on his pivotal role in the forthcoming change of power that he does not notice my pussyfooting accompaniment. Which is as it should be. When I choose to be low profile, I am a Black Velvet Fog on large cat feet. The Shadow who knows all the good stuff. The Furred Pimpernel. Oops, that last example is a little tacky in this venue.

Anyway, Mr. Matt pauses in the hall outside the parlor.

We hardly breathe until we hear the *scritch* of a cigarette lighter and Mr. Nicky's bold footsteps move from the back bar into the parlor.

I scent the acrid sweetness of a Havana. Not a Havana brown cat spoor, but an illegal cigar imported from Cuba. I am guessing the bar area holds humidors full of them. Cigar bars are ultra chic these days.

I can sense Mr. Matt's tension as we hear a flurry of movement and startled little mews in the parlor.

"Ladies and gentlemen," Nicky Fontana's voice announces, "this farce is about to end."

Mr. Matt whips around the corner and grabs the first semi-automatic he can lay hands on. "Don't move. Anybody," he orders.

I am not about to start obeying human orders now.

I leap up atop the table and take a battle stance, back humped, tail fluffed, hackles raised, teeth showing, claws out, my battle hiss a major media event.

Female *oohs* and *aahs* greet my entrance.

Meanwhile, Mr. Matt tosses a Beretta over my back to Mr. Nicky, who orders Miss Kitty to begin uncuffing his brothers.

I hear a lot of moaning and complaining on the bridesmaids' part, but Mr. Nicky raises his voice over the chorus.

"There is a murder victim upstairs. Unless we all want to be guests of the Nye County jail in no time flat, I suggest the fun and games are over for now and we all get our alibis ready. *Mi hermosos,* I am happy to say, are totally innocent in this case, as they were bound from the moment they entered the premises, thanks to you ladies. But you revenge-happy bridesmaids are all prime suspects, as are the occupants of the house. So bros, grab your Berettas and keep an eye on everyone but one another. We are not leaving here until we know who died, and why, and who might have done it."

By now the courtesans are exchanging anxious glances and counting heads. The bridesmaids gather into a large black-clad circle, and one by one sink like Southern belles onto the vacated parlor sofas, looking shaken, not stirred. But Miss Kitty, her girls massed behind her, is launching a verbal assault at Mr. Nicky.

"What do you mean, a murder? We have all been here and accounted for."

Mr. Nicky eyes the bridesmaids. "The women were all upstairs and loose for a good half hour and are major suspects. Lucky they cuffed my brothers. Cuffed their trouser legs too, apparently.

"Guys?" he asks his brothers.

They are all bending over as soon as Miss Kitty undoes their funky handcuffs, unwinding black corset strings from their ankles, faces scarlet with effort and anger.

"We were bound and out of action, all right," Julio is the first to say. "We had to play along with our so-called captors, but this was a damn-fool, stupid stunt and dangerous as hell. I hesitate to admit I know the lady of my acquaintance among them."

Nicky nods grimly. "I still need to know who each of you is, um, seeing."

One by one, the freed men reluctantly take a place behind the blond, brunette, or redhead girlfriend-cum-bridesmaid who went "nuptial" tonight.

Aldo joins Mr. Matt while Mr. Nicky finally answers the madam. "Miss Kitty, are you sure all you employees are accounted for? Between residents and invaders this is quite a gaggle of girls."

In fact, I notice now that some of the bridesmaids are draped in the occasional feather boa. The civilians and the professionals are not as easy to tell apart after the upstairs stroll. It strikes me that the dead woman could be either a bridesmaid or a, uh, hired escort. I do not think it is fair to demean these ladies with the usual descriptive expressions. My kind does not label willing females with any nasty words. In fact, a breeding cat is called a queen. We guys are just glad they go into heat now and then.

Miss Kitty does an actual nose count. "All my girls are here." She hesitates, then turns away from her cluster of employees to add in a low voice, "I guess I better go up and see the body anyway."

"Aldo," Mr. Nicky says, "escort Miss Kitty upstairs with us." He nods at the rest of his brothers, who are shifting uneasily on their notorious Bruno Magli loafers, not sure if they are escorts or jailers. "You guys keep all these women corralled while we're gone. We don't want anyone wandering off into trouble with a murderer on the loose."

I admire Mr. Nicky's tact. He does not say anything to point out more than is obvious: that one of these beautiful girls could very well be that loose murderer.

I am not invited upstairs to survey the damage but I trail the party upward, uncommented upon. At the top, I am joined by Miss Satin.

We brush vibrissae.

"How terrible it is, Louie," she whispers under her breath. "This is a house of merriment, not murder."

"My people are on it," I say. "I just have to make sure their suspicions are pointed in the right direction. Quick! I want to see what Miss Kitty makes of the body."

We sweep into the room just as Miss Kitty and her three escorts stand inside the door and gaze at the woman on the bed. From this distance, you could swear she was still alive.

"What a tragedy," Miss Kitty says. Her voice is wavery. "I thought at first you boys were spouting that murder stuff to give these crazy bridesmaids a good scare. Oh, poor kid. So young and pretty."

Mr. Matt has discreetly stepped nearer to take Miss Kitty's elbow. "Let me escort you down the back stairs to the kitchen. You can sit down, have a cup of coffee."

"With a couple jiggers of brandy in it," Aldo advises.

He and Mr. Nicky remain, looking down at the dead girl.

"Some bachelor party," Aldo says grimly.

I nod at Satin to follow Mr. Matt and the madam. Say, that phrase has a real ring to it, kind of like a novel title. I bet Miss Temple would really want to read that book!

Meanwhile, I eavesdrop while the guys talk turkey.

"Matt found the body," Nicky says. "I found him bending over the victim just afterward."

"Yeah, how did you two end up uncorralled up here?"

"We were the last two in. The phony driver ordered us into the parlor, but didn't stick around to make sure we went. Matt slipped up the stairs. The bridesmaids were so intent on tying up their special someones that I was able to do the same a bit later."

"So you two were hiding out up here, even when the ladies both pro and pro-amateur trouped up the stairs to eye the premises?"

"Right. Only Matt had the bad luck to hide out in the peephole closet in the murder room."

"Holy homicide! Where's the hidey-hole?"

Aldo approaches the mirror, checking where the frame does not quite meet the wall. In a moment, he has clicked the mirror door ajar.

"Matt saw the murder, then," Aldo crows. "We have a witness, one whose word is twenty-four-karat gold."

Mr. Nicky makes a face. "He is an ex-priest. He shut off the one-way mirror window. He did not see or hear a thing. I came to find him and found him all right, leaning over the body, gawking like a tourist and giving CPR."

"Shoot. That makes him a number one suspect. And you number two, little brother, because either one of you could be covering for the other. At least that is the way the cops will see it."

"I know that! I finally got through the poor reception and reached Van."

"Yeah?"

"She was living it up with Temple and her lovely and lively aunt and landlady in our penthouse. They are all coming."

"And . . . why?"

"I figure Temple is our best bet. We need to produce a likely suspect, or the murderer, who is not one of our party. You know the cops would love to nail a Fontana, any Fontana, with a current crime."

"The women are coming. *Our* women? To a brothel? Are you crazy?"

"They know we were hijacked. And . . . who better knows who

might off a woman than another woman? Unless you want to believe ex-Father Matt did it."

"Naw, not credible."

"You know how the police think in a case like this. Strangled. In a kinky room set up in a brothel. Maybe the ex-priest went berserk and killed an evil woman. Maybe he had molested her years ago in a distant parish and encountered her here and she was going to tell—"

I cannot restrain a growl of disbelief at these twisted interpretations.

Both Fontana brothers look at me for the first time.

"I agree with the cat," Aldo says. "That theorizing stinks. It is far-fetched in the extreme."

"But it is possible. The police look for past motives in a murder like this. For starters, I'll have Emilio guard the murder room, so nobody gets in there to mess with the evidence. We gotta protect ourselves from the murderer and the police. Even if the cops decide Temple's fiancé is not a suspect, I am. I am a Fontana and I was wandering around up here alone. Maybe I was a past client of the girl, they could think, and she could have threatened to expose me to my wife, say—"

"Hey, the murderer could *be* a past client! This is a rambling joint, but a guy like that would know the layout, and sure could come and go in the confusion. Maybe it even was a *girl* past client! Some of the dudes import their girlfriends for threesomes. Or more. Maybe some girlfriend got a lot more jealous than ours."

"And how do you know that about threesomes, big brother?"

Aldo shrugged. "Us older guys exist to do all the down and dirty research first and clue you punks in. As for you being blackmail material, heck, you never patronized any pros, Nicky. None of us needed to. We always had girlfriends, until you got married, and now I am going to."

"Our other brothers' girlfriends have gotten us all into a sordid mess," he said.

"I love little Miss Temple like she was our baby sister," Aldo says, "but you really think she can scope out a murderer overnight?"

"You have not seen her in action. She has this instinctive nose for vermin. When she gets here and finds out her fiancé is in a very compromising position, through no fault of his own but our brothers' girlfriends, you can bet she will move feather boa and fishnet stocking to find who really deserves to do the time for the crime."

Well. I am pleased to see my Miss Temple get full credit for her sleuthing ways. However, I never get a break. Mr. Nicky Fontana is completely unaware of how I have time and again assisted in Miss Temple's investigations.

Perhaps, in this pent-up environment, my true genius for crime and punishment will be more visible, and I will get the credit due me.

This will be my finest hour, particularly with my former light of love here to watch me play the hero. Miss Satin is bound to be impressed. Miss Temple and I will be a crime-fighting duo like Batman and Robin. Only it will be Catwoman and, and, uh, Robbin' Hood. Okay, that is lame.

Anyway, it will be something to see.

Chapter 27

Mental Clime

Max.

Short, simple. Not sweet.

So was the name Mike. And it had a faint, familiar ring too. Could a man have two names? Maybe first and middle. Max. Michael . . . whatever.

He wondered how much he could trust Garry Randolph, pleasant as the man was.

He knew he couldn't trust Revienne Schneider. She came into his room the next day wearing a cleverly cut pink wool suit with a long, belted jacket over the short skirt, still as leggy as a runway model.

He'd done thirty chin-ups on the shower rod that morning. His joints were aching, but the glow the pink suit gave her complexion was a nice liniment. What wounded man didn't enjoy a delicious nurse? One whose faltering memory was hers for the plundering, if he didn't watch it.

"You look remarkably well this morning, Mr. Randolph," she commented.

"And you."

"I haven't fallen off a mountain, merely come up one to stay a while."

"You're living at the facility now?"

"I could hardly meet with you daily if I wasn't."

"Daily. Somebody with deep pockets likes me."

"Deep pockets?"

He rubbed his fingers together. They ached, but were more flexible than yesterday. "Gelt."

She nodded. "Mr. Randolph . . . senior . . . spares no expense on your account."

He eyed her mouth. "He's a discerning old gentleman."

"You Americans! You're such serious flirters."

"Flirts," he corrected. Her response to colloquialisms was totally European.

"Flirts. You have a seriously bruised spine; two pins in your fractured legs underneath those casts; a concussion at the back of your skull; a skinned cheek. And a memory as solid as a, a . . ."

"Sieve," he suggested.

"A seine, I was about to say. A fishing net."

"A sieve is for flour. It's finer."

"You can be quite the pessimist."

"Realist."

"Really, Mr. Randolph. You need to get serious and help me to help you. Has anything about the accident come to mind?"

He checked the internal data bank. "Nothing. Except—"

"Except."

"I hit a cliff. A high, solid cliff."

It was true. He'd just had a flash of that dark looming wall.

Yet a mountain cliff ought to be white. And the object of his mental impact was black. And reflective. Black ice.

"That's good." She was leaning forward, watching him intently. "Something has come back."

The tremor of excitement in her voice echoed in his chest. If only he could trust her. He needed a coach, a passionate partner in his recovery. No. Not trustworthy. No one here was, except for Garry. Garry. Gary, Indiana, Gary, Indiana . . . it was some silly song. Garry. The name was all right, but he remembered the man by something else. A nickname? Ga . . . Gan . . . Ga! The memory search was painful.

She was removing his hand from his forehead, her face very close. European women wore perfume like mink wore pheromones, as an alluring personal miasma, touched at all the pulse points. His senses were spinning between pain and pleasure.

"Don't think too hard. Your brain can't take it yet. Let the memories flow. Don't even say them aloud yet."

Not self-serving advice for an undercover interrogator, if she indeed was one.

But a ring of pressure around his brow was pounding. Thinking had become a painful process. Jerky. Unreliable. He sensed that he had once moved like coiled steel, had thought as hot and fast as sheet lightning. Not now. Not . . . yet.

She'd put his suddenly trembling hand on her knee, covered in silky, opaque hose, her other hand atop it.

Was she seducing him, or saving him? And did he care which?

He loved the game of wondering, he understood almost at once. A worthy opponent. He loved the edge of fighting his own mind and body for supremacy. Or dueling a sexy, dangerous woman.

Maybe he was inventing a sinister history for her. Or himself. She was too obviously attractive to trust. Apparently, he distrusted fair surfaces most of all. Why?

"You can't expect to climb the wall of your mind in one day," she was saying.

It was an apt metaphor. He had a long climb back ahead of him.

His fingers flexed in the sandwiched warmth of her knee and hand.

"You hurt," she said. "All over. Everything. It's to be expected from an accident so severe. Better?"

He flexed his fingers again. He could feel her thigh muscles tense under them. Smooth, strong. As he would be again.

Ministering angel, detached professional, enemy in his weakest moments?

"Not . . . yet."

Her lips made a small moue, that subtly French expression. A French twist of the lips.

He felt a sudden pang. Mental not physical. He knew it was a warning from deep in his unremembered past.

Was it . . . worry? Danger? Or . . . guilt?

Chapter 28

Slippery Slope

If Temple's fingernails were bitable, she would have nibbled them off on the long, bouncing drive into the dark of desert. But they were disgustingly strong and her current coat of nail polish always wore out before they did.

Trying to read the map screen on Van's dashboard, while jolting over obscure roads was like translating Sanskrit when you didn't even know Latin.

"I'm really not sure why we're all rushing to a murder scene at a bordello," Temple said.

"It could be fun?" Electra suggested. "I kinda got into crime-solving at that Red Hat Sisterhood convention. We really should have called my Red-Hatted League chapter members in on this. We were a great team."

"No." Van wrestled the wheel around a tight curve and

slowed down. "The fewer people who know about this the better. There it is."

Kit and Electra craned their necks over the front seat backs to stare through the middle of the windshield.

A cluster of gleaming yellow and blue lights glittered like an electric oasis in the dark.

"They must have their own generator and well out here," Van murmured. "They'd have to be totally independent operationally. And the cell phone limitations wouldn't bother them."

"Why not?" asked Kit, the New Yorker who was always plugged into something. "Oh! Right. They wouldn't want customers getting rung during interesting moments."

"They must have some reliable way of communicating," Electra said. "They have to make appointments and such."

"Awesome," Kit said. "Imagine men driving all the way out to this wilderness to get a little nookie. This is the real West!"

"It's an adventure," Van said. "Some customers don't feel satisfied with entertainment that's too easy to come by. The Strip has everything at hand. Coming out here feels special. It's a marketing ploy. What's hard to get is better."

"How can sex for sale in Las Vegas be hard to get?" Electra wondered.

"Hard*er*," Van explained with a smile in her voice. "Selling sizzle is always a mystical process."

"I suppose," Kit said, "that what Minnesota-born and bred girls like Temple and me will have to keep in mind, when we see our intendeds in the ambiance of a brothel, is that such establishments are perfectly legal here."

"What you and Temple have to keep in mind," Van said grimly, "is that our nearest and dearest were kidnapped to this slightly seedy environment . . . and immediately phoned home to us for help."

"Yeah," Electra said, "but that was only *after* a dead body turned up."

"So says the cynic," Temple put in, "the five-times-married woman. I can promise you that Matt would have never gone willingly along with this prank."

"Nor Nicky," Van said.

There was a silence.

"I'm not sure about Aldo," Kit said, "which is what makes him so interesting. I can hardly wait to confront the dirty dog and extract suitable promises of 'making it up to me.'"

Temple sighed. They could joke about it, but this jaunt to a bachelor party had turned into a very sticky wicket. How was she going to clear everybody's favorite guy in less than twenty-four hours when they were dealing with a totally unknown cast of possible victims and predators?

Van nudged her knee. "We are going in there like gang-busters. We control the vertical and horizontal. They will all do as we say while we sort things out. Girls who are bridesmaids or bedmates, boys who are the innocent ours. We either run the investigation or we call in the police, right?"

Temple winced at the idea of calling in the police, which to her always meant surrendering to Lieutenant Molina.

But Electra pounded Van's headrest with a woman-power fist. "We are Charlie's Angels on the case!"

"Without a Charlie to dictate to us," Temple said. "We are the dictators. Way better."

"Way!" all three women shouted.

Van squealed the Rover around the last driveway curve its bright headlights illuminated, and they pulled up under the huge neon image of a sapphire-blue high-heeled slipper.

Chapter 29

Feline Fatales

Girrrrl power is fine, but I prefer Grrrrrowl power.

I hop out on the heels of the Misses Electra and Kit, undetected, of course.

There was a time when I lamented my midnight coat color,
which left me liable to be overlooked, and my long, trailing train
subject to being tread upon.

I contemplated aligning myself with the early flag of this
country, featuring a rattlesnake and a DON'T TREAD ON ME motto.

But over time, despite the many slings and arrows to my
overlooked extremities, I have come to appreciate the art of being easily assimilated into the dark of asphalt, the shadows, the
epitome of night.

The old man has been exploiting this inborn advantage since
he was an aspiring stud farm his own self.

I admit that now he is socially and sexually responsible, but he had a lot of bad years to make up for, including siring such by-blows as myself. By-blows is an old-fashioned phrase to designate unlawful heirs. Those of us of no account. Unwanted offspring.

I admit to an inborn intolerance of the double standard, by which the arranged mating of show cats produces prestigious lines, and by which we alley cat "accidents" are deemed worthy of quick quietus. That is a fancy word from Shakespeare for "put down." I too can sling around literary hash with the Old Bard.

So I consider this, my first solo case with my female human posse, a testing ground. I am free of male supervision for once. For once, *I* am Midnight Inc. Investigations, riding to the rescue of my old man, and I intend to prove my prowess.

It is no accident that I have invited Ma Barker, my partner's supposed mother, to aid me on the case. We girls are up for the challenge. If Ma Barker and her gang are established at the outskirts of the Circle Ritz, I believe Midnight Inc. Investigations will benefit from a large network of legwork operatives.

I do not expect the senior member of the firm to cede a chin hair on any reorganization of our assets. But I expect to win. If I solve this Sapphire Slipper murder on my own, with the semi-able assistance of Ma Barker, I will have a fine bargaining position.

So I tell Ma Barker to follow my lead and keep a low profile, and we trot after the Ladies' Number Three Lucky Detective Agency at our forefront. The humans can take the lead. We will untwine the tail of the case.

Chapter 30

Compromising Positions

Matt had observed the change of power in the Sapphire Slipper's parlor with a certain regret.

True, he'd held a Fontana brother's Beretta in his hand and had prevailed, but what use was taking over this scene when every woman in the place, and he especially, was a suspect for a particularly awful killing?

He'd watched a few of the TV forensics shows he could stomach.

Women were usually the victims; men were usually the killers.

He knew enough of the secular world now to know the earmarks of a sex killing: a sex industry woman stalked, controlled, brutally murdered. The setup was perfect. All these young bachelors out on the town for a night. The predictable implication of an orgy here in Nevada, the only place in the nation where illicit sex was legal.

A notorious local "family" up to their silk pocket scarves in murder most premarital.

A girl dead in salacious TV show–style: semiclothed, an elaborately erotic setting, costume and makeup by the Marquis de Sade.

Matt shuddered at the implied inhumanity of it all. Camera-ready.

And him a prime suspect, all because he'd opted not to be a Peeping Tom.

If only he had looked! Seen the crime and the criminal.

But no. He'd dutifully turned off the window on mayhem. Made himself into a suspect. And now Nicky was jubilant that his wife, Van, and her friends Kit and Electra and Temple, were coming here to the Sapphire Slipper brothel, to sort things out.

Oh. My. God.

The fact that Midnight Louie, Temple's cat, was here for some bizarre reason and rubbing back and forth on his pant leg was minuscule comfort.

If the big tomcat was sympathizing with his plight, he was in deep trouble.

His alibi was so hard to explain. Trapped in a brothel bedroom, he'd retreated to a built-in watching and listening post . . . and promptly disabled any watching and listening, so he knew nothing of the murder that had transpired afterward.

Either he was a totally naïve ass, or not a red-blooded human male.

Or both.

Matt couldn't decide which role was worse: innocent or prude.

If only he had decided to take advantage of the admittedly embarrassing situation to live and learn.

He might have stopped the murder. Caught the killer.

That fact that he hadn't felt worse than being a Peeping Tom.

A little scandalous curiosity could have saved a life.

Instead, a murderer had made him an unwilling accessory, by default.

A murderer had made him very angry. Righteously angry.

They were stuck here.

They were supposed to let Temple and her crew solve this mess.

Matt would be happy about that, but he'd be even happier if he took a hand in the investigation and found the killer himself. The killer who'd made him an impotent nonwitness.

Whoever had done it had malice aforethought toward the victim, and maybe malice toward every man and woman in this house of prostitution, whether unwillingly hijacked, or not. A disgruntled client? A sex pervert? Or something tragic, like a family member unable to accept a relative's working in the sex industry. He'd heard it all on his radio advice show.

It had been planned, beyond the bridesmaids' wildest schemes. Perhaps that very reservation had given the killer the idea for hiding a murder in the tangled webs of a silly prenuptial prank.

And it mattered that this was a bachelor party.

That had something to do with the motive and the means.

Matt may be an amateur at bachelor parties and bridal parties and brothels, but he knew a thing or two about murder from Temple.

He'd do everything he could to help her, as she would to help him.

But that might not be enough.

The murderer might be way out of their league.

They both might be too innocent for this situation, this conspiracy.

He'd have to get savvy fast.

Chapter 31

Wildest Schemes

"Okay," Temple said as the Range Rover cooled its engine in front of the brothel's well-lit porte cochere, "we need a plan. We need to divide and conquer, given that we're dealing with multiple suspects here. And we need to find out about any support personnel for the brothel. There must be a madam, for one. And a cook and bottle-washer.

"Van, you get the brothers Fontana and Uncle Mario. You and Nicky should be able to corral them, and they look like the least likely suspects, having been handcuffed from arrival until after the body was found. Barring a Houdini among them, they're in a fairly good position.

"Electra, you're the JP. You've had to deal with a lot of nervous brides, so you bird-dog this gaggle of eight bridesmaids for eight brothers, who have demonstrated a lot of nerve, including confiscating serious weapons. One of them could have used this wacky scheme to cover a murder.

"Kit, you're the veteran actress and jaded New Yorker. I hereby bequeath to you the madam and the house hookers. I'm sure you've seen it all, or at least acted it. If one of them recognized an opportunity for murder, and took it, I'm sure you can sniff out the guilty party."

"And you?" Van asked.

"I need to consult with Nicky and Matt about the scene of the crime, and on their own nebulous movements while hiding out of sight, out of mind, although it is hard to imagine either of those gentlemen being out of mind with all those loose women around. Though I may be prejudiced on this subject."

"Not at all," Van said. "Hiding those two good-lookers in a whorehouse would be a real trick."

"'Loose' women?" Electra asked. "Isn't that a prejudicial description for a legal profession in Nevada?"

"I was thinking of the screw-loose bridesmaids," Temple said. "They've made a royal mess out of trying to have some serious fun with the groomsmen. Somehow their crazy-brained daisy-chain scheme allowed a murderer a free hand to commit the perfect crime. No matter how bizarre the setting and the scheme that got everyone here, the murder sounds like the usual sordid and awful business.

"Everybody ready for her assignment? We'll have to consult periodically. We'll also need to confine each group so no one can confer without one of us overhearing. It's going to be a long night's journey into noon tomorrow, to paraphrase an O'Neill play title. And if we don't find a likely suspect, the police will charge us all with failure to report a crime. If Lieutenant C. R. Molina has anything to do with it, she just may do that anyway.

"Are we ready? Let's rock and roll."

Terrorizing Trio

Now that my crime-solving bed partner has arrived, all thought or notice of me has been shoved farther back than a no-name tie-up oxford in Miss Temple's shoe closet.

I cannot blame her for wanting to find and interrogate her latest significant other, Mr. Matt Devine, since he is up to his late-night golden tonsils in suspicion. I believe the least serious charge would be "interfering with a corpse," which has very gruesome and twisted connotations.

But Miss Temple has not even registered my presence, so I sulk downstairs after hearing all the good stuff. I spot Miss Satin sitting in the foyer and am heading for some ego-rebuilding strokes from a female of my kind, when I stop halfway down the stairs with a swallowed hiss of surprise.

The waiting Miss Satin has turned her head to reveal the

old-gold eyes of my feline partner in crime solving, Miss Midnight Louise.

I cannot count on having my wounded pride massaged by her, so I stop three steps farther on at the ghastly sight of another pair of black shoulder blades, these as sharp as a Swiss Army knife, cruising into sight and stopping beside Miss M. Louise.

Eek! That rangy, lived-in, scrawny form can only be that of my newfound materfamilias, the Mother McCree of the street cat world, my own dam, as they say in the horse world, Ma Barker. *Damn!*

I cringe against the wrought-iron banister and take deep calming breaths, intoning my mantra, *Kaaaaar-maaa. Kaaaaar-maaaa.* What can the so-called fruit of my loins be doing associating with the fruited loins of my maternal creator? And I do not mean Bast Herself!

Midnight Louise and Ma Barker in cahoots? This is not good! It is as bad as a Fontana brother bridesmaid and a brothel inhabitant canoodling.

While I sit transfixed between one story and another (and my own story for explaining my presence and keeping these opposing female forces from sinking tooth and claw into my unblemished hide), I witness something even more horrifying.

Along comes the latest lady of my acquaintance, totally unrelated to me by blood, at least . . . the cathouse cat, Satin.

Oh, great. I am not dead, but I am like a dead body about to be revealed to one and all: a helpless object of morbid speculation, soon to be dissected in every sordid detail of my life by a trio of vaguely related snoops.

I stare down on the three generations of females in my life, my once and future queens, watching as they begin the edgy get-acquainted dance of their kind and gender.

There is only one thing to be done, and I do it.

Turn tail and run.

Emilio definitely could use some expert assistance watching that dead body.

Chapter 33

Posthomicidal Nerves

Temple had never been inside a brothel before. She hadn't even been to a Chippendale's male strip show. She had no idea what to expect.

They walked into what seemed like the set for a play, a stuffy, period play like *Life with Father*, some fussy turn-of-the-twentieth-century Victorian parlor tricked out all in shades of blue.

One really crowded Victorian parlor!

Temple felt like singing part of the famous Christmas carol: twelve shady ladies, ten studly brothers, eight ditsy bridesmaids, four addled sleuths, three senior citizens, two roaming lads, and a cat in a sable-fur ruff. . . .

A cat? Black yet? *Louie, wherefore art thou, Louie?*

Not here at the moment, thank God and Bast. This was a fluffy bordello cat with green-gold eyes.

Temple recognized Uncle Mario, perching his bulk uneasily on a velvet-tufted chair next to a heavyset woman dressed up like Mae West in corseted glitter. And a second late-middle-aged person wearing a starched collared man's shirt with a garter on one upper arm and black trousers. Part woman, part man? Part bartender, piano player, dealer, or what?

For the overall atmosphere was Old West saloon. And the "girls" arrayed along one wall were a curled and feathered bevy all in blue, every shade of blue imaginable, from the faint saccharine hues to midnight velvet. And each woman along the spectrum ran the gamut from young and fresh to older and wiser and ready for every implication of midnight blue the law allowed.

It was all legal, and Temple thought it should be outlawed.

Back when she was a TV reporter, she'd run into the tawdry statistics about the sex trade. The "goods" were all spoiled. Strippers. Hookers. Many models. Childhood physical, verbal, and sexual abuse were the guaranteed ingredients that led girls and boys to the sleazy and often self-destructive side of the street. They may proclaim they worked this profession from free will, but their wills and self-esteem had been shaped by trauma most people never had to confront.

Selling oneself still was tragic, and Temple would bet that the reason for the dead woman upstairs would prove to be the result of some perverse, pathetic past, for both victim and murderer.

That concluded, she dismissed her gut reaction.

She had to keep an open mind to dig deep into this culture to find the twisted reason behind the crime.

So. Where were the prime suspects?

Nicky and Matt.

Chapter 34

Highly Suggestive

"We're not making progress with your memory," Dr. Schneider announced at her next visit.

A genuine assessment or a clever interrogator sensing his suspicions?

"Come, Mr. Randolph, stop glaring at me! I know you're impatient. Those casts must be as itchy as hell, and you're obviously not a man used to being pent up."

Reading and reflecting his emotional mood. Intuitive? Or manipulative?

"Bottled up, maybe?" She smiled shrewdly. "Is that the proper expression? You don't like your emotions to be obvious or to be read. Am I in your bad graces for noticing?"

"I didn't know I had any bad graces."

Her smile deepened. "Very few, but you've always known that. I'm glad that you remember enough to be suave."

"Thank you."

"I have decided to try a mnemonic device. Just a little game. It might . . . crack . . . some unconscious memories loose."

"Isn't that a bad thing to go poking around in, the unconscious?"

"I don't know. Is it in your case?"

"I'm not a 'case.'"

She shifted in her chair uneasily. "You're quite right. I apologize."

She folded her hands in her lap. She wore the shortest skirts of any doctor he'd seen, even on *Grey's Anatomy* commercial clips. He wouldn't dream of watching that show, not even now that he was a hospital habitué. Lord, he was starting to think in French words! The woman was a venereal disease, easily transferable.

He decided to put her on notice. "I apologize. I didn't mean to imply I expected more than the usual medical abracadabra from you, shrink or not."

"'Shrink'?"

"Like your skirt. Very skimpy. Miniaturized. Reduced from the normal size. It comes from the cannibal habit of shrinking the heads of their dead enemies. An American expression."

"You like my skirt?"

"I shouldn't? Why else do you wear it? Not for me, of course, but for men. All these poor, mentally confused men. You are quite the tease, Doctor."

"Most of my patients are too devastated to notice what I wear. Besides, are you so sure I'm not wearing what I do just for you?"

He snorted. "Those are three-thousand-dollar suits. You have them altered to your preferences. You were in bed with those suits long before you came to my bedside."

"Why not a special wardrobe for you? You are an obviously wealthy man. An adventurer. Charismatic. Oh, yes, you are, and you know it. My parents were civil servants. Why shouldn't I set my chapeau for you? Your mind is muddled. Any women you knew or loved are forgotten. Certainly none has appeared here to succor you in your illness. As far as I'm concerned, you may be the world's most eligible bachelor, and therefore, worth flashing."

He laughed. "You earned an advanced degree. You get paid plenty for your expertise and time. You know your way around the male ego, and inside a subconscious, not to mention a conscience. You don't need anyone, least of all me, ogling your knees. You like being an attractive woman, period. The reasons for that would be something I might like to explore, had I the time. Perhaps it was the low expectations of those civil servant parents."

"And your parents?"

"The American equivalent of civil servants."

He knew that was true, but not why it came out and sounded so right. And why he felt a sharp pang of failure and shame at mentioning his parents. And how he could have disguised that emotional weakness fast enough for her, which he hadn't.

"You are, you know," she said softly.

"Are what?" His pulse was pounding. What was he? What had he done to feel this wave of self-disgust and guilt? He was glad his face was scabbed, it might hide the inner turmoil better.

"Charismatic," she said. "Perhaps I should excuse myself from your . . . service," she added, avoiding the word *case*. "I am here to help, not irritate. Not to tease, and I have been, a little."

"What would be 'a lot' for you?"

Her laughter was free, loose, and apparently genuine. "I can only think of teasing answers to that." He found her knowing hazel eyes irresistible, and scary.

"How about," she went on, "I ask you these long-established

psychologically analytical questions, and you can have some fun at my expense? You will enjoy exercising your brain and your suspicions."

"What is this?"

"Free association."

"No associations are free," he said, dead serious.

"Ah. I agree. The purpose of this exercise is to startle your mind into remembering. Perhaps you don't wish that process to be shared. I could leave you the list, and you could . . . play with it mentally."

And take those lovely legs away? Not to mention the lovely acrobatics she was putting his mind through?

"I'm cool with it."

"'Cool.' Americans are always 'cool' with everything. All right. I start now. Freedom."

"No such thing. A common illusion."

"Responsibility."

"A snare and a delusion, and a major necessity for a human conscience."

"Everest."

"High and mighty."

"Women."

"Warm."

"Horses."

"Big, beautiful, and stupid."

"Money."

"Useful."

"Father."

"Priest."

Her eyebrows raised. So did his. "Where did that come from?"

"Mountains."

"Molehills."

"Love."

"Loss." Another telling answer. He saw her tuck that away.

"Trust."

"Virtue."

"Mirror."

"Deception."

"Woman."

"Dangerous." Her eyes were gleaming with psychiatrist's fool's gold: glints of supposed insight.

"Man."

"Original sin."

She looked up. "Not woman? It was Eve who ate the apple."

"A secure man isn't led into anything against his conscience by anyone. Adam was the weaker one."

"War."

"Senseless. But we all know that. Which makes it even more senseless."

"Champagne."

"Could use some about now."

She laughed and uncrossed her knees, putting her clipboard on the foot of the bed.

"So could I, Mr. Randolph. You have given me some very contradictory answers."

"You can't smuggle any champagne in wearing that skirt."

"I will come next time in an inexpensive peasant dirndl skirt to my ankles, with champagne. Would that do?"

He shook his head. "One would ruin the other."

"You don't compromise well."

"Do you?"

She eyed him hard. "No."

Then she stood. "I'll leave to contemplate your answers. I think you should do so as well. They are most interesting. But, then, I expected no less, and I know you wish to anticipate and meet my expectations in every way."

She was saying she knew he wouldn't tell her anything substantive? That he suspected her validity?

Or was she just flirting again? Damn, that was fun. He must have been celibate for a while before his accident. A flash of guilt again. Yes, he had been. And the guilt? That hadn't been fair to someone. A woman. Woman. Warm. Was that the woman who evoked that word?

Woman. Dangerous. He'd been thinking of Revienne, flirting back a bit, but he felt another twinge of warning. He'd known a very dangerous woman. Maybe more than one, if he was the undercover agent Garry Randolph hinted he'd been. Garry Randolph!

That name was so familiar and yet not quite right. *Grand* was the missing word, maybe. A pseudonym? *Garry Grand? Gandy. Gandhi?*

Answers were dancing like a cloud of annoying gnats flitting in front of his eyes.

Almost he could name them, each and every one of those trembling motes.

But he couldn't catch and trap and fix a word on a single gnat.

Chapter 35

Crime Scene

Miss Kitty, the madam, introduced the place's cook-bartender-piano player, Phylliss Shoofly.

Temple winced to recognize a play on the name of that right-wing Madonna of rectitude, Phyllis Schlafly. The pun was similar to porn performers' names Temple had run across. Velva Dixon, for instance. Or H. V. Load.

Phylliss looked like lesbian muscle. Every brothel needed one.

Temple rolled her eyes to think of Matt wandering around in this palace of subculture and the sex trade. Way more than he'd bargained for on a simple jaunt to a bachelor party.

First, to put this cast of dozens in their proper holding tanks.

"Let's be sexist about assigning rooms to our suspects," Temple said. "Van, you round up everything with the last name of Fontana in the bar area. Electra, you herd the bridesmaids into the kitchen. Kit, you and Miss Kitty and Miss Shoofly can stay here in the parlor with the resident ladies."

"Where will you be?" Kit asked.

"Upstairs, in my ladies' chambers."

As Temple turned, she jerked to glimpse Midnight Louie sitting in the archway. No . . . this was a fluffier, smaller black cat with halo of turquoise marabou for a ruff. What was the lurking Louie up to? Not like him to avoid the spotlight. Had he seen this hotsy-totsy house cat named Baby Blue? Probably. Maybe he was like any human male in a bordello distracted from business by the scenery. Heck, that was why the men went there!

Temple moved into the foyer to take the front stairs and spotted the two missing men sitting together on the top step, neither looking distracted by courtesans. In fact, both looked equally grim and chagrined.

Matt took Temple's hand to steady her as she sat on the steps below them. All this excitement on top of a few glasses of champagne was wearing.

"Nicky Fontana," she said, "what makes you think I can find a murderer in this mess?"

"I need you to?" When Temple was silent, he added, "Matt needs you to?"

Temple glowered. "What's all this about Matt being in danger of imminent arrest? Are you trying to panic me?"

"It's true," Matt put in. "I ended up hiding from the armed and dangerous bridesmaids in the one room that produced a dead body."

"So you witnessed the murder?"

"No."

"So you heard the murder?"

"No."

"Yet you were there?"

He nodded miserably.

"What is this: see no evil, hear no evil, speak no evil? You admit you were in the room."

"Not quite, Temple. I was in an adjacent . . . chamber."

She glanced at Nicky. "Just how kinky was this room setup anyway? 'Chamber'?"

"A voyeur's room," he answered. "Two-way mirrored wall."

Temple drilled Matt with another disbelieving look. "Then you could at least see something even if the 'viewing chamber' was soundproof."

" 'Viewing chamber' sounds so funereal," he objected. "No, I couldn't see anything because I shut the interior blinds. I was as good as blind and deaf, and while I was waiting in the dark, someone brought that poor girl into the outer room and strangled her with a fishnet stocking."

"Do you have any idea how long you were in there?"

Matt glanced at the inexpensive stainless-steel watch on his left wrist. "Doesn't glow in the dark. Felt like the anteroom of eternity."

Temple eyed Nick Fontana. His watch was a Rolex and had dials inside of dials on the watch face and a bunch of indiscreet diamonds scattered here and there.

"Mine glows in the dark as well as prepares sushi," he admitted. "We both hid out for half an hour. We heard the patter of high-heeled feet coming and dove for the most concealing place possible. Matt happened to be near one of the kinkier setups when the bridesmaid and hooker posse arrived, that's all."

"And where were you?"

"In the hall linen closet. It was extremely commodious, as you can imagine, and soft. I also could hear gales of girlish laughter as the 'good' girls inspected the nightly haunts of the 'bad' girls."

"You Fontana boys always land on your assets," Temple grumbled. She turned to Matt. "If only you had one perverted bone in your body, you could have peeked."

"I know! I blew it. I might have saved her life."

Temple didn't have an answer to that truly tragic possibility.

"Maybe not," Nicky said.

They both stared at him while he explained.

"It was pretty populous up there for over a half an hour while the 'bad' girls were showing the 'good' girls around. It was like a sorority house giggle-in. I'm guessing that someone dragged the dead girl into a room everyone had already looked at, and strangled her. After everyone was through 'inspecting,' the killer dumped her on the bed so it would confuse the time of death and who had done it."

"You're assuming one of the other women did."

"Maybe not. We two guys were roaming around up here undetected. Why not some other guy, someone who knew the place a lot better than we did?"

"The only guys present here now—and then—were the ones trucked in by Gangsters. And how was that managed anyway?"

"The drivers were switched," Matt said. "No one would notice through the heavy tint glass on the exterior and interior limo windows. When we arrived here and went in, Nicky and I were the last to leave the limo. By the time we hit the foyer, we saw something was wrong inside the place. We tried to duck back outside to regroup, except the 'chauffeur' was waiting just outside the closed front door to discourage us with a big automatic weapon." He glanced at Nicky. "What would you say it was?"

"I thought an Uzi at the time, but since the driver wore nothing but black fishnet stockings, black high heels, a black jacket, and visored cap, I wasn't exactly registering the make and model of the weapon she was toting. Her legs, however, were extremely high caliber."

Temple grimaced. "Good thing Van isn't hearing this sexist—and worse, useless—evaluation. Did the driver rejoin the bridesmaids' ranks?"

Nicky and Matt exchanged a look and shrugged as one.

"We weren't downstairs after that to count noses," Matt said.

"I'm presuming there are eight bridesmaids, but whether the driver was one, I don't know," Nicky added. "My brothers' girlfriends come and go."

"Probably why this set has contracted wedding fever now that Aldo has broken custom and popped the Big Question."

"I've been married forever," Nicky objected, "and that never motivated my brothers' girlfriends to go nuptial."

"It's the fever of the fresh catch," Temple said. "Aldo is also the oldest, thus the most confirmed bachelor. If he goes—"

"So could the whole tribe." Matt nodded sagely. "It's a form of mob hysteria."

"Don't mention 'mob,'" Nicky said with a superstitious shudder. "There's a hidden planet here. Those girls could have been egged on, unbeknownst to themselves, by one of Uncle Mario's rivals. Fontana family public embarrassment would not only be satisfying, but would put us all under a microscope and severely hamper our lifestyles."

Temple clapped a hand to her forehead. "So we not only have loony lady friends, but opportunistic rivals. It makes more sense that a rival crime family murdered an innocent bystander to put the Fontanas in hot water than a miffed girlfriend going overboard at a hokey-jokey bachelor party and strangling a strange woman. The first thing is to identify the victim. I suppose I'd better see her."

Each room had its own indented entryway, so the various doors were not visible from staring down the long, half-lit hallway. When Matt and Nicky led Temple to the murder room, she gave a little jump to see a tall, pale figure on guard at the door.

"No ghost," Nicky said. "Just Emilio. I thought having someone guard the body was a good idea. We shouldn't cross the threshold because of compromising the evidence more than it already is. Can you see enough to be useful?"

Temple had leaned inside to crane her neck left and right, and down and up, avoiding the bed and its occupant.

"That huge mirror wall in the rococo frame is the one that's see-through from the other side?"

"Yes," Matt said. "It's a small room, maybe eight-by-ten, with mini-blinds on the inside window. There's a table with a low-level lamp. And a chair. I sat on it; but it felt creepy."

"Kind of like taking a seat in a porno movie house," Nicky suggested. "Not that I frequent such places," he added quickly.

"Like any place illicit," Matt said, "it had a nasty feel to it."

"So you stood?" Temple asked.

"No. I moved to sit against one wall. I didn't need or want to see anything through that secret window."

"Was the floor carpeted, like the bedroom?"

Matt thought. "Yes, I guess. It wasn't cold anyway."

"It wouldn't be," Nicky said, "out here in the desert, but the steel-blue carpeting continued through the false baseboard on the section of wall that was a hidden door. How'd you find it?"

"The seam was a bit off. And I was desperate. Those women hooting up a storm in the hall were heading my way. I had no idea proper young women could be so rowdy, and bawdy."

"Oh, Matt," Temple said, "they probably ate up a tour of a bordello by its residents the way I'd devour a backstage tour of a major Vegas magic show. I'm a little weird that way, preferring magicians' illusions to peeks into a bordello. Women find 'naughty' very interesting."

"Men too," Nicky added.

Matt said nothing, just sighed pointedly.

Temple studied the room. "Definitely on the kinky side. You're sure the mirror above the bed is not see-through?"

"No," Matt and Nicky said in unison.

"No, or not sure?"

"It's pretty irrelevant. When I found Matt in here bending over the girl on the bed, doing CPR," Nicky said, "I just checked on her condition, dead, and his, in shock, and got us the hell out of there."

"What did you learn from bending over her?" Temple asked Matt.

"That her eyes were blue, to match the decorating scheme. Maybe it was a color-coordinated murder. And the thin black scarf around her throat flared at the ends so I could see it was a fishnet stocking. They are stockings, aren't they, not panty hose?"

"I'm not an expert on fishnet stockings," Temple said. "They have a long rep as sexy entertainer accessories, on the trashy side, although they came back into high fashion briefly a couple of years ago. The manufacturers are always trying to get women back into hose again, even in this suffocatingly hot climate. Didn't work with me."

"Does with Van," Nicky said. "She's an executive woman; dresses to the nines."

"I dress to the Easy Eights," Temple said with a smile, offering her bare calf and foot in its medium-heeled mule.

"Speaking of the Not-Easy Eights," Nicky said, "we need to discover if this corpse is one of my brothers' significant others, or one of the resident ladies."

"The madam didn't recognize her."

"Okay, she might be somebody entirely unknown, but then how did she end up here?"

"How did most of us?" Temple asked. "You twelve guys were hijacked."

"An imported body," Nicky mused. "That's kinky. I suppose she could have been imported in the limo trunk without anyone the wiser. Where do you hide a semi-naked dead woman you want to ditch?"

Matt added, "We need to identify her. Is she known to the people who are here now? Not that they wouldn't lie. How can we try to identify her without entering the room again?"

Nicky flourished his cell phone, hit a button and rapidly clicked through close-up and distant photos of the seminude dead woman. "While I was guiding you out of the crime scene, I took these. You were pretty stunned. Giving CPR to an almost nude dead woman would do that. Damn cell phone may not get great signals way out here, but the photo feature works swell."

Temple shivered to see the woman's features close up in the small screen, as blank of expression as a doll's face. She was young and pretty enough to be either a sex-for-hire object of desire, or a Fontana girlfriend. Such a waste.

"First thing," Nicky said, "I'm going to search around here for her clothes. I doubt she arrived here undressed, and even a resident would start with more than some inciting lingerie at least. Maybe she was undressed just before, or after, her murder."

"Why?" Matt asked, appalled.

"Confuses the issue of who she . . . was," Temple said, "and therefore, who might have killed her. Whoever did it must have acted on impulse. You couldn't set up a situation like this."

"Well," Nicky pointed out, "eight vengeful bridesmaids did. Maybe one of them figured she could off a rival while she was at it."

"But your brothers surely weren't ever customers here?"

Nicky frowned at Temple. "I'd say no, they don't have to patronize brothels. But there are a lot of them and I certainly don't keep up with their entertainment and personal lives."

"And there's always Uncle Mario," Matt put in.

"Of course!" Temple eyed Nicky. "An older man might need more . . . exotic stimulation."

"Hey. I do not speculate about my uncle Mario's affairs, criminal or personal. You'd have to ask him."

"Or the madam," Temple said hopefully, trying to avoid a

fate worse than death, a fate that might *be* death if she inquired too much into Macho Mario's virility. "That Miss Kitty is getting to be on friendly terms with him, come to think of it. I've spotted them canoodling in the bar."

"You're the detective," Nicky told her. "Your fiancé and I are your prime suspects and none of my family is absolved. Go to it. Dig up all the dirt on all and sundry that you can."

Chapter 36

Mama Molina!

"Hey, Ma!"

Mariah came tearing into the bedroom, throwing her backpack on the bed's foot.

"Slow down, *chica*!" Carmen pushed her pistol and remote close to the pillows.

Mariah had moved from tween to teen keeping Hispanic slang, but not other words. Hence her mother was no longer "Mama" but "Mom" or "Ma."

"I forgot! Next week is What Your Daddy Does. I was wondering if you could—"

"No *problemo*. Uncle Morrie will be happy to show up and help."

"'*Problemo!*'" Mariah whined. Whine was the new "beg." "You've already been there and done that. That is so boring! To have cops for both days. Can't I, can't you—"

"You don't like Uncle Morrie? Honey, he has kept us going when I've been off work. You don't realize what he's done for us, for me."

"He's good. I like him fine. Only I thought, wouldn't it be cool if . . . if we did the same thing as for the father-daughter dance next fall? You know."

She was trying to make Mom come up with daughter dearest's obvious and only conclusion. What She Really, Really, Really Wanted.

Only Carmen's head had ached all day, in pulsing tempo with her stitches. Next fall was a long, long time away. This was only May and school would be ending soon. Luckily, Carmen would be on her feet by then. In a few days. Good as new. Hah!

"Honey . . ."

"I want him! Matt. It would be so cool. I mean, he's famous. He's on the radio."

Mariah was not alone, Carmen reflected. Thank God he was finally taken. Temple Barr had won the brass ring that lonely, late-night, radio-listening women all over Vegas lusted for, including her alarmingly hormonal daughter.

She thought as fast as she could.

"I don't know, honey. He said okay for the fall dance, but this is coming up so fast. He's a busy man."

"He works nights, and this is a daytime gig. I mean, middle school. Come on, Mom!"

Mariah's cheeks glowed rosy with emotion, warming her dark eyes. She had the as-yet-unmade-up beauty of the young.

"I'll think about it."

Mariah made a face, but left to make supper for them. Something microwaved that would be tippy on Carmen's lap tray and leave oily, red-dye-tinged sauce on the paper napkin and on the bedspread, if she wasn't careful.

Carmen sighed. It still hurt.

Damn. Matt was Temple's official guy now. She couldn't keep drafting him for absentee father duty. Even the fall dance was a terrible imposition. He was an ex-priest, for God's sake. Children were the last thing he had signed up for.

She wondered if Temple wanted any. If they would have any.

None of her business. Mariah was her business. Mariah and her phantom dead dad. The cop killed trying to assist a stranded motorist.

The fake. The figment of her mother's imagination.

Now Carmen was lying about the present, about her unauthorized breaking and entering at Kinsella's house, and worrying about Dirty Larry using his knowledge of that against her.

Oh, what tangled webs we weave, and all that.

What Your Daddy Does Day.

Somehow Carmen didn't think Our Lady of Guadalupe grade school was looking for a *Who's* Your Daddy Day.

War was hell, but family relations could be hellacious.

Chapter 37

Three Cat Night

My worst nightmare has come true.

I am trapped in a strange place by a gang of three.

I have no escape route, no allies, no alternatives.

I have been hounded upstairs, where I had hoped to take a restoring snooze in the establishment's linen closet while I let my little gray cells get cooking on a subconscious level.

Unfortunately, a closet is a cul-de-sac.

My back is to the wall.

My front is to a trio of female relatives on the warpath who have tracked me down and used their carnivore claws to pull the door to my sanctuary wide and now stand shoulder to shoulder like linebackers to ensure that I am going nowhere except where they say.

Now I know how the Fontana brothers have been feeling all evening.

Only *my* pursuing Furies are all feline and all claws and teeth.

"There he is!" they howl as one.

"Sonny," cries a voice. (That one is okay. It was the moniker of a mob guy in *The Godfather*.)

"Daddy," cries another voice in syrupy, sarcastic tones. (That one is *not* okay. I am not a family guy unless it is spelled with a capital *F as* in fierce, fearless, feline, footloose, and fancy-free.)

Alas, I am not footloose and fancy-free now, for a third yowl comes: "Lover boy."

What is a guy to do, held hostage in a house of pleasure along with a lot of other dudes?

Rolling over and playing dead is not an option.

I fan my shivs and snick them back into their sheaths. "Ladies, please. There is enough of me to go around."

"In your dreams," jeers Midnight Louise.

"You could use a street diet and some sparring time," Ma Barker says.

"You are a one-queen kind of guy, I know it," Miss Satin says, all moony-eyed.

Oh, Cheese Whiz! Here I am, trapped, caught between three generations of clinging females. At least I am outdoing the Fontana boys all by my lonesome self. At least only one of these dames has any serious designs on me.

One is bad enough.

I had better get some designs of my own on them. Quick!

First I spring to my four furry feet, claws unsheathed.

Then I growl, "What took you so long?"

"Us?" Midnight Louise spits in disbelief. "You are the one who was napping on the job."

"Tut-tut." I strut forward and brush past them, brush past Satin, that is, and into the hall. "I was not napping. I was planning the best dispersal of our agents."

CAT IN A SAPPHIRE SLIPPER · 189

"And what have you planned, oh, sage snoozer?" Louise asks.

"We need reliable reports from all fronts on my Miss Temple's interrogations. She is usually pretty sharp, but your eyes and ears are better equipped to spot telling signs among such a bevy of potential baddies. Satin, you will join your sister residents in the parlor. Midnight Louise will hang with the bridesmaids in the kitchen.

"Ma Barker, your alley cat instincts have not been blunted by the decadent comforts of domestic life. You still live by your eyes and ears and nose. I want you to give the murder room the going-over of your life."

"And where will you be," Miss Midnight Louise asks, "while I have been confined to the kitchen with the women?"

"I will be in the bar with the men. I can break their macho codes and tell when they are lying, and when they are just bragging to save face."

"It is true that they will swagger more in your presence," she concedes. "And bragging men often give away far more than they mean to. Your assignment roster makes a certain kind of accidental sense."

What? Miss Midnight Louise agreeing with me?

"Good. We clear on our assignments?"

Docile head nods all around. By gummy bears, executive authority agrees with me!

I watch two sets of fluffy tails, unnervingly upright, salute as Louise and Satin turn and head downstairs, looking more like littermates than mother and daughter.

"That cathouse girl has some moxie," Ma Barker growls to me under her breath, which is rank. Regular hard kibble should help that. "You do not worry about my pad prints being all over the death scene?"

"The authorities know we are notorious carnivores. They may rag on my Miss Temple and Mr. Matt and the Fontanas for not securing the crime scene better, but who can stop an alley cat from checking out dead meat?"

"Your lady friend, Satin, may know better what's what in a bordello bedroom."

"Yes, but I want a virgin nose on this scent."

Ma Barker emits a curt cough. Now I know where she gets her oddly canine name. "You are dreaming, boy, but I will give it my best once-over."

Chapter 38

Devised to Disguise

The police professional always interviews suspects in a murder case separately, one at a time, Temple knew.

The police professional did not usually have to deal with bulk lots of suspects numbering eight or more. Nor did one have—Temple checked her bangle-style watch—less than twenty hours to do it in if Matt was to make his midnight radio advice program by the next night, Tuesday.

It occurred to Temple how thoughtful the Fontana brothers had been to hold the bachelor party on Matt's one night off, Monday. She was sure that was a concession to her and her own engaged state.

So now she sat around several long kitchen tables with her aunt Kit and an octet of strange females aged from the mid-twenties to the beautifully preserved late-thirties. Everybody was swigging various flavored and antioxidant-laden bottled water.

There were four brunettes, three blondes, and a magenta-black redhead.

She was encouraged that blondes were in the minority, not that they were stupid, only they were so darn hard to tell apart. A Blond Miasma that went with the hair color blinded all onlookers' senses. Temple knew that now from personal experience, not just non-blond prejudice. She'd been a bottle blonde for a few weeks, thanks to an undercover assignment for her personal pain-in-the-bleach bottle, Lieutenant C. R. Molina. Now she was rinsed and conditioned to a lively strawberry red, which was a vivid version of Aunt Kit's faded fiery locks.

Temple was a public relations freelancer now, but her former jobs as a Midwestern TV reporter and PR person for a repertory theater in Minneapolis—and her former experiences in amateur theatrics—made her a perceptive group interviewer. As a reporter, she'd learned to spot or hear any hint of insincerity, and a little acting experience only honed that gift. Kit, being a former acting pro and now a novelist, was equally sharp in this respect.

Their quick conversation outside the kitchen had cast Temple as Good Cop, Kit as Bad Cop. Temple had decided they should have a go at it before Electra relieved Kit.

"I'll have to go some," Kit complained, "to reach the heights of your Lieutenant Molina in the role." This was laughable because Molina was six foot in shoes with flat heels and Temple and Kit were five foot each, period.

"*Ooh*, don't call that annoying non-woman 'mine,'" Temple whispered before they pushed through the swinging barroom doors into the serving area. "Hi, guys," she addressed the women sitting at two of the four tables in the area. "My name is Temple, and I'll be interviewing you. My aunt Kit will help."

"Oh, she must be the old hag who nailed Aldo," someone said.

"This is going to be fun," Kit whispered, donning her Leona

Helmsley bitch-goddess manner in the next, loud sentence. "Who said that? You, the mouse-brownette with the cheek mole shaped like a turtle? Beauty marks went out with Little Orphan Annie's freckles, sweet jowls. Get it lasered off. I'm here to extract your names, addresses, and occupations, so just spell it out for me."

The now-abashed girlfriend produced, "Meredith Bell. I'm a lifestyle coach."

Temple noted that down, along with the physical characteristics Kit had nailed.

The rest of the wedding party-to-be if no one was arrested were: Wanda, honey-blond and a massage therapist; raven-haired Judith, a runway model; white-blond Jill, a pharmacist; the mahogany redhead, Alexia, a horse trainer; Tracee, a dark brunette Pilates instructor; Evita, an auburn-haired ventriloquist; and Asiah, an exotic black beauty with blond hair, who was, surprise, a showgirl.

Temple didn't even want to know which woman went with which Fontana brother, but she did ask and note down the pairings. She couldn't help thinking that Kit and she would be overwhelmed by these long-stemmed beauties in the wedding party, although Alexia and Jill were more petite.

Several of the women needed strength in their professions: the massage therapist, horse trainer, Pilates instructor, and showgirl. Yes, the showgirl. Those huge, glamorous headdresses weighed about forty pounds each. It wasn't just Third World women who could balance heavy weights on their heads to earn their daily bread. . . .

"Okay," Temple told them. "I think you know that a woman is dead upstairs. Apparently she's not one of you."

"No," came a chorus of answers. "We've been together all night, except Asiah, who was driving the limo. She had to come along with the men, see them in, and guard the front door until we had them under control."

194 · Carole Nelson Douglas

Temple eyed the woman, who still wore the barely rear-covering blazer of a chauffeur over modest black palazzo pants now.

"You were the only one who came along to the Sapphire Slipper later, with the abducted men," Temple said. "How'd you get driving duty?"

She answered offhandedly, "I like to drive. Dark and desert don't bother me. I got to eavesdrop on a lot of hunky guys letting their hair down. And I got to tote the Really Big Gun at the end, making sure none of the arrivals scampered off when they realized the setup was definitely not what they'd ordered."

"Where did the firearms come from?" Temple asked the tables at large.

"Prop shop fakes," Tracee, the Pilates expert, said. "Pretty convincing. You can rent anything in Vegas."

"Why did you do it?" Kit asked. "Just to ruin my wedding, or what?"

"Nothing personal," Jill said quickly. As a pharmacist, she was used to soothing customers. As a pharmacist, she could have administered a narcotic to the victim that made her easy to strangle.

It occurred to Temple that the bridesmaids had used a formidable amount of planning and cooperation to pull off this faux abduction. Maybe it was more than a declaration of dependence on perennial boyfriends. Maybe it had been devised to disguise a murder.

Chapter 39

Mass Matrimony

"Who are you, anyway, to ask us all these questions?"

Electra, the bridesmaids' "housemother," had taken over for Kit, who now babysat the house courtesans. "Now, dear . . . it is Evita the ventriloquist, isn't it? How would you like it if you were onstage and your dummy did all the talking?"

"We are *not* dummies," huffed Judith, the runway model. "Would dummies have hijacked every Fontana male in town?"

"Of course not. I'm just saying that being grilled by my friend here, Temple Barr, is a lot better than answering to teams of police detectives in small, clammy, air-conditioned rooms that smell of cigarettes and vomit."

"*Euuw*," exclaimed several of the women, Temple among them.

"You do recognize," Electra went on, "that a young woman is tragically dead, someone your age, murdered upstairs? That the police would be hauling everybody off in paddy wagons for rude and uncomfortable grillings if you didn't have the finest little private eye in Vegas here to get to the bottom of things."

Electra had been doing great until unreeling that last phrase.

Temple didn't bother denying that she was fine and little, or a PI. Whatever gave her a modicum of control over these herds of suspects.

"The idea is," she told them, "we figure out who the victim is, and who killed her before the police and forensic teams come clomping in to put you and your boyfriends in custody. The idea is to keep Aldo's and Kit's wedding on schedule for next Saturday, and all you lovely bridesmaids free to waltz down the aisle with your handsome tuxedoed escorts, free of suspicion and free to be roped into matrimony by all of you.

"Wedding fever strikes a family like the Fontanas only once in a blue moon."

"We know that!" Jill, the ethereally pale pharmacist, was almost in tears. "We thought this joke would put them on the spot. That they'd be impressed by what guys like the Fontanas admire."

"Which is?"

"Nerve and organization."

"Great! You proved that. So keep it up and help me solve the murder of that girl upstairs. She's not one of you, obviously."

"No." Tracee, the Pilates instructor, counted noses around the table. "We're all here, after Asiah came inside from parking the limo and guarding the front door."

"Oh, and when was that, Asiah?" Temple asked.

"I don't know," the lanky black woman said. "We weren't on a timetable, other than picking up the guys at eight sharp."

"How'd you manage taking over that limo?"

"Hundred-dollar bill and a tongue kiss to Manny G., who's fifty and prefers sitting in front of a twenty-one horseshoe to sitting behind the wheel of a behemoth on a trek to the desert."

"He'd let a strange woman take over his ride?"

Asiah dug her talons into a tiny quilted purse she kept on a long chain, rather like a Chihuahua. "I have my chauffeur's license. I made some dough that way while working on the modeling career. Leggy chauffeurs get premium pay in Vegas. I've driven Donald Trump."

"Hopefully, off a cliff," Electra muttered to Temple.

"And thanks, Tracee," Asiah added with a toss of her blindingly blond long tresses, "for pointing out that I was the last one in. Real sisterhood, bitch. I hope the Down Dog breaks your back someday."

"Hey!" Wanda, the massage therapist, was obviously the peacemaker of the group. "Let's not panic and snipe at one another. At least none of *us* is dead. Are you sure someone killed the girl upstairs now, while we all were here, Miss Barr?"

"Just Temple, thanks. Save the formality for the cops, because they will have to be called. I can't say, Wanda, when she died. Right now, I need to find out who she was."

"Not one of us." Alexia, the horse trainer, noted with a shimmy of her roan mane.

"How do you know?" Temple said. "Maybe she used to date one of your boyfriends."

"That's just it." Judith, the model, toyed with a sealed pack of Virginia Slims cigarettes she was obviously dying to open. "We're all veterans. We've dated our guys long enough to get tired of being long-term girlfriends."

"How long?" Temple asked, and got bombarded with a blitz of years. "Nine." "Five here!" "Seven!" "Six." "Four." "Five." "Eight." "Two," Asiah finished. As all the others looked at her with disbelief, she added, "That's a *looong* time for me."

"So what's with the mass rush to matrimony?" Temple wondered.

198 · Carole Nelson Douglas

They eyed one another, wordlessly consulting on whether to tell her the truth.

"We've met one another," Tracee said finally. "Hung out with one another and our guys. Heck, our periods are even in sync."

The others nodded glumly. Temple had heard of that: women in close proximity or in families tended to ovulate, and everything else, at the same time.

The Fontana brothers' girlfriends formed quite a little "family" of their own.

"So when Aldo broke the circle, so to speak," Alexia said, "when he announced he was marrying a stranger, we all just went bananas for commitment."

"Wait a minute!" Temple shouted into the muttering of bridesmaid indignation at being left at the altar unwed. "Who was Aldo's girlfriend? Before."

The silence that greeted her very apropos question lasted a long time.

For, of course, she was the obvious prime suspect: the woman who could never join this jolly little group again. The one Aldo never moved up from "girlfriend." The one Temple's aunt Kit had replaced.

"There wasn't one, at the moment," Wanda finally said.

"How long a moment?"

"For about a year. She was a performer at one of the acrobatic shows."

"Was?"

"She fell and broke her neck."

Temple felt her stomach flip over. Fell. Dead. Like Max, maybe, who lived to tempt fate with spectacular aerial stunts. That was the nightmare, anyway.

"How awful," Electra said, her voice throbbing with empathy.

"They'd been together nine years," Jill added, choking a little.

"I see why—" Electra didn't finish her thought. Why Aldo

had flipped for Kit and decided to marry her. He knew what loss was.

And all these women knew it too. Time could be short.

Temple, being advertised as the city's "finest little private eye," had to ask herself an unpleasant question. Had Aldo's girlfriend just had a tragic accident, or had it been murder too?

Chapter 40

Memories of the Fall

"Garry," Max asked the man he believed had been his mentor and "handler" since he was seventeen, "why do I have a psychiatrist assigned to me?"

Garry was wheeling him through the gardens again, after having checked the wheelchair and Max's pajamas for recording devices the size of a flea, or not much larger. He had graduated from the butt-baring hospital gown.

"They claim it's standard practice for victims of head injury and memory loss. That makes sense. This is a world-renowned facility. I've looked into Mademoiselle, or Fraulein, Doctor Schneider's professional and personal background. She is highly qualified. Degrees from Heidelberg *and* the Paris Psychiatric Clinic. She travels all over the world, at stratospheric fees, to discreetly aid some very global players. Rupert Murdoch has used her, not personally."

"Who's paying her in this case?"

"We are. You, actually."

"How much?"

"Fifty thousand dollars for three weeks, a renewable contract."

"Fifty thousand? For a little knee patty-cake? I must have a lot more money than I know, but I don't think I'd spend it on this. Fire her."

"It might look suspicious if you didn't get the best of everything, Mr. Anonymous world-class, rich man mountain climber. Or that I wasn't as concerned as the doctors about your memory loss. Which I am. She might do some actual good. And what's with the knee patty-cake?"

"My patty, her knee. But she put it there first."

"Do you think she's trying to pump you?"

"Please put that more genteelly, Garry. I can't tell if she's a sincere therapist, or a sinister inquisitor-cum-watchdog masquerading as a sexy lady. She's clever. Mentally agile. As with a lot of Frenchwomen, flirting is a genetic marker. Mostly, I think her sessions are worthless for liberating my memory, but good for my ego."

"So she could be worth it under the label of 'morale'?"

"Under the label of 'not looking suspicious, and doing what they tell us.' She does exercise my wits."

"Your casts are coming off soon. Then it's physical therapy."

"No. I want out. You say I have good instincts. I'm sensing an . . . atmosphere here. I'm being watched. The minute these casts are cracked open, you break me out. Say we're using a private therapist at my fabulously equipped retreat in . . . Bahrain."

Garry chuckled. "The details may be escaping you, my boy, but your style is perfectly intact. You always could charm the snakes *into* the basket."

* * *

He hadn't wanted to trouble the old man. He knew he was being watched by a lot of people, people patients weren't expected to notice, like cleaning personnel, nursing aides, certainly Mademoiselle Fraulein Doctor Schneider. He was also going crazy kept down and inactive by these damnable casts. Did he really need them? Were they a ploy to keep him prisoner?

Then the memory of his body soaring toward that shiny black wall from unsupported space returned. He was lucky to be alive. Like a drunk driver, she'd said, too out of it to tense up and get really hurt. He wheeled himself to the window, back and forth, a form of pacing he couldn't manage physically.

Was he really that in command of his mind and body, enough to convert that fatal hit into a minor accident? Certainly he hadn't managed to keep his memory. But memory loss in severe accidental injuries is common. What wasn't normal, at least for his expectations; it wasn't coming back. The memory. His legs weren't the problem. He was relatively young. They'd heal. He was an athlete of sorts, even if he didn't buy the role of mountain climber.

He expected more from his memory. From himself. *Damn it!* Now was not the time to have a little brain crash! He paused to stare up at the postcard peaks rising like a colossal shark's maws around him. He shivered. Cold. Icy. Killing. Everything he didn't like in a landscape. Everything he didn't like in a woman.

Chapter 41

Ladies-in-Waiting

Temple moved on to the parlor, where Kit had corralled the Sapphire Slipper's staff.

Kit came snowshoeing over the thick wool carpet to Temple like a happy puppy.

"I've been getting acquainted with the girls," she whispered. "What a tragicomic bunch of life stories! They're a whole play by Eugene O'Neill via Neil Simon. They make *A Chorus Line* look like *Little Orphan Annie*. I'm getting an idea for a revue here. A play. A novel!

"A bunch of women are trapped in snowstorm in *The Best Little Whorehouse in Texas*, only it's in Nevada—maybe the mountains, there's snow there, right?—and there are *no* men in the cast. Just the women talking: whores and wives and would-be wives. Wolves howling in the distance—"

"A perfect offstage role for the Fontana pack," Temple interrupted.

"Wolves? No, these would be real wolf voices, tribal brutality at bay, the Taliban, maybe—"

"Kit, I hate to derail the creative muse when it's mingling *Medea* with *A Funny Thing Happened on the Way to the Forum* with *White Fang*, but I just learned something pretty awful, and—worse—maybe relevant."

"About what?"

"About who," Temple whispered, grabbing her aunt's thin wrist and pulling her into the archway to the bar, where Fontana Inc. awaited under the supervision of Van von Rhine. "The girlfriends said Aldo's significant other died a year ago. She was an aerial performer and fell during practice. Broke her neck. Did you know that?"

Kit had sobered instantly, plunging from creative mania into deep concern.

"Yes. He told me, of course. He said he liked that I did something safe. What could happen to a writer?"

"No wonder the poor man freaked when you were mistaken for me at the Red Hat Sisterhood convention and attacked with a garrote."

"I think that only made both of us realize we didn't want to be apart."

"Maybe you're not so safe. We assumed you were attacked because you wore a pink hat and are my physical double."

"Yeah?"

"But what if it was because you were seeing Aldo morning, noon, and midnight?"

Kit had always been a fast study. She bit her lip and looked around the not-so-innocent rooms that surrounded them. "That's what you learned from interviewing the Fontana brothers' ditsy girlfriends?"

Temple nodded. "Maybe one's not so ditsy, but got fixated on Aldo—"

"Maybe crazy like a fox." Kit nodded too. "Maybe you better interview these real 'foxes' fast to get an idea of what's really going on in this henhouse."

"Maybe, and amen."

Temple found that the sisters of joy, gathered en masse in a Victorian-style parlor with no men around to make them bill and coo, looked a lot like of dispirited hens on a rococo roost. All that blue together was starting to look . . . tired. Even tawdry.

Not only their feathers, but their faces seemed to droop.

"Wouldn't you all normally be hard at work now?" Temple asked as she sat on a plump, tiger-striped ottoman.

"Depends on what you consider 'work,'" one noted in a desultory voice.

"Earning money," Temple said briskly. She wasn't going to be trapped into thinking of them as "exotic." It wasn't a coincidence that another euphemism for their ancient profession was "workingwoman." And not a coincidence that employed women from the 1890s streets of New York to modern-day Baghdad were called "no better than whores."

Except here in Vegas a workingwoman could get stoned on the job in a whole different way than in a fundamentalist Muslim country.

And in Nevada, the authorities policed these "chicken ranches." The women were healthy, protected, and drug- and disease-free. Elsewhere in Las Vegas, the roulette wheel was in fine fettle and you pays your money and you takes your chances, as the carnival barkers say.

She had set aside the troubling question of Aldo's dead

significant other and was regarding the young women gathered around, all mostly under thirty or nearing forty at the outside, with a teacher's fond expectations.

Temple understood that they had been primed to perform.

"The first thing we need to establish," Temple said in a slow, serious tone, "is who the dead girl upstairs is. You know that the police will have to be called. When they are, they'll come here in force, along with a lot of forensics staff.

"It won't be as gory or glamorous as *CSI: Las Vegas*, but it will sure disrupt everybody's lives. The more information we can dig up now so you can give it confidently and truthfully to the police, the better off everyone will be."

"Except that dead girl."

The first to talk back was a skinny black woman.

"True," Temple said. "I'd better get your names."

"They're simple. We use the alphabet so our clients can remember to ask for us again."

"Alphabet pseudonyms?" Temple asked doubtfully.

"We even sit in alphabetical order."

"So the clients know where to spot you the second or twelfth time around?"

"Right. On the far left of the first sofa is Angela, then Babette, Crystal, Deedee, Fifi, Gigi, Heather, Inez, Jazz, Kiki, Lili, Niki, and I'm Zazu."

There were a lot more blondes of every shade among the residents than among the bridesmaids, curled, or tousled, or spiky. It made the girls harder to tell apart.

"So everyone who's here is someone who should be here?" Temple asked.

There was a pause, almost as if a moment of mental communion occurred, then all the bedheads nodded.

"Then who is she?" Temple got up to show the dead woman's cell phone image to everyone in reverse alphabetical order, studying their reactions.

"Nobody we recognize for sure," said the first one, Zazu, who wore a blue peignoir over skimpy French underwear. At least Temple assumed it was French, since she had never seen the like, even online.

The others agreed in turn, in different words, but just as definitely.

"That hairdo is way too long and loose for one of us."

"Men like piled and teased hair that's easy to disarrange."

"That there's a receptionist pageboy. No guy would ask her for anything but directions."

Their instant summations were unnerving. Temple realized that their world was one of appearances and snap judgments. So they were judged by the customers, and so they judged everyone.

Like Kit, Temple found the house girls amazingly open and even chatty once the ice had been broken. They reminded her of teenagers at a pajama party. Theirs was an all-female society. Of course men came into it every night, and then they performed their agreed-upon sexual pas de deux with whoever paid.

But the real culture of the Sapphire Slipper wasn't the hordes of men who arrived and departed, but the ongoing daily gossip, pampering, laughing, interaction of the women. Temple had sensed the same sort of high school camaraderie in the dressing room of a strip club she had once visited undercover.

These women had never gotten past the trauma of their families, the casual bonding of girls in passage, the sharing of fripperies and laughs, the bored, knowing, eyebrow-raising worldliness of girls who'd had to grow up faster than was good for them.

In a strange, warped way, they were convinced that anyone who subscribed to a monogamous, straight way of life was either deluded or a liar.

To answer the famous song line, "Is that all there is?" they

were sure that this, their commercially intimate lives, was all
that there was.

It was only in going over her notes of their names and de-
scriptions later that she noticed the *E* and *M* girls were missing
before the string jumped to Zazu at the end.

Chapter 42

Happy Hooker?

Temple adjourned to the bar off the parlor with a sense of relief, probably false. She felt on common ground here, however bizarre the situation.

A sober group of men surrounded several of the round tables, sitting on leather club chairs.

The liquor labels fronting the mirrored back of the bar were all high-end. Heavy crystal ashtrays suitable for cigars centered every polished tiger-maple tabletop.

Temple would have to say that if she were a resident sizing up the night's customers, she'd be one happy hooker. Matt's Polish-blond hair stood out among the dark Italian ones like a headlight, but not one guy here was shabby, including Uncle Mario, whose teeth were as snow-white as his silk tie against a black shirt. The man's old-style gangster look made portly into muscle and balding into moneyed.

The younger Fontanas were hipper in every respect, but still radiated a slightly Old World air of elaborate courtesy that won over women everywhere.

Van von Rhine was the other blonde in the room, and Temple had missed seeing her at first. She was perched on a navy leather barstool and had faded into the faceted glitter of the mirrored bottles behind her.

After Temple had surveyed the scene, Van waved her over. "How's it going?"

"I'm learning a lot about hordes of strangers." Temple joined Van at the bar, deciding that an elevated seat would command more attention from this armada of men.

She skillfully hopped up via the crossbar, which anyone who is five feet tall masters early. She felt like a judge at a bench, which was just the inner buttressing she needed to play the authority card here.

"You seem one short."

They frowned, straightening their ties and their postures.

"Not short in height, in number."

Emilio dashed around the archway. "Sorry, I just heard from, er, Fifi, that it was the guys' turn for grilling."

"Who's guarding the murder room door?" Nicky asked as their uncle nodded with grave disapproval.

"Um, three of the girls. That way they watch one another. I'll get back up there as soon as Miss Temple lets me go."

And she bet that he was a lot more eager to pass the time with three courtesans than here.

Smiling at the tables, she said, "I'll need to use you guys as a sounding board. First, I'd like your impression of how the abduction was managed, and what you all did, and where, when you arrived here."

There was the expected universal, awkward silence.

"Did any of you suspect something was wrong before you arrived here?"

Dark heads shook.

"The right limo was gassed up and idling for us. We hopped in," Aldo said.

"Like lambs to the slaughter," Macho Mario growled dolefully.

Imagining him as a lamb was quite the funny-bone tickler. Temple bit her lip and caught Matt's eye, who gave his answer. "I didn't know what normal was for these events, so it all seemed uneventful to me."

"There was one surprise," Aldo noted.

"What was that?" half-a-dozen basso voices wondered.

"Your cat," he told Temple, "hitched a ride in my groomsmen-mobile. I didn't recall anyone inviting Midnight Louie to be a ring bearer."

"Have you seen him since you all were ushered inside?" She hadn't yet encountered him in the living fur, which was odd.

"No, ma'am," Emilio said smartly. "He must have run off and hid at all the strangers and commotion."

That didn't sound like Louie, who had a habit of running *toward* strangers and commotion. Where was the big lug now?

"I saw him upstairs," Matt put in. "In fact, he *led* me upstairs."

Several of the boys laughed lustily. "Hey, there, Matt, maybe he wanted to rush up to where the action was," Ralph jibed.

"The action was dead," Matt said.

A pall fell like a winding sheet over the naturally boisterous Fontana spirits.

"Sorry, man," Ralph said. "We only heard about the body on the bed. We didn't have to find it."

The other brothers nodded somberly, but Temple was sure they'd expected to find lots of bodies upstairs at a brothel, live ones. And, frankly, she doubted that dead ones would much upset seasoned wise guys. But she'd never tell Matt that. He'd be shocked.

You could play along with the Fontana boys' pussycat facades, but you should never forget their Berettas weren't just a
high-tech fashion accessory.

Temple pulled out Nicky's cell phone and asked him to take
the images of the dead woman around to all the tables. There
was much tsking and glum murmuring among them, but no
Fontana claimed to recognize the girl.

Wonderful! Total strikeout. The victim was utterly unknown
by anyone now in the Sapphire Slipper. Not likely. How was
Temple going to find a murderer among this cast of dozens?
And by tomorrow afternoon, yet?

Start at the point you know, she told herself.

"Okay. This question is for all you younger generation
Fontanas. How's your relationship with your current girlfriend
and how long have you been associated?"

There was a stunning silence. Most guys don't talk relationships even when plied with vodka and needle nose pliers to
their private parts. Why were they going to breathe a word in
this communal setting?"

"Please, guys. You were the ones deemed worthy of nicking,
which set this whole insanity in motion. I don't have time to
take you aside one by one for a private tête-à-tête. The police
may be more private about interviewing you, but they'll be a lot
less understanding."

Macho Mario snorted. "The police aren't understanding at
all. Okay, girlie, you didn't ask, but I'll come clean. I've been a
widower for twelve years. I ain't never been to the Sapphire
Slipper. I can still get my own girlfriends at any bar in Vegas."

"Have you ever dumped a girlfriend since you were an eligible bachelor again?"

"For one thing, I have never been eligible. I have lawyers
who see to that. For another, I know that a guy my age and
weight can't be choosy. I also know my rep attracts the little

dolls. I have never been known to say no to a little doll, hence they do not leave me unless a wedding ring comes along from some new beau. Then it's no hard feelings, aloha."

Macho Mario's unabashed confession got the brothers rushing to spill their guts.

"It was Aldo," Armando said. "Flipping over your aunt. That got our girlfriends all stirred up. Then they try on the bridesmaid gowns and say they hate them, and only a bridal gown will do. Vera Wang, yet."

Rico shook his head at their oldest brother. "When Nicky tied the knot, we all thought he was just young and didn't know better. No offense, Van. And, although he was the youngest, he'd always wanted to settle down early, go straight, have a hotel of his own, and kids. Or kid, in your case. How is little Cinnamon, anyway?"

"Safe at home now, and in preschool otherwise," Van said, "which is more than can be said about any of you, then or now."

The brothers managed to look both sheepish and suave, en masse.

Van nudged Temple in the side. "Fontanas do 'guilty but innocent' so well. I'd like to see your stone-cold police lieutenant, Molina, handling this gang in an interrogation room."

"No, you wouldn't," Temple answered. She addressed the Fontanas again. "All your girlfriends hate their bridesmaid gowns?"

"Oh, yeah."

"Mamma mia, does she!"

"Already offered it as a car rag for the Viper."

"But Kit and Van put a lot of thought into them," Temple objected. "The colors are sophisticated, the lines elegant, and there's no bow on the butt. What more could they want?"

There was a long, sullen silence.

"Bridal gowns," Temple answered herself.

"This wedding stuff has made them snap," Eduardo said. "Simple as that."

"How long have you been going together?" Temple asked absently, still mourning the fact that Van's and Kit's brilliant choice of bridesmaid gowns was not only a washout, it had incited a rebellion.

Their answers echoed the women's. "Six years." "Three." "Four." "Three." "Five."

"Uh, guys. That's a pretty stable amount of time. Didn't it ever occur to you that they might be expecting some more permanent commitment?"

"They have jobs," they chorused again.

"Jobs, hell. Careers."

"Nobody was clamoring for bambinos, and that is sure not gonna happen for Aldo and Kit."

"They liked a good time, and we had 'em. Why ruin it?"

As the Fontana boys listed their grievances against their suddenly martially minded significant others, Temple mulled recent polls she'd seen that *women* were slow to tie the knot nowadays. That they no longer needed men to support them financially, or even to give them babies. They were totally independent. Then why did these eight go over the edge?

This whole scheme was beginning to look like a prank that had gone very wrong when someone used it as cover to kill a young woman nobody here knew. They all said they didn't, anyway.

Temple turned brisk. She wanted some one-on-one time with Matt. He was the most at risk.

"Okay, guys. Were any of you not in full view of the others at any time after you left the limo out front?"

Another long silence. Fontana boys did not squeal.

Van stepped in. "Only Nicky and Matt. They were able to split off from the main group because they weren't the objects of the kidnappers' affections and objections. And the staff here didn't know a Fontana from a Fontana from a tall, blond stranger. Nobody missed them."

That meant that she and Temple were the only ones whose significant other was in the murder suspect runoff.

Oh, goodie.

Chapter 43

Command Post

Temple decided that she needed a command post.

Imagine: her acting like Lieutenant Molina. Actually, she was beginning to sympathize with the problems of the police force.

"I need to interview suspects separately someplace private," Temple told Miss Kitty when she returned to the parlor.

The Sapphire Slipper girls were playing computer games, including solitaire. Weird.

"We got plenty of private rooms upstairs. Take your pick. They're not going to see any action tonight."

"The murder room did."

"Don't use that one then."

As if she would!

Temple returned to the bar, went up to Matt, and tapped him on the shoulder, jerking her head to the exit.

Hoots and laughter followed them out into the parlor, then whistles and kiss-kiss sounds hounded them into the foyer.

"I'm glad they're all having so much fun with that dead girl lying alone upstairs," Matt said.

"She's not alone. Emilio's gone back up there already to guard her door."

"I guess that's a girl's dream death in this town: Fontana brothers at your door."

"Matt. Chill! I know it's rough to find someone dead. You tried to revive her. It was too late."

"I said the prayers anyway. That's never too late. Good God, Temple, can you imagine what it's like to be feet away from a murder, and not know it?"

"Like a baptism of fire on the battlefield," she said seriously. "No, I can't imagine that. No one here admits to recognizing the girl. That is so . . . unbelievable. Was she brought in just to be killed in this mob scene, so the motive is forever obscured?"

"You're right. I can only help her now by making sure whoever did this doesn't walk out of here tomorrow free. We need to get the police out here. There may be evidence in that room, on that body, that would reveal the murderer."

"There's surely evidence there that would implicate you. And Nicky. And the press will be all over any lurid headlines involving Fontanas. I'm thinking this death was planned to take advantage of the mock-kidnapping."

"But the only ones who knew about the abduction in advance were the girlfriends, although the brothel staff knew a big party of men was expected.

"Thank you, Mr. Clarity. At least all those people are strangers to us, not our nearest and dearest, or friends, anyway."

"So what did all the women tell you?"

"Nothing. Less than an embarrassed Fontana brother. None of them admitted to knowing the dead woman's face."

"It's an easy lie. Simon Peter found it came trippingly to the tongue in the Garden of Gethsemane, three times."

It took Temple a full minute to switch to childhood New Testament studies to remember the betrayals of Christ that night by Judas, the designated turncoat. And by St. Peter, the best and the brightest disciple. Peter, the rock upon which Jesus would found his church, denied even knowing Christ three times before the morning cock crowed, as Jesus had predicted.

The lesson was that, in moments when stand-up courage is called for, everybody can be weak-kneed. That might be the case here. A houseful of the sex queens of denial. Certainly the hookers denied the tawdry reality of the their life work. The girlfriends denied the charming elusiveness of the Fontana brothers that domesticity might destroy. The brothers denied growing older and up.

What did she and Matt deny?

That a murder was more than something to solve to get him and Nicky out of an awkward position? That Max Kinsella going missing so suddenly just made him an ex-boyfriend better out of the picture, and not another puzzle that would tear at their separate and joint needs and desires.

Oh, shoot!

Temple had examined the rooms upstairs (wild) and downstairs (standard hotel), and decided on using the office adjoining the cigar bar.

This was where male clients were put on hold while the logistics of the girl and the room and the fantasy were rotated on the madam's office computer. Yes. Sex for sale was micromanaged these days.

Temple could imagine male clients eyeing each other warily. *What are you here for?*

It felt very nineteenth century, and so did the ambience of the Sapphire Slipper.

Sex. The Final Frontier. Then and Now.

The office had flocked purple velvet wallpaper, a neat compromise between the blue theme of the whorehouse and the presumed red-blooded male vitality of the clients. A miasma of blue smoke haunted the intimate room.

Temple commandeered the rolltop oak desk and the rolling, golden oak, leather-upholstered desk chair, both big enough for Judge Roy Bean. She felt like Alice sitting on a mobile mushroom, but no need to tell anyone else. Her first task: to discover who were the usual denizens of the place, and who had been imported for this travesty of a bachelor party. Who was out of place, in one way or another? Besides the naked and the dead.

Sitting here, alone, Temple felt the despair Matt must have known on discovering the body. She could picture him chest-tapping and blowing into those still-warm lips, trying to coax life back into a frame it had only so recently deserted.

Matt, bent over a seminude woman, kissing her back to life.

She was proud of him. She might have been too squeamish to try to raise the dead with the pound, pound, pound of hands on chest and the pinched nostril Kiss of Life.

She knew he had given it his all. And so Nicky had found him.

Sad that trying to undo death made you look like a suspect.

Nicky Fontana had tremendous faith in her, enough to gamble his brothers' lives and freedom on it. He counted on her to get him and his enterprise out of any hot water before the Las Vegas law's zeal for arrests could boil over to scald clan Fontana.

This was a third-degree burn. Every male Fontana on the planet was front and center as a suspect, just for being here, especially Nicky, and even Aldo, Kit's late-life love. *Damn!* Had someone meant to ruin Temple's life and that of everyone she cared for? No. That was paranoid. This murder was a fluke intruding into the serene unwinding of her life and that of those she loved. And who loved her.

This murder was a hate crime. Sudden. Opportunistic, not caring about anyone she herself cared about. The motive was likely old. And ugly. And well concealed. Easy to assign to someone unconcerned and utterly innocent. So it was diabolical. Dangerous for the very randomness of the act.

Temple put her fist to her mouth and breathed a sigh on it. It was really pedal to the metal time.

No time for amateurs.

And no time.

She had to come up with a likely suspect before the police had to be called out here in a fistful of hours. Maybe ten.

Max would have known what to do here, where the Obvious intersected with the Devious. That's what magic acts were all about: the outward motions seemed open and obvious, but deceptions lay behind every apparently simple move and motive.

Temple was surprised to be missing Max as much she was. Not as a bed partner—a neglected love life, no matter how electric once, couldn't compete with a long-smoldering attraction suddenly cooking on all burners—but as a thinking partner.

Max had let her in on the mental gyrations of a counterspy. Taught her how to see beneath the illusions most people throw up around themselves in self-defense. Beneath the deceptions of people who truly mean to do other people ill.

A lot was on the line in Vegas's legal brothels. Competition among women for customers, everybody's—courtesan and client alike—sexual potency and self-esteem, the crass bottom line of giving or getting one's money's worth.

Max, being a professional deceiver onstage, was almost impossible to deceive.

Yet he was gone, too suddenly. Had he finally been deceived?

Or was he finally finishing the ugly business that had put his life in danger, and had contributed to their drawing apart despite themselves?

Temple didn't know. With Max, one never could.

And one could never count him out. He knew how to breathe life back into dead relationships. She missed him. Wouldn't count him among her dead and gone yet.

How could she? He was perfect. Immortal.

Wasn't he?

Dead of Night

Max was having a great dream.

He was doing a trapeze act with a girl in a red velvet swing.

They must have been in the circus. The arena was high and surrounded by applauding throngs. He knew it was a dream because he couldn't hear the roar of the crowd, could only see those wonder-struck, ravening, open mouths *oohing* and *aahing* at his daring swings back and forth.

He was perfect, immortal, his hands changing holds, swift and sure. He was dancing on air, hanging by a hair . . . and by a hand from his own lifeline.

The girl in the red velvet swing above him had dainty legs hidden by a froth of Victorian lace beyond the knee. She was winking at him, peeking over her full short velvet skirts, and she had red hair. It was a coppery, strawberry red, and it clashed with her valentine-red velvet swing ropes.

Which suddenly turned into DNA spirals of thick, coagulating blood.

A bronze-scaled snake was swiveling down those gory ropes, toward him, just as he thrust out his hand to catch the swing and spin off into the distance, safe.

The snake undulated toward his grasping, muscled forearm, suddenly naked, the arm, not the snake. The snake's fangs dripped slowly. Like an IV.

The crowd now surrounded an operating table. Max was laid out on it in a skimpy white hospital gown. No, not an operating table, a morgue dissecting table, and the snake's yawning fangs were turning saw-toothed to become the coroner's cranial cutting saw . . .

His still-living limbs flailed, seeking a secure purchase, on the trapeze or the red velvet swing.

He heard metal clattering, felt the pain of being cut open without anesthetic, twisted away from the treacherous arena, tore the girl from her red velvet perch. They fell struggling into the abyss, sawdust and sequins sparkling like a reverse night sky at the bottom of the circus ring. One ring to rule them all. Three rings, including the Worm Orobouros. Opal. Unlucky. Emerald. Fragile.

"Wake up," said a voice.

Hands shook his shoulders. Someone shook him hard enough that the back of his skull rapped a hard surface.

God!

Are you sleeping, are you sleeping, *dormez-vous?* Morning bells are ringing. *Ton. Ton. Ton.* Morning bells are ringing. *Frère Jacques.* Brother John. *Auprès de ma blonde, je désire dormir. Auprès de ma blonde . . .*

A tiny flashlight beam was drilling into his left eye.

"Wake up, Mike!"

That "Mike" did it. Woke him up to a lie. A fresh lie he recognized. He instantly knew where he was, who he was supposed to be, and that something bad had happened.

"Revienne?" he asked the dark behind the dentist's drill of light into his brain.

"Mike." Her voice, with that ambiguous, charming, accented English.

Are you sleeping, brother John?

"*Mon Dieu*, Mike! He was trying to kill you. Can you get up?"

He sighed. Not easily.

She hadn't turned on the room's general lighting.

"An assassin! *Mon Dieu*. The only explanation. Here, in such sanctuary. If I hadn't been thinking about you, hadn't had an insight on your therapy, I'd have never come by so late. Mike. Say something. Speak."

"Was it an . . . injection?"

"*Oui. Ja. Da.* Yes! In your veins. We must find the needle. It fell to the floor when you struggled and he ran. We need it for testing."

We.

Testing here? Not bloody likely. He felt the floor for a dropped hypo and found nothing. Time to move on. He pushed himself up using the strength of his arms, the ones so invincible in the dream. They were pretty stable. Good. His legs?

"The leg casts," she said as if reading his mind. "Perhaps you can do without. But not here. Not yet."

Her breaths came fast and frantic in the silent room, betraying the rapid search and reject of her brain cells. "Murder. Here! That is of all places supposed to be safe! *Mon Dieu.*"

He thought, irrelevantly, that a fervent "*sacré bleu*" would be a nice alternative.

"Nothing else to do," she muttered to him, to herself. "We must leave. Gather forces. How do I move you? Mike! Is your brain clear now? Can you do as I say?"

Yes. Yes. Do I want to?

"An assassin has breached this . . . what is the word? . . .

citadel of civilization. I can't believe it yet. Who are you? Why? Who'd want to kill a helpless man?"

Not quite helpless.

"We must get you out of here."

We again?

"I must . . . must . . . take you out. It's the middle of the night. You have a seizure. I'm taking you to the laboratory for treatment."

Laboratory? Ouch.

"No, not an emergency. Everything is fine. Just an . . . adjustment. I am, of course, authorized. Can you get yourself back up on the bed?"

So he was on the floor. Someone had wrestled him there.

She heaved. His arm muscles took hold and helped.

"Good. *God.* Good. It's all right if you look drugged. They're used to serious conditions here. They're used to me, moving around. I will take you out. Just . . . let me do it. Say nothing. Do nothing. Mike, do you hear me?"

More than you know, sweetheart.

"*Mein Gott!* They will kill you if they can."

He didn't like hearing that, but he didn't doubt it. Now. So she spoke fluent German as well as French. And what else? For now, her shock and stress rang true. He could let her lever and scam his hampered body out of here. He agreed. They had to leave.

After that, away from the drugs and control—and, unfortunately, his only contact, Garry Randolph—he would be stronger, his mind clearer. He could decide what to do next, and what to do about her.

For now, it only mattered what she could do about him.

Chapter 45

A Fine Kettle of Fish

It is hard to realize that I am best out of the way for the moment, and that the others are probably better off for it.

Perhaps Mr. Max Kinsella and I face the same quandary.

We are soul mates in several ways. (Now that he is not here to joust me for bedspread room I am finding more and more that we have in common.)

Like a master magician, I set my assistants about their appointed tasks. Some may not even know that I am pulling their strings. Or whiskers, in my case.

It is better I stay upstairs so that Miss Satin and Miss Midnight Louise, who are virtual twins (if not mother and . . . *shudder* . . . daughter) can roam the downstairs area like mobile bugs. Not the big, many-legged roach kind of bug, I hasten to explain, but as furry listening devices.

They are much larger than the real thing, but also as easily overlooked. If you are perceived to be "mute," you are also considered "dumb." This is where the phrase "dumb animal" originated. A big mistake, but your average Homo sapiens are experts at that kind of underestimation.

I also realize that the axiom Out of sight, out of mind pertains here.

While everyone downstairs hustles, tattles, lies, and dodges as my Miss Temple investigates their motives, means, and opportunities, the dead woman lies in a tawdry, disheveled state up here behind a guardian accoutered in Ermenegildo Zegna tailoring and Beretta and Rolex accessories, a high-end combo she had likely never seen in her brief life.

I shiver. They have lowered the air-conditioning to preserve the body. Even my luxuriant hair is not proof against chills.

Mr. Max also lies in a forgotten state in some people's minds. I know my partner is not letting the mystery of his possible fatal accident lay unexamined, but even she recognizes that we must ride to the rescue of Mr. Matt, who is not mysterious at all and firmly on the suspect list.

A pity his sterling scruples and blind Justice have put him in a perfect frame: too noble to peer at a nearby, possibly sleazy sex scene and therefore an ignorant and useless witness. Too compassionate to forgo saving a possibly dead person, and therefore caught red-handed performing the Kiss of Life on the body. Thus leaving DNA traces all over it.

Such behavior is likely to look suspicious, if not downright psychotic, to the police professionals who will soon descend on our parlor play of the moment.

It strikes me that Miss Temple, who spent most of the past year defending Mr. Max from Lieutenant C. R. Molina's relentless suspicions, has traded one fiancé for another, and for the same outcome. She must now defend Mr. Matt from Lieutenant C. R. Molina's relentless suspicions.

At least, it occurs to me, Miss Lieutenant C. R. Molina likes Mr. Matt Divine, maybe more than she realizes.

Hmm. Sad to say, but it might best serve our cause (Mr. Matt Devine) if said homicide lieutenant got her size nines out here and took over this messy, confusing crime scene straight out of that movie musical, *Seven Brides for Seven Brothers.*

Brother! I am sure glad that we feline dudes do not do matrimony.

Chapter 46

Wheel of Misfortune

The ladies in the front parlor were still playing Game Boys. Apparently, they'd never updated to the latest techie toys.

The odd appropriateness of their choice of amusement hadn't occurred to them, although it had certainly stunned Temple. She supposed they had a lot of odd hours to while away in their profession.

Miss Kitty was knitting, and Ms. Phyliss Shoofly was torturing the ivories on the upright piano in the bar. She was playing the title song to the musical, *Cabaret*.

Apparently not just life, but death, was a cabaret, my friend. Because life here clearly went on, with time to be killed as well as paid for.

Temple paused on the threshold, studying the women's odd combination of undress and gussied up with such fripperies as fingerless chiffon gloves, garter belts and hose, teeny-tiny thongs, high heels, and low-cut mini-corsets.

The various shades of blue reminded Temple of Matt's "Virgin Mary blue," the pastel not-quite-turquoise shade found on Catholic holy cards of the Virgin and Tiffany jewelry boxes. That was an odd combo of the sacred and the secular.

Here the blues ran the gamut from a military navy blue speaking of bondage and discipline to ruffles of the palest sky blue, speaking of sugar and spice and everything nice. Yet it all was exaggerated, whether butch or babyish. It all went to extremes, like elaborate theater. Like a cabaret.

"I'm surprised you don't play solitaire with real cards," Temple remarked as she came in and sat down on one of the few free chairs.

"Cards?" one woman jeered. "If the guys knew we had cards in the house they'd hole up with them and start gambling. We want their concentration, and their money, on us."

"Is that why the Sapphire Slipper is so far out on the desert?" Temple asked. "To keep the men captive?"

"Sure," answered Miss Kitty, rising and moving among the courtesans. "Pretty and pleasing as my girls are, gambling is a more magnetic vice. It's hard to lure big spenders away from the tables. That's why I keep a cigar bar stocked with world-class spirits, and why my cook can whip up big game dishes as well as cow and crawfish. And, of course, my girls are the best in the state at their specialties."

"Do you often rent the whole house to special parties?"

"Sure. Conventioneers. PACs."

"Political Action Committees?" Temple couldn't help sounding shocked.

Miss Kitty's plump features folded into a complacent smile. "We put the Action in PACs."

"So nothing about this booking set off any red flags?"

"Only the green flags of moolah. The girls enjoy a big party.

There are group scenes. Some customers request special, high-dollar attention."

"Would you say you and your staff were disappointed when you discovered this was a kidnapping party?"

"Hell, no. Surprised at first, sure. But then we eyed the 'victims' and thought this would be a laugh riot. My girls are ready to do vixens-in-charge any time."

"And it didn't bother you that the men were captives?"

"Pretty willing captives, once everything became clear." Miss Kitty leaned against a floral-upholstered easy chair. "I'm going to set out some sodas and chips in the kitchen. The girls are used to a bedtime snack about now. They burn a lot of energy before the wee hours. As for what goes on here, Miss Barr, we aim to please our customers, and I've never known a man to object to some sexy teasing."

Matt would have, Temple knew, but he wasn't caught in the same net as the Fontana brothers. As for the brothers, once they recognized their girlfriends, they would have gone along with the mock-kidnapping. They would know that sampling the house goods was only a tease. The whole idea was to claim the brothers, once and for all.

All for once, and once for all. Like the Three Musketeers' "all for one and one for all."

It was just a bit of nonsense and fun, until the dead girl had landed in their midst.

Temple punched up the photos on Nicky's cell phone.

"Look. I'm going to send these pics around again. One of you might recognize the girl in them on a second round. Nobody else has a clue."

Game Boys idled in laps. Whitened teeth bit into reddened and plumped-up lips. The phone passed from woman to woman, each one expertly clicking through the three photos Nicky had taken, then shrugging and shaking her head. The screen was small and the quality was iffy.

The dead girl was not a game.

Babette handed the phone back to Temple when the circle had been completed. "Can't say I recognize her. She could be a Fontana girlfriend."

"They're all accounted for."

More shrugs. Game Boys were in play again on several laps.

"Listen," Temple said, annoyed by the indifference. "Something is fishy here and I want answers. I'll be a lot easier to deal with than the police. I bet they like to rake hookers over the coals."

"We are legal," Angela said.

"We are courtesans, not hookers."

"We don't lure men, they come looking for us. We are a cut above."

"Then if you're a cut above, why can't you spell?" Temple asked, cuttingly.

"Huh? Who says we can't?"

"Well, you don't know your alphabet."

"ABCs? We know a lot more than that."

"Then why are E and M missing from your roster?"

"E is a sucky letter for glamorous names. I mean, Emily, Eleanor, Evelyn, Edith. Sound like freaking dead schoolteachers. That's not the kind of school we teach."

"And M?" Temple pointed out. "Surely M is promising. Mitzi, Muffin, Mimi . . . I guess you may be a cut above but you're not very creative thinkers. Might that carry through into the bedroom?"

She had them riled and spitting. Playing Bad Cop was fun. No wonder Molina did it. They protested in a blizzard of comments.

"Hey, that's not fair!"

"You don't know nothin' about us."

"That M is taken. Reserved. We can't use it."

Finally. An interesting response.

"Why?" Temple shot back.

The sudden silence said a lot. Kohled eyes consulted kohled eyes. A communal sigh and continued, now sullen, silence.

"What name is the M for?" Temple goaded. "What's the matter? Can't you spell it?"

"It is an odd spelling," Inez said quietly. "But then, she's an odd girl."

"Miss Fritzi Ritzi House Favorite, you mean," Lili said.

"She has a shtick," Zazu added.

"What is the name?" Temple asked again.

"Madonnah. M-a-d-o double n-a-h." Zazu again. She didn't seem to have issues with the missing girl.

It took Temple a second to visualize the spelling. "Like the rock star, only different."

"She has a Madonna shtick," Niki said. "Always changing her hair color and style, her nails, her makeup. Even her own mother couldn't keep up with recognizing her."

"Her shtick is being a prima donna," Lili said. "She doesn't have to sit in a presentation row like the rest of us, selling her wares. She picks her johns from watching on the surveillance camera. We hardly see her."

"Then," Temple said, picking up the cell phone, "these photos *could* be of her. Care to look again?"

"We haven't heard she's here again," Kiki objected.

"She sounds like someone who could have slipped in anytime," Temple pointed out.

They shrugged and passed around the cell phone images again.

"Can't say. Could be her. Even we didn't glimpse all of her looks. We just know she's in the house when there are these secret assignations in the Starlet room."

"She's Miss Kitty's pet."

"Like Baby Blue, the cat?" Temple asked.

"Like, I don't know," Crystal said. "Like some weird recluse.

Maybe she has a special talent in the sack. We don't know. She comes and she goes, and we hardly know when or where. If we run into her in the break room or the hall or the bathroom, she's like a freaky geek. No chitchat, no zippers help pulled up and down. Just in and out. She does her job that way, she'd get no johns. But they love the shtick and keep asking for her."

"Madonnah," Temple repeated.

Deedee handed the cell phone back to Temple as it finished its rounds. "Could be her. Who knows?"

Miss Kitty might, Temple thought.

"Thanks," she told them. "Sorry I was so rough on you. I need the info."

They stared at her. "Honey," said Zazu, "you is a declawed kitten."

Temple was not encouraged, but she *was* wondering how Matt would take knowing he'd given CPR to a hooker called Madonnah.

Chapter 47

Loving Dangerously

Matt snagged Temple as she was passing through the bar to the kitchen for something bracing for further interviews, like a Red Bull energy drink. It was no surprise that she'd spotted a large stock of those in the refrigerator.

"Does the busy interrogator have a minute?" he asked, stopping her by the doorway where the opportunities for overhearing were minimum.

"Oh, Matt. It's so impossible. Meeting every Fontana girlfriend and trying to remember who goes out with whom and unravel how they came up with this scheme and who might have had an ulterior motive."

"And you haven't even factored in the resident 'courtesans' yet."

She groaned. "Whoever set up this murder, if it was indeed set up, knew how to confuse the issue three times over. I finally beat a lead on the identity of the victim out of the resident courtesans."

"That's great! Why are you moaning about not making progress then?"

"She was a real mystery woman, made a shtick out of always being in disguise."

"I thought those abundant Venus on a clamshell locks were a little unreal."

"She worked under the name Madonnah, spelled with an *h* on the end and was almost never seen. She picked her johns, not the other way around. The others were not too taken with her prima donna ways. So . . . one of them could have killed her in a fit of jealousy."

"That's why I think you should let me interview the courtesans."

"You?"

"I *am* a professional counselor. The theory being that many sex industry workers have abuse issues, I might pry things out of them easier than you. A lot of women like this call into 'The Midnight Hour.' "

"It's true that they probably think women like me are hopelessly naïve about the world as they see and live it." Temple glanced back toward the parlor, where bare parts of half-clad courtesans were visible through the archway. "These pros would eat a good boy like you alive."

"Maybe not. I know how to get past well-varnished facades. And I'm not as good as I used to be."

Temple lofted an eyebrow. "In the behavior sense, not the bed-avior sense."

"See? I'm more qualified than ever for the job. Let me try."

She considered his request, realizing that he still regretted the call girl's death at the Goliath. Apparently, their tête-à-tête that night had been a revelation to both. Matt's priestly years of celibacy made him a mystery to worldly women like hookers,

Temple bet. They'd probably sense that he didn't have the ordinary male vulnerability to their wiles and seductions and mind games. He was firmly neutral in that department, almost like a gay friend. Yet not gay at all.

"They'll be enchanted with you, and probably let their hair and their guards down," Temple decided. "Pick a room upstairs to set up in, and go to it."

"Not upstairs, not their working environment. If they have private quarters, there must be a gathering room there."

So it was that half an hour later the first courtesan, glancing significantly at her sisters in suspicion, announced that she was having a visit with "Mr. McDreamy Midnight" in the break room and slunk off through the Fontana boys' bar—applause and whistles—through the girlfriends' kitchen—hoots and the clatter of tableware—to the low rambling annex where the women of the Sapphire Slipper actually bathed and slept and did their nails.

Temple hoped that she was doing the right thing. Which was hard to determine in a brothel.

Chapter 48

Break Dancing

Darned if the brothel "break room" didn't resemble any small business cafeteria, if it was for a funky, loosely run operation.

Matt took in the Formica-topped vintage dinette sets scattered over the vinyl tile floor. Their chrome legs and trim were age-dulled, but their cheerful seat covers in maroon, purple, yellow, and red plastic resembled a field of large, gaudy mushrooms.

A big white refrigerator was the elephant in the room, dwarfing a roomy microwave on an adjacent wheeled cart. A similar cart hosted a small TV. If small Lucite trays holding fingernail files, polish, and glue, lip gloss and mascara wands weren't lying on the tables, Matt would have felt as at home as in a convent kitchen.

But the Age of Innocence was past, and this kind of communal living had nothing churchly about it.

Matt's impression of the resident courtesans had been that they all looked alike. This open call interview session Temple had dreamed up for him would force him to discover differences and, perhaps, suspects.

It was likely one of their own, after all, who lay murdered upstairs. He shivered, more because Miss Kitty had kicked up the air-conditioning when it was obvious they'd be stuck out here with the body for a few hours. But that was like trying to stop the Red Sea from parting with an air machine.

"Howdy, Mr. Midnight. My name is Angela. We're coming in alphabetically, so you get the heavenly body first."

Angela paused in the doorway in typical temptress pose, one arm up along the frame, the other hand on her hip. At least she wore something, a sheer peignoir over a corset with garter straps and thong panties. Matt would never get what was hot about such outfits. Must be hangovers from Victorian repression. Analyzing that kept him from ogling Angela's celestial form, which did look slim and firm and shiny in a Barbie doll sort of way he found a little too perfect.

"You know me?" Matt asked as she swaggered over on her four-inch spikes, jerked open the refrigerator door and regarded the contents long enough to give him a good rear view.

She finally found a can of some new-wave high-energy drink and joined him in sitting at the gray Formica-topped table.

"I never thought you'd be a customer out here at the Sapphire Slipper," Angela said.

"I'm not. I was hijacked. We town guys all were."

"I *looove* your voice on the radio. It'd be a real kick to hear it whispering in my ear some night. Tables turned."

He ignored her come-on. "So you've actually heard my program?"

"We all have, honey, coming down from a night's work in here. Unwinding. Gettin' down. Who do you think we tune in to? Mr. Mellow Midnight."

He knew he had long-haul truckers and night casino staff in his invisible audience, but he'd never dreamed whole brothels of shady ladies would tune in. "You close at midnight, then?" he asked, surprised.

"That's our hours, noon to midnight. It's a long drive back to anywhere from here, and even good-time guys and hookers gotta sleep sometimes."

He eyed the hall off the kitchen. "Those are your quarters?"

"Yup. You wanta see?"

Matt thought it might be illuminating. "Yeah. Do all the . . . places have this arrangement? The guest bedrooms up front and fancy, and a, like, dorm for the residents in back?"

She stood and leaned over him, as her lips enunciated the words only inches from his. "No, my Midnight Man. Some of the lower-end places have the girls work out of their living quarters. In a way, it's more convenient."

But this was more convenient for a murderer, to kill on what amounted to a stage set, far from where the residents actually slept.

Matt stood. "My curiosity is purely academic."

"Yeah, sure." She smiled enticingly over her filmy blue shoulder as she led him down the dim, plain hall. She reminded him of the huge plaster figure atop the Blue Mermaid Motel, a knowing creature in her element, relishing that he was out of his.

It took five minutes to figure out the courtesan's quarters were as bare and practical as a convent. How unnerving that women consecrated to no sex and women living on nothing but sex ending up in such spare, unsensual circumstances.

He saw single beds without head or footboards, cheap motel dressers bought by multiples with matching bedside tables. Blinds on windows. Everything institutional, although stuffed animals lined up against the plain beige walls and the dresser tops here were littered with gaudy rhinestones and garters, not the simple string of rosary beads and a small photo of the old folks at home. There were no photos of anyone but these women, taken at formally happy moments, in a line in the parlor, laughing in the break room. They were family.

Nuns, of course, were an old and dying breed. These women were a breed as old as prehistory probably, and not dying out at all.

"Knowing the layout of the place will help put the murder in perspective," Matt commented as they returned to the main room.

"'The place.' You can't even call it a chicken ranch. A brothel. A bordello. A whorehouse. You give all that advice out night after night to sad and lonely people, but you never give us spirit-lifters out here on the desert a moment of thought or credit. Send some of those road-weary truckers thinking too hard on their lonely lives our way, Mr. Midnight. That'd be some real good counsel."

"If you'd give them the same personal attention you're giving me right now, I can see your point."

"You can see a lot more than that, but you're not looking. Engaged, I hear, like tall, dark, and Aldo. That doesn't stop guys from coming out here."

"How'd you get that information?"

"Those ditsy girlfriends. They chatter up a storm. Not used to being rounded up in a group and kept isolated out here in the desert."

"The resident girls aren't chat-happy?"

"This is our workplace, hon. It's hard work catering to men who expect a hundred percent every minute for their money. We get worn-out. No time for pajama party gossip. We *are* the pajama party."

"Do you have any . . . protection?"

"You speaking sexually? We are *all* condoms *all* the time. Every place, every act."

"Um, no. I meant a . . . union."

"Not here. We do have an 'association' and bylaws. We're

242 · Carole Nelson Douglas

freelance workers like your girlfriend. We accept jobs, see them through, get paid, kick back a commission to our landlord for room and board and providing the necessities, and move on in a few weeks to another place, another part of the country."

"You like that?"

"Which parts?"

"The rootlessness."

"You bet. Not everybody can travel for their job and get paid for it. There are a lot of laughs going on all over this country. We work the hot spots. East Coast, West Coast, and Vegas. Atlantic City, the Gulf Coast some. Gambling brings out high rollers or would-be high rollers. Both winning and losing brings 'em home to the Sapphire Slipper."

"What brought Madonnah back to the Sapphire Slipper?"

Angela forgot her seductress act to think before she spoke. Sincerely. "I don't know. Our schedules are our own. That's one of the best parts of the job. Thinking about it, that probably is her upstairs. Like her to slip in unnoticed, but she sure didn't leave that way this time. I don't know why she came back before she was expected. Maybe because she liked doing the unexpected. She was—"

"What?"

"A loner. Kept to herself. We don't have to bond like Lassie and Timmy here, but sisterhood helps. She kept aloof."

"Stuck-up?"

Angela shook her head. "Not that. Just deep inside her own troubles maybe. Like she was just visiting. Always. Just visiting. Tuned out, that's exactly what she was doing. Only it was the planet, not just our little ole whorehouse."

Matt digested Angela's analysis. These women saw a lot of men, and women, at their worst. He trusted Angela's instincts. That's what hookers and midnight radio shrinks relied on. Their instincts about strangers in the night.

"Thanks," he said.

"Next!" she announced as she flounced through the doorway.

"And you are—?" he asked the busty brunette who paused in the doorway to show off her saloon girl figure.

"Babette, Daddy."

He hated that "Daddy" thing. "I'm Matt."

"We know who you are. We're your regular listeners. It's a thrill to have you on our turf, to see you in person, and isn't that a nice sight? Are we what you like?"

"I like women," Matt said. "All ages and stages."

"Yeah?" Babette was nearing forty as far as Matt could tell. The maternal sort, with all that natural or assisted mammary development. There was a courtesan here for every druther. Even it was mother. Babette heaved her boobs atop the table and crossed her arms in front of them. "What can I do for you, baby?"

Ten minutes later he was ushering Babette out to bring in Crystal.

"Why the alphabetical names?" he asked the thirtyish woman. She was lean with a narrow harsh face and wore a lot of Goth gear he tried to ignore. He was sure her looks determined her shtick.

"We use different names in different places. Vegas attracts a lot of johns. The alphabet helps keep them grounded to who's who and who does what."

"And the dead woman . . . ?"

"Madonnah? Guess she turned out to be a kind of Jonah, didn't she?"

He was surprised to hear this Wicked Queen woman make a biblical reference.

"Oh, I was raised on the Holy Book," she said, her dark eyes glittering like the iridescent spiky black tattoos on her upper arms. "Whomping my bare bottom with it until I bled."

"Did you know Madonnah's real name?" he said, unwilling to go there.

"She *said* Mary Jo once, but I've heard Miss Kitty call her

Nonah once too. I don't know which is the real one, but we take names close to our own. Like Jazz was Jasmine."

"And you, Crystal?"

"Crystal is beautiful, fine glass and it cuts."

He noticed the scars on her forearms. Self-cutting. She noticed him noticing and sneered. "Cathy. What a wimp that little bitch was."

"Crystal shatters," he reminded her. "But you are far from being a wimp."

"I'm not a fan," she said. "You don't live in a real world."

"Agreed. Not that real a world. So you thought Madonnah was a wimp too."

"Did I say so?"

"Yeah. Loud and clear."

"You think you hear things, over the airwaves. You think you see things." She glanced at her scarred and tattooed arms. "I could show you some things, if you had the guts to come up to my room."

He didn't, and he knew it. "No one can go there but you, until you're ready to come out."

"Scared?" Jeering again.

"Damn right. You win. At last."

She drew back, not liking the ease of her victory. "I have nothing to tell you."

"Not anymore. Thanks for the insight on Madonnah. It might help."

She stood, glowering. "I don't want help."

"No, but I thought you might want *to* help. A little."

"She was okay. I guess."

Crystal turned in a crackle of black taffeta skirts and left.

Matt wiped the invisible veil of sweat off his upper lip before . . . Deedee came in.

Temple would pay for setting these brassy, sassy, glassy women on him, but not in the way Crystal would want.

Matt took notes, but Deedee, Fifi, and Gigi were as featherweight as their names, which really were: Dolores, Frances, and Geraldine. Too many girls were still named after their grandmothers. They had seen Madonnah around for three years. She kept to herself, was a little nervous. Seemed like she wasn't really cut out for the Life. Didn't have much fun, but delivered for the johns.

Matt turned over a page in his Hello Kitty notebook, courtesy of Miss Kitty.

These big-eyed kitty drawings reminded him of the slitty-eyed real cats prowling the Sapphire Slipper. He'd never admit it to Temple, but he found Midnight Louie's presence . . . encouraging. That old tomcat always knew where the rats were hidden. Matt thought he'd glimpsed the old boy hanging around that sleek Sapphire Slipper house cat, Baby Blue. He hoped Louie would not let blatant sex appeal divert him from his forever mission of protecting Temple.

Then there was the matter of the Bed between them. Matt knew Louie was used to taking his leisure on Temple's California king mattress. Matt wasn't about to share her horizontal time with a cat, especially not after they were married. He supposed he and Louie would just have to duke that out between them. Matt was a reasonable man, but he knew who would win that contest. Black topped blond except in Temple's human love life.

"I'm Heather," breathed a Marilyn Monroe–Jackie Kennedy voice from the doorway.

She was a provocative blend of the two. Matt was reminded of a photo of MM he'd seen, wearing a dark Jackie K wig (way before she'd become Jackie O, which made her Jackie K-O in some weird way), and pearls and palazzo pants and a soft flowing blouse.

The odd thing was that Marilyn had never looked more relaxed than in that prism high-fashion outfit. Otherwise she was molded, pinched, corseted, and confined until overflowing like these SS women.

Matt found himself confounded by this eternal cultural icon of madonna-whore. The really weird part was both celebrated women had been deemed to play both those roles in their tumultuous private lives.

"Heather," he said, playing for time. "On the hill?"

"Not Scottish. Maybe Heather as in 'heathen.'"

"Another fan, I guess. You know my history. You have the advantage."

"That's nice." She slithered around him, touching his shoulder with a false fingernail, before she sat. "I like the advantages."

"What about Madonnah?"

"Her? Didn't belong here. Didn't want to play the game. Games. She didn't even listen to your show."

"No!" Matt feigned horror. "I thought I was the house DJ after-hours."

"Not just you." Heather pushed herself up to grab a bunch of chilled grapes from the refrigerator.

Matt thought: *Roman orgy.* Was he programmable! Putty in their practiced hands.

"We loved your *clients*, is that what you'd call them?" Heather had a lovely English accent. Maybe her real name was . . . Helena. He could be bewitched if he didn't know better. "Charming people. You are always so considerate of them. Reminds us of our own jobs. Consideration. Quite a lost art, don't you think?"

He nodded.

"It won't help you solve bloody murder, of course. The people who do that are always inconsiderate. Look at Sherlock Holmes. Snooty sort! Hercule Poirot! Another airy-fairy! But not you."

Heather, with her hooked nose, too close-set eyes, and rugged complexion had managed to seat herself on his lap to fondle his shirt buttons.

He laughed. "Of all the seducers at the Sapphire Slipper, you're the one having the most fun. What about Madonnah?"

Heather gazed past his shoulder, imperiously. "No. No, Madonnah. No fun fast, as the Americans say. A very sober girl. Scared sober, I should say. Not like you, Bertie Wooster Baby. You'd like to be scared out-of-your mind drunk."

"Not now. Not here. Thanks very much. Mind the gap," he added in the robotic tone of a London Underground recorded message as he stood to unlap her and show her out the archway.

She growled and snapped at him, but went.

Mind the gap! Matt couldn't believe he was ably parading prostitutes in and out of his lunchroom office like an Inspector of the Yard. Temple had a lot to answer for.

Inez was a Latina beauty with a tender manner. He could see her reared as a good girl, wearing a white mantilla and clutching a white First Communion prayer book and rosary at Mass . . . until some junior high gang-banger deflowered her in a back car seat and it was all over, the days of white and roses. Her culture was black and white, bad and good, and she was suddenly done wrong and irremediably bad.

So she went the way she'd been pushed.

She was a lovely girl, and his heart ached for her, but she wasn't used to observing and making judgments, just living in her narrow aisle of deserved (she thought) purgatory.

He sent some Hail Marys after her, but doubted they'd catch up to her scurrying spike-heeled steps.

It was starting to weigh on him, like too many confessions heard in a row, the lives lived and not lived here. The ghosts of gaiety and ghastliness that make up the all-too-human condition.

What was he learning?

That the courtesans were gypsies, birds of passage who often bunked together but made no lasting ties. Not with the johns and not with one another. They shared the intimacy of sisters and lovers everywhere they went, but went everywhere alone.

That didn't seem likely to lead to murder. Yet, maybe where sex was so casual, death would be too. Matt couldn't fathom these women. He'd picked up that they liked their tawdry notoriety. They burbled about Web pages and blogs and steady customers always welcoming them back wherever they went. About MySpace.com and YouTube.

He found the lifestyle all too depressing. Sure, some of the women showed obvious signs of the childhood abuse that leads to sexual acting out. But some really seemed more like entrepreneurs, peddling their flesh with gusto and even glee of a sort.

Still, they were hooked on the midnight sob stories he heard on WCOO-AM radio.

Still, there was always one more rich john who would drape them in goodies, or a lonely one who'd leave consoled, or a reluctant one, like Matt, who needed to be cajoled. It was unnerving to think that he could have sex with every one of these women, or even several at once, all for what was a reasonable price for his income level.

But he'd been reared a Roman Catholic, not a Roman emperor, and orgies were not for him. Nor celibacy, anymore. Thank God.

And still Jazz and Kiki and Lili and Niki and that ole devil Zazu to go. It already felt like a long night, and no one was having any fun yet.

"What is it with the names?" he asked Jazz.

"Haven't you ever wanted to reinvent yourself?" She was a fresh-faced pixie of a girl, with acne spots peeking through the pancake and the Clearasil. Maybe . . . twenty-two.

"I think we all do, sometimes."

"Well, we can be whoever we want. Someplace else, we're somebody else. Someplace else I use an English accent and go by Dana. "'Wot'll ya 'ave, Ducks?'"

Jazz giggled at his expression. "You don't have to take that personally. You're better-looking than I'd thought, though. Most radio guys sound like Dr. Kool on the airwaves and look like Moby Dick the whale off the air. We get a lot of DJ guys. With us, on the other hand, whatcha see is whatcha get. We're more honest."

"Looking good isn't that important."

"Say you! I know. I mean, I've seen hookers with faces to die for. Bodies too. Models, only they're too well endowed for the human hanger trade. Some of those don't do too well at this. Snobby, I guess. They scare the guys."

"What about Madonnah?"

"Madonnah? She wasn't bad-looking. Never the kind of girl to play Queen La-ti-dah in the back of the house. Not that enthusiastic about her work. You got to work it, you know. Flash it, flaunt it, make a guy want to spend hard cash on some fun with you. She didn't seem like a girl who was in it for fun."

"She didn't make much money then?"

"Enough, I guess. It kept her on the circuit. Some of the girls you know from the skin out. Some you never know. She was one of the never-knows, that's why it was so weird she was killed. You wouldn't have thought anyone was that . . . what's the word?"

"Passionate about her?"

"Yeah. She was laid-back. Despite our profession, that is not a salable quality."

Jazz bounced out in her gymnast-pixie way to make room for Kiki, Lili, and Niki.

Matt was asking for the others in groups now, figuring K, L, and N wouldn't have much new to tell him. And he was wearing out from the parade of bouncing, flagrant party girls. Sultans and polygamists bewildered him. But the impulse to combine proved unwontedly provocative.

"Say, Mr. Midnight. I guess you're up for a group scene!"

One was a blonde, one was a brunette, and one was auburn-haired. He knew he'd never remember who was Kiki or Lili or Niki, so he thought of them as gold, bronze, and copper.

They wanted to swarm him, but he made them take chairs at the table like civilized girls.

"This is serious. One of you is dead, and the police will soon be interrogating all of you for real."

"So you're our practice run," the blonde suggested. "Ask away. We are all way too friendly by profession to commit murder."

"Killers don't advertise," he answered. "They don't have the look written all over them."

"You know what you have written all over you?" the brownette asked suggestively.

He didn't encourage her with an answer, but she rushed on uninvited. "You look like Mr. First Time in a house of pleasure. Could we give you a welcome party!"

"Is there a lot of that?"

"Welcome parties?" asked the redhead, Niki. "Every night."

"I mean clients wanting multiple courtesans." He was beginning to appreciate the old-fashioned dignity of the term *courtesan*.

"They almost all want it," blondie said.

"But they can't all afford it," brownie added.

"And some just don't dare to admit it," the redhead finished, eyeing him as no doubt the latter.

"Do you get a lot of bachelor parties here?" he asked.

They shrugged in triplicate, and chorused, "Some."

"It's not like we get the Fontana brothers in one big bunch ever." Kiki was the blonde.

"What a shame this gig was a bust," Lili, the brownette, said. "None of the houses in the state can put up a sign saying, 'The Fontana Brothers Were Here.' That would be a huge notch on the bedpost, let me tell you."

"I'm relieved to hear that my almost-in-laws are so upstanding."

Niki, the redhead, loosed a shower of laughter. "What you just said!"

Matt realized any Nevada chicken ranch was a House of Double Entendres, and he was unwary enough to deliver them COD.

"Always glad to amuse," he added. "Now. About your dead associate."

"Associate," Kiki mocked. "I guess that's what we do, girls. Ass-o-shi-ate."

"This isn't fun and games. Madonnah is dead. You girls must feel something about that. Maybe a john was after her for some reason. Sneaked in and killed her."

"Look," said Lili. "Nevada is the only state where sex trade workers are guaranteed clean and protected. We can't come in here and work unless we check out weekly. So we don't have violence and all that stuff that comes with working the streets with pimps. It's a great gig, and when we're off elsewhere, we make real sure we're fit to come back here. So there are no tooth-gnashing johns raving about scabbies or herpes or anything bad. It's more likely *they*'ve got the diseases, and we see that what breeds in Vegas, stays in Vegas, thanks to c-o-n-d-o-m-s."

"Not a hundred percent effective. Maybe she had a baby once—? Doesn't that ever happen?"

A silence, then Niki spoke. "We don't talk about that if it does. It's as much a secret among us as it is out there in Henderson or some hoity-toity suburb. We mind our own business. And Madonnah minded her own even more than we did."

"She doesn't seem like she was part of the gang."

"She wasn't," Kiki said. "Some of us are like that. Private. Good-time girls maybe had bad times once. We don't ask, and we don't tell."

"That makes it tough to solve a murder."

"It makes it tough to get anything on any of us, too," Lili

said, standing. "We're done here, Mr. M., unless you want to pay for something personal."

He shook his head. He'd actually managed to put names with faces during their talk, but what they offered was pretty nameless and faceless anyway.

He sat there for a minute, enjoying the silence. Madonnah had been an odd duck here, though none of them had put it that way. He suddenly realized that she had a room here, and he wanted to see it. He could ask Miss Kitty and make a big, public deal of it. Or—

"Miss Zazu, I presume," he said, rising as a tall, angular black woman entered the room without posing in the doorway.

"I hate cops," she said.

"Good. I'm not one. I'm just the preview." He didn't bother sitting again.

This woman wouldn't domesticate and with her five-inch hooker spikes she was taller than he. Taller than most men.

"I'm betting," he said, "that you're like the others. You didn't have much to do with the late Madonnah."

The dark eyes set in ivory whites blinked. She lived to contradict. "We talked some. Madonnah weren't so standoffish as those cows think."

Ah. A rebel in the house. "Could one of them have killed her?"

"Didn't have the balls."

"I'd like to see her room."

Those corrosive eyes flicked him with disdain, like he was some kind of ghoul.

"None of the others knows anything about her," Matt admitted. "When someone gets murdered . . . somebody thinks he or she has a reason."

"None of the others bother knowing anything about her. They likes to pretend they get down. They flash. They players. You wanta see her crib? C'mon, motormouth man."

Matt wasn't sure he should walk the long hall with this bad

girl but he wanted to find some trace of a personality for Madonnah. Anything.

"You're the only one seems to have a reaction to her."

"I watch. She was one lone sistah. She always watched others, but she not watch herself." Zazu paused. They were in the demi-dark, only closed doors facing each other for another sixty feet. "I didn't watch close enough."

She resumed walking.

"I'm sorry."

She stopped, stared at him like a cat from the dark. After a long pause, she resumed walking. "Maybe you is."

He let out a breath.

"Maybe not," she added.

Matt found her dead seriousness a relief from the forced whorehouse gaiety the other women broadcast. Here was someone who didn't beat death off like an encroaching moth around a porch light.

"Her room." Zazu stood in the hall while Matt opened the door—with his jacket bottom to avoid leaving prints on the knob, just in case; they were already all over upstairs—and stepped inside.

Light flared on, weak through the standard opaque glass dish that concealed a cheap one-bulb ceiling fixture. Zazu had reached inside to flip the wall switch. She must have been in here often enough to not worry about prints. These rooms looked like cells: stripped to essentials. Madonnah's didn't have even a framed photo, a goofy giveaway key ring of a Care Bear. A personal set of nail polish.

"Nothing much here," he commented.

"Sometime nothing much says a lot." Zazu was looming behind him, in the room without making a sound.

Despite, or because of that, he used a tissue from the plain discount-store box on the bedside table to open drawers, gawk in the closet.

"Bathroom's down the hall. We don't get private accommodations, not even for tending our privates."

This woman didn't sugarcoat things. "It's a public business, isn't it? Not many secrets."

"No secrets. Or . . . almost none."

"You know one? Or two?"

"Maybe. I don't tell."

"Not even if it would help find Madonnah's killer? I found her, you know. Tried to breathe life back into her. Too late."

"Y'all's not even supposed to be here!"

"That's true."

"Why'd she die when y'all came here when you weren't supposed to be here?"

"You're saying it's our fault?"

"I'm saying you had a part in it, and you can't get outta that."

A bitter taste burned in his mouth. The saliva of a dead woman he couldn't raise. The salt of an accusation he couldn't lay to rest that rang both false and true.

Zazu was the last of the good-time girls he had to interview, and she had been a heller.

But she left him alone in the dead woman's bedroom.

Matt looked around again, carefully. Women's bedrooms weren't his area of expertise. Another big box of tissue with aloe and vitamin E sat on the dresser. He pulled several free and stuffed them in his side jacket pockets.

This wing was fairly new, but it had a makeshift look. The closet had sliding doors, one mirrored. He used a tissue to ease it open, trying not to regard his own full-length image as it glided past. *Picture yourself here.* He could see the Sapphire Slipper Web page come-on now. *No.*

But *come on*, he wasn't snooping on his own behalf. No scruples needed.

The farther half of the closet was full of stacked cardboard boxes, probably house supplies, storage. The wooden clothes pole held mismatched empty wire hangers, some colored, some white, most the bronze color favored by dry cleaners.

A few T-shirts and dresses and skirts hung there. It was the faceless Styrofoam heads on the shelf above that entranced him. Wig stands. Marilyn Monroe blond, Cleopatra black, rainbow-streaked, long, short. He wasn't familiar with the singer Madonna's various chameleon "looks," but he did realize that these wild wigs would make a good shtick for a hooker. And a natural disguise.

He'd read that a prostitute's greatest fear was seeing her own father walk through the door, maybe an indication of how much she feared the father figure, or how much he may have abused her. This woman had been determined not to be found, no matter who walked through the door, and apparently her wig trick had worked, until tonight.

Matt bent to pull her luggage out into the room. A medium-sized hardcase one, probably for the wigs, and a couple of backpacks. All were scuffed and scratched. He guessed she traveled by bus rather than air. The luggage tags held empty forms, never filled in.

They were empty, not even a stray gum wrapper left inside.

At the dresser, the drawers stuck in the dry air and came out only when jerked, and then they opened crooked. He dropped the tissues back in his pocket and lifted her personal lingerie. Plain cotton, with what Temple called camisole tops instead of bras. The large plastic makeup bag on the dresser top was marked inside with red and black lines, as if it had been lashed. But it was just the unintended strokes of lip liner and eyeliner pencils, all in bold colors: scarlet, black, blue.

As his tissue-holding fingers riffled through, he noticed that everything was well used, not new, the exteriors smeared, not neat and clean like Temple's. These were working tools, not playthings.

A tall bottle of lotion next to the tissue box must be makeup remover.

This time Matt stared at himself in the mirror above the dresser. Here was where Madonnah saw herself bare, and, he'd bet, no one else did.

He went to the door. It had one of those center-knob lock buttons, so she could have privacy. He grabbed a couple of tissues from his pocket and turned the lock.

Back at the dresser, he found her working clothes in the second drawer. Black and baby blue corsets with garters and marabou feather edgings. Stockings ranging from nurse white to sheer black to fishnet to sheer with lavish tattoos printed on them and even rhinestones. He counted. There were six fishnet ones; even pairs, none missing. Filmy thises and thats. A box of tangled jewelry, mostly black and glittery or rhinestones or lengths of pearls.

The bottom drawer held spike heels, all four inches tall, exaggerated, in shiny patent leather, white or black or sliver or red. All the heel tips were worn, and they were tumbled together. The soles looked remarkably clean. Never worn outdoors.

Her purse was in that bottom drawer too, under the shoes.

Matt pulled it out and put it on the dresser top.

It was an inexpensive black microfiber shoulder bag. It had an outside zipper, an inside zipper on that flap, an exterior three-quarter zipper that revealed credit card slots and a driver's license window and pen-holding nooses, all at easy, organized access.

Every slot was empty, except one. The driver's license was from Indiana. The photo of a youngish woman with brown hair and bangs reminded him of the mousiest wig on the shelf. Obviously what she wore when traveling.

There was another zippered compartment at the back of the

lining It was empty except for a penny and a few crumbs of something long since inedible.

He pushed his fingers behind each empty credit card slot. Nothing.

But this was a purse of a thousand compartments. He was sure that had she flown with it, airport security would have missed a couple of places in this bag of tricks.

He found another zipper inside the outer inner face of the bag.

There! His half a gum wrapper! And on the plain back, a phone number jotted down in faded pencil. It looked like something even the owner had forgotten.

So he committed it to memory, not knowing where the area code was from.

He dropped the purse back into place in the bottom drawer and pushed it shut with his borrowed tissues.

As he stood and looked around a last time, he couldn't help thinking the room was so devoid of personality and effects that it resembled a simple convent bedroom for postulants who had left all worldly goods behind. The late Madonnah, had her wigs been headdresses and her clothes habits, reminded him more of a nun than a courtesan.

Matt pulled a couple fresh tissues from his pocket and unlocked and opened the door. He felt confident he'd left as little trace on the room as she ever had.

Louie's Imps

As soon as my Miss Temple has finished with that old gang of ours I head to the Midnight Inc. Investigations rendezvous spot, the upstairs hallway.

The presence of a dead body and a live Fontana brother on watch discourages all but the stout of heart from venturing up here.

Luckily, my breed is expected to venture where no man has gone before, or will go again, so I duck into a doorway niche to another bedroom and wait for my troops to reassemble.

Ma Barker is either still in the murder room and needed a distraction to dart out again, or she had departed before the Fontana brother called to the downstairs family powwow had returned to his post.

Her I am not worried about. In either case she will think of something, and act on it.

Nor do I worry about Miss Midnight Louise. I know she has been soaking up every bit of gossip, every inadvertent verbal slipup, every guilty whiff of sweat from the assigned bridesmaids below.

Besides her well-honed street smarts from her life among the homeless, she has a personal aversion to dames who are overdependent on the regard and support of the male of the species, any species. So I can count on her to not take any of these Fontana squeezes at face value, and know that if she has run across a hot clue she will follow it on her own.

Therefore, I am not surprised that the dainty Satin is the first of my three operatives to return to base operations.

"Turn up any hot clues?" I ask.

I do not expect an affirmative, seeing Miss Satin is new at the shamus stuff.

"I did not find any, but Mr. Max Devine seems to have."

"Matt! It is *Matt* Devine."

"Max, Matt, what is the difference? No more than Kitty, Kit."

"Let me tell you, there is a big difference to those names among the humans I associate with, and, come to think of it, between Kitty and Kit too."

For while Matt is Miss Temple's current swain, I explain, Max is the previous one, now missing.

Miss Satin shrugs her vibrissae as her muzzle makes a charming moue.

"Humans are way too anal-retentive. We cats like to bury our leavings both physical and emotional as soon as possible. You are lucky that your untimely impact with a Brinks truck impressed you on my memory, so I developed a sentimental attachment."

I am starting to get that I am not a priority among most of the females of my breed. Except at breeding time.

"So what is Mr. Matt's hot clue?"

"I was able to tail him unnoticed to the courtesans' break room and slip into the bedroom of the one known as Miss Madonnah.

She was a mysterious lady. Never looked the same twice. Apparently she's the number one candidate for the murder victim. He unearthed something in the purse in her bottom dresser drawer. It was a gum wrapper with something written on it."

"What?"

"It was Juicy Fruit, a particularly cloying and unmistakable scent."

"Not the variety of gum! What was written on the wrapper?"

"Something short. I was hiding under the bed and couldn't see it without leaping up and out, and pulling Mr. Matt's arm down, and that would not be a wise undercover move."

"Actually, it would have been great. People expect us to make unexpected attacks on their extremities and you might have been able to read the message."

"Unlikely at that speed. His lips did move as he attempted to memorize it. Humans often do that sort of pantomime."

"Memorize it. It must be a number!"

"To what?"

"Perhaps a Swiss bank account. Who knows? We must find out more."

"I suppose it could be a number to the safe," she muses.

"Safe? What safe? Where?"

"In Miss Kitty's office, inside a hidden closet."

"I suppose she does handle a great deal of cash. Many of the gentlemen callers would not want their stay recorded on a credit card."

"No, but the corporate name is Desert Deposits, so it is not a dead giveaway."

I shudder. "That sounds like coyote droppings to me. I had a bad experience with that once."

"A coyote, or droppings?"

"Both," I reply tersely. "What else might be kept in the safe?"

"The courtesans' IDs. Oh, and probably the surveillance films."

CAT IN A SAPPHIRE SLIPPER · 261

This makes my neck hairs stand to attention.

"There are surveillance tapes?"

"Not in the bedrooms, of course. That would be illegal, but in the bar, parlor, and foyer, just to keep a record of our clients. In case one is naughty."

"I have news for you: they all are 'naughty' just for being here."

"I mean, if one is rough with a courtesan, or is drunk. Miss Kitty is careful to back up any testimony she might have to give. Humans can be brutal."

"No kidding! The safe is very interesting. You must find out what kind of number Mr. Matt found."

"Humans do not exactly confide in us."

"But he will surely communicate this to Miss Temple. I must remain here until the rest of the crew checks in. Go back downstairs and glue yourself to Miss Temple or Mr. Matt, without attracting attention."

"That is silly. I always attract attention."

I give her and her turquoise cape the once-over. Good point.

"Make it look like you are hanging around for food or flattery," I advise. "They will never suspect a thing."

Chapter 50

Missing Max

Garry Randolph had two roles to play that awful morning.

One was genuine. Heartfelt.

His charge was gone, had vanished. Overnight. His "nephew, Mike Randolph."

This grief he didn't have to feign. Max was . . . was . . . *is* . . . so much to him. Pupil. Peer. Partner.

The clinic bedroom reeked with treachery. An overturned IV stand. Far under the bed, a full hypodermic needle. It rested in Garry's capacious suit coat pocket now. Not for him, or his physical type, the sleek fitted suit. For him the large, lumpy one, capable of holding as many magicians' tricks as a suit coat the size of the Colosseum in Rome. . . .

"But what happened here?" he asked the supervising doctor, acting as ignorant as he felt for once.

"These head cases can get strange obsessions. The man, who knows what he was thinking, simply ran. Fled who knows what demons in his stressed brain?"

The man, thought Randolph, ran because his life was threatened. Garry had no doubt the syringe would prove to be filled with something fatal.

Max! Out of his head but still possessed of that rare, acute prescience Garry had seen in him as a terrorism-wounded boy of seventeen. A middle-class American boy catapulted into the worst the world had to offer, the worst of global politics a man or boy could face.

Garry had faced it too long. He yearned for a happy ending. The restoration of memory. The restoration of peace. Hope. Happiness.

Now, here, he was called upon to exert all his old, devious skills.

"Perhaps," he suggested to the night physician, "we should talk to his psychiatrist about this."

"Gone?" he said, hearing himself sound honestly astounded forty minutes later.

His heart didn't know whether to soar or sink.

So the able Dr. Schneider had gotten Max out of here. For what? Debriefing? Rescue mission? Laugh at that one. For . . . sex? Max had been attracted, as any man who wasn't brain-dead would have been.

Was she a lure? Probably. He'd have to seriously investigate her past. Meanwhile, Max was free of the fatal injection, on the run in his plaster casts, with a woman whose motives could be anything from humanitarian to homicidal.

The old Max would have found out which in a heartbeat.

The new, disoriented Max . . . ? *Aiyyyee!*

Garry wished he had Max back in Las Vegas, where they only wished him dead.

Here, in Europe, they had ways of making Max *wish* he *was* dead.

Chapter 51

Gossip Girls

It is only natural that sour should follow sweet.

Barely has Miss Satin's fluffy tail vanished around the corner then Miss Midnight Louise's nose peeks around the same corner.

"Having a secret tryst?" she inquires. "This *is* a cathouse, but—"

"Knock it off, sister. If you have as much solid information to report as Miss Satin, you will be doing very well."

"An information exchange, eh?" Louise sits to wrap her tail around her paired front feet.

This demure pose does not fool me for a minute. She too has something hot to report, or she would not be so laid-back about Satin's presence.

"The bridesmaids are not all sweet and sincere as well as demented," she says.

"How so?"

"Once Miss Temple had finished questioning them, they broke into smaller gossip groups. Some of them have not just been tapping their toes waiting for the Fontana brothers to propose. A couple have been seeing other dudes."

Well, knock me over with a peacock feather and fan me! Could Vegas's most desirable bachelors be losing their magic touch? I hate to see a good footloose and fancy-free guy like me go down. Especially eight of them.

"Who has been two-timing our favorite suave swingers?"

"Speak for yourself," Midnight Louise says. "Every Lothario must have his day of reckoning, including you. They were whispering about it, but no names were mentioned. Since Judith, Tracee, Evita, and Meredith were the ones whispering, I suppose that Jill, Alexia, Wanda, and Asiah are all suspects."

I frown, knowing it gives me a mature, commanding appearance. "But a truly clever turncoat would be among the gossipers, pointing the finger at some innocent party."

"So we are back to square one," Louise says.

"Not necessarily. At least we know at least one is not on the up-and-up. You had better eavesdrop on them from now on."

After Miss Midnight Louise leaves, none too happily, I sit and mull the puzzle pieces that are coming together. Madonnah had something to hide. So does a bridesmaid who is not really as upset about being unproposed-to as the other girls may think. Maybe such a disgruntled ex would want the brothers Fontana caught with their Berettas in a brothel.

Maybe there were two crimes in the offing tonight: Madonnah's death and the Fontanas being framed for it. It was only bad luck that the most innocent party, Mr. Matt Devine, should be cast in the role of prime suspect.

It is quiet up here, so I can think plenty, and my mind goes around and around the maypole without coming up daisies. Or whatever.

Then I hear a violent sneeze down the hall, and two seconds later a lean black form bolts around the corner and pastes itself against the wall.

Ma Barker's ears are as flattened to her head as her whole form is to the floor. One might take her for a big grease spot. Her street skills are awesome.

I hear a nose being blown down the hall.

"Big lummox," Ma says, sitting up and letting her scraggly hackles lie back down. "I figured he would never leave, so I had to goose him out of my way."

"How did you manage that?"

"I scratched a snowstorm out of my hide and wafted it upward with my tail. Humans' eyes close when they sneeze, you know. Only for a second, but that is all I needed to dash out and disappear."

I am impressed by the Sneeze Diversion, but it would not work for me. My skin is not dry and flaky from years of street life in the desert heat. I can recommend a good anti-dandruff shampoo, but then Ma Barker would lose her edge, and the treatment smells bad.

"So what did you learn communing with the corpse?"

"Is that what you call it? The corpse was as mum as day-old bread. Starting to get a bit fragrant, though. Only to an expert nose. I am sure some of the forensic geeks on *CSI: Las Vegas* could tell us just which insect larvae was going wild in there."

"Please, Ma. No gruesome speculations. I want hard evidence."

"Not much to see in there, and too much to smell. I did detect the presence of lilac cologne. And I found the second fishnet stocking."

"No! Where was it?"

"In the adjoining peep room."

"No! That is even worse for Mr. Matt!"

"That is no skin off my nose, which has been skun by better than you. But I knew you would be distraught, so I dragged the item out and rolled it into a ball and put it under the bed."

"That is evidence tampering."

"I thought your Job One was to get this Devine guy off."

"With evidence, not shenanigans."

"There are no fingerprints to be found on fishnet anyway."

"What about claw marks?"

She flashes her shivs and then retracts them nail-by-nail, smooth as a magician doing a baton roll through his fingers. "They call me the Hooded Claw in the 'hood."

Oh, great! That makes me Son of the Hooded Claw. Sounds like some cheesy old serial movie.

Fortunately, I have established a reputation for fine sleuthing as well as slicing fisticuffs in this town.

If the other fishnet stocking was in the murder room, they must have been worn by the dead woman, not an imported garrote, but a tool of opportunity. That looks like someone who came to the Sapphire Slipper tonight, unexpectedly ran into the victim, then did her in with her own intimate accessory.

Unfortunately, that theory makes the Fontana party and their scheming girlfriends and innocent ride-alongs all still the prime suspects.

Chapter 52

Just Kidnapping

When Temple told Aldo she'd like to interview him alone in the Victorian boudoir, Kit raised an eyebrow.

Heck, the eyebrow almost jousted with her hairline.

"I'm looking for some context here," Temple told the room, including a scowling Macho Mario and a thoughtful Matt. "Only the eldest will do. Of the brothers, that is," she said quickly to shut Uncle Mario's already open and about to object mouth.

Aldo rose, shot his jacket sleeves over his pristine white cuffs, paused to whisper in Kit's ear at the parlor archway, then glanced into the kitchen.

"I may need a bodyguard to pass through that gauntlet of pissed-off girlfriends."

The joke lessened the tension behind . . . and the dawning tension ahead as the girlfriends' chatter became dead silence.

They all broadcast an air of heightened interest as a Fontana brother crossed their sight line.

In the foyer, Aldo took a deep breath. "Everybody is twitchier than a Valentine's Day Massacre trigger finger. Uncle Mario does all the talking for the family when things get tight."

"It's just me," Temple said.

"Right now, 'just you' is our designated savior. Don't fool yourself. The cops will be furious we kept quiet about the crime scene so you could play detective. We're all in deep scaloppini."

"But what a way to go," Temple said as he followed her upstairs, kissing her fingers to the air like a chef. "Pasta, olive oil, and lots of sauce."

"We may find all those ingredients in the Victorian Room upstairs." While Temple tried not to blush—racking her brains for any uses of pasta in kinky sex—although the olive oil and sauce she got, Aldo went on. "Why the Victorian Room?"

"I figured it wouldn't be wired. None of them are supposed to be, but you never know. Recording would ruin the illusion. But I'm counting on you to check it out first."

"Right. Wait here."

Aldo slipping into the room's saccharine pale blue décor resembled a white-clad black panther invading a froufrou shop. It took more than ten minutes, but he examined everything from four-poster canopy to carpet to furniture to walls and ceiling.

He stepped out into the hall to report.

"All is as ersatz, authentic Victorian as could be desired. No wires, no peepholes. So." He folded his arms and eyed her with an arched eyebrow. "What did you really have in mind here?"

Temple grabbed his arm, ducked inside, and shut the door on them.

Aldo did not look worried. Nor did he look hopeful.

He didn't have to. She would never even *flirt* with her aunt Kit's guy.

"You're right," she said. "The police will tear this charade to pieces, making all of us look guilty and no doubt dragging every one of our names through the media. After my first round of interviews it's becoming evident that, while there are a ton of suspects on the premises, there's also plenty of room for outside skullduggery."

"Outside as how? Sapphire Slipper employees?"

"First and foremost, yes. The place had to be reserved; that was a forewarning. The girlfriends think they were clever and that their designated caller sounded like an executive secretary making arrangements for a bunch of businessmen on a company-paid rampage, but it might well have sounded suspicious to the staff here. Then there's the question of how these babes in the woods managed to subvert your regular Gangsters' driver and take over."

"That *is* odd." Aldo pulled out his cell phone. Although it was as loath to connect up here as anybody's, he could still examine his call lists and other information. "Ah. A new hiree was on last night. Marlon Gherken."

"Could he have been planted?"

"Sure. The Gangsters' manager runs the daily operation, not us. She'll be the first person I talk to when we get back to Vegas."

"*She*'ll?"

"Gangsters is an equal-opportunity employer," Aldo said piously.

"Could she be a pal of one of these girlfriends?"

"All my brothers' girls live and work in Vegas, some in the entertainment industry. That means they know a lot of the workforce here, casually or closely. Yeah. She could be related somehow. But why such an elaborate setup for one murder? I'd have to say that it was something on this end, the bordello, that made this murder happen here and now."

Temple heaved a sigh and sat on the edge of the frilly feather bed. She fell backward into the linens like Alice in Wonderland into a flower soufflé. After Aldo hauled her upright again, she spit out an errant down feather.

"That's what this scenario is," she said, "feathers in the wind. We're drowning in a miasma of details, and a pile of personalities, half of them strangers, and I can't pin any one of them down."

"Sit on this toy rocking horse here, you won't sink into that."

Temple followed Aldo's advice, after removing a small black leather riding crop from the saddle. "Ick! I can't stand cruelty to rocking horses. Aldo, I was crazy to think I could come out here to get Matt and Nicky off the hook. This case is going to rest on forensic evidence, and we just have to hope that killer left some."

"Besides Matt and Nicky doing such a good job of that? CPR in a whorehouse. Way to go."

"Aldo! The murder weapon was an article of clothing as common as cinnamon buns in a bakery to this scene. A fishnet stocking. Please!"

"That's a little too pat," he said. "You know it screams kinky sex crime."

"You don't think this was a sex crime, half-naked woman and all?"

"They're all half-naked here. The guy clients too. Nah. I don't like it. Why, I can't say. That's your job, Toots."

" 'Toot, Toot, Tootsie, Good-bye,' " Temple quoted the title of the ragtime song. "Go back to the guys' barroom and ask your brothers about the hiring of this Marlon Gherken. Who, when, and why. And have Electra send up the girlfriend who cops to setting up this event with the Sapphire Slipper and Gangsters. All I can do is follow the trail of the arrangements that made this Murder in Shades of Blue possible."

He stood, shooting his sleeves again. No wonder the Fontana brothers' clothing always looked smooth and sharp. They shook their coats like Big Cats shrugging off a nap. Temple admired the effect, but thought that being married to such an unself-consciously self-conscious man would be tiring. Matt looked better ruffled, especially if she did it.

She sat back on the hard settee, curious to discover which insecure little witch would appear.

It was the endlessly upbeat Meredith Bell, lifestyle coach.

"Aren't these rooms a hoot?" she asked on entering. "I mean, talk about cheesy fantasies."

"Is that why you booked the place?"

"No. I booked the place because most of the legalized broth-els are farther north, upstate. Lots of freelance ladies work Ve-gas, which has zillions of available hotel rooms for hanky-panky right on the Strip. Nobody needs to drive to a double-wide in the boonies to get his pathetic rocks off."

"Apparently you thought the Fontana brothers did."

"*Did not!* That was the fun part, taking the Romeos of Las Vegas Boulevard someplace tacky. It might remind them of what they were treating us like: modern conveniences, but not worth committing to. Guys today! With the sexual revolution, they have it all: women who love them and let them walk all over them."

"Girls today seem to want their freedom too."

" 'Seem to.' Most women don't do casual sex well, no matter what face they put on it. Who wants a come-and-go alley cat that can pick up all sorts of diseases, not to mention never show up again some day, when you can have a responsible resident house cat."

Temple wasn't going to delve into that one, with this woman or with Midnight Louie. "So why were you elected to call the brothel?"

"I deal with all sorts of people in my job. I'm good on phones, or in person. I'm . . . just convincing, I guess."

Horrifyingly so, Temple thought. Why is it that people who

guided other people were always so infuriatingly self-certain? Except for Matt, which was what made him the brilliant counselor he was. His own uncertainties showed through.

"How did the scam go?" Temple asked, settling into her uncomfortable corner of the settee.

Meredith, a woman who looked like she did daily yoga routines, didn't even notice the harsh seating.

"Perfectly," she said. "None of us know more about brothels than we could find on the Web, but I knew this place encouraged large parties and accepted exclusive reservations."

"When did you make the reservation?"

"Ten days ago. I had to be sure to get the whole place to ourselves. Luckily a lot of their business is impromptu and Monday is a dead day and night. I just put on my executive assistant voice, gave 'em the credit card number, and we were set. The Sapphire Slipper, and the Fontana brothers, were all ours for twenty-four delicious hours."

"Whose credit card?"

Meredith straightened her spine and shook her silky blond ponytail. "Alexia had Eduardo's. We thought the punishment should not only fit the crime, but underwrite it."

"And what had Eduardo done to incur a three-thousand-dollar tab?"

"Let her see his credit card number when buying her some low-end sop to her self-respect."

"Hmm," said Temple, wanting to kick the smug Miss Bell in the supple shins. This juvenile scheme had put Matt in harm's way. "What was this 'low-end sop'?"

"A gold charm bracelet with all their little sweet nothings on it. A piano for the piano bar where they met, a fox for being 'such a foxy lady,' an Eiffel Tower for their first dinner together at the Paris, a gondola for the Venice, a peacock for the Crystal Phoenix rendezvous . . . I mean, a peacock, for God's sake! Couldn't he at least have found a real phoenix?"

Since the phoenix was a mythical beast, Temple thought a peacock made a good substitute. She also thought this particular peahen was a piss-poor substitute for a real girl.

"Actually," Temple said, "most men I've seen wouldn't spend that much time or thought or money on memorializing sweet nothings."

"Aldo managed to come up with the real deal: a high-carat engagement ring. And for some strange woman out of left field."

"That is my maternal aunt you're talking about, and although she is a woman she is not strange, nor out of left field."

"You know what I mean."

Temple sighed. "Yes, I do. All you girls got poison-green jealous and decided to use the innocent excuse of Aldo's engagement and forthcoming marriage to pursue your own grievances. Aldo's significant other *died*. He was not only a free man, he was an unhappy one. Now he's happy . . . or was, until you and your crew had to turn a genuinely joyous outing into a petty revenge weekend. And I guess you're happy now that you messed up my fiancé's life and reputation. What's an innocent bystander sacrificed here and there?"

"You can afford to get on your high horse. You're engaged."

"Fair and square," Temple said. "No coercion, no kidnapping, no nuttiness involved. No setting anyone up for a murder rap."

"We didn't know what would happen! We had no idea someone would die. We were going to give the boys the naughty night of their lives. We were just kidding. Obviously."

"Obviously, someone found your juvenile idea of 'kidding' via kidnapping the perfect backdrop for murder."

Meredith's relentlessly upbeat expression collapsed like a tissue-thin tent.

"You have to understand," she said, upset. "In Nevada, brothels are these sort of slightly sleazy near-neighbors. All the girls were dying to see inside one without having to actually put out. Heidi Fleiss is even starting a Stud Farm for women up near Pahrump. Regular women are finally getting to do all the edgy stuff guys have done all the time. Going to a chicken ranch is supposed to be a harmless, fun thing. That's what we thought we were getting into."

"Sex for sale?" Temple asked. "It never occurred to any of you that there could be something seamy about it, even in a health-approved setting? Sex is about power. And where there's power, there's abuse, even if it's subtle and concealed by a lot of flash and cash. Whether on the Strip or way out here in the desert. Isn't that what you women really wanted, the power to protest? To have the men under your power, even in jest and even for twenty-four hours? Surely a 'lifestyle coach' should know that."

Meredith had no answer. She shrugged. "It seemed like harmless fun, like a coed pajama party."

"With pros."

"The guys were going along with us."

"Until someone died."

"She wasn't even one of us."

"Her 'lifestyle' wasn't worth worrying about."

"No, but . . . she was just the hired help. I mean, we didn't need her life messing up ours."

"Well, get ready for a surprise. Her death is going to mess it up a whole lot more than you can imagine."

Chapter 53

Babes to Boots

Temple's head was throbbing.

No wonder the golden age of mystery had been in the Agatha Christie, Dorothy Sayers, Ellery Queen era of the 1920s, '30s, and '40s, the days of cozy, closed-cast murder scenes. Everyone present a suspect. Victims and suspects isolated, so no messy outsider could be pegged as the evildoer at the last moment. A culture clash between the girlfriends and the victim that could have turned lethal. Upstanding citizens could snap when confronted with extreme lifestyles, which is why Matt was such a tailor-made suspect. Upright, uptight clergymen were long fabled as spectacularly snap-worthy. And Fontana brothers were always prime suspect material.

The more desperate Temple was to relieve Matt and Nicky of suspicion, the more frantic she was to wrap this up before it tainted Kit and Aldo's wedding, the less of a way out she saw.

Nobody here except the Sapphire Slipper residents had any overt connection to the brothel, unless Uncle Mario and brothers were all lying like Milano wool-silk rugs.

One of the girlfriends, of course, might have a slightly shady lady background. She might have a sister in the biz. Who knows? Trouble was, Temple was supposed to find these things out.

She decided she was right to start at absolute zero, since that was all she had anyway. She was doing what those brilliant amateur detectives of almost a hundred years ago had done: observe and trace the time line of the crime.

It had started with the real bachelor party, so she should start with a bachelor and work her way through logically, from person to person.

So which Fontana brother had set up the party? Not Aldo, but someone had to be the front man. She asked Aldo to find the culprit and bring him to the Victorian Room for an interview.

She waited alone in the room's tawdry elegance. Despite its reputation as an elegant brothel, the Sapphire Slipper was more pretension than class. Temple had used the brothel's office laptop to survey the competition's Web sites. (Also to snoop at how it presented itself and use any inside information she could come across.)

Reception was fine, and their cell phones were now registering signals. They had agreed, though, that further isolation would help all involved with the police when they were finally called.

Most legal Nevada brothels were located in the cactus and sagebrush of the boonies, no more than single-wide trailers offering visions of low-end furniture glory.

Compared to that, the Sapphire Slipper was an oasis of sophistication. The "courtesans"—that was the official title for the girls according to their organization site—were freelance workers who set their own prices and menu of offerings. They were rigorously certified as disease-free, and always used condoms. They didn't languish for months or years at a particular "venue," but traveled the country like carnies, checking into familiar stands for two to four weeks at a time.

Apparently variety was a big advantage of the brothel menu.

Temple tried not to be judgmental. She understood the argument that legalized prostitution protected both client and provider way more than streetwalking, but she couldn't picture a life of such casual sexuality. Then she considered the angst she felt in changing lovers, from Max to Matt, with marriage always a likelihood in the equation. . . . And thought maybe that feeling less and experiencing more was not a totally insane way to go.

A gentle knock on the door startled her from her musings.

For a moment she felt like a resident expecting a client. Who would he be? Which one of the men from downstairs? That darling blond guy? Hell, no. He was taken.

This would be a tall, dark, and handsome, Fontana-style. The only mystery about this guy would be which one had been stuck setting up the party venue that had been usurped.

Temple imagined the fury uncorking at the place that the Fontana party was *not* at this very moment, including pathetic Quincey *not* being able to wriggle out of a fake cake in true bimbo form.

"Come in," she said. "Ralph!" She gazed at the second youngest Fontana brother.

"Hi." He shrugged. "Yeah, the church elders stuck me with setting up the village idol worshipping. I hear you want to know where we all were *supposed* to be right now."

"Have a seat," she suggested.

The only place was the other end of the Victorian love seat, which was hard of back and sitting surface, despite being upholstered in baby blue.

"Man, this is one uncomfortable mama of a couch," Ralph said, arranging his lanky frame. "I guess it's because they want to get right to the bed."

Temple eyed the high-mattressed, rococo affair with ruffled canopy. "That doesn't look any better."

"There's always the floor," Ralph said with distaste, running the edge of his Italian sole over the saccharine floral-design area rug. "No, I guess not."

Temple cleared her throat. She was not here to discuss ideal reclining spots with a Fontana brother. "Where were you all supposed to be?"

He described the place, the G-Strip Club, the plans for the evening. "It was going to be the usual bachelor party nonsense, a lot of booze, razzing the groom-to-be, a stripper bride popping out of a big cardboard cake. We didn't have a lot of time to set it up."

"That club is in Las Vegas proper. Or improper. When the ride there took so long, weren't you suspicious?

"We were *paesanos* having a good time. The champagne and banter flowed. I just figured the driver was giving us a chance to mellow before we arrived."

"The driver. *Hah!* Who was this?"

"Whoever was assigned to chauffeur us in the Rolls-Royce Silver Cloud, our smoothest and creamiest limo. The silver exterior finish is so perfect it seems like warm mirror to the sight and touch. The leather inside is softer than kid, the color of champagne. The inlaid woods are Swedish blond."

Temple was almost drooling.

"Nicky calls it the Vanmobile."

Well! She didn't need to know that!

"Um, Ralph. I understand the driver was a new hire."

"Chauffeurs come and go, like headwaiters. Essential, but temperamental."

"You remember this guy?"

"Gherken. They go by last names, like ritzy English butlers. Never saw him before, but he seemed competent. One of our regulars had called in sick and this guy just happened to be applying. He had a good rap . . . I mean, reference . . . sheet."

"What do you mean by good?"

"Employed as a getaway driver by the Ciampi family in Chicago. Not Irish. They tend to drink while waiting."

"But not Italian?"

"Not . . . anything," Ralph said, narrowing his eyes and fingering his discreet gold earring. "The guy was . . . blah. Bland. Not memorable. Every Mr. Smith you ever saw. Except his last name was Gherken. You talked to him, it sounded like you were asking for a pickle. On the other hand, our clients are always pretty jolly out on the town, and like a good laugh."

"Funny," Temple said. "You hear the name 'Smith' and get suspicious. You hear a ridiculous last name and you think it's got to be genuine. Who'd make up a moniker like that?"

Ralph sat up, worried. "You think he was in on it! But it was just chance he got the Vanillamobile and our party."

"Anybody talk personally to the 'sick' driver?"

"He was bribed?"

Temple said nothing.

"You mean he might have been mugged."

"Or kidnapped himself."

"Or killed. *Jesu bambino!* He could have been killed himself. And we shouldn't call out of here to find out, unless we're ready to call the cops too." Ralph stood. "It would look suspicious if we want to use the excuse that none of our cell phones worked. Much as I hate to do it, I'll talk to the guys about turning ourselves in."

Temple had the satisfaction of astounding a Fontana brother. Usually it was the other way around.

Meanwhile, she was waiting for her next interviewee. This person was the bridge between the "before" and "after" of the kidnapping, least seen, least appraised.

Aldo led her in. The woman who had actually added some black palazzo pants to her butt-skimming uniform blazer.

As a showgirl, Asiah had the height and department-store-mannequin-broad shoulders to convincingly mimic a man in silhouette through a tinted glass darkly. With her platinum-blond hair under a cap and her hot-chocolate skin, she was the perfect substitute for a male driver, especially since the Fontana party owned the limo and the company.

They were likely to pile in on their own without an attentive chauffeur opening and closing each door behind them. They were on home ground; less wary. They were all men; the bachelor party crew didn't need the niceties of a formal evening out to impress a woman. And that had been their blind spot, as their girlfriends had foreseen.

It was hard to imagine the spectacular Asiah squired by the most conservative Fontana brother, Ralph, but opposites do attract. And Temple had a hunch mild-mannered Ralph might go for a drop-dead, in-your-face gal like Asiah.

In fact, Temple felt a little nervous about interviewing her. All the Fontana girlfriends were taller than she, but that wasn't hard to be.

"What sold you on this kidnap caper?" Temple asked.

Asiah's wide smile showed shark-white teeth. "I figured my guy could use a walk on the wild side."

"The wild evening out was the reason, not making them regret not proposing marriage?"

"Girlfriend, that was a fine reason for the others. Me, I just liked the rush. Driving those Fontana boys somewhere off the beaten track, fooling them, being in control of that huge limo and all those men. What a blast!"

"You French-kissed the driver to seal the deal?" Temple sounded squeamish even to herself.

"*Soul*-kissed, sweetie. I love turning the tables on everyone. Even my girlfriends, if that had come up. I crave adventure."

"Did you have a room picked out for you and Ralph?" Okay, that was a totally salacious, irrelevant, and immaterial query.

"*Um-hmm.* But I don't wanta embarrass a sweet little thing like you. You are so darling! And so is your man. If you ever take your fiancé here on a sentimental journey, ask for Room XXX."

Wow. They did need to decide on a honeymoon destination. . . .

"Asiah, you obviously like living on the edge and are a sharp lady. Didn't you have any suspicions that this scheme was working too smoothly? That someone could have been using this girls' night out scenario for something sinister?"

"Is that what you think? The whole thing was a setup?" She crossed her long, long legs and sucked her shiny paprika red–glossed lips to consider it. Nothing shy about this woman. *Ralph?* "Now that the murder's been done, sure. Then . . . we were pumped. We were into it. It seemed like harmless fun."

"And the dead woman?"

Asiah's expression sobered. "Not planned. Not anticipated. That is one ugly development, and it isn't only the Fontana boys who will be in the hot seat when the law comes into it. It'll be all us girls. We look stupid, if not like right-on-target suspects."

"Is it possible some of you are?"

Asiah shook her platinum-blond hair, still serious. "Could be. I never thought of that, even after the body was found. Girls just want to have fun, you know."

"Not always. These girlfriends were tired of just having fun. That was the point. They wanted serious commitment."

"Not me. I've got a great job, a great guy, a great life."

"How did you all get together for this? Did you have occasional hen parties, or what?"

"Or what. Sometimes the boys double- and triple-date. If they have tickets for a major show or sports thing. If it's a sports thing, some of the girls get bored and do their own thing nearby. So we get each other's cell phone numbers and texting addresses."

Temple found it depressing that they didn't bother with e-mail or street addresses. It was a mobile world now, with people always wirelessly wired to other people. Some teens couldn't seem to breathe without being in touch with someone all the time. It was a manically social way to be alone in a crowd.

Of course, cell phones didn't always work everywhere at all times, as this place proved.

"So not all the girlfriends were peeved about not being engaged?" Temple asked.

"I'm the most independent one. Yeah, the others would have liked to have been asked, at least. Shown something eye-popping in a box besides a bracelet."

"Who was the ringleader, then?"

Frowning, Asiah crossed and uncrossed her legs. "I really . . . can't say. We seemed to come up with it all at once when we heard about Aldo's marrying that New York woman. I mean, if Aldo fell . . . that was a big change for the Fontana brothers."

"So there'd been no mutters of trouble among the women before then?"

Asiah shrugged those skinny linebacker shoulders. "I heard one or two were dating other men."

"Who?"

"Wanda. She's Rico's girl. A guy'd be crazy to let a professional massage therapist get away from him. But she was taking it personally. Maybe she wanted to rub only one guy the right way."

"When you say 'therapist'—"

"I mean professional. She wasn't in the sex industry, although any therapist gets a lot of male clients. They have bigger muscles and often need to show one and all how they use them. Leads to strain and pain."

"Who was the other girlfriend dating outside the family?"

"That mahogany redhead sports gal, Alexia."

"She's a horse trainer, right?"

"Right. Some folks think that's glamorous, being out in the hot sun all day, with sweating horsehide and circling horseflies and poop piles the size of beehives on the ground. Not my way to chill."

"Whose girlfriend is she?"

"Ernesto's. He loves the track, betting. Every guy's gotta have a guy-type hobby. You're getting married, you better keep that in mind."

"Do you know anyone else who was dating out of the Fontana circle?"

Asiah put long forefinger to lip. Temple noticed her nails were short. She probably wore long false nails onstage. "State secret. They knew enough to keep it off the Internet."

"They're afraid of the Fontana brothers?"

"That mob history is just that, history. No, but they didn't want to risk one good thing while trolling for another. It was all Aldo's fault. His engagement was a shock."

"To me, too," Temple said.

"Yeah, your aunt has avoided the JP pretty long herself, a lot longer than Aldo, right?"

Temple saw the speculation flashing in those shrewd espresso-brown eyes.

"Family secret," Temple said primly. "We Northern Europeans have our clannish ways too."

"Yeah, *Clan of the Cave Bear*!" Asiah pretended to shiver in below-zero cold and laughed up a storm. "I was just the driver, along for the ride. I don't know much."

"Who was the ringleader?" Temple repeated.

"Gotta know that, huh? I'd say . . . Miss Jill."

"She's the—"

"Little. Natural white-blond. One of those Northern European stock people. Jill Johanssen. Was real hyper about being in on the caper. Don't know her well. Giuseppe's girl. Pepe is crazy about her. If anyone was going to crack and go nuptial, I'd have said it would have been him. She was everything opposite he was: small, pale, tightly wired in a cute, brisk way."

"And her profession is?"

"Oh! Pretty boring stuff."

"You other women are hard to beat."

"True. She was a pharmacist. Don't ask me how she met him."

"Maybe in a drugstore line," Temple said, smiling. "Thanks for the info."

"You're welcome, babe. I gotta be back on the Strip tonight for two shows at the Rio. Crack us out of here, girl! Or you'll have a riot on your hands."

Temple nodded as Asiah eeled out the door.

Jill. A pharmacist.

Access to all sorts of drugs.

Maybe the dead woman hadn't been strangled. That took a bit of time and struggle. Maybe the foam-flecked lips and bloodshot eye whites Temple remembered with a shudder from the other strangled murder victim she'd seen recently could have been caused by ingesting a poisonous substance.

Maybe someone had knocked Madonnah out first with an injection. That made sense in the milling, populated upstairs where the killing had to have happened.

Or did it? Maybe the body had been trucked in, like the Fontana bachelor party, from Vegas. In the limo's trunk.

Or the "boot," as the Brits called it.

Chapter 54

Meeting Mr. Wrong

Molina's instincts had made her crave neutral ground, but she couldn't think of any.

She'd called the Oasis Hotel, where he purportedly held a security job now.

Darned if she didn't get a secretary. To avoid leaving the telltale physicality of a written message, she had to identify herself.

"Certainly, Lieutenant. I'll page Mr. Nadir at once. He should call you back in a couple of minutes, if nothing urgent is under way."

Molina snorted after the woman hung up. Nothing would be more urgent to Rafi Nadir than this call.

She paced in the homicide unit's tiled women's restroom, holding one hand to her touchy stomach. No one usually came in here between shifts. It was 7:00 A.M. Monday. She'd come in early to make this call. Her wound still squealed at any stretching movement. She was worn ragged from concealing her condition and lying to everyone about her absence for a week a month earlier.

Still, she needed to pace, cradling the cell phone against one shoulder, waiting for it to ring.

"Carmen?" His voice was low. He was holed up somewhere semiprivate too. *Lord!*

"We need to talk privately," she told him.

"Not much of that in Las Vegas."

"What about your place?" Better his than hers.

"I'm not where you visited before—"

"I know."

"All police, all the time," he said.

"You got it."

"I'm on night shift."

"Morning. Nine A.M."

"Ten."

"Done," she said.

"Tomorrow. Tuesday," he said.

Same old, she said, he said.

"You got it."

"You want to hint what this is about, Carmen?"

"What has it always been about?"

"Fine. Tell me when you get there. You want directions?"

She'd let him tell her, a pulse in her neck throbbing. She really didn't feel up to this. But if she waited to feel better about it, it would never happen.

Now it was Tuesday morning, and everything about the visit made Molina uneasy.

She'd debated between taking her personal Volvo or a cop car. She hated having her personal license plate on display outside Rafi Nadir's house, but a police plate was worse. It was daylight. She'd have preferred the dark of night. But he worked then. Couldn't be helped.

She'd driven the neighborhood first, looking for parked cars with people in them. *Nada.* Nobody under surveillance.

The house was modest, not more than fifteen years old, the first edge of the wild housing boom that had hit Vegas and environs like a whirling dervish and had not stopped until the mortgage bust. Now the Strip was booming with obscenely priced high-rise condominiums, like Miami Beach, and sales had nearly stopped.

Rafi's house was distinctly low-rise. Still, it was as respectable as her twenties bungalow in Our Lady of Guadalupe parish. She could have afforded something modern and sleek in the suburbs, but she'd wanted Mariah to know her Hispanic roots, to be part of a real community that only church, school, and home within walking distance can provide. Call it old-fashioned . . . being a single mother gave her the opportunity to do what she believed in, no questions asked. By nobody.

She walked up to the door, facing north, smart in this climate. On the other hand, when you barbecued supper in the backyard, you broiled too. The idea of Rafi barbecuing was so funny, she smiled.

Unfortunately, she was caught in the act when he opened the door before she could ring the bell.

"So this is a social visit," he said, raising dark, heavy eyebrows.

"Sorry. I was thinking of something else."

"And that makes you smile. Come in, anyway."

She entered like a cat, slowly, sniffing out the atmosphere. Also, she didn't move that fast with eighty-some stitch scabs still pulling at her side and stomach.

The new carpet was a pale sunset color, beige-peach. Developers and people who wanted to sell their homes loved those blah neutrals. The walls were off-white. They were in a cathedral-ceilinged main room-den with an eating bar dividing it from the small kitchen.

Everything was tidy. Tidier than Casa Molina. No kid, no cats, no working mother in residence.

Rafi was wearing khakis and a black T-shirt. There were dark circles around his eyes—swarthy skin was prone to that—but he looked trimmer, tauter. Funny, he was looking better and she was looking worse.

"You still like calorie-free Dr Pepper?" he asked.

"I can drink it."

He popped two cans and brought her one.

After eyeing the seating pieces, low, beige, and cushy, she opted to hike one hip on one of the three barstools drawn up to the den side of the eating bar. She wasn't about to mire herself in upholstered furniture when she couldn't be sure of pushing herself up again without a slight struggle or a grunt of pain.

Rafi leaned on the counter behind the raised eating surface like a bartender.

"So what do I owe—?"

"We need to talk, I told you. I don't want to do this right now. About you meeting Mariah. It's not a good time for me."

"And Mariah, when would it be a good time for her?"

"In my book? Never."

He just watched her. That was different. He'd never been wary before.

"I don't suppose there's any point in denying anything," she said after a bracing sip of Dr Pepper. She hadn't had one since . . . well, since the day she'd decamped without warning, without word. Leaving L.A. fourteen years ago.

He sighed. "Why'd you do it, Carmen? It was bad enough what we were both going through in the department. Then, bang. You're gone. Most of your things are gone. No reason. No message. No way to trace you. A cop knows how to disappear."

"Isn't it obvious?"

"The kid? But you didn't run home. I didn't think so, but I checked. Why run? You thought I'd want you to get rid of it? You, pregnant? That's one possibility I never even dreamed about. You made plain from the first no kids, no accidents. I can see that a pregnancy would shake you up, but you could have at least consulted me. That's all I can think of. You didn't ask. Maybe I would have said have an abortion then. I don't know. That's the problem. I had a right to know."

Her forefinger pulled a drop of condensation from the soft drink can into a long tail on the eating bar Formica. "That's the thing. I didn't think you'd want me to abort. I thought you'd fixed it so I got pregnant without my knowledge and cooperation."

"Me. Got you pregnant? How? Sure, foam and condoms have failure rates. That's why you used a diaphragm too. God, it was like having sex in a bubble bath every time. Sure, we hadn't talked about it. But . . . man, I had enough problems on the job, like you did. Baby was the furthest thing from my mind. You were escaping the tension starting up your singing gig, and I was helping you. Don't you remember? We'd comb those funky L.A. vintage shops, trolling for movie star leavings. We invented 'Carmen.'"

It was his turn to write an invisible word in a drop of cold water. "Yeah, we were stressed. The brass was loading us with shitwork, the Anglos were on both our tails. Why would I want a baby in a situation like that! I don't want a baby now."

"You do. You want access to my baby!"

"She's a kid. Not a baby. Very fast getting not to be a baby, Carmen. And she's my kid. She's got my eyes. Freaked me when I first saw her. Maybe some chin too. You got pictures?"

"Pictures?"

"Baby pictures."

"Yes. But I didn't think to bring them. Sorry, daddy dearest."

"So why did you think I made you pregnant deliberately?"

"I couldn't believe it when it happened. You know we weren't ready. I sure wasn't. I couldn't believe my diaphragm had failed. I examined it up against the bathroom fluorescent. There was a minute pinhole in it."

Silence.

Rafi slammed his pop can off the counter. It clattered to the cheap vinyl floor and rolled, spewing brown fluid like tobacco juice.

"And that's it? Convicted without trial, without an interrogation even? You think I was running around with a needle sticking holes in your diaphragm? Are you crazy, woman? We didn't need that. I didn't need that. Why the hell would you even think that?"

Suddenly her reasoning seemed weak, stupid, insulting even.

"I was doing better with the force. They were getting the message that they needed some token women, and I wasn't buckling on the 'hood patrol like they'd thought. Hoped."

She looked up from drawing in her new water blob. "I knew I was in line for a promotion. And you weren't. I knew you wouldn't be happy about that. I figured you had figured it out too, and wanted to put me out of the running."

He took all that in, ignoring the still rocking pop can.

"You knew and you figured. Wrong. No, I wouldn't like the gender card dealing me out. Yeah, I'd be mad. But I wouldn't have sabotaged you. Some of my Anglo 'peers,' maybe, if I'd have a chance. But not you. That's it? Our whole lives off track because you assumed I'd trick you. Usually it's the woman who pulls that 'Gee, I'm pregnant' stuff."

"That was the last thing I'd wanted, and I was really pissed, because I couldn't ditch all that Catholic upbringing. I couldn't do an abortion."

"Sorry now?"

"No."

"I'm not either."

She caught her breath, which hurt like Hades.

"Yes, I'd like to meet my daughter besides on a crime scene. I got to know her a little at that Teen Idol reality TV show. I'd decided she was an okay kid even before I figured it out. Yes, you can break it to her gently. Doesn't she wonder about her father, for crissakes?"

"No. I told her he was a policeman who'd been hit and killed by a drunk driver while helping a stranded motorist."

"At least that's a likely story. And what'd you do for photos of the hero dead dad?"

"I clipped a newspaper story, told all about it. The funeral, everything. I told her that was the only memento I could bear to keep."

"At least you told her that he was a cop." Rafi laughed in disbelief. "Written out of my own life. You did a good job."

"I can't keep you out of mine, though, can I?"

"I just want to meet my daughter. Spend some time with her. What you did put me in a tailspin, Carmen. I blew everything. Yeah, I did that, but did you ever stop to think what disappearing like that without explanation did to me? I followed up on every unidentified female body around L.A. for years. I didn't dare report it, because you took your stuff, but I couldn't believe you'd leave me without a reason."

"I had one."

"A freaking fairy tale." He looked up at her, hard. "I'm not letting you off the hook. I have parental rights, and I want them. I'll keep it quiet, if you will. I didn't deserve what you did to me."

"Maybe . . . not."

"You can be lukewarm about it, but it's almost fifteen wasted years of my life. I've got some friends now. I don't have to fall back on the freaky edge of being a bitter ex-cop. I've got a new job and I'm pretty good at it. Private cops get better pay and more respect. There's no reason you shouldn't let me have a small part in my daughter's life."

"No."

"No? You're not fighting me on this?"

"No."

"Something's happened."

"Maybe."

"You're not going to tell me. Someone pressuring you to let me into Mariah's life?"

"Only you."

"A thrown pop can isn't much pressure, Carmen."

She managed a small smile. "It wasn't much of a temper tantrum, either. No, I've reconsidered, realized that I might have been wrong. I have no reason not to believe your version of events, unless you give it to me."

He laughed again. "'Version of events.' Cop talk is not the only way to communicate, you know."

"I know. But I need some time."

"Time! I've wasted almost fifteen years."

"A little time. There are a couple of loose ends I have to tie up, at work and at home. Then we'll . . . arrange something. Since Mariah met you while you were on guard duty, it might be best to build on that, not tell her right away. She'll be mad, but you said you bonded a little at the reality TV house. That'll win her over. She's crazy about a TV singing career."

"She's got some pipes. Next she'll be going for *American Idol*."

"So she says."

"Kinda like you. Determined. You got determined in the wrong direction about me."

She pushed herself upright, sighing. He never suspected she was in pain.

"I guess."

"We need to talk more about that. It's important."

She looked at him for the first time. The man she'd been in

like with, at least. Maybe not right for her for the long haul, but worth something then, or they'd have never gotten together.

"You're looking good, Rafi." She smiled as his wary facial tension collapsed with utter surprise. "That hotel security job sounds like a new start. That's what Vegas is for. The gambler."

He came around the barrier to see her to the door.

"You're way different from what I thought."

She turned on the threshold. "Maybe you are too."

He was still gaping after her when she left, a little giddy on inner and outer pain, pain pills, and revised attitudes.

Chapter 55

Ex Marks the Spot

Time was flying and Temple was getting desperate.

She found it mildly suspicious that Ralph set up the bachelor party and it was his girlfriend who bribed the driver to turn the limo over to her. But Asiah had been pretty open about the bribe and also about her lack of interest in roping a Fontana brother into matrimony.

Temple meandered back into the kitchen, sensing the tension in the parlor and bar areas as she passed through. The police would have to be called soon. Then, at least, some of the suspects could be cleared enough to be sent home.

Matt had stood as she'd passed through the bar, his face tense. It was now almost noon on Tuesday. He had to be on the air, live, by midnight.

She needed a sign, something to put her on the trail of a disloyal or maybe just royally misguided girlfriend. They were listlessly hanging out around the large homey kitchen table and sitting on the quartet of stools at the eating bar. The radio was playing country and western plaints. The girls looked tired, bored, and rebellious.

One of them must have gone very wrong, but which one?

Life coach Meredith; Wanda, the honey-blond massage therapist; raven-haired Judith, the runway model; white-blond Jill, a pharmacist; the mahogany redhead who trained horses, but maybe hoped to control her Fontana brother, Alexia; Tracee, the superfit Pilates instructor; Evita, a ventriloquist who could certainly call in sick for a missing chauffeur, or Asiah, right Jill-on-the-spot to drive the huge silver boat and its unknowing cargo to a totally wrong location.

But Temple didn't think it would take a ventriloquist to ensure that a driver call in sick. All the women had probably shown up at Gangsters to hook up with their guys a time or two. All would be familiar with the operation, even with the drivers.

The women eyed her with weary disinterest. Wanda yawned.

Eeny, meeny, miney . . .

All at once, Temple's glance was drawn by a motion on the carpet. A fat black tail extended from under the kitchen table. Two feet away, so did a fluffy one. And another narrow one and a fluffy one. Her first glimpse of Louie, showed him in cat cahoots with Midnight Louise and cathouse mascot Baby Blue, but whose was the fourth tail?

The tips were twitching ever so slightly. In time. If the radio hadn't been playing, Temple could have heard the tap, tap, tap of feline impatience.

Not impatience, signaling!

Because every tail pointed in one direction: to the breakfast stool on which one Fontana girlfriend in particular sat slumped and unhappy.

"Come with me," Temple said. She knew better than to

ignore a four-feline Ouija board reading. "You might be able to answer a few questions."

Temple wasn't sure what ethnic gene occasionally produced blinding white hair in children that lasts into adulthood. She'd seen a few only in Minnesota, so it was no wonder that Jill's last name was—"

"Johanssen, right?" Temple asked, spelling it out.

"That's right!" Jill sat up a bit straighter. "That's amazing. No one gets the double s and the *en* ending."

"That's because I'm such an ace detective," Temple said, dead serious.

Jill began fidgeting with her nails, which were filed short and square, not typical for a Fontana brother girlfriend. Nor was her petite frame. Or her profession of pharmacist. Jill was striking but not sensational.

"I hear Giuseppe is crazy about you."

Jill laughed uneasily. "So they say."

"Don't you know?"

"What girl does? Especially with those guys? I mean, they have all these glamorous girlfriends."

"Including you."

"I'm not glamorous. The others, sure. I'm the odd woman out." Jill glanced at Temple's platform mules. "You know what I mean. You're a shrimp too, and they're all sailfish."

Temple narrowed her eyes. "I know you did it."

"I didn't!"

"Didn't what?"

"What you think."

"Which is?"

"Whatever you think."

This was getting nowhere. Temple's interrogation skills were nil. Of course, she had no authority.

"Listen, Jill, the police are going to regard every man and woman in this bordello as a murder suspect. Lives and reputations will be wrecked, including yours. Maybe it started as a prank, but it's a matter of life and death now."

Temple leaned closer. "Come on, Jill, I know you did it. The police will figure it out a lot faster, given your profession."

Jill drove her stubby fingers into those silken strands of platinum hair. Her complexion was almost as pale.

"Yes, I did it! Yes, it started as a joke. No, it's not any fun now. I could lose my license—!"

"What did you use?"

"Foxglove, the herbal source of digitalis."

"Digitalis?"

Jill nodded.

"And that wouldn't kill somebody?"

"No! Not in a small dose in food. The idea was just to produce vomiting and diarrhea."

"Then you didn't realize—"

"I didn't think anyone would realize I did that. If the murder hadn't happened out here, no one would have even suspected."

"Suspected?" Temple was confused into echoing her perp.

"Who would have cared *how* it was done, or by *who when*, if it all was just a big fat prenuptial joke?"

"You mean that *you* drugged the regular driver, not the murder victim."

"Yes!" Jill looked up, big blues bug-eyed in horror. "You didn't think—you'd never think that I would've helped murder that woman?"

Temple felt that question didn't merit an answer. Of course that's what she'd thought, had even hoped in her haste to solve this crime so none of her friends—and her fiancé especially—would be implicated.

"How did you get the regular driver to take something?"

"I visited Gangsters that late afternoon, swore him to silence on the fact that we girlfriends were making a surprise appearance at the end of the bachelor party, and even gave him a taste of the cake we were all going to pop out of, devil's food. There was enough foxglove in that so that all he could manage to do was call in sick six hours later. We figured the new driver didn't know what was what yet and would be easier to con. Asiah gave him the same story, this was a surprise prank, and got him off the lot in time to slip into the driver's seat before the bachelor party arrived."

"For a pharmacist to play a prank like that . . . it could cost you your license. Why'd you do it, Jill? It was a pretty stupid idea."

She picked at the clear polish on her fingernails. "I'd never fit in with the other girls. They lived such glamorous lives, did such glamorous things. I just wanted to prove to them I could be a good sport. I didn't care if Giuseppe proposed. He's probably going to dump me anyway." She shrugged dispiritedly.

"What part of 'crazy about you' don't you understand? Don't you get it? Giuseppe probably *liked* that you were different from the usual arm candy. I can't say that the Fontana brothers are sobersides, but they aren't just tall, dark, dumb hunks either."

"Oh. I thought he was just joshing me. About something long-term. I thought if I was part of this fun game the other girlfriends were playing, I could hang on a little longer."

"You and he need to have a long talk after this is over."

"I doubt we'll be still talking then."

Temple sighed. "There's no reason that exactly how the bridesmaid crew got the original driver out of the way has to come up—"

Jill was all eyes, saucers brimming with bright blue hope.

"*If*," Temple added, "I can hand a murder suspect over to the police when they get here. And they will."

Temple looked at her watch. "Too damn soon."

Chapter 56

A Real Pickle

I wind up in the kitchen with my kisser in Satin's empty food bowl.

The bored bridesmaids are chowing down chips, no doubt trying to outgrow their gowns before the ceremony at week's end, just out of spite.

That seems to be their inbred reaction to crisis: flight or spite.

I am getting pretty spiteful myself . . . the more my stomach registers "empty."

That the only remaining traces in Miss Satin's bowl sniff of Midnight Louise and Ma Barker, not to mention Free-to-Be-Feline, does nothing to slake my bad mood.

I hang over the bowl, hoping the gesture will inspire She Who Feeds to action. But though the room is packed with shes, none seem the least bit maternal.

Then I hear the soft suck of the rubber seal on the refrigerator door.

I immediately gaze at this Moby Dick–size behemoth with interest.

I spot the old demi-dame who does odd jobs at this place pulling out a package that reeks of roast beef. Rare, just the way I love it.

I amble over, trying to turn the frog in my throat from the dry desert air into a respectable purr. I am prepared to massage the calves in those black slacks, even though I am not sure of their owner's gender. I am not biased. I am an equal-opportunity mooch.

I am just about to abase myself with a total stranger (sorta symptomatic of business as usual here anyway), when I watch Ms. or Mr. Shoofly slip out the back door, a hunk of sliced odiferous beef in one hand, and a longneck beer in the other.

The bridesmaids are the usual self-absorbed and notice nothing.

I am fast enough on my feet to slip through the door under the cover of moving black pant legs.

Alone at last: me, the meat, and the night. And whatever.

The alluring odor is slipping away into the dark beyond the glow of the lamp-lit windows. Yet the cover of darkness is my native element. I slip-slide along behind the butch butcher of the Sapphire Slipper. I do not see why the odd odd-jobber here takes a snack break alone in the dark, but I would not trust those bridesmaids to refrain from stripping away every last, small solitary pleasure a guy might want either.

I do not appreciate the sand that is getting in between my toes. Not everyone here is shod in cowhide.

A flashlight finally flares into action now that we are out of sight and hearing of the cathouse. I can spot where we are heading, the roast beef and I. It is a low outbuilding, probably where the brothel's vehicles are housed. I suspect most customers drive themselves, or are driven here by cabbies who get a cut of the deal. I overhear that a regular session can run four hundred clams. Or oysters.

But Miss Kitty and Ms. Shoofly must require vehicles to do the shopping and other homely chores a bordello requires. I am betting the laundry is done on-site. *Umm,* warm sheets fresh from the dryer and more than a dozen beds to make up every day. Miss Satin must be in catnap heaven when it comes to soft, warm places to snooze here.

Meanwhile, I am grinding the sheen off my nails and the skin off my pads trekking over raw desert cacti and choke weed.

At last Shoofly yanks open a barn-type door and vanishes beyond it.

I follow, secure in being behind the flashlight beam.

Well, this is a fine kettle of fishiness.

"Here," Shoofly's raspy voice whispers. "Some grub."

"Beef? Just beef? No bread?"

"Beer is better than bread."

"It is warm."

"I did not want to grab a cool one from the fridge and get all those girls thirsty all of a sudden. Will you quit your griping? You were supposed to have been long gone. At this rate, you'll be picnicking here for the police to find."

Another flashlight points into the darkness. I spot the silhouettes of a Jeep Tracker, a van, and Gangsters' own sterling-silver Rolls-Royce.

"Who ever parked the Rolls and disabled the engine did the same to the company cars."

"Your leggy black showgirl pal did the parking. I am guessing a Fonanta brother slipped out to disable the vehicles once they'd taken over the house party. Did you not hear anything?"

"I was lying low in the Roll's trunk, the way I got here. I just popped the emergency release and was free as a bird. I knew once the inside scene got going, nobody would remember the limo."

"Too bad. Someone did. They take something from the ignition?"

"Not the usual cop movie mischief. Something's got all these motors dead. I might get the Jeep going."

The man's voice stopped as I was forced to overhear beef-chomping sounds. Not mine. I then and there resolved that this unknown meat thief, and worse, should face immediate custody.

"What a mess," the guy complains.

"What, the meat too dry for you?" Shoofly is snickering. "A big-time player like you? Want some *pickle* with that?"

During the ensuing string of curses I realize who this is: Gherken, the newly hired substitute chauffeur who let Asiah "bribe" him into letting her drive the Crystal Phoenix gang straight into the waiting arms of mayhem and murder.

"If worse comes to worse," Shoofly is speculating, "you can always ride out of here on the horses you came in on."

"Unlike when it arrived, that limo is not leaving here without a complete going-over for tracking devices and clues. It may be impounded on the spot. No way am I hiding out in that trunk anymore. Besides, it stinks of Fontanas and cigars."

Aha! I smell a rat!

Maybe I even smell a murderer.

I have opportunity. I have gotten the meat of the matter, so to speak. Or smell. All I am missing is motive.

But first I have to figure out how to point my slow-tempo human associates in the right direction. That might be tough . . . until I recall a trick from one of my favorite bedtime stories.

No, it is not a mystery, although it was almost a murder case.

Piece of catnip.

Chapter 57

Peace of Paper

"It's our only clue," Matt said.

He and Temple were cloistered in the madam's office, if one could be "cloistered" in a brothel. Apparently, lots of people could.

Temple sat on the large, golden oak desk chair, feeling like a shrunken Alice on a massive seating piece meant for Miss Kitty's full sensuous bulk.

"Maybe it's a Social Security number," she suggested.

"These women are paid in cash. Madonnah had no personal identity except a fake-looking driver's license and this number. Ten digits. It's got to be a phone number."

"We could try it on the office safe first, with Miss Kitty present."

"There are no break spaces to indicate turning left or right."

"Doesn't mean Madonnah didn't have them memorized. She wouldn't want to transcribe a safe combination exactly."

"No, but why would she care about the safe in a place she only visited once in a blue moon?"

"If she was so anonymous, there might be something revealing in the safe. Miss Kitty strikes me as a benign madam, someone her girls could confide in."

"Like a mother superior, sure. Only she kept the records and kept the money."

"I want to call it. The cell phones work much better on this floor. If whoever answers sounds funny, I hang up."

"You could leave a trail," Matt warned her. "These days cell phones are as traceable as landline calls."

"Look, Aldo is right. We *have* to call in the authorities. Annoying them is on the brink of turning into antagonizing them."

"You call. A woman is always given more leeway."

"At what? Being mistaken for a ditz who can't dial the right number? That's sexist."

"Yes, but yes." He smiled ruefully. "You're the one with press and stage experience. You ought to be able to pose as a dirty rotten liar way better than I would. I'm still learning the ropes."

Temple took out her own cell phone. "I'll call, but on my nickel and my responsibility. I'm a known meddler. You're a prime suspect. It'll look better if I mess up things than if you do."

He nodded and watched as Temple punched in the ten digits. Her eyebrows lifted as her lips mimed a ring.

"Oh," she said. "Hello." A pause. "My number? Isn't this one enough?" Another pause, her eyes darting as she improvised. "It's just that I don't know what happened to me." Her eyes widened. "Yes, Nevada. The usual place. No, not my phone. I couldn't get to it. Wait! I'm . . . feeling faint. I think someone drugged me—"

Temple dropped the cell phone, putting her finger to her lips to ensure Matt's silence, then bent to hit the End button.

"What the heck—?" Matt asked.

"That was a very weird contact. The man on the other end expected confirmation. The call was instantly traced, Matt, or he knew who had that number. He knew right where I—she—was. I faked a problem and got the hell off." Temple took a deep breath. "What does this mean?"

"It means you could have been talking to her murderer. I'll tell Aldo to call the Nye County sheriff. It's always good to go through jurisdictional channels, and that way the bias of the Vegas police toward the Fontana family doesn't come into instant play."

"I'm not sure we're ready. Matt, this sheriff's department may not know the Fontanas, but it doesn't know us, either. You, me, Electra. We'd catch a break from Molina's people, because they know our . . . my . . . penchant for crime and that we're harmless."

"Not this time," Matt said. "This time not a one of us looks harmless. We look like scofflaws with something to hide. The sooner we face that particular music, the sooner we get a chance to evaluate just how screwed we are."

Temple fidgeted on the shiny, varnished oak chair seat. "The sheriff's department could be worse than Molina and her minions. I've got another idea for backup we might need. Let me see your cell phone."

"You didn't want it used for calling out."

"I'm not using it to call out. I'll use my Miss Marple snoop sister personal cell for that. I just want to cop a number from your address book."

"Address book? It's more an address mini-list."

"*Ooh!* I'm number one. How long has that been going on?"

Matt's face flushed. "You're the one who said I had to have a cell phone. So—"

"And Electra. Ambrosia . . . ?"

"My boss at the radio station, remember? Her on-air name."

"And some more radio station names. A couple Chicago numbers, your mother and—?"

"None of your business."

She lifted her eyebrows again, but said nothing. Then, "Molina. Hey, all we have to do is dial direct."

"You have her on your instant dial too."

"Guilty."

"Janice Flanders," she read off without expression.

"Never know when I could use a good police sketch artist," he said.

But they both knew he'd briefly dated Janice when Temple was unavailable.

She nodded. Hit a few more buttons, then dialed.

Matt frowned, trying to remember who else was in his scanty cell phone address book. His agent, Tony Valentine, of course. Danny Dove, Temple's choreographer friend who'd become an odd combination of counselee-mentor for him lately. Who the devil else?

The phone was ringing, and from the way Temple slightly raised her voice, he knew it was a long-distance call.

"Temple Barr calling on behalf of our mutual friend, Matt Devine," she said confidently. "Sorry to bother you, but Matt's in a spot of trouble in a brothel in the Nevada boonies and—" She laughed, almost flirtatiously. "I thought that would get your attention. So help me God and Judge Roy Bean. Right. Heart of the West. I, we, need to know what this phone number means." She repeated the digits. Then listened. And listened. And listened some more.

"No shinola! That would explain what happened when I called it. Yes, I did. Just now. I'm sorry! There was no other way to learn what we're dealing with on that end. On this end? Murder. Matt tried to give the victim CPR and was discovered in a compromising position with the body. Female, right. That too. Are you online? Yes, about thirty. Hard to tell. Really made-up."

Temple glanced at Matt. "Well, it happened more than twelve hours ago. It's a touchy situation. We were hoping to— Yes, I know that's loony. Yes, I know you know me. Molina? Over my dead body. We're sixty miles from Vegas anyway and in a different county. Really. Yes, I have seen some of *Smoky and the Bandit*, but only accidentally while using the remote control. County sheriffs are really that obsessive? Okay, okay, I'll have Van von Rhine call the LVMPD. You bet I don't want to be the whistle-blower here! This call was bad enough.

"Yes, *all* the Fontana brothers and their significant others, as a matter of fact. It was a bachelor party. Aldo. Getting married, yes. The girlfriends crashed the party. My aunt from New York. She's not that old! You'll call and cancel? That would be great. I kinda hung up by pretending to pass out."

Temple cringed. "I know it was a stupid stunt. Helicopters? Well, we do have more people here now than would fit in even the most elastic stretch limo. That much an hour for gas? Man, fuel prices are outrageous. There oughta be a law." Temple cringed again. "Yes, I know I've broken several. Thank you for calling that helicopter thing off. It might have stampeded the lizards."

Temple flipped her phone shut and grinned at Matt. "I've irritated some real heavy hitters in law enforcement, but I've now got a motive. A damn good motive. Next stop is Miss Kitty's safe."

Chapter 58

Not So Safe

"Sorry, Red. I don't open my safe until the police get here."

Miss Kitty folded her ample arms over her truly commanding chest.

She filled the golden oak desk chair now, and Temple and Matt sat on the maple side chairs drawn up to it.

"We need to present the police with a fait accompli solution," Temple said. "There are folks who have places to be tonight and I imagine you have rooms booked too."

Miss Kitty stirred on her executive throne. "True. But I don't break a confidence. My business reputation depends on it."

"Even when the other party is dead?" Matt asked.

The madam heaved out a frustrated breath.

"We know you recognized Madonnah when you first saw the dead woman," Temple said. "It would have simplified everything if you'd just said so. I wasted hours trying to find out who she was."

"I don't break a confidence. In life, or in death. Even I didn't recognize her at first, and I knew the girls' hadn't seen her latest 'look,' so they wouldn't say anything. She really was a woman of a thousand faces. Had to be, poor thing."

"Look," Matt said. "I'm the prime suspect here, just because I tried to breathe some life back into Madonnah. It's obvious she had something to hide." Matt glanced at Temple. "She knows what it is, but she hasn't told even me yet. And we're engaged to be married. Whatever this information in your safe is, it could help find Madonnah's killer."

Miss Kitty's barely there eyebrows lifted. "Engaged to be married? Would you hold your bachelor party here too?" Apparently the group take was hefty.

Matt glanced at Temple again. "Uh . . . not really."

Temple shrugged and appealed to Miss Kitty. "He cannot tell a lie. That's why the police would make garlic mashed potatoes of him."

"Where did you find such a rare specimen of the gender?" Miss Kitty asked.

"Formerly in the priesthood."

"Oh. Really?" Miss Kitty gave Matt an accessing glance that only a madam could. "What a waste."

"Not now," Temple said. "But we can't let the poor lamb be led to the slaughter for doing a good deed."

"I suppose not." Miss Kitty's sigh again inflated her décolletage. Then she went to the closet door and fiddled inside until there was a metallic clank. The standing safe door yawned open while she retrieved a small metal box.

She brought it to the desktop, then reached to pull a key to its lock from between her bosoms.

"This is Madonnah's life. It's all in here. I was her keeper, I guess you could say."

"Why?" Temple asked.

"Everybody has to trust somebody," Miss Kitty said gruffly.

"The police won't want us handling the contents," Matt said. "Why don't you just tell us what it is. Temple already suspects."

"Knows," Temple told Miss Kitty gently. "I called the phone number Matt found in her room."

Miss Kitty's plump hand rested on the unlocked but unopened box. "It's not much. Her real driver's license and Social Security number. Birth and high school graduation certificates. A license tag for her dog, Clancy." Miss Kitty's lips curled with bitterness. "He died protecting her, little pound mutt. He was the only person who cared about her."

Silence held. Matt segued into his radio voice: soft, even, inviting confidences. "It was that bad?"

"Worse." Another deep sigh. "A lot of these girls are just party animals. A lot of them were introduced to sex, drugs, and rock 'n' roll too soon, or too roughly. But victims? Not the way they tell it. They're having fun being sex queens, making two hundred bucks an hour, traveling around, building up nest eggs until they retire at forty.

"A couple are 'ordinary' wives and mothers who take an annual 'vacation.' Me, I don't judge. I took my own path to here and now. I know the girls here are clean and doing what they do from free will, as much as any of us have it. Right, Father?"

Matt look disconcerted. "I'm not clergy anymore."

"This is so not your scene, though, right?"

"Right. I don't judge either."

"Did you, when you found her, did you—?"

"She was still warm. I tired to revive her. Then, yes, I said the prayers for the dying."

Miss Kitty's lavender-blue-white head nodded. "My job is simple: keep order, keep the money, pay the girls, make it fun for the client. With Nonah, I let it get personal. I tried to keep her safe. That's not in my job description. That's not my business. But I tried."

Temple leaned forward on the hard chair. She wondered why the office furniture was so ungiving, when everything else in the place, except the Victorian sofa, was overupholstered, cushy.

"That's why she got to preview the night's clientele by the surveillance system," Temple said. "Why she made a shtick out of using the name Madonnah and changing her hair and makeup and looks so often. Why she locked up the remnants of her real life in your safe."

Miss Kitty nodded. "Somebody had to know. Somebody had to keep her secret, otherwise, the loneliness would have destroyed her."

Matt was growing more puzzled by the minute. "Now that the secret's out and she's dead, let me in on it. I don't get it. I get that she led a tragic life, and that you were her only friend," he told Miss Kitty. "But I still don't see how that got her killed."

This time Temple sighed. "She was in the Witness Protection Program, Matt. She had to ditch her real identity and life. Choosing to be a traveling prostitute was clever. She could tart herself up until unrecognizable, change her location frequently, do anything but have friends, be truly intimate with anyone. Why'd she pick this life?"

Miss Kitty was answering all questions now. "She didn't want any connections with anyone. No long-term coworkers, no hope of friendship or romance that would have to be broken off anyway. She'd had a rough time as a kid and ended up as the mistress of a drug dealer. She witnessed a triple murder, and testified. There's a chain of dealers all over this country, and it would enhance their reps if she was caught and punished. She said she liked it here. She was in control. The men were grateful. Pets aren't allowed. Abuse isn't allowed."

"Someone found her," Matt said.

Miss Kitty nodded. "Someone found her and managed to get

in and kill her. You bachelor party guys, and gals, were just innocent bystanders."

"Or cover," Temple said, catching Matt's eye.

"Funny," he said. "I don't feel very innocent, or very much like a bystander anymore, or like I'd settle now for being 'cover' for anybody."

Chapter 59

Mincemeat

Okay.

I got a party of one picnicking on smuggled-in rare roast beef in the outbuilding.

Inside the Sapphire Slipper, it is not a picnic, as several of my favorite humans and a whole passel of other Homo sapiens are twitching to the ends of their opposable thumbs about what the oncoming authorities will make of them when the murder at the Sapphire Slipper is everybody's business, and especially the cops'.

I need to get Mr. Rare Roast Beef wrapped up in a nice ex-portable package before the county sheriff, the real-life Vegas CSI techs, and the law personnel who don't know any of us from a Geico caveman (or those who *do* know my nearest and dearest all too well) get here to really mess up the crime scene.

All this guy out here needs to do when reinforcements arrive

is retreat to the cover of the tumbling tumbleweed that surrounds this bit of salacious enterprise in the desert and he will
be home Scottsdale-free. Heck, he may shortly *be* in Scottsdale
if I do not stop him.

I could persuade my human cohorts to lean on the ambiguous Ms. Phyllis Shoofly and make he or she confess to aiding
and abetting a murderer. But how?

I could betray the guy's presence without allowing him to run.
But how?

Everybody has focused on the brothel, on keeping the suspects in the brothel along with the body and crime scene.

Nobody has considered that the crime had an inside and
outside man.

Maybe that is because of the intimate setting of the murder
on a mass scale. Maybe that is because there are so many
likely suspects inside, no one has seen the bigger picture. They
cannot all be detecting geniuses like me.

Chapter 60

Monkey Business

"Sorry to report this just now," Morrie said, eyeing Molina for more than physical stress. He'd charged into her office as soon as she'd returned from Rafi's. She hadn't even had time to process her talk with her ex.

"I bet. What is it?" She sat gingerly on her desk edge.

"It's out of our jurisdiction, is what it is." The detective sat her usual mug of coffee on the oddly empty desktop. "But the, er, visiting personnel are persons of interest."

"Jurisdiction?"

"Nye County. Near Beatty."

"That isn't even on the same planet as Vegas, really. Chicken ranch land."

"Right. That's the point."

"The county sheriff can handle it. That's what they're for."

"Murder."

"*Hmm.* Intriguing. But if some wayward Vegas boys got themselves into trouble way out in Nye County, it's none of our affair. Literally. Why are they bothering us with this at all?"

"Most of the persons of interest in the murder are well-known Vegas habitués."

"Lots of the horny gamblers who fly in here motor out to a chicken ranch. What's new about that?"

"These aren't tourists. They're residents."

"Residents? What residents?"

"They would be the Fontana boys."

"Fontana! What were those city slickers doing out in the boonies?"

"Uh, bachelor party. Hijacked bachelor party, they claim."

"One of the litter was murdered, hopefully?"

"Now, Carmen, don't wish for something you wouldn't like to live with. You know they add a lot of ambience to the town."

"Ambience that Vegas tried to dump in the nineties. Who was getting married, anyway?"

"The state police didn't fax wedding party assignments." Morrie kept his eyes on the sheet. "Matt Devine is there, though, and Macho Mario Fontana."

"Matt? In with that crowd?"

"It *was* a bachelor party."

"He's getting married?"

"I don't know about that. He may be, given his new closeness to Temple Barr, but I'd guess this bachelor is known to us."

"Known to us? Do not play games with me, Morrie. I'm a little on edge right now, as you well know."

"I thought you'd remember."

"Remember? Why shouldn't I remember? I was stabbed, not robbed of brain cells. Fontanas. Bachelor party. I missed attending because of eighty-six fresh stitches, not that I would have gone anyway. Oh, that's right!" She slapped her forehead. "My own unauthorized adventures made me temporarily forget that saccharine public announcement you reported on at the Crystal Phoenix six weeks ago. Aldo Fontana is engaged to Temple Barr's aunt. Kathy . . . Harrleson, isn't it?"

"Kit Carlson," Morrie corrected in a discreet murmur.

"That's it. The Pony Express rider once removed." Molina frowned. "Aldo must be several years her junior. Must be the chlorine in the water those Minnesotans drink. My question remains. What does this have to do with Matt Devine?"

"Apparently he's the number one suspect. Found the body."

"And the body is—?"

"Someone called Madonnah. One of the girls at the Sapphire Slipper. Tried CPR on her, so Devine's DNA—"

"That's what happens when idiot ex-priests visit brothels with the Fontana brothers. This sounds more like a Marx Brothers movie, if it weren't for the dead body. I suppose your favorite redhead is accounted for and present too?"

"Now she is. Seems a female rescue party motored up after the murder. So we've also got, on the premises, Nicky Fontana and Van von Rhine, the eight Fontana girlfriends who hijacked the bachelor party, Macho Mario himself, Electra Lark, the bride-to-be aunt, a dozen or so bordello girls, and assorted staff. And, uh, three extra black cats."

"You can have 'extra' black cats on a crime scene?"

"One of the black cats is a resident. The other three are visiting from Vegas."

"And we know this how?"

"They've been identified as Temple Barr's cat, Midnight Louie, and the Crystal Phoenix mascot, Midnight Louise, plus an unnamed old alley cat, also black. The resident cat is called Baby Blue."

"I suppose their paws are all over the crime scene too."

"It's possible. That's why our crime scene technicians need to go over the place before the body and any suspects are removed."

Molina just shook her head. "You know I don't need another Temple Barr Flying Circus of Crime and Cats just now, Morrie."

"Yes, ma'am."

"Stop addressing me like a military woman. You've seen my midriff bare. You can call me Carmen."

He straightened uneasily. No one on the force was allowed to use her first name. "You want me out there wrangling this, don't you? Is that the reward I get—?"

She leaned close, over her desktop, eyes like indigo ice.

"That's the reward you get for being the bearer of this bloody awful news. Don't worry. I'll have to go too. God, jolting over those desert roads! How does Barr know just when to turn up bodies to inconvenience me the most?"

"Talent?" he asked.

"That was a rhetorical question, Alch. Saddle up the Crown Vic. I'll call Grizzly Bahr. I'm sure he'll want to eyeball this one himself."

"Because of the complication of postmortem CPR administered by one of the suspects?"

"Because of all the seminaked ladies on the premises." Molina managed a grin. "He does like to get out of the autopsy room sometimes to view some live bodies instead of dead ones. Especially if they're comely.

"Come to think of it, this crazy quilt of a case might get my mind off grimmer matters."

"What's scratching your ass today is more than your stitches," Alch said.

She nodded, the phone already auto-dialing the coroner's office. "I just saw the father of my child. Tried to set up a civil 'arrangement.'"

"Good for you—"

She waved him silent. "Dr. Bahr. Got a case that might need your personal touch." She listened as he spoke. "One corpse, female." Another pause. "I know that's nothing new in Vegas, but this one isn't in Vegas. It's out at the Sapphire Slipper. Yes, that place is still out there, and going great guns, apparently. Our involvement? The joint is crammed with Vegas persons of interest, including all of the male members of the Fontana family. Yes, mentioning 'male members' is ironic under the circumstances. Oh, you've been pining for some fieldwork, have you? Alch and I will drive over and your van can follow us out there."

Alch was astounded. "Grizzly Bahr is leaving his den of death and disintegration?"

"A dozen or so live shady ladies will motivate and move even the most morgue-entrenched coroner."

"Does he know you nicknamed him 'Grizzly'?"

"I doubt it, Alch, and you aren't going to tell him. I'll inform the captain. He will just love this! And me deserting my newly neat desk I've maintained for more than a month after you cleaned it up during my week off. You get the CV from the garage. Matt Devine!" She snorted. "In a hooker hotel. This I gotta see with my own eyes."

"And supervise?"

"That'll be the best part."

She was feeling a lot better.

Chapter 61

Louie Puts Up a Red Flag

Can you believe that I, Midnight Louie, must come up with a scheme to draw attention to myself?

Me, who is usually bigger than life and as hard to disguise as the MGM lion?

Having assistants at hand during this case has permitted me to hang back above the battle and remain out of sight while I deploy my operatives. It has permitted my three female operatives to assume at various times the identity of Satin, the house cat, and be taken for granted and totally ignored while collecting information like a trio of furry, black, mobile, eavesdropping "bugs."

Now I need to step up to the plate my own self and lead the many befuddled humans in the house to the lurking perp at the perimeter. I return to the back screen door of the kitchen and proceed to sharpen my shivs on the mesh, making a nerve-wracking rending sound.

But the kitchen radio is playing and the assembled bridesmaids are doing their nails in the courtesans' bizarre and glittery colors.

I yowl.

Finally, one yawns and shivers. "Listen to the coyotes."

"It sounds like it is right on top of us," another comments.

They never even glance toward the back door, not even Ms. Shoofly who is not only a guilty party, but presiding over a huge, noisy fry pan of sizzling bacon and scrambled eggs at the stovetop.

Not one of my ninja trio is in the kitchen at the moment.

I want to scream like a catamount. This case is next to closed, and I am shut out and ignored.

In desperation, I amble outside to prowl the bordello's perimeter, finding a way up to the first-story roof via the courtesans' bedroom annex. I am forced to blunt my shivs on stucco before I manage to scramble onto the roof's asphalt shingles.

Panting, I approach the dormers for the guest bedrooms. All are draped, or shaded, or blacked out. I finally am able to claw a ripped screen open. The broken edges currycomb my sides as I eel through, cutting a pad on a loose nail.

By now I am panting, bleeding, and furious.

I must head-butt a heavy Roman shade aside until it slips its bottom moorings. I plummet to the wooden floor inside, not landing on my abused feet. I do not know which is worse: more foot trauma or knocking my teeth on some thick circle of leather embedded with spikes.

Eek! My own black facial leather has touched a recreational dog collar! Spitting out the awful taste, I box my way out of the room in the darkness into the hall.

Luckily, it is lined with night-lights even during the daytime, a touch I am sure the Sapphire Slipper clientele much appreciate both coming and going.

I find my way into another room, this one decorated more like a bedchamber than a doggy discipline school. I jump back when I glimpse a black cat in the mirror.

Oops. That is me, but my hair is a mess. I look almost as ragged as Ma Barker.

Now. I gaze around as my eyes adapt to the dim light.

I need a signal. Something like a white flag of surrender. Something that will draw every human eye to my form and will sufficiently intrigue someone in this mob of guys and gals and my usual associates to follow me to where the criminal is hiding out.

It certainly will *not* be a canine collar!

Something bright catches my eye. It is light, small, but memorable.

Just the thing!

Chapter 62

Leading Questions

It was now high noon and Temple was getting butterflies in her stomach.

Van von Rhine called the LVMPD to report the situation, which meant Molina would soon know about her latest and most bizarre crime scene involvement yet. Aldo and Nicky comforted her by saying that Nye County would have had to call in the Vegas CSI unit anyway. Temple's investigative calls on Madonnah's hidden number must have stirred some powerful forces into action. The idea of helicopters, plural, had really upset her.

Van worked under her maiden name, so at least the volatile surnames of Fontana and Barr need not come up right off the bat. And it would look better for all concerned if they called the authorities before the distant Big Guys showed up.

Matt was standing close behind Van to back up her story,

and intervene if Lieutenant Molina got involved and went ballistic. The homicide detective had always liked *him*.

All of it made perfect sense, but Temple couldn't bear staying with the barroom crowd and listening to Van's end of the conversation. They now knew the "why" but not the "who," which made this a pretty half-baked effort on her part.

She'd been imported to the Sapphire Slipper to solve the murder, and without a murderer identified, everyone, including her nearest and dearest, was still a prime suspect. Plus, the first scheduled clients were driving out of Vegas even now to add to the Sapphire Slipper's already overcrowded population.

Temple was a proven failure.

She ambled through the parlor and the dozing courtesans into the deserted foyer to brood. No one noticed or missed her. Even with the hectic events of the past few hours and all the new faces she'd met, nagging worries about Max danced in and out of her mind.

You can't worry about the whole world, she told herself.

She was so exhausted she'd start hallucinating soon.

And then something came floating down the stairs from the deserted second floor. The supposedly deserted second floor.

Her mind refused to believe her eyes.

A disembodied crimson thong trimmed in marabou feathers floated down toward her. Madonnah's ghost was up and walking? Or crawling, rather. Even creepier!

The apparition was already breezing past her to the front door when she finally made out the black feline form whose neck it adorned. Finally! After all these hours out here, she had been granted a glimpse of her own elusive cat!

It had to be Louie. His broad-cheeked tomcat face squeezed out a snarl as his paw scratched a gash into the door's dark wood.

Temple started laughing, hysterically. Louie in boudoir wear? A flaming red thong? Louie a panty sniffer? A pantywaist? A red-hot thong-head?

She almost doubled over from laughing, but figured that the small resident cat probably had a petite box that no one had remembered to change lately, and Louie might desperately need a potty break.

She went to the door, and opened it.

Into the shockingly bright daylight Louie bounded. The bordello was like a casino in that all sense of "outside" disappeared when one was inside. Time stopped. Night was eternal.

Louie had just reminded her that a bright, sunlit world surrounded them. The light also showed how alarmingly tight the wisp of nylon was around his neck.

"Wait! Louie! That thing could choke you if it caught on something."

He stopped, as if understanding her. Temple ran to catch him. He darted off, around the building's corner.

Darn! Trust a cat to act independent just when he most needed a little human help. Temple stomped over the hard, shifting sandy ground through the desert scrub.

The building's exterior looked rough and tawdry in daylight. The courtesans' quarters off the main building's kitchen was just a string of linked single-wide trailers.

Louie led her around them into higher brush and cactus that raked her bare calves. Temple stopped, blinking in the hot sunlight.

"Louie, you dork! I am *not* chasing you over the equivalent of the Ethel M Chocolate Factory cactus garden. I refuse to follow you another step."

Silence. Then a pathetic yowl from out of sight.

Temple glanced back at the Sapphire Slipper. The front entrance was almost out of sight. She sighed and trudged forward again, surprised when a rough-sided wooden structure came into view.

She edged closer, hearing something faint and tinny.

A radio?

Someone was out here? A caretaker? No one had mentioned . . .

The sound cut off, as if it had been a mistake.

A gash of bright red near the worn wooden barn door ajar on its shaky hinges made her tiptoe over the sand.

Louie had found something out here he was returning to. Maybe food. She saw shreds of what looked like cooked meat on the sand near the door. Or, he had found *someone*.

Chapter 63

Radio Silence

The last thing I expected to hear from the barn was a blast from the past.

But there it was, for a few unguarded seconds, some soul anthem, "R-E-S-P-E-C-T."

I realize at once what has happened, especially since the radio went dead again, fast. Our resident killer has gotten one of the three disabled vehicles going, and the radio had been left on when it was stopped.

The reviving vehicle could be the brothel Jeep Tracker, or its van, or it could be the Gangsters' Vanillamobile. That station sounded like something the long-stemmed Asiah would listen to once the limo's dividing window was up and no sound would flow through to the main body of the stretch Rolls.

Whatever the vehicle and whoever the driver who had tuned into that station, now an escape vehicle is coming to life, and my

Miss Temple and I are caught like deer in the headlights. Well, headlights are not very strong in daylight, but the fact is something inside the barn is primed to start moving again soon and we must get our rears in gear too.

I wheel around and dash toward my Miss Temple at a gallop, finding she is only twenty feet behind me, which is good trotting for a short-legged breed like her, but not good enough for effecting a fast, quiet, and unseen retreat.

I hear the barn-door hinges squeal behind me, and watch Miss Temple's face register dismay in front of me.

Talk about caught between a car and an accident waiting to happen!

I expect Miss Temple's face to register some joy or relief at my presence on the scene, but she is busy freezing in midturn and looking behind me and putting her palms up in the air to test the desert breeze.

I do a one-eighty and would put up my dukes too, if I didn't need them to stand on at the moment.

The villainous Gherken is poised with the shadow of the barn behind him, wearing a sinister five-o'clock shadow and a lean and hungry look that would do a wolf proud. A very real Uzi is pointed at my Miss Temple. And he does not even need fishnet hose to wield it with scary style and confidence.

"Just what I needed," he says. "My ticket out of here."

The nasty black metal nose of the Uzi beckons us into the barn.

We go.

I do not know if the villainous Gherken notices me, or cares, but as soon as I am back in the shadows, I dive into the barn's deeper darkness, trying to work the stupid lingerie off my neck. All it will do now is attract the wrong kind of attention.

"You picked the perfect time for a stroll," he tells my roommate. "Good for me, bad for you."

I can see him check his watch.

"You are coming with me as a shield. The johns will be wheeling in any minute now, but I intend to be on the highway by then."

He looks around and spots the ditched thong.

I hunker down behind the Tracker in shame and fury as he uses my former neckerchief to tie Miss Temple's hands behind her.

"You will ride shotgun with me," Gherken says, dragging her into the front passenger seat of the Rolls. "We are leaving in style. If you're good and I can spare the time, I will drop you off somewhere in Death Valley. Even alive maybe, baby."

He gives out the evil laugh beloved of villains everywhere. My Miss Temple tries to get her feet out the door before it shuts, but he kicks her ankles back in, making her bite her lips in protest.

She buys me just the time I need to slink onto the black floor carpet and squeeze my capacious guts through a slit the size of Satin's tail into the limo's main body. Luckily, the Brits were still making those high-end snooty cars as roomy as Checker cabs back when this vintage beauty was created.

Okay, two of us are taken hostage now.

Much better.

I notice that the villainous Gherken has left the dark window behind the driver's seat up.

Excellent. I could use a little traveling music.

Luckily, I saw Fontana Inc. and their expert fingers and enviable opposable thumbs manipulate the limo's many functions from the long thin control console set into the padded leather ceiling. Of course, this useful unit was not designed for a guy of my height, one foot at the shoulder.

It will take multiple bounds up and a delicate touch on the controls, but there is only one simple function I crave.

The engine starts with that leopard purr of a really big, fine vintage motor.

The walls of the Sapphire Slipper should be shaking and baking now.

So this villainous dim-bulb, Gherken, thinks that the sound of one of their legendary limos starting up will not draw a sharp Fontana ear, much less ten of them?

I add my purr to the Rolls's throaty roar.

Jump. My shivs have split ends, but I punch a spot I noticed before. *Manx!* There are more tiny controls on human communication devices lately than on a Victorian high-button shoe! If I ever have to rely on text messaging, I am a dead dog.

It takes only the pointed end of one shiv to manipulate this console. Too bad I was never much of a game boy, although I know my way around a television remote.

Jump.

Punch.

Miss.

Jump. Punch. Very near miss.

The limo is inching onto the rough desert pathway, trying to sneak past the bordello.

I have lift-down!

I hear a stir at the Sapphire Slipper's port cochere as the Rolls glides by on a muffled growl.

I have three inches (not to get personal) and am going for four.

Jump. Punch.

This is a jerky process, but then we have a jerky driver.

Jump. Punch.

I let out an ear-piercing battle cry unmistakable to my kind. It is so ear-piercing I could open a shopping mall kiosk with it.

Jump. Punch. Jump. Punch. Seven inches. *Jump. Punch. Jump. Punch.* Nine inches. We are getting into X-rated territory now . . . *Jump. Punch.*

And Miss Midnight Louise lofts through the lowering side window into the moving limo.

Jump. Punch. Jump. Punch. The Rolls is picking up speed. Gherken knows he has been seen. Satin, panting a bit, tumbles inside beside me.

Jump. Punch.

I hear an exterior piercing scream and spot eight shivs clinging to the three inches of window still up. A mighty leap for mankind and also for Ma Barker.

Miss Midnight Louise plants her forepaws on the leather door upholstery, sinks in her shivs, and grabs her granny (maybe; I do not lose my wits even in a life-and-death crisis), by the nape of the neck and throws her into the limo with us.

"I must lower the chauffeur's window next," I advise my troops.

Out the open window, I spot Fontana brothers, bearing Berettas, running to pursue us. The Rolls is accelerating to full speed.

Jump. Punch. Jump. Punch. Jump. Punch.

I am getting the rhythm. The dark glass behind the driver goes down like the evening sun, fast at the end.

The villainous Gherken's neck is pale and bare and great meat for the three midnight-black, blood-lusting brides of Dracula I have summoned.

Through the clear windshield, I see a white car with a red blinking light on the roof careening toward us, followed by two white vans swerving alternately on two wheels, with a big hairy man behind the wheel of the lead van, grinning like a Hell's Angel.

The Rolls is gathering real speed. It is the Power Ranger of the Gangsters' fleet. Reinforcements will be too late once it hits the highway, although a helicopter can pursue it. But a high-speed chase in such a cumbersome vehicle is bound to hurt someone.

I order the attack. "You go, girls!"

Before you know it, Gherken is wearing a fang and claw

necklace and screaming his head off, his hands also off the steering wheel, just as the *zing* of Beretta bullets takes out all four tires on the Rolls.

We Rolls to a lamentedly lumpy stop.

I leap into the front passenger seat, right into Miss Temple's lap, and plant a big, wet juicy one on her sadly furless little cheek.

"Louie, *ow,* that scratches! And, watch it, your claws are sharper than broken glass. Louie, are you all right?"

Now I am.

Chapter 64

Peace in the Valley

"Asylum?" he asked.

"Alyssum," her voice answered, laughing. "Sweet alyssum. It's a flower."

He was lying on the mountainside, every sinew and joint aching. Somewhere half a mile above was the civilized comfort of the clinic. He was mired like the Cowardly Lion in a field of flowers, his legs weighted by plaster casts.

If he hadn't been a mountain climber before, he damn sure was now. His chest heaved for air, and his shoulders and arms shook from using the metal crutches as pitons to dig into the tough sod and pull his plaster-weighted legs behind him.

She wafted the small blossom under his nose again. "I need to get to one of these high mountain farmsteads. Ask for food, beer, a saw."

"Not water?"

"Beer is water here. I need a road." She sat up to eye a snake of paved darkness twisting up the Alps, and sighed. "I need a reason to say I'm stranded. I'll probably have to trek back a gallon of unneeded petrol."

She stood, shaking out her chic suit. She looked like someone stranded. "I'll get you out of those casts. You think you can put weight on your legs again?"

"I'll have to."

"You Americans. Always what must be done. Never what is pleasant to be done."

He thought on that parting remark long after the hip-high grasses and knee-high flowers had swallowed her pink-suited figure.

Here, he was truly helpless, his body anchored by the means of its recovery. Yet his mind soared like the distant clouds. He rubbed his left inner elbow. He still smelled the acrid rubbing alcohol scent, felt the *ting* of the hypodermic needle tip tasting his vein, as a serpent smells, with the bitter end of its toxic tongue.

Death rode on that thin, hollow steel reed; he knew it. His death.

This woman had interrupted that, and by duplicitous means had wafted him away from the clinic, from his would-be killer and also from the only man he trusted.

That made her the only woman he trusted.

That made trust a necessity rather than an option.

He knew this Max person he was didn't like necessity as a partner.

He inhaled the heady scent of mountain wildflowers. Their only escape route had been on foot. For now, he was helpless and, rid of the leg casts, might be more helpless still. Yet his mind was working, weighing. His mind wouldn't let him sink into complacency.

Complacency. "The refuge of the inferior mind."

That motto rang true, like history. He'd been warned against complacency. Over and over again.

Twilight was falling on the valley below before she returned.

"Did you think I wasn't coming back?" she asked.

"I didn't think. That's the advantage of being an invalid."

"I deliberately stopped us by this haymow. It'll be as cozy as an inn. But, first—"

She knelt in the long grass, the action releasing the scent of crushed wildflowers as he lay back on his elbows.

"They had a saw."

He viewed the sturdy, ragged edge of a small, hand-size hacksaw and winced.

"I've only time to do one cast before the light fades. You were due to have them removed two days from now anyway. Think you can bear an early exodus?"

Her language was quaint, laughable. *Exodus.* "Saw away. If you hit skin, you'll know."

Still, he steeled himself, feeling the hard-edged plaster rocking back and forth as she sawed. She knew where the seam lay, and attacked the cast on his right leg top and bottom, then pulled, then sawed . . . finally the cast opened like an almond shell. Two halves, clean. The setting sun made the revealed white skin of a man's leg glow in its angled rays. The dying light revealed a horrifying degree of muscle waste in a mere six weeks.

"Ye gods," he murmured, "it's so pink and puckered and ghastly."

There was a silence.

"My leg," he said firmly.

Chapter 65

Come Into My Parlor

The siren screams of police and emergency vehicles racing to the Sapphire Slipper continued into early afternoon.

A number of Vegas cabs and private SUVs that were driving up hastily turned around. Inside the Sapphire Slipper, the resident courtesans had a new client to lavish exclusive attention on.

"That was the bravest thing I ever saw," Babette said, stroking Midnight Louie's fevered brow.

At least his tongue was very warm anyway.

"He's so cute!" purred Kiki, Lili, and Niki, tickling his tummy.

"Look at these nails!" Angela and Heather intoned together. "Shredded. And his pads are *bleeding*."

They looked with accusing fury at Lieutenant C. R. Molina, Detective Alch, and Coroner Grizzly Bahr.

"I will tend him immediately, my dears." Coroner Bahr

hovered over Louie's lush nurses. "Some styptics and gauze bandages should set the little guy right. And then I'll see to you ladies."

"What about the D.B.?" Molina asked.

"In a minute. This, uh, Good Samaritan needs tending."

Temple shook her head at Louie's moment in the spotlight. She was sitting on a blue sofa with Matt down on one knee, attending her kicked ankle.

"It's swelling already, and bruised," he decided. "You'll need to elevate that."

"Oh, for God's sake," Molina said. "You've already proposed, from what I hear. You may pick up the bride-to-be and put her down on the long sofa in the bar area. There's an interrogation going on there that you may be useful for. Coroner, I really think you have more pressing matters upstairs. I sent the crime scene crew up first. Leave the alley cat for the vet."

Soon all have dispersed but the Sapphire Slipper nursing unit. Louie deserted his cooing chorus of ladies, squirming until they were forced to let him down to limp after the exodus to the bar.

Matt had been focused on Temple from the moment the limo stopped. He'd taken her out of the front seat, spotted her scraped ankle at once, and picked her up, so this was her second stint of bridal carting.

No one noticed them much, though, Temple saw. The barroom was jammed.

Fontana brothers were lined up on and between the barstools. Their girlfriends were scattered at the round tables. Molina had joined two serious, suited men at a table with four semiautomatic pistols on it.

"I take it," she was saying, "that these are the firearms that shot out the tires."

One man nodded. "You'll want to confirm that, for the record."

The other man looked up and Matt turned to confront him, shocked. "Frank." He turned back to Temple. "You knew."

She nodded as the man walked over. He was tall and lean with scissor-sharp features and a receding hairline.

"Matt. I do find you in the most interesting places these days."

Temple smothered a smile. Frank Bucek was also an ex-priest. He'd been Matt's teacher in the seminary, but was now an FBI agent. The other agent was getting the girlfriends' names and addresses, so they made a confidential trio conferring on the sidelines.

"Okay," Matt said softly, still obviously shocked. "So you were the one Temple called from my cell phone address list. How'd you get here so fast?"

"I was in L.A. And your . . . fiancée, is it, from the good lieutenant's comments in the foyer? . . . had a bout of curiosity that set a huge fuss in motion." Bucek grinned. "Congratulations, kids. Am I invited to the wedding?"

"When we decide on a place and a time," Matt said. "But—"

"I'll buy you both a celebratory drink in town later, and give you some big explanations in private. Right now, we have a last piece of the puzzle I need to pry out of these women before we leave the crime scene to the able lieutenant."

Temple was about to scream if she heard Bucek put one more praising adjective in front of Molina's title, but then she was a bit wrought up from seeing the limo driver's eyes nearly scratched out by a posse of infuriated domestic cats, led on by the awesome cries and growls of her own cuddly bed partner.

"My midnight radio show—" Matt began, his brow furrowing.

Bucek leaned close. "Carmen is not in a good mood, for many reasons I can guess and some I can't, but I did get her to promise you'd flee the mass interrogation in time to make your live radio commitment." He glanced at Temple with some amusement. "You she has plans for. But it's a small price to pay for Matt getting sprung from a brothel ASAP."

Temple just shrugged. "How can I help you, Agent Bucek?"

"Tell me which one of these lovely ladies was mad enough at a Fontana boyfriend to help set up a mob hit."

Temple caught her breath. Putting Madonnah's murder in those terms took the whole last eighteen-hours' chaos from the comedy of errors it felt like to the tragedy it was.

Sitting on a leather sofa with her legs up and her foot on Matt's thigh like a shoeless Cinderella, now that he'd sat down again, made her look about as effective as a poetic Victorian invalid on a fainting couch. Elizabeth Barrett Browning, say. Temple had to twist her neck to eye the eight women she'd come to recognize and know.

She'd suspected one of them had been involved with more than engineering a surprise prank. The FBI man was relying on her crime-solving instincts to tell him who.

Wow. This was the Big Finale and she already looked like a limping fool who'd walked into a trap and become a hostage.

Actually, Louie had done the walking and she had followed, but he was being coddled by courtesans and she was merely being ankle-massaged by Matt . . . which was enough to turn her knees to hot melted butter. As well as her brain.

"Agent Bucek, I haven't a clue to who the guy who abducted me really is, except that he was a hit man hiree who replaced the real driver, and it suited him, in turn, to be replaced by a Fontana girlfriend. He probably rode out here concealed in the Rolls's trunk never expecting to be found out in a million years."

"That's okay. We know him. We just don't know which girl aided and abetted, and whether she really knew what she was doing. Whether she was a victim, or a villain. Can you help us?"

Lord, she wanted to! Every Fontana except Macho Mario

had believed in her smarts. She eyed the old guy, having a big cigar lit by Miss Kitty while the other agent gave him the sixth degree, at least.

But if she wrongly dissed a loyal Fontana girlfriend, sold her out to the Feds. If she was wrong, and got an innocent woman in trouble. . . .

"If the girl won't confess, we'll never get this right," Bucek said.

Temple eyed them all. Neurotic Jill, so insecure. Buoyant Meredith, the life counselor who might have failed in her own choices. Headstrong Alexia had been mentioned as possibly bolting the fold.

But only one was a likely suspect.

Temple beckoned Bucek to bend down to her.

She whispered, "It's kinda obvious. Asiah, the substitute driver. She wore fishnet hose with just high heels and a skimpy blazer."

Bucek glanced at Matt. "You do travel in style these days."

"Later, she'd changed to palazzo pants. I'm betting she had them in the trunk and changed stockings for pants right then. Did she spot the fake driver then and go along with whatever story he was handing out . . . he was part of the prank, say? I'm betting he was inspired to grab her stockings as a murder weapon after she left the vehicle. It would keep her quiet afterward about what would look like complicity in the murder, wouldn't it?"

"That it would." Bucek eyed the girlfriends.

"The African-American woman with platinum-blond hair."

He nodded. "We'll be discreet about cutting her out from the herd when we do our interrogation at the LVMPD. Who's the unlucky boyfriend?"

"Ralph, the second youngest. Another thing. Asiah told me she was totally uninterested in marrying her Fontana boyfriend, that she was along for the ride for the thrill of it."

Bucek nodded.

"She's a showgirl. She has a curtain time tonight too."

He glanced at Matt. "She doesn't have friends in high places. She'll miss her high kicks tonight, and for a lotta nights. Thanks. Listen to Matt on that ankle. Maybe you'll stay out of trouble for a while."

"Amen," Matt said.

Chapter 66

Farewell, My Lovely

"Keep in touch. Phone sex is a favorite sideline around here," Miss Satin notes from her position on the floor by the door.

I am about to be hustled back to town, along with Midnight Louise and Ma Barker, in the Rover with the Misses Von Rhine, Barr, Carlson, and Lark.

Usually I consider being the only male among a passel of devoted females as my birthright, but this feels like I am being shuffled away from the best parts of crime and punishment. Like grilling the suspect.

"Phone sex is not what I consider 'keeping in touch.'" My vibrissae plays footsie with her vibrissae.

"Maybe I can visit you in Vegas sometime. I kind of bonded with your family."

"Maybe by then I will have the details about our joint collar. I expect my Miss Temple will not rest that ankle until she knows the who, what, when, and why of all this. I am glad to have encountered you again, however briefly. And I am glad that we were all able to bring matters here to a conclusion, to an end, to a climax, so to speak."

"Forget it, Louie. I am done with that nonsense."

"Nonsense!"

"You should forget your romantic aspirations and worry about your roommate getting off scot-free. That body upstairs is ripening by the minute, and the trouble your associates could get into with the officials is getting stinkier by the second."

"Yeah, but us nailing the perp should banish any bad odor that might cling to my associates."

"Us?"

"You, me, Ma Barker, and the number one daughter."

"I thought you said Midnight Louise was someone else's baby."

"Probably is, but now that she thinks she has found mommy dearest, who am I to disillusion a pathetic orphan? Would you want to?"

"Midnight Louise does not strike me as pathetic. In fact, in some ways she is more worldly than you, Louie! This is all that remains of my one and only litter?"

"What do you mean, one and only?" I ask with bated fish breath.

"My ladies are very conscientious about birth control. I have been fixed."

"No! You still waft the tempting perfume of a lady who can work up a heat storm now and then."

"Dream on, Louie. I, for one, am pleased to know that none of my darling babies are out on the byways facing horrible dangers."

"Well, I am out and about, and I face plenty of danger in my job."

"That is different. You always were a scrapper. I think you

were born with a silver can opener in your mouth. Certainly you have a silver tongue, and have seduced your human into life-long devotion. Not all of us are that fortunate. Look at your own mother."

"Ma Barker runs a street gang, not a small achievement at her age."

"Come on. She has mentioned the posh 'retirement home' you are setting up for her and her gang. You know she is too old for the streets."

"But I am not."

Satin shrugs her slim shoulders under the turquoise cape, which sets the marabou feather trim in vibrant motion. She is not fixed enough for me!

"I would like to visit this Circle Ritz retirement home some-time. I do not intend to go out with my sapphire slippers on in a bordello. I might want to invest in the right property."

Hubba, hubba, hormones! If the well-seasoned Miss Kit Carl-son can get inspired by the right dude, perhaps Satin is not a lost cause. I live to defy the odds.

Chapter 67

Traveling Music

The hay was fresh and frothy. Clean-cut.

He awoke breathing unrecycled air, hearing birds chattering, and a meadowlark uncorking an aria. All he needed was the Disney mice wrapping his withered legs with elastic bandages.

The illusion shattered as he realized he needed to piss, badly, and was in no shape to get himself up, hobble off, and do it. Pink and puckered indeed.

As he looked around, he saw he was alone. He could manage a discreet shift to the side. Then use his ass and elbows to move far away.

Thriller films never dealt with the ugly realities.

Then he was free to crab-crawl until he found his partner in flight. A quarter of the way around the haystack, she was seated, tying two loaves of bread and a jug into a large light-weight wool shawl. Their latest travel rations.

She noticed his crablike approach and hefted her saw.

"The last cast. Then we see how well you can hobble."

At least his more recent hospital garb had not been gowns but flannel pajamas, the legs snapping open along the inside and outside seams like infant wear would, he imagined.

She unsnapped the pants over the leg still in a cast. In the bright morning light she cut away that cast in about fifteen minutes.

"A quick learner," he said.

"Thank you, Mr. Randolph. So, I imagine, are you. You survived a night on the icy Himalayas with two broken legs. How will you do in the more temperate summer Alps with two half-healed legs?"

He eyed the gnarly walking sticks she had cajoled out of some upland farmer's cottage. He hadn't stood unassisted for as long as he could remember, but a maimed man was a dead one on this steep slope, no matter how tepid the daytime climate. He could ditch the flimsy, aluminum crutches.

He turned to face the upward slope of the meadow, took the sticks in his hands, ready to push down until he rose up. The cudgel-like canes chewed into divots of sod as he levered himself up twelve degrees, then twenty. Then forty-five. Sweat was raining off his brow and chin. His arms were shaking with strain. Sixty.

She slipped under the angle of his body to position a shoulder under one of his. Early hospital training.

Up. More. More! For a moment he tottered fully upright and almost tipped over backward. But the thick wooden cane bases dug in under his weight. He was standing, his arms and shoulders bearing most of his weight.

"Good," she said, slapping him lightly on the iron bicep. "You'll regain leg strength."

Nice of her to think so.

They edged sideways down the steep meadows, his weight forcing the thick sod to give so his homemade crutches could get traction.

After an hour he was exhausted. He collapsed to the ground. They drank dark ale until it was gone. The rush of a mountain stream lured her away, to return with bottles foaming with bubbles.

He didn't think about where they were going, or about what they were eating and drinking. This was on-the-job therapy. The mountainside was a million-dollar retraining program.

By night all his muscles were shaking, and he was moaning, whether awake or asleep. She fed him bread, some water. In the morning, she returned from another foraging expedition with sausage and cheese. He didn't ask where, when, how. A lone beautiful woman who spoke several languages would be able to concoct a dozen stories to win sympathy and supplies.

He knew he'd never worked so hard, and was glad his arms and shoulders were strong from the shower rod chin-ups. He never complained, she never coddled.

By the second day he could get up and down by himself. By the third he was using only one cane and wanted to approach the farmhouses with her.

"That will be harder to explain," she objected. "They'll want to take you to the nearest village, and we'll be discovered."

"You mean it'll be harder for you to cajole goodies out of these remote farmers with a man along."

"Goodies?"

"Good food, good drink."

"You have a point." She pulled the untidy knot at her nape out of its tie, freeing her shoulder-length honey-blond hair. "I've been neglecting to appear vulnerable. I've simply been paying so far, after a tale of a hiker with a sprained ankle. But we'll need fresh clothes soon and it will be good to have further inducements to help. Unless, of course, I'm dealing with a farmwife, who will be suspicious of a city-dressed hussy wandering the mountain meadows."

He shook his head ruefully. "Say that your husband had been in a clinic recovering from an accident and you had taken me for a ride. Our car engine failed on one of the high passes. No one came by or stopped, so we had to go in search of assistance and got lost. It's about time we took someone's offer of a ride to a nearby village or town. Just how much money do you have on you?"

"My euros are almost gone, but limitless." She produced a continental credit card, rather proudly. "I thought to take my wallet from my purse before we left the clinic."

"Bury it. Whoever wanted to kill me can easily trace your credit card."

"But . . . how will we buy food, transportation, housing?"

"We won't buy. Let me worry about it." He was calm, relying on skills he assumed would reappear when needed.

Her reliance on her credit card was rather endearing . . . or a clever plot to convince him she was a babe in the woods when it came to survival on the run. She *was* a babe in the woods, he thought, and she must have interpreted his grin correctly, because she snapped the credit card away from his fingers.

"I can hide it on my person."

"Not well enough to fool a pro. Lose it. It's a death sentence. For me, certainly, given the likely lethal hypo meant for me. And, now, because you're with me, for you too."

"We'll be helpless without it."

"But alive. Trust me. It's totally compromised. By now they know you've vanished too. If the hypo people aren't after us, the authorities are."

And Garry Randolph, maybe. He hoped. His talks with Randolph had given him the confidence to see past his injuries and memory loss, to see himself as wily and competent and apparently well trained for this rough flight down the mountains.

Was there anywhere he could head where Garry would find them? Probably, but he didn't remember it. Yet. There was muscle memory, which would help his damaged legs work better and better as they got stronger and stronger; there was also mental recuperation, which would slowly repair the severed pathways of his memory. Hopefully. And there was gut instinct. He guessed that was his best ally at the moment.

"Get some suitable walking clothes for us at the next farm-house. We need to clean up and dress the part before we actually bum a ride from anyone."

"'Bum' a ride?"

"Beg." He cocked his thumb. "Hitchhike."

She nodded at the gesture. Narrowed her eyes and tilted her head. "'Clean up.' Does that mean we'll have the clichéd mountain stream bath of unacquainted couples on the run?"

He nodded. "Excellent therapy. Might motivate my legs to do a better job at moving me around. Fighting the running water, that is."

"You may not remember much, Mr. Randolph, but what you do remember is choice."

With that she tossed her freshly loosened hair and moved through the long grasses to the steep wooden roof of a farmhouse in the distance, one with a ramp that allowed cattle and other stock into the warmer living area during the long, snow-deep winters. It had been done that way here for centuries. Despite the three days' struggle down the mountain meadows, Revienne Schneider looked cool and very hot at the same time.

She was either an *über*-competent woman with unflinching devotion to a patient, a doctor with a passion to save and rehabilitate broken lives and minds, one repelled to her soul by an attempt to kill a helpless man . . . or she was his worst enemy: an agent who saw the death plan had failed and had accompanied him to gain his trust so they, or she, could try again.

Either way, they both seemed to thrive on challenge.

Chapter 68

Sanctuary

The farmer's horse-drawn cart had seemed like a tumbrel in the French Revolution to Max, hauling him to the guillotine. He was tired of lying on a bed of straw, no matter how fresh.

Revienne, however, relished being off her aching feet. They hung, bare, over the cart edge, swinging with the bumpy motion. Naked, rather. With pink painted toenails. A pretty sight, except for the angry red places on heels and toes where her shoes had rubbed them raw. She'd never complained.

Revienne was able to ignore him completely for the first time during their flight. He studied her exhausted profile. Brow, nose, and chin were feminine, but strong, determined. If secret assassin she was, who would she work for? Not for money, he decided. Principle. Which might seem comforting at first, but fanatic principle had proved itself a far worse influence on the modern world than mere personal gain.

He hadn't realized he was whistling until her profile lifted and she glanced his way. She smiled. "That tune is familiar."

He thought about it. "Not to me."

"Ah, a secret message from your subconscious. Whistle a bit more."

"I've forgotten it now." His subconscious would not perform for free.

She shook out her hair. "It doesn't matter. It was something Irish. Their tunes are both lilting and somber. Come now, less somber and more lilt. Admit it, you're as happy as I am to be off your feet."

"I didn't know you were *on* my feet."

A frown in that alabaster forehead. "I am not perfect at the English language."

"It was a joke. I agree. Laughing is better than moaning."

She nodded, looking away again to the deserted sweeps of green. "They say the nearest village is Zuoz. Small, but a tourist attraction when the big German buses come through."

"Good." He eyed a pile of fabric beside him. "Clothes?"

"At the last farm a son had left for vocational school in Zurich. It's hard to keep the young ones in the mountain villages these days."

He shook out a pants and shirt, and shuddered at the heavy, narrow denim pant legs. They were a new kind of cast, ones he'd have to force his long-sheltered legs into. Painfully.

"I'll get them on to the knees." She'd read his mind. He'd have to watch that.

He nodded.

She glanced at the hospital pajama bottoms. "These off?"

His only underwear? No way. "The pants can go on over these."

"It'll be bulkier, harder."

"Just get the two legs up to my knees. When the cart stops, I'll lower my feet to the road and . . . shimmy into the damn things."

"Shimmy?"

"You'll see," he said sourly. Not his most graceful moment, he could foresee, but it couldn't be helped.

In another half hour, he spotted the spire of a simple church in a fold of road and hill below. Gable roofs appeared next. The horse slowed from a walk to a crawl. He pulled the lightweight wool shirt over his pajama top and over his hips.

He stared down at the mountain path beneath the heavy wheels. It still seemed to pass at a dizzying pace. To jump off would be a dangerous moment for his weakened legs. He sensed that he had jumped off far more dizzying heights, absolutely fearless. A throb of self-disgust shivered through him.

"Not until the cart stops utterly," Revienne said. Ordered. "You are still an invalid, and under my care."

He recognized good counsel, at least, and waited impatiently, judging every shift of the wheels for the moment when he dared to stand on his own two bare feet again, clothed and on the road to independence. And danger.

The cart and its burden of hay finally rocked almost to a stop. His hands grabbed the thick wooden edge, his mind gauging the drop, his shoulders supporting him until the flats of his feet were on the rutted dirt, then his rear supported him on the edge, easing off. . . .

She raised a hand, forbidding movement, then . . . lowered it.

Max took the plunge, felt the soles of his feet touch a solid surface and the arches settle down into solid contact. He felt pure jubilation, like the first man landing on the moon. Such a simple step for a whole man, such a great step for a semi-cripple.

His arms and shoulders were strong enough to cushion any shock. He released an arm to grab the quaint, knotty cane.

But. You couldn't shake yourself into a tight pair of jeans without all your weight on both legs with both hands needed at the sides and . . . front. Shit. This was worse than the delicately negotiated mountain stream sitz baths.

"Let me," Revienne said, brusque as any nurse. "The farmer's son was not as tall as you, but was also very lean."

She grabbed the heavy fabric at the sides and pulled up with each fist in turn, until they rode on his hips and would go no further. The fly was a buttoned affair and she bent her head and hands to the task.

"As I said," she murmured halfway through, "young Johannes was not as big as you."

"Dr. Schneider," he rebuked.

Her face looked pink behind the veils of her loosened hair, and he could tell she was biting back a . . . giggle.

She stepped away and pulled the shirt down over the skimpy pants.

His face felt red too, as if he was a green boy again. Had he ever been? He recalled an old riddle about what walked with four legs in the morning, two legs at noon, and three legs in the evening. . . . He could remember stupid riddles, but not the riddle of himself.

"I'm glad you're feeling better," she said. Primly. "Now. We must go and do what you said you would know how to do when we were among people again."

If he remembered what that was.

Revienne was devouring half of a roasted chicken across from him, wiping her mouth with a linen napkin and gulping white wine, then pulling meat from bones a moment later.

An accordion was playing in the background. An accordion! He hadn't heard an accordion in decades, if ever. As far as he knew. Red-faced, stout people were drinking beer and wine and eating all around them at the small bistro adjoining the village's central, and only, inn. The language flowed like the wine and beer, soft and fluent. He caught words, some English and German, and something different. Swiss-German.

Revienne's loosened blond hair was catching in the chicken grease at the sides of her mouth. No skinless fowl here. He'd eaten three pork chops, sauerbraten, dumplings, and cooked greens until he felt gorged. He'd ordered beer, not because he craved it, but because it would put weight on him faster. He'd lost a lot; he could tell. Odd, he knew how the man he really was should feel, but not who he really was.

He knew who Revienne Schneider thought he was.

"You must be a very bad man," she'd said through her first, ravenous bites of chicken and dumplings and thick brown bread. Her eyes glittered at him like a wild animal's. "An adventurer. Utterly no scruples. This is very good." She paused for breath and to wipe her mouth. "You have no conscience at all. Pass the butter. Please."

It was white as snow and as soft as whipped cream. He knifed off a glob to put on his own rugged loaf of bread before he handed it over to her and she took the whole mound.

"They're tourists," he whispered over the board heaped with varieties of cheese between them. "I'm only using each card for one item. I'll ditch the one for dinner and lodging tomorrow. Literally bury it. It will cost the man a minimum of euros. He'll get a notice and change the card number. We must eat and rest."

"Yes." She drank more wine, pulled the hair back from her face. "I need a bath. And of course you would not put two rooms on the poor tourist's card, so we shall have to sleep together."

Her eyes were as fevered as her face. Her tone was half accusation, half something more interesting.

"I don't think I could heft this body into a bed tonight, princess. You'll have it all to yourself."

"'Heft'? What is this 'heft'?"

"Lift."

"Ah." She looked around. "We must look like savages."

"They're too absorbed in their own dinners to take much notice of us."

"You're sitting."

"Yes."

"That is an improvement."

"My hips ache like the very Devil. Why do you think I'm chugalugging so much beer?"

"Chuga?"

"Swallowing fast."

She nodded. "I'm hungry still. I'll give you a massage tonight."

She was back on the subject of his legs. And hips.

"I have very good hands. Strong hands."

He drank some more beer, wanting to put on weight, feel no pain, forget about her hands on his legs and hips. She was a possible enemy. Of course she'd offer . . . things. His job was to forget his own pain and confusion, and not take any wooden nickels.

Where did that expression come from? It sounded as old as the hills, which were alive with the sound of music . . . which was not Austria, but Switzerland, which was not where he belonged.

Where did he belong? He remembered the song he'd been whistling earlier. Something about a minstrel boy and a war? Ireland. Did he belong there? He felt another deep throb of recognition, accompanied by a surge of mixed sensations: love, hatred, anger, guilt, pain. Man, the real him must be some dysfunctional bastard. Though that didn't seem right, either. Garry Randolph didn't seem to think so.

Revienne ate some cheese, then stuffed some into the backpacks they'd bought on the stolen credit card.

"Come," she said, whispering across the table. "I don't want you unsteady on your feet with too much beer. After all those meds it could hit you hard, and I'm not strong enough to get you up the chalet stairs to our room."

He grabbed his new cane, hand-carved tourist bait that leaned against his rush-seated chair. He didn't bother to tell her he'd been off meds for some time. Still, the stairs took two turns, there was no elevator, and the new walking shoes made his gait clumsy. He was exhausted by the time she turned the key to their room.

He leaned against the wall just inside the door while she turned on the lamps—no overhead lights in the boonies— looked into the empty freestanding wardrobe and under the double bed piled high with a down comforter.

"The bathroom is down the hall," she said. "This is not the American Plan part of the world. But don't worry." She hoisted a deep white pot from under the high bedstead. "There are emergency accommodations. Mike, don't look like that! You're still an invalid; you must take the simplest route. I am a medical doctor, you know. I've seen everything."

Yes, but not his "everything."

"You use the bathroom first," she decided. "I'll help you to and fro. Once you're in the bed, I can use it."

It took them an hour to accomplish their separate turns at the simple room with a bathtub, toilet, and sink. It was early, so they had no competition. Max used a cloth to wash off the three days of sweat and outdoor elimination, and donned the beige shorts from a village shop with relief. Luckily Swiss mountain men wore the equivalent of short shorts in the summer, almost as good as boxers. He felt like Tom Selleck in *Magnum, P.I.* shorts, but at least he could dump the hospital jammies in a knapsack for burying farther down the road.

The black, long-sleeved spandex turtleneck top was as silky as a second skin. The moment he put it on, he felt more relaxed. Something to his taste, apparently.

It didn't make sense to struggle into the new, baggier jeans the stolen credit card had bought as well. Not for sleeping. Revienne would just have to see his pale legs, with the dark hairs rubbed off by the cast. He recalled her threat of a massage and chose to consider it a promise. He was, as she'd pointed out, an invalid.

The bedsheets were Egyptian cotton, maybe a thousand-thread count. Smooth as a baby's cheek. The foot-high comforter was the only blanket or coverlet, and all that eiderdown was housed inside another silky, high-count shroud.

Max took deep, satisfied breaths. His stomach was full, his magic fingers knew how to lift a tourist's credit card so smoothly no one would ever notice, the beer was making him drowsy, and he was going to let Revienne's strong doctor-trained hands massage his abused legs.

He was half-asleep when she finished in the bathroom. She came back smelling of freesia soap and began running her hands over his aching leg muscles all the way up to the place where his butt began, where it hurt so good. . . .

This person named Max didn't trust many or much, but tonight he fell asleep in the cradle of civilization.

Woman.

Warm.

Chapter 69

Endurance Vile

After all and sundry have had a couple days to recover from being cooped up together in a residence high on bedrooms and low on other creature comforts, I amble up the Strip to visit my partner in Midnight Inc. Investigations.

Miss Midnight Louise can be found by my old office area among the canna lilies, overlooking the koi pond at the Crystal Phoenix.

Although she professes to despise the way I do things, I notice that she enjoys the shade under the tall, spreading foliage, and the way the wet fish scales shimmer in the sunlight.

Since she is house detective here now, not I, I do not comment right off that she is tolerating riffraff in the pool area. At least three skinny dames in skinnier bikinis have designer carryall bags containing yappy purse pooches beside their lounges.

When I innocently observe that she is leaving the canine intruders unmolested, she just shrugs.

"They may expose themselves to dangerous sun rays if they wish. Besides, those are not dogs so much as animated purse lint."

I sit to clean the hairs between my toes. In human circles this would be regarded as an uncouth pursuit, but among our kind it is considered good grooming.

"Are your split shivs recovering?" she inquires.

"Yes, thank you. They will be their old Ginsu-sharp selves in another week."

"What brings you over here? The wedding is not for two days. I presume you plan to crash it, as you did the bachelor party."

"Of course not. I am an invited guest."

"*Hmm.*" Her brief purr is decidedly unimpressed.

"I have been busy about town sorting out the details and progress of the case."

"And—?"

"I have it on the best authority—"

"Whose?"

"FBI agent Bucek's."

"Go on."

Somehow I feel like a footman reporting to the queen when I am the kingpin here.

"He honored Miss Temple's Circle Ritz and my abode with a visit and all the inside info he was free to spread around."

"Who else was there?"

"Miss Kit Carlson and Mr. Matt Devine."

"So he did not exclusively call on Miss Temple and you, but Miss Temple and her nearest and dearest, and you happened to be there coddling your claws."

"Louise! I am as much a part of Miss Temple's less formal investigative cases as those of Midnight Inc. Investigations."

"Oh, stuff a catnip mouse in it, Daddy-o! You know you are just trying to appear all-wise and knowing. Can it. I am wise to you in a way you will never be wise to me."

Those are fighting words. Louise is lucky my shivs are dull, but the back of my tongue is not.

"I can just leave you in the usual blissful ignorance," I say, pausing to polish one of the shivs in question with the tongue in question. Then I shut up.

"All right, spill it." She settles onto her haunches with a yawn that fools no one.

She is dying to hear who was really who and what was really what in the shenanigans at the Sapphire Slipper.

"First, the perp. He may be a nameless nebbish to us, and have made a really lame attempt at escape, but it turns out he has a murderous rap sheet as long as a kinkajou's tail."

"He is supposed to be what passes for a professional at this?"

"I share your amazement. Good hit men are hard to find in Las Vegas nowadays, I guess. This guy was from the East Coast mob."

"And his inside contact was the lady known as Asiah?"

"No, she was his fortuitous outside contact, as my Miss Temple figured out. She set up the deal with him for the girlfriends, thinking he was just what he was masquerading as, a driver for Gangsters. She didn't know he hitched a ride in the Rolls-Royce trunk, then hid in the garage until he snuck in later to fulfill his contract and kill Madonnah. Miss Asiah didn't know until she saw the victim was strangled with one of her fishnet hose that he'd implicated her. Ma Barker found the second stocking in the peep room later. Miss Asiah knew to look for it in the bedroom and tossed it in there to put the blame on Mr. Matt."

"Naughty! There must have been an inside contact."

"Right. The Shoofly character took over as general factotum at the brothel about eight months ago."

"Who is this General Fact-totem? Something to do with the military and the Indians?"

"Naw, it is just some general person useful for domestic slavery work."

"It sounds like someone had this plan in mind for a while."

"Right. Madonnah was really Norah Rudinsky. She got close to some drug-lord mobster and testified when he was caught. Just like we heard, she was in the Federal Witness Protection Program. They have been trying to kill her for three years."

"Why now? The case is closed, surely, and her mobster boyfriend is upriver until his toenails grow long enough to decorate for Christmas."

"Sure. But the mob needed to make an example of what happens to anyone who squeals on them. The fact that this opportunity would put a former rival like Macho Mario and kin in trouble just made revenge all the sweeter."

"So Shoofly is likely to go to prison for quite a while?"

"As soon as they figure out what gender he or she is."

Miss Midnight Louise licks her vibrissae with the tip of her dainty red tongue and considers.

"So they have the pseudonymous Gherken for murder one, and Shoofly and Asiah as accessories. Will the showgirl get big time?"

"Maybe not, but Ralph is through with her, although he was pretty upset about the trouble she got herself into. She did it for kicks really, not knowing something was up."

"Not even when a woman was murdered?"

"Maybe then. She changed into pants when she came into the bordello for good, Gherken was lurking and smart enough to grab her discarded hose from the trunk for the murder weapon. Then she kept her mouth shut, not knowing how they'd turned up around Madonnah's neck."

"Is not one pair of fishnet hose like another?"

"Apparently not. Asiah's were from Frederick's of Hollywood, and they had a lurid little label on the back rear seam. They were the trashy, real thing. The other girls, including Madonna, had more fashionable seamless fishnet hose."

"So the only one of the bachelor party to take a loss is Ralph?"

"Yeah, but a dame gone bad is worse than no dame at all. You hear anything on this end about how he and your other protégés here at the Crystal Phoenix are taking the girlfriends' prank turned deadly?"

Miss Midnight Louise looks around, as if the fish have ears. "I know, Louie, that the male of the species does not like to listen to the idle speculation called gossip—"

"In this case," I say quickly, "I will be idle."

She rises to look around again, then bends my ear, quite literally, with a cupped paw.

"Wedding plans proceed apace, but the Fontana brothers are still mightily annoyed with their abducting girlfriends. The rumor is that they all have been fired as bridesmaids."

"No! But who will they find to escort to the wedding on such short notice?"

"You think Giuseppe, Rico, Ernesto, Julio, Armando, Emilio, Eduardo, and Ralph cannot find alternate dates on the spin of a dime?"

"No, but there is the matter of the bridesmaids' gowns. They are already altered to fit a bevy of lithe beauties."

"Do not worry, Louie. Miss Van von Rhine and Miss Temple Barr would not permit Miss Kit Carlson's nuptial moment to be tarnished by the actions of a flock of jealous and impulsive girlfriends, one of whom is currently in custody."

"Of course not. So who will replace the eight bridesmaids?"

Miss Midnight manages to look both smug and coy.

"Let us just say that 'something blue' for the wedding is a set of eight garters and their wearers, out from Beatty way."

I gasp. Yes. Literally. Like a fish, like the oh-mouthed koi crowding to the pond's edge to mock me with their piscine kisses.

Midnight Louise goes on. "Miss Kit Carlson will wear the ninth garter as an honorary badge of courage for having her bridegroom held in durance vile at the Sapphire Slipper."

I nod. There is a certain satin-smooth justice in the solution to the wedding party problem, for, of course, bridesmaids behaving badly must not be rewarded.

Chapter 70

Family Circle

Temple and Kit clasped hands before leaving the Circle Ritz for their dinner date at the Crystal Phoenix.

"My mom is going to flake out," Temple said.

"My sister is going to go ballistic."

They took a deep, simultaneous breath.

"Do you think," Temple asked, "it's all right to have the guys waiting in the wings?"

"We can always cancel the introductions in case things look too . . . dreadful."

"Leave them waiting in the bar all evening, deny them dinner, and then brush them off at the last moment?"

"That would be rather tacky," Kit agreed. "But better tacky than homicide victims."

"My parents would never overreact so badly."

"Yeah?"

"Well, maybe so. So you think we're better off not wearing our rings?"

"Absolutely not. Karen would spot them instantly. We want to ease the Old Folks at Home into the current realities, not give them strokes."

"She's your sister. Almost your age."

"I'm almost *her* age," Kit said icily, "were I about to give such privileged information out hither and yon. I'm sorry, Temple, but you do not look like a hither or a yon to me." Kit thought for a moment. "They probably don't even have sex anymore."

"Kit! These are my parents. I don't want to think about such things, the lack or presence of them. Please!"

"Why not? That's all they're going to think about us. About you deflowering that nice ex-priest and me succumbing in the vulnerability of my 'certain age' to a sleek Italian gigolo."

Temple paused to think. "Actually, those scenarios sound rather hot to me."

"Me too," Kit said with a giggle. "Wanta trade? Just kidding, kid! Only a good sense of humor is going to see us through tonight. Why do my sister and her husband seem like parents, even to me?"

"Because that's all they've ever been to me. Parents." Temple swung Kit's hand. "I feel naked without my ring."

"Me too, but we must *not* feel *naked* in front of your parents. Parents sense that kind of vulnerability and exploit it like cardsharps. We are independent women of the world and no one tells us who to sleep with."

"Right. My latest bed partner has been a big black cat."

"Do not go there. Parents will immediately think bestiality. Trust me."

"Come on! How bad can it be, Kit?"

"Worse than we can imagine. Look. We arrive. We chitchat, we idly mention our significant others. . . ."

"Nothing 'idly' about that for me. They're sure to think I'm still being hoodwinked by that rat, Max."

"Are you?"

"Only when I stop to think about it."

"Oh, Temple," Kit said, squeezing her hand. "I'm sure he would never have left you if he'd had a choice."

"You mean dead or alive?"

"I mean dead or alive. But you'd never leave Matt standing forever in the wings, waiting for an interrogation by your parents, would you? They can be *soooo* Midwestern."

"So can we. Sometimes. Let's go do it. Maybe we can make them feel guilty for a change."

"Excellent plan. We are women of the world."

"We live in Manhattan and Vegas. They live in the Grain Belt."

"We drink martinis and absinthe, they drink—"

"*Absinthe?*" Temple asked. "Isn't that illegal?"

"It was banned, but one or two brands are now allowed on sale, and I also do smoke the occasional cigar."

"No!"

"That's very hot in Manhattan. Cigar bars. A girl has to adapt."

"Let's adapt our way into the worst shock and awesome disapproval Karen and Roger Barr can deliver."

"Right." Kit linked arms with Temple in a Yellow Brick Road sort of way. "Off we go."

Of course, Nicky and Van had seen to it that the Barr party had the best table in the house, overlooking the Strip shooting due north far below on a shimmer of glitter and neon and fairy dust.

Temple was wearing her solid Austrian crystal pumps with a black cat on the heels with a silver knit two-piece suit. Kit was electric in a teal satin dressy suit.

Temple choked when she saw them sitting at the table, eyeing the Strip, Dad in a navy sport coat, Mom in a lightweight blazer.

"Just think *American Gothic*," Kit whispered, tightening her grip on Temple's hand.

Temple had to laugh. She hadn't seen her parents since leaving Minneapolis with Max to come to Las Vegas more than two years ago. She'd left under a blue-black cloud of parental skepticism and dismay, but she was almost nine years past twenty-one and had the right to follow her heart.

They surprised the Barrs, who turned to see them standing there, smiling, thanks to Kit's little joke.

Karen gave a little cry and stood up to hug Temple. "Your hair! It's . . . faded. But otherwise, of course, you look wonderful."

"A cosmetological accident," Temple murmured, not mentioning she liked the lighter strawberry blond-red so much she might keep it. An engaged woman had a right to change her hair color.

Her dad gave her the awkward fatherly hug perfected in the Midwest for occasions from weddings to funerals. Next it was Kit's turn to be embraced by Karen and shake hands with Roger.

"This is a fairly subdued hotel," Karen said after they'd all seated themselves again. First, Temple and Kit insisted the Barrs keep their seats facing the view. They'd been set on giving them up. "For Las Vegas."

"It's a client of mine," Temple said.

Her mother was gazing at the padded closed menu as if it needed dusting. "That's nice, dear. Roger, I hope you brought your bifocals, this menu is as thick as a phone book."

"I know what I want," he said, pushing the glasses in question up his nose. "I always get a New York strip steak and a baked potato."

Kit and Temple exchanged agonized teenage glances. Too bad they were both so far past the teen years.

Temple eyed her mother. She wore a figured silk blouse and rose slacks under the beige blazer. Her father wore a sport coat and long-sleeve shirt, no tie. Their clothes were perfectly suitable for a fine restaurant in casual Las Vegas.

Why, then, did they look so stuffed shirt?

"I see," Temple's mother said, "you've opted for going barelegged."

"It's always hot here, outside at least, and I hate pantyhose. And this is a desert climate. . . ." Temple let her apologia trickle off.

"Me too," Kit said. Karen eyed her over the menu. "I never wear hose in Las Vegas. This is the West."

"But in Manhattan," Karen began.

"Oh, in Manhattan. Yes, of course. All the time. Sliding into the hot, broken-down cab seats, out of the hot, broken-down cab seats; panty hose, every second. Racing crosstown on the crowded sidewalks, all of us women in panty hose. Every minute."

"You chose to live there," Karen said. "What is this cerviche stuff?"

"Spanish," Temple said hastily. "Undercooked and overexpensive. Not that we have to worry. Our meal is on the house." She didn't add that it was raw fish in lime or lemon juice. Minnesotans didn't eat anything but vegetables raw.

Her father frowned over his glasses frames. "We're perfectly capable of paying."

"I have a permanent free pass to all the Phoenix's restaurants."

"Food is very cheap here, Roger," Karen explained. "They practically give it away."

Temple took a deep, deep breath. Not these high-end days. A dinner for four here could run close to three hundred dollars. If they had cocktails and wine with the meal, it would be more. Temple desperately wanted cocktails and wine with the meal.

She met Kit's eyes as the waiter breezed by with a question. "Cocktails?"

"A green apple martini for me," Kit said smartly. "Temple will have one too. Karen? Roger?"

"Do you have beer?" Roger asked.

"A hundred and forty varieties, sir. What would be your pleasure?"

"Schlitz would be fine."

The waiter was momentarily tongue-tied.

"Anything Scandinavian," Temple offered.

"Certainly," the waiter said.

"I'll have a daiquiri," Karen said.

The waiter blanched and asked, "And wine for dinner?"

"A nice Chablis," Roger said decidedly.

"Very good, sir," the waiter boomed, as if just asked to deliver a jeroboam of champagne.

Roger beamed. "Nice fella."

"This *is* a hospitality industry," Temple said cheerily.

"Are you eating enough?" her mother asked. "You're not drinking too much?"

"Green apple martinis are a health food," Kit said. "No nasty salty olives or onions, just fresh Granny Smith apples and a touch of vermouth."

And a few jiggers of gin.

"They do have a strip steak," Karen told Roger encouragingly. Then she smiled at Temple. "I'm glad we managed to come for Kit's wedding. It's so good to see you. You haven't been managing any visits home."

"It's been so busy—" she began, sounding lame even to herself. Her mother certainly wouldn't want news of Max Kinsella. Even if it was bad, which it was, as there was still no news of Max Kinsella. Which would be good news to Karen Barr, so Temple was going to be very vague about how and when Max split, and they split up.

"I can't believe it," Karen went on, eyeing Kit. "You, getting married! After all this time single. And you had to leave that miserable New York City madness and come to Las Vegas to visit Temple to find Mr. Right. Is he . . . retired here? I understand a lot of people do that."

Aldo? Retired? Temple was glad her martini had arrived and she could take a tart sip and cough slightly. *Only in a circular water bed.*

"No," Kit said. "He's in business with his brothers." She sipped, savored, and added, "One of whom owns this hotel-casino."

Minnesota eyebrows raised in tandem.

"The Fontanas are an old Las Vegas Family," Kit added demurely.

Roger folded away his reading glasses. "How 'old' can a Las Vegas family be," he joked. "They didn't start up the place until the 1940s."

"If that's when you arrived here, then you're an old Las Vegas family," Temple explained. "They also call this end of the country the 'New West.' It's all spin."

"Is it exciting," Karen wanted to know from Temple, "to be doing public relations work in a tourist destination like Las Vegas?"

"Oh, yes. Sometimes too exciting."

"And cultural too," Kit said. "Temple handled the opening of the *Treasures of the Czars* exhibition here just last month. Fabulous Imperial artifacts and stacks of uplifting, interesting information about the new order in modern-day Russia."

"And, then," Temple added, "I do PR for a lot of conventions that come to town. My most recent was for the Red Hat Sisterhood. They're—"

"I know who they are," Karen said excitedly. "Some of my friends belong and have been trying to talk me into joining, since Roger's retired and you're gone and your brothers are all busy with young, growing families."

Temple counted two possible digs: her moving away and her not producing children. Her brothers were in their forties, as Temple had been either an accident or an afterthought, and coming from a family with five kids, they had gone forth and had three each, defying statistics of the times. Not that her brothers had done the actual *having*, which made it a lot easier to do.

Karen was watching Temple closely, no doubt with Max in mind.

Luckily, the waiter buzzed by, recited the evening's specials, and they spent the next ten minutes *oohing* and ordering.

"Won't tournedos of beef be a little rich for your stomach?" Karen asked Roger in an undertone once the waiter had left.

Temple was proud of him for venturing beyond the usual New York strip steak.

"That's what seltzers are made for," he answered. The red-gold beer in the iced glass must be mellowing him. "When is your fiancé joining us?" he asked Kit.

She lifted her small evening bag from the tabletop. "As soon as I call him on my cell phone. I wanted us to have some time to relax and chat first."

"Kit," Karen said, "we won't bite. I'm just so tickled you finally found the right man."

Kit tried not to squirm. Temple knew that her getting married had just happened. It wasn't a lifelong search. Aldo was there, feeling a bit burned out after the loss of his longtime girlfriend, and along came Kit, full of postmenopausal zest and a tad of hormone replacements.

"Oh, now isn't this something?" Roger asked as the waiter lofted the appetizer tray Temple had ordered for them to share. One of the four delicacies was fried in batter, which she knew her dad would go for.

He grinned at the women and, after a glance at the many plates and pieces of silverware, moved half the batter-fried items to his plate.

Kit flashed Temple a happy smile. Papa had his beer and batter and would be cool from now on in. Mama, on the other hand . . .

"That looks fatty," Karen said.

"They only use olive oil here," Temple said. "That's the kind that's good for your heart."

"Oh? I thought that cheap food was oilier in general."

Temple was glad they'd never see the bill. Her mother was thinking of the days of cheap three-dollar buffets laden with sugary, greasy comfort food, back in the unenlightened eighties. Las Vegas was a class, and costly, act these days. Sure, there were always economical fast-food places in every Strip hotel, but even those menus were healthier and more palatable.

Temple sipped her sweetly tart martini, feeling a little mellow herself.

"So," said Karen to Kit, sipping her daiquiri, a vintage cocktail with a funny little hazelnut bobbling in it, "how did you meet this Aldo?"

"Through Temple," Kit said brightly. "She introduced us."

"Oh, that's nice, dear. Meeting through family is always best."

"Yeah," said Kit, thinking, no doubt, of the whole, big, slightly mobbish Fontana family, from Uncle Macho Mario on down to Nicky.

Speaking of which, at that moment Temple was surprised to see Nicky and Van stroll over, a very handsome couple blending dark and light looks.

"Everything all right here, folks?" Nicky asked, his bright white teeth flashing against his smooth olive skin.

Van, always the elegant Hitchcock blonde, merely smiled.

After introductions, Roger took the beef tournedos by the horns. "So it's your brother that's stolen our Kit away."

"My eldest brother," Nicky said, grinning.

"You must be just a baby," Karen suggested.

"The youngest, yes."

"Your mother must be quite an interesting woman."

Temple could see her mother calculating thirty years of childbearing. If she only knew how many brothers there were, she'd be really impressed. Unlike Mama Fontana, Karen had ended her streak of four sons with a lone girl. That family position left Temple cosseted and fussed over and bullied and controlled way too much.

It was nice to be from Las Vegas now, on her own, making her solo choices. One of which . . .

"Is Matt coming along for dinner too?" Nicky asked, turning to Temple as if giving her a cue.

He didn't mean it that way, but it gave Temple the perfect opening. She looked at her parents in explanation. "I have a significant other coming to dinner too. Matt Devine is a local celebrity. He hosts a syndicated radio advice show."

There!

Karen dropped her fork, which had been attacking the remaining battered items that she'd appropriated to her appetizer plate. She might inveigh against fatty foods, but a Minnesota blizzard-ridden winter made them a number-one crave. "*Matt,* not Max?"

"Max has left Las Vegas."

Karen just stared.

"They drifted apart," Kit said, "and Matt drifted into view. Quite a nice view he is too. Shall I call the boys now?" She pulled her cell phone from her purse as Nicky and Van eased away.

"Boys?" Karen said weakly, still numbed by the fact that Temple as well as Kit was producing a new beau.

Kit dialed. "Hi, handsome. Yeah, you can steer your Italian tailoring up to the restaurant. The waiter knows you'll be ordering a bit late."

Karen's jaw was again agape. She glanced to Temple, then at

the two empty place settings. Two, not one. Her jaw moved as if she was going to speak. But her first question would have been about Max, and even Karen Barr knew that would be a fatal move.

She sipped her daiquiri. "This is very good. I haven't had one in years."

"Then have another," Kit urged. "You don't often meet a new prospective son-in-law and brother-in-law on the same day."

"Temple?" Karen gazed accusingly at Temple's ringless left hand, and then Kit's.

"We're letting the gentlemen install our engagement rings again tonight," Kit said, "for your viewing pleasure. We're very sorry about surprising you with two engagements, but we thought it would be better to do in person instead of over the phone."

"But we haven't met this Matt person," Karen said.

"That'll be taken care of tonight," Kit answered. "Don't worry. He's a matinee idol dreamboat. Smart and rich too. What mother wouldn't be over the moon about it?"

"Has he been married before?" Karen asked. "After a certain age, it's hard to find . . . uh . . . ."

"Non-preowned models?" Temple asked. "Nope. Never married."

"And he's how old?"

"Thirty-four."

"Never-married men that age can be . . . difficult."

"Nope," Temple answered. "See for yourself."

"He makes all this money from just talking on the radio?" her dad asked.

"Think Garrison Keillor," Temple said, "but cute."

She wanted to avoid the ex-priest part until her parents had gotten used to the idea of an Unknown Quantity in Temple's life. Max had not been welcomed, but at least they'd met him.

Kit had been playing lookout while Temple fended off her

parents' questions and now she grabbed Temple's hand. "Here they come, our Greek gods."

The attractive hostess strutted across the floor with the guys in tow, the tall and dark Aldo in his usual yummy pastel silken Italian suit, shirt, and tie; Matt wearing less formal clothes, but relaxed and pale for the climate, enhancing his blond good looks.

Barr Père and Mère were satisfyingly speechless as Temple and Kit stood for the greeting pecks on the cheek . . . as the men were introduced and took their seats . . . as the waiter breezed by to take the newcomers' drink orders. Then they spoke.

"I'll have another daiquiri," said Karen.

"Very good."

"And I'll—" Roger gazed at his empty beer glass. "I'll have a scotch on the rocks."

Kit and Temple crossed glances. *Yes!*

After the drinks had been delivered and the new entrée orders had been taken, the sixsome was alone at the table and the conversational ice was as solid as on Lake Minnehaha in mid-January.

"I guess we should toast the happy couples," Roger said finally, looking eagerly at his lowball glass gleaming gold with Johnnie Walker.

"First," Aldo said with a smile, "we must repeat the ring ceremony for our honored guests." He flourished a velvet box from his side jacket pocket. Matt's was produced from his inside jacket pocket, on the heart side, a detail Temple didn't miss.

The small boxes opened, dispensing major glitz. Rings slipped onto fingers they had previously fit like a dream.

Roger raised his glass and everyone followed suit, Karen last. "To our loved ones, and their loved ones."

It was a darn good toast. Temple stared at her father. He winked. "Drink up, Karen, you don't want to miss the Love Boat."

And then the chatter started. Man-to-man. Woman-to-woman. Cross-gender, cross-table. Aldo, incredibly, knew about broomball, that skating-rink sport Roger got a kick out of. Hockey with brooms. Aldo said bocci ball was a lot like it. Temple doubted it, but gave him high marks for creativity.

Matt explained Temple's important public relations coups to her mother, without mentioning any stray murder-solving or neck-risking. Karen became fascinated by the people and issues that surfaced on Matt's "Midnight Hour" counseling program and his Chicago appearances on *The Amanda Show*. She watched that program, liked Amanda better than Oprah, who was getting to be "too much Oprah everywhere all the time." She wanted Matt to e-mail her when his next appearance was coming up.

E-mail? Her mother?

"We've got a phone-Internet-TV setup now," Karen told Temple when she spied her daughter's amazement. "Roger is going to set me up with an e-mail identity and a Web page."

They asked Matt about his own parents.

They lived, he said, in Chicago, not mentioning that it was separately and had been that way forever.

Chicago! Great city. Just four hundred miles from the Twin Cities. Where would Kit and Aldo be living?

Las Vegas and Manhattan. No way was Kit giving up her Greenwich Village redone condo. It was a very profitable investment. She was still writing a new novel now, but the industry wasn't what it used to be and she was considering herself not so much semiretired as having a long ongoing narrative to write with Aldo. A trip to his native Italy, maybe some cruises. They'd both worked hard and it was time to enjoy leisure time.

"We should take a cruise," Karen told Roger, resting her hand on his.

"We could go together," Aldo said. "For a honeymoon, a second honeymoon for you two. Temple and Matt could come."

Karen looked hopefully at Temple. She hadn't seen much of

her daughter for more than a year, and maybe now she realized that it was her fault for being so negative about Max.

Temple felt her throat closing up again. She was happy this evening was going so well for everyone, but Max hadn't deserved her parents' disapproval. She'd never regret a moment with him. And if he was dead now, with no one to know where or to mourn him, she always would.

Matt put his hand over hers and leaned close. "We'll do what we want about the wedding and honeymoon," he assured her. "Your way."

She just nodded, not trusting herself to speak quite yet. It was nice to bask in astounded parental approval, but she'd never disown her own past. And Matt would never expect her to, as he could never renounce his past either.

They sat quietly for a while, listening to the others talk and discover common ground, content to be by their unspoken selves. Just . . . content.

Chapter 71

Nuptial Nuances

From the May 12, 2008, *Las Vegas Review-Journal*

The wedding of the spring season was not a big-time celebrity do, or a shocking film-star wedding-chapel prank that became tabloid fodder for a week.

No, it was a lavish yet tasteful affair involving some less spectacular, but intrinsically Las Vegas names.

The Crystal Phoenix Hotel and Casino's Crystal Court main floor reception area was a wilderness of ivory roses, tiger lilies, and bronze, mauve, and orange orchids. Baby's breath floated like the airy spray from the plinths of freestanding metallic wall fountains where low-lit sheets of water shimmied over the textured surface like silk moiré come to life.

The famed French crystal chandeliers had been lowered over the wedding site, providing a dazzling yet intimate ceiling of unimaginable iridescent glitter, as if the guests were inside the Hope diamond.

The white carpet was pristine and flanked by rows of ivory velvet Parson's chairs for the guests.

An archway, covered like a Rose Parade float in a solid carpet of ivory roses, had every hotel guest rubbernecking the eight Men in Black (tails) milling nearby, especially since they were all Fontana groomsmen. The man-about-town clan of eligible bachelors lost one of their own in the ceremony to follow, but they willingly relinquished their trademark pale and perfect Italian tailoring for the day to become tall, dark, and handsome in midnight black.

Ladies, this was more sumptuous viewing than the Red Carpet at the Oscars!

The bridesmaids seemed to appreciate that fact, clinging to their handsome escorts' arms. They were a pretty bevy of young women, radiant in shades of silver, gold, bronze, pewter, and pink and copper gold. Oddly, none of them can be identified, as none have been seen about town with the respective Fontana brothers they were paired with, and, like Cinderella clones, they all fled the festivities before this reporter could get their names.

While all were here to celebrate (or mourn) the nuptials of the eldest Fontana brother, Aldo, the only other married man in the clan of bachelor brothers played best man, with his wife as matron of honor. Mr. Nicky Fontana is the youngest of the brothers and owns the Crystal Phoenix, which his wife, the Continentally elegant Miss Van von Rhine, manages. Together they have made the Crystal Phoenix the biggest little boutique hotel in Las Vegas. The Crystal Phoenix led the way to "high-end" Las Vegas hotels long before the Bellagio, Paris, and Venice arrived on the scene.

The groom's uncle, Mr. Mario Fontana, whose name has many long local associations, was resplendent in a striped silver-and-black satin vest under a white dinner jacket. He escorted a lady who would only identify herself as "Miss Kitty." She was a natural platinum blonde (that is, of a "certain" age), putting her Mae West proportions to great advantage in blond silk chiffon. Her appearance at the wedding caused much speculation about the widowed paterfamilias and his current affiliations.

The maid of honor, the bride's niece, is that well-known publicist around every major Las Vegas media event, Miss Temple Barr. She was escorted to her position by a rising Las Vegas star, Mr. Matt Devine, better known as "Mr. Midnight" on his WCOO-AM late-night, nationally syndicated, radio advice program. In an unobjective aside, this reporter must admit that Mr. Matt Divine makes Blond the New Black.

Miss Temple Barr was a vision in a short, trained gown made of changeable silk organza, which was a bipolar blend of metallic red bronze and lavender mauve. Her shoulder-length corona of red-gold curled hair was a crowning glory in need of no additional diadem.

Now for the happy couple. Mr. Aldo Fontana wore silver-gray tails, British-formal with yet an air of elegant Italian gusto.

And here comes the bride, Miss Ursula "Kit" Carlson of Manhattan, actress and novelist. This is her and the groom's first wedding, though both have passed the first flush of youth. She wore a gleaming ivory cut-lace leather Thierry Mugler suit that rocked, rolled, and took no prisoners. A petite woman, like her niece, she obviously believes in living large. The suit skirt was conventionally short in front to display her Jimmy Choo bronze ankle boots, but had a cut-lace leather bustle that changed into an ivory fall of lace that dusted the champagne-beige marble floor and white carpet as a train.

Officiating as justice of the peace, was Miss Electra Lark, owner and operator of the Lovers' Knot Wedding Chapel. She wore a white instead of a black robe for the ceremony.

Perhaps the star of the show was the flower girl, an adorable toddler with her father's dark hair and her mother's poise, Cinnamon Fontana, her dotted Swiss pale green frock sashed in brown satin. Her bouquet mixed the same sophisticated metallic shades as other floral displays. The ring bearer was a black cat with the box affixed to a bow-tie collar. The best man lifted him to extract the rings, then placed him back on the white carpet, where he remained as obediently in place as a well-trained dog. The Fontana magic can tame even the feline nature.

After the vows were exchanged, the groom kissed the bride long enough for his obviously restive brothers to indulge in boyish banter.

The assembly adjourned to the hotel's pool area for the champagne reception and dinner, and a spectacular display of fireworks that outshone the Strip's neon glory and outroared the Mirage Hotel's celebrated exploding volcano for half an hour.

Wedding and hotel guests alike acclaimed the affair as the Wedding of the Century. So far. Mr. and Mrs. Fontana will honeymoon in Paris and London, then return to maintain residences in Manhattan and at the Crystal Phoenix's new European-style multimillion-dollar condominium building, the Crystal Palace.

Oh, yes, you will be wondering: Miss Temple Barr caught the bridal bouquet, despite the fevered attempts of seven attractive young women who occupied first-row seats for the ceremony. It struck this observer that the bride "threw" her throw.

Is the toothsome Mr. Matt Devine the next candidate for a Crystal Phoenix wedding?

Chapter 72

Resurrection

"My poor boy," Garry Randolph murmured, lowering the week-old edition of the *Review-Journal* his Las Vegas contact had sent.

The social scene reporter, although a bit gushy, had written vividly enough to paint him into the entire scene, especially since he'd glimpsed some of the players. Well, her especially, Temple Barr. Max's Temple Barr.

He slapped the paper against the small glass-topped table on his hotel balcony. The vast ripples of Alpine meadows beyond it were too magnificent and generous to absorb a fit of pique.

Still, Max was a son to him. He wanted to witness his wedding, a happy ending to all those unhappy years since Max's cousin Sean had exploded from an IRA pub bomb.

Even if Max had been here now, Garry wasn't sure whether he'd show him this news from what had been his most recent home. The boy's body was compromised from the attempt to kill him even as he attempted to fake his death. His mind was . . . able, still quick and brilliant, but emptied of all its personal data, even the guilt of Sean's death. That, at least, was a blessing. And his spirit was intact.

Garry grinned. And he could still disappear, like any good magician, as he'd learned from his mentor for both stage and spying purposes.

Damn! The magician once known as Gandolph the Great again slapped the folded paper to the glass tabletop as if trying to flatten a fly. *Why had Max vanished, and that sleek lady psychiatrist with him?*

Another attempt on his life in the Swiss clinic? Most likely. Why leave with her? Had she made the attempt and he'd taken her as hostage? But a man with his legs in casts was hardly able to take a hostage, even a female one. Even Max. Had she and her henchmen abducted Max? More likely.

Who would be her henchmen? Members of the rumored group of worldwide magicians, the Synth? Synthesis was an important concept in the kabbalah and ancient systems of magic and alchemy. Las Vegas had hosted a small, secret nest of Synth members, but—from what Max said when he infiltrated them in his own persona—they were petty plotters, more disgruntled unemployed magicians playing at conspiracy than any real force.

Or so Max had concluded. Had he miscalculated? Certainly someone had arranged for him to hit a wall at high speed at the nightclub called Neon Nightmare, the very pyramid-shaped building in which the Las Vegas chapter of the Synth met.

Pyramid. Another link to ancient magic systems. Perhaps he, Gandolph, should take these theatrical villains much more seriously. He was tired of returning to his old European spy grounds as Garry Randolph, calling in debts and trying to lay to rest Max's ghosts, Sean and their personal femme fatale, the psychotic IRA operative Kathleen O'Connor, now finally at rest in an unmarked grave in Las Vegas.

What was happening now could create new ghosts, perhaps for Garry Randolph himself.

So far he'd followed the tried-and-true paths. In Switzerland, Ireland, and Las Vegas. But with Max missing, Gandolph the Great was coming out of retirement, albeit secretly.

It would need more than spy work to quickly find and save Max this time.

It would require a bit of that old black magic that Gandolph knew so well.

Chapter 73

Au Revoir, Max

Somehow, during the night, he'd managed to turn himself over from sleeping on his stomach to his back.

Pretty impressive for an invalid.

The morning sun was slanting through the drawn sheer curtains, slashing light across the golden birchwood floor, on the pristine white comforter.

His stomach rumbled, craving more food.

He stretched out an arm. He'd never sensed her again in the night, not after the massage that had put him out cold. No, out warm. No dreams. No nightmares.

His hand sunk into a foot of airy feathers, nothing more.

He pushed up on his elbows, giving his leaden legs a bit more rest.

Nothing there. He was alone in the room.

Alarm racing down his limbs.

Wait. It was morning. She was waiting her turn at the bathroom, or already in it. In fact, his bladder was burning. He'd slept too hard to use the chamber pot under the bed. But he sure needed relief now.

He'd have to—*unnh*—spin and get his feet to the floor. There was the cane. Put his weight on it, stand. Shake a little. He'd go to the hall bath in his shorts. If he met anyone, tough. No point shrugging into the jeans again until he was ready to go out in them. His legs were stiff from being unused all night. He walked like Frankenstein's monster, as if the casts were still on them.

But his joints were loosening by the time he got to the door. Peeking out into the hall, he saw it was deserted. She must be in the bath then.

His steps and the clunk of the cane sounded like *The Return of the Mummy*. He swung his legs stiffly ahead one by one. The knees would take a while relearning to bend.

There was no splashing sound beyond the old wooden door, so he exercised his knuckles and knocked. Maybe he could talk her into a morning massage. It had really helped him sleep.

No answer.

He tried the knob, which gave. The bathroom was empty. He pushed himself inside, looked it over hard. Not even one vagrant blond hair in the sink from washing her hair last night. Some Swiss neat freak had freshened up the place for the day already.

Whoever he was had been a sensible guy. He took a leak while here, hand-brushed his dark hair, then clumped down the hall, pushed his tender legs into the jeans. He noted that her backpack was gone, packed his own, took a look around to make sure nothing was left behind, and went downstairs to the "expanded Continental" breakfast room. That would mean muesli as well as bread, fruit, coffee, and tea.

A German couple with a teenage daughter were chewing their cuds at one table. The buffet offerings looked picked over. Max finally thought to glance at the cheap watch with a cuckoo clock on the dial he'd bought on their first nicked credit card spree last night.

Eleven! In the morning?

Where the hell was she? Out on the town? It boasted a square the size of King Kong's handkerchief, a fountain, some quaint shops, and that was it.

His heart was pounding. He lurched through the pocket lobby and into the streets. Still narrow, hilly, mostly empty, leading to the square where the tourist buses stopped on their overland way from Italy to France. This village was a remote way station between twelve-thousand-foot peaks.

Why would she leave? Now? She was just softening him up, damn it.

Or . . . she had been taken.

His crutch.

Someone had caught up with them, wanted him on his own, more vulnerable.

Or, she had joined someone who'd always followed them, now watching him from a distance, waiting to see what he did, where he went, when he was alone again.

It didn't make sense, either scenario, with Revienne cast as either villain or victim.

He knew what he had to do: keep moving, keep supplying himself with stolen and soon-ditched credit cards, get to a large city. Find some way to arm himself with more than a hokey carved cane, although no ideal weapon came to mind.

"Max" had been facing a lot worse for half a lifetime from what Garry Randolph had said. And his legs were really pretty good, considering. Too bad there wasn't a tiny bit of level ground in this whole damn handkerchief country . . . !

He recognized the fear underneath his anger at this sudden change in circumstances, this desertion. That he didn't know who he was or where he could go and he didn't dare tell anyone that, because then he'd be revealed as vulnerable and enemies could come circling like mad dogs.

Around him the life of the square bustled on. The shriek of the huge buses' brakes, the rush of babbling tourists in and out of shops, the tinkling fountain, all the ordinary sounds scraped his nerves raw.

No one noticed him. As far as he could tell.

He felt like a kid lost in a department store. *Mommy!*

Ridiculous! He didn't need a keeper, or an anchor. It was time he was truly on his own, then.

High time.

Maybe he'd retrieve his survival instincts by finding out what had happened to Revienne. Why would she have deserted him after hauling him so far, with so much effort? Maybe she hadn't. Maybe she'd been snatched.

Maybe *she* was also a target. After all, she'd been interrogating him for days.

He started over the cobblestones, so quaint and damnably uneven, leaning as little as possible on his cane. A truly lame man stood out. A tourist enamored by an Alpine souvenir didn't.

He'd start in the shop where they'd bought the new clothes. He'd have to concoct a likely story for his inquiries.

His wife had left the inn to get some extra film for the camera. Wait. No. Everything was digital these days. Some . . . sunscreen for the thin mountain air. Blond, you remember? Very sensitive to sunburn. Had anyone seen her this morning? His beautiful blond wife.

The description felt alien, but a magician was an actor at heart. He could sell any illusion.

His beautiful blond wife.

Like his sanitarium patient name, Michael "Max" Randolph, that just didn't feel right. Not the blond part. Not the wife part.

From his unease in the role, he gathered he wasn't the marrying kind.

Midnight Louie Has Issues

What is a self-respecting PI to do?

Here I thought I was off on a festive stag jaunt with the Fontana boys, and we end up surrounded by mad and murderous dames, and worse, rescued by dames.

There is no sanctuary for us manly dudes these days, not even at a notorious Nevada chicken ranch. And that is another thing. I do not get why they call these establishments "chicken" ranches. They are not ranches and they do not have any chickens I noticed hanging about the place. Besides, chickens are not usually notorious, unless they are running around telling everyone the sky is falling.

It seems to me that if the done-wrong bridesmaids wanted to make a point about being overdue for matrimony, or at least engagement rings, a bordello is not the logical place to do it.

Although I do understand the "last stand" notion of a bachelor party, in which lewd dudes drink and ogle and carry on, hopefully knowing when to stop, although some do not and that is when weddings are canceled.

Not this wedding. It was quite the classy event, I thought. Of course, me and my extended family (and, *oi!* it is ever-extending, all on the distaff side), are delighted to be guests and are always dressed in formal black to play key roles for such occasions. Miss Kitty saw to it that Miss Satin came along in a lacey off-white cape, and Midnight Louise managed to sneak Ma Barker in for the food line poolside, although the fireworks had her hackles at attention most of the evening.

The only black cat I am missing at this event—besides my old man out at Temple Bar on Lake Mead—is Mr. Mystifying Max.

And what is my esteemed collaborator doing on her own authority, putting him in dire circumstances in a far place?

That is cruel and unusual punishment for a poor guy who broke both his legs and misplaced his memory. That psychiatrist strikes me as highly suspicious. You will recall that the treacherous, or at least disloyal, Persian honey, Yvette, claimed to be French. And you see how she turned out. A little German on the father's side is not going to cure the French part. Those French females are all femmes fatales.

I suppose I am going to have to nibble my nails over what is happening overseas, where I am not likely to go or be taken. This is a cheesy operation, if I say so myself. There are gambling meccas on the Riviera, in Bangkok and Macao, on cruise ships. Why could we not have the occasional holiday case there? Midnight Louie, Intercontinental Op.

My only consolation is that I can look forward to escorting my Miss Temple to her own nuptials. I have become resigned to domestic change. These human beings are terribly independent and self-involved and not trainable, and they will not listen to reason.

It is like herding lemmings.

I, and my millions of kin worldwide, still try our best to make them behave.

And so I will continue to do, as little as I am appreciated for my efforts.

Midnight Louie, Esq.

If you'd like information about getting Midnight Louie's free *Scratching Post-Intelligencer* newsletter and/or buying his custom T-shirt and other cool things, contact Carole Nelson Douglas at P.O. Box 331555, Fort Worth, TX 76163-1555 or at www.carolenelsondouglas.com. E-mail: cdouglas@catwriter.com.

Carole Nelson Douglas
and Nitpickers

Usually, Louie, I don't interfere with your closing comments at the end of our books.

You are, after all, mentioned on the cover and the spine, just like me.

I am politically correct in your case. I've never found anybody lesser for having four feet instead of two. I realize you contribute a lot to our mutual enterprise.

But you must recognize that some people, perhaps not felines, are very much interested in Max Kinsella's fate and future. I might point out that having one member of the cast at large in Europe is quite enough.

If you were so longing for a Continental outing, you should have arranged for a history as an international counterterrorism agent and for someone to try to assassinate you.

That said, I think you have truly stretched yourself in this

396 · Carole Nelson Douglas

adventure. You're becoming quite the executive, overseeing the situation and sending your agents out to do the leg, and ear, work for you. Also, you are playing much better with others.

I am even gratified to hear that you're accepting the inevitability of a change in your domestic landscape with good grace.

On the other hand, I'm also worried that something is very, very wrong.

This is just too good to last.

Here's a preview of
Carole Nelson Douglas's

Cat in a Topaz Tango

Available August 2009

Louie Left Out

Ring bearer.

Who do they think I am?

Frodo?

I *am* short and I *do* have hairy feet, but do I look like I eat seven meals a day?

Well, maybe a wee bit.

Anyway, it was bad enough I was shanghaied into my Miss Temple's maternal aunt's wedding party recently. After all, the event was over the top to begin with, just in having eight legendary Fontana brothers for groomsmen, not counting the eight good-looking bridesmaids they squired.

And, granted, I got a little local publicity for being Johnny-on-the-spot, but I got no credit for outsmarting the murderous

Copyright © 2009 by Carole Nelson Douglas

individual who almost ruined the wedding beforehand by taking out the maid of honor, my very own Miss Temple Barr.

All this wedding talk and reminiscence is making me gloomy. My Miss Temple was "this far" from being the *matron* of honor. The way a maid gets to be a matron is by marrying someone, as she and Mr. Matt Devine are discussing so often these days.

I do so miss my previous rival for turf on the royal bedspread here at the Circle Ritz.

Mr. Max Kinsella was the perfect boyfriend for my Miss Temple.

He lived and slept somewhere secret off the premises.

He customarily arrived discreetly by the patio doors, which is my usual modus operandi.

Although he gave lip service to a future of marital bliss, he led two to three lives and his past career as a magician and undercover counterterrorist kept him on the run and single.

He was so studly he could satisfy with a riveting personal appearance and then stay gone for whole days at a time. There were no nightly assignations to muss the bedspread and my territorial imperatives.

He remained totally protective but at a discreet distance, leaving me to do the daily bodyguard work and also lie guard on said bedspread.

In other words, for a significant other, he did not significantly get in my way. He exemplified the highest ideals of the Alley Cat Code: friendly, fierce when necessary, and fancy-free.

Mr. Matt Devine, however, is a much more domestically inclined breed of cat. Having no secret missions of an international nature, he lays about the place, especially in *my* spots!

He discusses "their" possible move to his apartment right above us on the third floor, no doubt hoping to erase all bedroom memories of Mr. Max Kinsella. I am not as young as I used to be. A three-story climb is much more demanding than a two-story climb. Show a little consideration for the aging frame.

So move. Fine! I will continue to occupy Miss Temple's rooms all on my lonesome then. I am happy to entertain guests of my ilk in complete privacy. I could use a bachelor pad as much as the next guy. Just because Mr. Matt Devine is from a churchy background and actually considers matrimony holy does not mean those of other denominations, such as myself—I am a devout follower of the Egyptian female cat deity, Bast—must live by his rules.

But this is an empty threat. I have come to appreciate a feminine touch about the place, and also frequent ear stroking. The thought of being edged out of my Miss Temple's bed if not her affections is most distressing.

I fling myself through the flimsy patio doors that Mr. Max was always urging her to fortify, and scramble down the single old leaning palm tree that is my land bridge to the ground-floor parking lot.

The asphalt is hot on my pads as I skitter across it to the hedge of oleander bushes. They are poisonous eating to critter kind, which is why Ma Barker, my long-lost mama, and her feral gang shelter in here for the time being. No wise street dog will disturb them here. I could use a friendly ear.

Instead, one of my own ears is boxed as soon as I am in the safe shadows within.

"Disappointing boy!" my venerable dam spits in that very now-ringing ear. "This is what you call a safe haven? With gourmet food and distilled water? We have seen nothing but aluminum pie tins full of those awful dried green rabbit droppings."

"I have been busy, Ma. I have not had time to train the human waitstaff on what to serve in which manner. They constantly involve me in the criminal community. And Free-to-Be-Feline is a prime New Age health food."

"Food! It is already in a condition to be eliminated before one can touch fang to its odious smell and texture. When can we expect something juicy and tasty that does not run away on four legs?"

"Soon, Ma! The only crimes transpiring around the Circle Ritz these days are crimes of passion," I add sourly. "As soon as I can interrupt these proceedings for a few minutes, I will get your needs tended to."

"You had better, son. We might just have to rumble nights in protest if you do not push these people into line. Free-to-Be Feline! If we were really free to be feline, we would run this town."

You would think I had led them into forty days and forty nights in the desert. Or was it years?

I slink away, caught between the conflicting needs of my kind and my kind of girl.

A Moses of my people I am not.

By Carole Nelson Douglas from Tom Doherty Associates

MYSTERY

MIDNIGHT LOUIE MYSTERIES

Catnap
Pussyfoot
Cat on a Blue Monday
Cat in a Crimson Haze
Cat in a Diamond Dazzle
Cat with an Emerald Eye
Cat in a Flamingo Fedora
Cat in a Golden Garland
Cat on a Hyacinth Hunt
Cat in an Indigo Mood
Cat in a Jeweled Jumpsuit

Cat in a Kiwi Con
Cat in a Leopard Spot
Cat in a Midnight Choir
Cat in a Neon Nightmare
Cat in an Orange Twist
Cat in a Hot Pink Pursuit
Cat in a Quicksilver Caper
Cat in a Red Hot Rage
Cat in a Sapphire Slipper
Cat in a Topaz Tango
(forthcoming)

Midnight Louie's Pet Detectives (anthology)

IRENE ADLER ADVENTURES

Good Night, Mr. Holmes
The Adventuress* (Good Morning, Irene)
A Soul of Steel* (Irene at Large)
Another Scandal in Bohemia* (Irene's Last Waltz)
Chapel Noir
Castle Rouge
Femme Fatale
Spider Dance

Marilyn: Shades of Blonde (anthology)

HISTORICAL ROMANCE

Amberleigh†
Lady Rogue†
Fair Wind, Fiery Star

SCIENCE FICTION

Probe†
Counterprobe†

FANTASY

TALISWOMAN

Cup of Clay
Seed upon the Wind

SWORD AND CIRCLET

Six of Swords
Exiles of the Rynth
Keepers of Edanvant
Heir of Rengarth
Seven of Swords

* These are the reissued editions.
† Also mystery

Praise for Carole Nelson Douglas and Midnight Louie

"Douglas's humor and keen plot twists keep this long-running series purring."
—*Publishers Weekly* on *Cat in a Red Hot Rage*

"A catastrophically cool crime caper."
—*Publishers Weekly* on *Cat in a Quicksilver Caper*

"Fans of the series will not be disappointed, and new readers will delight in the fun."
—*Romantic Times BOOKreviews* (4½ stars) on *Cat in a Hot Pink Pursuit*

"This feisty feline detective is fast gaining a reputation of being one of America's top investigators. . . . If either Mike Hammer or Columbo had a cat, it would be Midnight Louie."
—*Cat Fancy* on *Cat in a Neon Nightmare*

"Douglas just keeps getting better at juggling mystery, humor, and romance. . . . Established fans will welcome another intriguing piece of the puzzle."
—*Publishers Weekly* (starred review) on *Cat in a Midnight Choir*

"Never a dull moment."
—*Library Journal* on *Cat in a Leopard Spot*

"If Midnight Louie prowled only the predictable streets of genre fiction, all the murders in his ersatz world would be resolved. But each new installment in this exuberant series compounds the complexity, leaving us between books with mysterious bodies and looming menace."
—*Kirkus Reviews* on *Cat in a Kiwi Con*